VOLUME ONE

SISTERS
ARE FOREVER

LIKE
AN EAGLE

JOANN KLUSMEYER

innovo
PUBLISHING

Published by Innovo Publishing, LLC
www.innovopublishing.com
1-888-546-2111

Providing Full-Service Publishing Services for Christian Authors, Artists &
Ministries: Books, eBooks, Audiobooks, Music, Screenplays, Film & Curricula

**THE OZARK MOUNTAINS
HISTORICAL FICTION SERIES
FOR ADULTS**

VOLUME I

**SISTERS ARE FOREVER
&
LIKE AN EAGLE:**
An Anthology of Southern Historical Fiction

ISBN: 978-1-61314-696-5

Cover Design & Interior Layout: Innovo Publishing, LLC

Printed in the United States of America
U.S. Printing History
First Edition: 2021

Has God called you to create a Christian book, ebook, audiobook, music album,
screenplay, film, or curricula? If so, visit the ChristianPublishingPortal.com to learn
how to accomplish your calling with excellence. Learn to do everything yourself, or
hire trusted Christian Experts from our Marketplace to help.

CONTENTS

Carl and Lorena Morgan decided that their five beautiful sons made a complete family. There was, however, a family situation that made them rethink their decision. The problem was, were they strong enough in their love of family to risk this preposterous thing?

The preacher had promised, at the funeral, that she could "rise up with wings like the eagle," but how could that be possible? Pregnant as she was, and living on a thirteen-acre strip of hillside land, what hope was there for her and her seven children after a revenuer's bullet had taken the life of her husband, the town moonshiner? In addition, her oldest son was "taken in" because he tried to defend his pa. As she stirred the batter for the cornbread that would be supper for her children, she hoped she would be able, with help from above, to rise up like the cornbread she was preparing.

SISTERS ARE FOREVER

1

Seven-year-old Carl Morgan Junior picked up the shiny double-bladed ax and swung it at the base of a persimmon sapling. The limber tree trunk quivered from the blow but stood fast, so Junior swung again.

Six-year-old Freddie Morgan watched respectfully then suggested hopefully, "You get that'n cut down I getta cut the next'n."

"No, you ain't. Six years old, that'd be not old enough to be handlin' a ax. You'd most likely chop off a foot," Junior pointed out.

"Aw, them's the words Pa said to you and you went and took the ax 'hind his back. Iffen you don't let me cut down a tree, I'm gonna tell on you."

"Now, Freddie, you know Pa said them words to me when I was six, like you. But now I got to be seven. They's a lot'a difference 'tween six and seven."

Junior took another swing. The ax blade glanced off the springy tree and struck a flint stone. Sparks flew.

"Wow!" exclaimed Freddie. "Georgie, you and Stanley see that?"

Five-year-old Stanley, and Georgie, who had just turned four, nodded, wide-eyed.

Junior paused, basking in their admiration. "I just done that for the little 'ens to see."

"You gonna do it again?" Georgie wondered, hopefully.

"Reckon not. I gotta be cuttin' down this here tree," their brother explained.

Junior shouldered the ax and again aimed it at the base of the tree. The blow almost severed the small trunk.

"Freddie, you get a holt onto that'n and twist it off. I gotta be cuttin' another'n. Pa gonna be back askin' where at his ax is."

"I won't tell," Freddie promised.

"Likely you'd not have to, him havin' ears to hear me choppin' with it. Freddie, count them logs we got done a'ready. We most likely got logs enough for the floor."

"Let me count 'em," offered Georgie.

"Aw, you can't even count. Get out'a my way."

"Can, too, count. One, three, eleventeen...."

"That ain't right. Now get back," Freddie demanded. "I been to school and you ain't."

Georgie obediently stepped back, pulling Stanley with him.

"We got thirteen of 'em, Junior. That'd be near what you allowed we'd need?"

"Yep. Now Georgie, you and Stanley don't be touchin' this here ax where I lay it down. You'd hurt yourself for shore. Freddie, you drag them logs over to the tree and hand 'em up. Georgie, you can bring along that rope."

Junior Morgan caught the lowest limb of a massive oak and, wrapping his legs around it, pulled himself into the tree. The second limb, a good eight feet off the ground, grew straight out from the trunk of the tree and made a branch with a level fork. A perfect site for a treehouse.

"Hand me up that little'n first and the rope. I gotta tie the first'n down real solid."

Freddie took the rope from Georgie and draped it over the end of the smallest tree trunk. The two younger brothers watched, wide eyed, as Freddie carefully raised the stick and the rope to Junior, who was straddling the limb above. The three boys on the ground watched closely as their brother tied the first floorboard of their treehouse to the limb of the tree.

"I wanna come on up there," Freddie announced.

"You can't. Them little boys ain't big enough to reach them poles up to me."

Georgie took his thumb out of his mouth. "Can I come on up?"

"No, 'cause we'd be havin' to quit work to help you and we ain't got the time."

Freddie handed another small log to his brother who carefully fitted it into place. To make it lay better, he knocked off a few excess chips, which fell down on his brothers.

"Georgie, you pull Stanley back away. Iffen he'd get a hunk'a bark in his eye, he'd go bellerin' to Ma and she'd make us stop."

"Why?" asked Georgie.

"I ain't never figured it out why but that's what a ma always does. Ain't no matter what's bein' done, ya always gotta quit when a little'n gets hisself hurt."

"We ain't got but two logs left," reported Freddie.

"Two's all we gonna need. Hand 'em up."

By now, the ground crew had completely lost sight of the floor builder, due to the six-by-eight-foot platform of small logs covering the limb.

"I'm gonna come on up, now," Freddie announced.

"Come on."

"Me, too."

"Me, too."

"Freddie, you wait down there and boost the little 'ens, and I'll catch their hands and pull 'em on up"

"Me, first," Georgie insisted.

"First," echoed Stanley.

"No, me first," Georgie yelled and shoved Stanley backward.

A stern voice came from above. "Cut that out, Georgie. You gonna have him yellin' and Ma gonna be runnin' out here for shore."

"But I said 'me first' first."

"Yeah, you did," Junior agreed. "Hand 'im up, Freddie."

Freddie grabbed Georgie around the waist but couldn't lift him up to the first limb.

"I know what, Freddie. You come on up here and I can push him up to you."

Whereupon Freddie and Junior changed places.

From his place on the ground, Junior now instructed, "Listen, Georgie, you hold out your leg so as you can catch onto that limb. Freddie ain't gonna be holdin' onto you for very long, you bein' so heavy."

With a grasp and a jerk, Junior boosted Georgie upward. Freddie grabbed Georgie's upraised hands and pulled. Georgie's leg wrapped around the limb like a possum tail over the henhouse door.

"You got a good holt?" Junior asked.

"Yep," came the answer, as Georgie climbed on up to the second limb and crawled out to the platform.

"Me! Me!" squealed Stanley.

After sizing Stanley's height against the height of the first limb, Junior made a stirrup for Stanley's foot and Freddie reached down, but Stanley didn't catch the limb with his free leg.

Freddie's grip slipped and the small boy dropped back down into Junior's arms.

With a stern voice, Junior refined his instructions. "You gotta help out, Stanley. Freddie can't be holdin' on to you all day. Now, you seen how Georgie done it so you know what you gotta do. Here we go, again."

Junior hoisted Stanley up again and Freddie reached down. Stanley raised his leg but failed to catch the limb. Down he came in a pile on the ground, yelling with indignation.

"Don't you be cryin', Stanley," threatened Junior. "Ma'll hear and then we gotta go in."

Stanley whimpered and pouted his lower lip. "Me, first, too," he pled.

"What we gonna do?" wondered Freddie, turning to Junior for the answer.

Junior looked around, sighing wearily. His eyes rested on a small wagon used for light, one-horse hauling. The wooden box of the bed was tight for hauling grain, and it stood about three feet off the ground.

Junior's practiced eye determined it to be about the right height.

"Freddie, come help me get that cart over here and he can climb up on it. Then it'd be easy for us to get him on the rest'a the way."

As instructed, Freddie jumped down. Georgie yelled, "Me, too. I gotta help."

A quick response came from his brother. "No, you ain't. It was trouble enough gettin' you up there," Freddie pointed out, so Georgie now had permission to settle back to enjoy the show.

The three brothers walked up the incline toward the waiting cart.

"Ride?" suggested Stanley, hopefully.

A quick decision and Junior answered, "Yeah, get on in it. Won't be no heavier with you in there, once we get it to rollin'."

The two bigger boys leaned against the endgate of the wagon but the ends of the double-pole tongue just dug themselves into the soft ground.

"Freddie, you go around and lift them tongues whilst I shove on it. Bein' downhill, likely it'll go easy once it gets goin'. I'll break it loose, and when it gets to rollin', you just swing them ends on around the side of the tree and drop the tongues to stop it a'rollin'. Ready?"

"Ready," Freddie answered, as he positioned himself between the poles and lifted them.

Junior applied his shoulder to the endgate, dug in his heels and the wagon began to roll. Freddie ran to keep ahead of the wheels, holding tight onto the bouncing tongue poles.

"Go to the tree," shouted Junior.

"I can't!" yelled Freddie. "It's tryin' to run over me!"

The cart rumbled down the incline and passed under the treehouse platform, then headed for the bluff overlooking the Tuscalara River. Junior's mind accurately projected the certain outcome.

In wide-eyed horror, he gasped and shouted above the gleeful and excited laughter of Stanley and Georgie. His command was somewhat muffled by his brothers' excitement.

"Drop 'em, Freddie! Drop 'em!"

"Huh? I can't hear you."

A few decibels louder, he repeated, "Drop 'em! Let 'em fall down!"

The cart was now nearly fifty feet from the overhanging bluff of the pasture. Junior ran ahead to help turn the cart away from the river, continuing to shout, "Drop 'em, Freddie! Drop 'em! You hear me?"

"Yeah, but I can't. It's tryin' to run over me."

"Drop 'em, anyway!"

At this moment the right front wheel of the cart struck against a large rock, spinning the cart completely around. Freddie was sprawled onto the grass by the tongue poles, skidding on his chin and elbows.

The cart proceeded merrily on toward the bluff, endgate first. Junior reached the speeding wagon and barely touched the tongue pole before it bounced out of reach.

Stanley crouched down into the corner of the cart, clutching its sideboards screaming, "Mama! Mama!"

In desperation, Junior screamed, "Come on, Freddie. We gotta catch it!"

Freddie, green from the grass stain and red from blood streaming from a cut lip, obediently jumped up and ran after Junior.

At the very edge of the bluff, the wagon bumped against a tuft of grass and hesitated for a moment, then it sailed out and over the fast flowing river. It seemed to hang motionless in the air before settling downward, the tongue shafts whirling.

Stanley's terrified scream carried out over the water and seemed to echo against the opposite mountain.

Junior, white as chalk, and Freddie, a mixture of red and green, watched the wagon settle onto the swirling water of the fast-moving river.

It spun around, righted itself, then headed downstream. Stanley's terrified screams became faint and indistinct as the wagon disappeared around the bend of the river.

2

Lorena Morgan closed the cabin door softly and walked toward the bluff to her own private thinking place. Two-year-old Jamie would sleep for at least two hours and she really needed this time alone, this being the first moment that she knew, absolutely for certain, that she would bear another child. Yesterday she thought so, and today she was sure, for hadn't she been at this stage five times before?

There was even a name for the feeling. It was the quickening. It was that moment, just an instant, really, that a woman felt herself projected into the future. It was the feeling of being part of all mankind. It was that delicious wave of elation at the beginning of the creation of a new life.

Except that this moment brought her no elation.

This first, uplifting wave was followed by the rock hard impact of knowledge that this child within her did not belong to her. The wonderful miracle of a baby growing under her heart had nothing to do with her. The child was not hers now, nor would it ever be.

Slowly she sat down on the rock ledge, drawing her feet under her skirt. The rock was massive and sloping, offering a perfect view of the miniature silver bridge over the restless river, a tiny, green-pastured farm or two, and the distant slope of Five-Mile-Hill.

The bluff also overlooked the Tuscalara River with its racing, swirling water and often it seemed to relieve her anxieties and weariness, just by the sight of it. Its currents and movements were alive and restless, yet orderly and contained. The river entered her life from somewhere to the east and disappeared just around the bend in the west, but for a moment, it passed before her and it was hers. As it passed her bluff, it was her river, and she was content to sit and watch it flow.

She was sitting there on the ledge watching the river and the sky above, hoping for its peace to settle onto her, when she heard Stanley's screams.

"MAMA! MAAAMMAAA!"

She turned instinctively toward the sound and saw, in bold relief against the blue sky, a square shape similar to a small wagon. The strange shape hung in the sky for an instant, then began to settle onto the water. From this shape came more screams.

Lorena watched, fascinated at the illusions a mind can create. Then she walked to the edge of the bluff for a closer look. She saw the shape swirl around on the water and rapidly head downstream, bearing the outline of a small boy clinging to its sideboards.

"MAMA! MAMA!" came the hoarse sound, piercing her illusion in a most unnatural way. Then realization clutched at her heart. This was no illusion! She gasped and ran back to the cabin, to the bed of the still sleeping Jamie. What now? Where was Carl? She turned this way and that, but it was as though her feet were glued to the floor. *Think, Lorena,* she demanded.

As a reflex action, she grabbed Jamie into her arms, hugging him. His sleeping head lolled over on her shoulder, his black lashes heavy against his rosy cheek.

She put him back on the bed where he sighed, turned over and continued to sleep. She tapped her chest with her fists, seeming to try to keep her beating heart from stopping.

3

Junior and Freddie watched the wagon sail into the air and splash down into the water. They turned, as one, and ran to the calf shed in the lower pasture.

"Pa! Pa!"

"What you boys doin' down here?"

"Pa, you gotta...."

With fatherly concern, Carl began with what was the most obvious problem. "Freddie, what you done to your face? Here, we gotta clean you up. Junior, something punch him in the mouth?"

"No, Pa. You gotta get Stanley. We...."

"Now, Junior, I told you and Freddie to quit sneaking off'a the others just 'cause they're littler. I told you...."

"Pa, listen at me! Stanley got in that little wagon. You gotta come...."

"Now, Junior, I got work to do. You boys ought'a be able to get him out. Freddie, what did you do to your chin?"

With eyes wide and frightened, Freddie shook his head vigorously, "No, Pa. You got no time to be talkin' at me...."

Seeing they finally had their father's attention, Junior plunged in again.

"Yeah, Pa. Freddie's sayin' the truth. Stanley got in the little wagon and it rolled over the bluff!"

"Bluff? The wagon? Stanley? Good Lord a' Mercy!" Carl stuck his head out of the shed and yelled, "Marcel, come help me get Stanley out'a the river!"

"The what?" came the unbelieving response.

"Grab a couple's horses and run!"

Marcel McCann, brother-in-law to Carl, was fence-mending along the bottom calf pasture. Being no stranger to emergencies, he dropped his tools and jumped onto the nearest mare. "Come on, Buck," he yelled to the white pony nearby, and the pony came trotting after the mare.

"What you needin' with the horses, Carl?"

"Stanley rolled into the river in the little wagon. Gotta get 'im!"

Carl paused from running long enough to swing onto the white pony as it came galloping past him, directing the animal onward with a slap on the rump. Guided by a hand on his mane and knee pressure on his neck, the pony ran for the road. The mare and Marcel came lumbering after.

"How far did he go?" Marcel called.

"Don't know," was Carl's answer. "Somewhere 'afore the Mississippi, I'm hopin'. Figure that sharp turn there in town could ground 'im. It'll either stop 'im or...anyway, that's where I figure he'll be."

The pony and the mare galloped down the steep bluff road onto Dogwood Valley Road. From there they clomped across the silver bridge.

They stretched flat out as they tore down Main Street where a small group of people, attracted by the screams, stood by the bank of the river.

"They's a kid in the river! A little'n. I seen 'em goin' past like he was a little Noah in his ark."

"Who is he? Why, he's just a little fella!"

"Could get lucky. Looks like the bend'll stopped 'im. Got 'im stuck in the sand bar."

"Preacher's a'swimmin' out after 'em, now."

"Ain't no end'a the surprises that come down that river."

"He come down from up river? I speck I know who he'd be. I'd bet a dollar to a toothpick he's a Morgan."

Just then Carl and Marcel came galloping up, the animals hanging their heads and blowing their breath, their sides heaving from the exertion.

"Yep, and here comes his Pa after 'im. Preacher's got your kid, Carl, swimmin' on in with 'im on his back. See yonder?"

Carl and Marcel watched as Preacher Joe McCrey's strong swim-stroke brought himself and the boy closer. Stanley Morgan caught sight of his father and uncle and began to cry at the top of his voice.

"Why you reckon that kid's a'squallin', now that he's been got?"

"Aw, he'd just be cryin' to get sympathy out'a his Pa."

Carl reached for his soaked and whimpering son.

"Much obliged, Preacher."

"Don't mention it."

Stanley patted his father's face with one hand and pointed with the other, sniffling, "Out there, Pa. I want my mama."

Bystanders chuckled and patted Stanley as he sobbed dismally into his father's shoulder. Marcel's practical eye gazed into the river, studying the position of the wagon.

"Reckon we could pull that wagon out right here. I'll get on home and get rope and a harness. Buck, here'd, he'd be most able to pull it out."

Joe McCrey cut in, "Did you take notice of the wheel that got popped off?"

"Huh?"

"The thing that tipped me off to watch for the wagon was a wheel rollin' over and over in the water. Popped clean off the axel. The right one. I could loan you a rope to pull the bed up into the churchyard till you could get a wheel down here. Speck the one that come off is probably rolled down to the Mississippi by now, judgin' from the speed it was travelin' when it went past here."

The preacher, being already soaked, swam back to the beached wagon towing a thick rope. The tongue shafts had buried themselves in a sandbar, rearing the small wagon bed into the air. He tied the rope securely to the axel, directly behind the remaining wheel.

At his signal, the pony strained against the pull of the current as Preacher Joe steered the damaged wagon to the riverbank. Many willing hands helped pull it up from the reach of the current.

Little Stanley laughed and waved to the crowd as the mare and the pony clippity clopped up Main Street toward home. Bystanders waved and thoughtfully stroked their chins. They nodded and agreed, once more, that Carl Morgan was going to be lucky if he raised all those sons of his. They also agreed that they had seldom seen more life in any set of boys than they saw in them.

From the top of the hill, Lorena saw them coming and ran to meet them. Marcel allowed he'd be going on along home now that everyone was safe. The incident, though dangerous, was just one of many he had experienced.

Lorena hugged her drenched son and laughed and cried. Junior looked from one to the other, grinning, and a very relieved Freddie stood by his side. Jamie, now awake from his nap, stood staring.

Carl looked around. Junior, Freddie, Stanley, and Jamie. Someone was missing.

"Where at is Georgie?"

Junior and Freddie looked at each other wide-eyed, then turned as one and sped toward the bluff.

"I'll hand 'im down and you catch 'im," Junior instructed as they neared toward the site of the new treehouse. They could hear Georgie's angry yells long before they could see him.

Later, when the boys were asleep in their lean-to room, Lorena confided, "Times I think I ain't gonna be able to stand happenin's like today, lookin' out there and bein' so scared I could die, and then not knowin' what to do about it."

"What do you want done?"

"Well, could we maybe scold them boys?" she asked hopefully.

"Which one?"

"Well...."

"Look at it this'a'way. Nothin' would'a happened to 'em, 'cept they was playin' with Stanley like they was made to do. They weren't big enough to lift 'im up in the tree. Gettin' that little wagon was a good idea Junior had and Junior knowd what to do to stop it. Freddie didn't let go like he was told to, bein' scared hisself.

"But I figure Freddie done paid the price for not knowin' how to drop them tongues, by the loss of skin on his chin. Georgie got scared, out there alone, but he weren't in no danger and he done nothin' wrong. Stanley could'a got hisself killed but it weren't no fault of his, and we was lucky to get him back. Which one of them boys you think we ought'a scold?"

Lorena sighed and Carl continued, "Ain't nothin' I'd'a liked better'n blisterin' the hide off someone. Trouble is, I can't figure out who to whip."

He grinned his handsome grin and pulled Lorena toward him. "Don't you be frettin', honey. We gonna whip up on somebody next time. I promise I'll whip someone next time they pull somethin' like this, lettin' Stanley fall over the bluff."

4

It was morning.

Lorena opened her eyes to the dawn, soft and silent on the mountain. The next sound she would hear would be her sister's big, red Shanghi rooster from on top of the shed roof. She slipped quietly from the bed and went into the kitchen of her cabin.

She sat at her table by the window and watched the sky turning rosy behind the gray strips of rising river moisture. Dawn was her favorite time of the day for thinking, for planning, and for just being alone. It was also her time for sorting out thoughts and feelings.

During the first of the discussions about the child Lorena now carried, the ground rules had been set. Lorena had bravely told her sister, "That baby will be yours right from the first. I daren't think on anything else."

"But, Lorena..." InaMae had attempted to protest.

"No, and that settles it. Iffen it was me havin' no babies and you the one to be able to have a new one every year, then you'd be the one doin' this for me, bein' the kind of sister you are."

InaMae had been overcome with emotion. "Oh, Lorena, how was I so lucky to have you for a sister! Who else'd come right out and offer on somethin' so personal as a baby."

Lorena had quickly protested, "It'd just be a matter of sharin' what I could do. Wouldn't that be the onliest way to look at it?"

They had embraced and wept together and Lorena had known at that moment, the hard part was yet to come. But it was difficult to see why it should be so hard. She and Carl had made five boys together and had decided that was enough for a family. There would be no more.

Yet there was now to be another. At this moment the new life still belonged to her. But, no, that was not right because she had promised InaMae and she still felt that whatever was to be done should be done right from the first. She must force herself to remember that it was InaMae's baby that was on his way.

At the time of the discussion, Lorena had laughingly told her sister, "Reckon you know your baby gonna be a boy. From the looks of things, I'd say that'd be what you could count on."

InaMae had chuckled. "Likely a boy'd be the best anyway, on account of me havin' a boy name picked out. His name gonna be Marcel, just like his daddy."

Lorena had nodded. Yes, she had been happy with a boy, too. Carl Morgan Junior had fit happily into her plans. A cattle farm needed a strong son coming on. Then Freddie was born, and was not two sons better than one?

But then when Mary Lorena should have been born, they had Georgie. Then, the next year, Stanley had taken Mary Lorena's place in the family.

Darling boys. Try again? Everyone in town was having baby girls. Seemingly, the time was now right for Mary Lorena, but Jamie had been born and that was enough.

Beautiful boys, they were, pink cheeked with heavy black hair and their eyes like chocolate ice cream, clear and glistening. Carl Junior was getting tall and well-muscled, and Freddie was close behind. Georgie was losing his baby fat and Stanley was hardly more than a toddler. Jamie was a baby. Actually, Jamie was a little more than that, but he was her last and she dreaded to see him grow away from her.

These were her family, and they were all of her family, she reminded herself, and the one she now carried belonged, from this moment on, to her sister.

The Shanghi rooster began to flap his wings. He was joined in the flapping by this year's crop of young fryers. Then the flapping turned into the half-crows of the young ones as they warmed up to the morning serenade. Finally came the full-fledged, full-throated crow of the tall, brightly feathered Shanghi signaling the arrival of the morning.

As she watched, the rosy sky turned lavender and Lorena arose and began to mix the dough for the breakfast biscuits. Today she would tell InaMae and tonight InaMae would tell Marcel. It should be a woman's privilege to be the first to tell her husband about their baby.

InaMae and Lorena lived a short distance apart, just down the hill on the huge mountain property given to them by the girls' parents. As girls, they had been courted well, and finally they had chosen Carl and Marcel, a pair of young men who had been boyhood friends. The four had made their promises before a minister in Jacksonville and their fathers would have been tempted to be angry about the double elopement, had they not been so pleased with their choices.

They had moved onto the mountain acreage bordering on the south edge of the Tuscalara River, constructing cabins from the oak and sycamore timber produced by the mountainside. The cleared patches of land had been seeded in rye and native grasses to nourish the animals that would be reared there.

The young men had worked together on the land, growing their food crops and buying calves. These young animals were grown to the heavy beef weight desired by the current market and to be shipped to northern cities such as St. Louis. The fattened cattle were sold at the auction in Jacksonville and new, young calves were bought to replace them.

It was a good living well adapted to the slopes of central Arkansas, and as Carl's sons began to make their appearance, the two men had purchased adjoining bottomland acreage for a calf pasture. Grass grew thick and deep in the black soil along the river, perfect for fattening the cattle.

And now, in her kitchen, Lorena made sandwiches of the biscuits and eggs left from breakfast to pack in the lunch pail for Junior and Freddie. The boys had been fed and their necks and ears examined for cleanliness. They had been checked for the actual presence of underwear and their hair had been combed. It was a morning ritual before letting the two bigger boys out the door.

Now was the time to tell InaMae. Georgie and Stanley would need something to occupy them for an hour or so.

"Georgie, you and Stanley come here. I got somethin' I been wantin' done and you'd be the ones to do it, bein' the two biggest boys I got with me."

Two pairs of chocolate ice cream eyes looked at their mother, expectantly.

"I got me some fat meat here, and you boys need to get them little fishin' poles and bring 'em in here. You seen how the big boys catch them crawdads and put 'em in the big pail?"

Two heads nodded eagerly, and Lorena continued, "You boys are gonna catch enough crawdads to make a pie for supper." The heads nodded again. "Now you run and get them poles so's you can get at it. You'll be havin' to work a long time to get crawdads enough."

The door slammed behind them as they dashed to the shed for the poles. Excitement pushed them along. Never had they been allowed to fish for crawdads alone without the bigger boys telling them what they could or couldn't do.

Lorena cut the fat meat into tiny chunks and put the bits in a bowl made from half a gourd from which the seeds had removed.

Lorena gave last minute instructions. "Now, Georgie, you carry the pail, you bein' bigger, and we gonna set this meat right down here in the pail. Stanley, you carry both them poles. You boys don't be goin' no place but to the crawdad hole. You hearin' my words?"

The boys nodded and glanced toward the door, suggestively.

Their mother was not to be hurried, and she continued, "Now, you boys ain't goin' down to the river. You don't never go down to the river without Pa. You hearin' that?"

Two heads nodded and two sets of bare feet began to edge toward the door. Lorena could not resist adding, "You boys be careful, hear?"

If there was a reply, it was drowned by the slamming of the door.

Lorena sighed and looked around her. All she had left was Jamie, and, now, what was to be done must be done. She gathered him in her arms, crooning, "Come here, sweet baby. We gonna go see InaMae."

"InaMae?" he lisped.

"Yep, we shore are."

The morning was crisp and cool, typical of an early morning in May. When the sun fully cleared the mountaintops, the air would be hot and steamy, but that would be at least an hour away. In the distance, she could see the tiny figures of her sons, happily making their way to the crawdad hole, a pool of water captured from the stream coming down the hill.

After the short walk, Lorena tapped on the cabin door and, knowing her sister to be alone, stepped into her kitchen. Jamie pulled loose from his mother and ran to his aunt.

"InaMae! InaMae!" he squealed joyfully as she gathered him into her arms.

Lorena sat down at the table and her sister poured coffee. Reluctant to start with the needed words, Lorena reached for a leftover biscuit and spread it with bee tree honey. InaMae waited. She would never ask Lorena, and Lorena knew she would never ask the one question that burned in her heart for an answer.

The older sister took a bite from the biscuit and looked out the window. What was coming was very hard to do. Why was it so hard to say the thing she had come to say about a baby that had never been hers? She sighed deeply, turned her eyes from the window, and looked into her sister's eyes. Words failed her so she just nodded.

For a moment, InaMae was motionless. Then she leaned forward and whispered, "Yes?"

Lorena nodded again and tears began to flow. She was angry with herself because of the tears. She had promised herself they would not appear.

InaMae lowered her head in anguish and looked at the floor. Her words were soft and low. "Lorena, I got no right to hold you to a promise you made, you not knowin' how you'd be feelin' when the time come."

Lorena shook her head. "No, that ain't it. I knowd how it would be when I made the promise. Ain't nothin' changed from then. Come Christmas time, your little boy gonna be comin'." She forced her mouth to smile.

InaMae ran to her sister and fell to her knees. "Oh, Lorena, Lorena," she cried and buried her face in her sister's lap. "They be anything you want done, like you bein' tired or such, you let me know. You want supper fixed or maybe your washin' rubbed out, you tell me. It'd be a relief to me to be at it. You wantin' more biscuit and honey?"

Lorena smiled through her tears. "You already thinkin' your baby ain't gonna get what it wants to eat, you pushin' food at me?"

InaMae laughed from relief. "Eat another biscuit!" she demanded, playfully, then grew thoughtful. "Christmas! Just think! Baby Jesus was born on Christmas, so it'd be just about the best time of the year for a baby. Oh, Lorena!"

Georgie and Stanley sat on the bank of the shallow crawdad hole. Georgie had put down the bucket and importantly took the poles from Stanley.

The fat meat was slick and greasy in his small fingers but he managed to pick up a piece of it. He held the bent wire fishhook in one hand and the chunk of meat in the other, pushing the meat toward the point as he had seen Junior and Freddie do. The meat squirmed from his fingers and squirted into the water. Two pairs of eyes followed the arc made by the meat as it splashed in the shallow water of the pool, and before it had settled to the bottom, three large crawfish had clamped their pincers onto it and had begun to feed.

The boys looked on in amazement. "Law sakes! You see that, Stanley?"

Stanley nodded. "Law, yeah!"

Georgie grinned, "Now we gonna put a piece of meat on the hook and bring one of them fellers up."

Stanley nodded in agreement, "Law, yeah."

This time Georgie was successful at getting the meat onto the hook, then handing the pole to his brother.

"Here, Stanley, you take this'n."

Stanley reached for the pole and lowered the bait into the clear water of the pool. A six-inch crawfish immediately advanced toward the bait. A large pincered claw reached out and clamped onto it.

"Law, sakes, Stanley. You done caught one. Pull 'im on out!"

Stanley pulled quickly and with all his strength. The short pole flipped into the air, tossing the crawfish behind him onto the grass. It began to crawl rapidly back toward the pool.

"I get 'im! I get 'im!" promised Stanley, running after it.

"No, no, don't you do that! See them pinchers? Law, them things'd chop the finger right off a your hand. Likely. You gotta do 'em this'a way," whereupon Georgie poked at the crawfish with a stick and the brilliant red claw clamped on it. He carried the stick to the pail and tapped it on the rim. Their first catch of the day thumped against the bottom of the metal pail.

"Now, you can put that bait back in the water, Stanley. 'Member not to jerk it out so fast so the crawdad don't go flyin' off like that'n done."

Stanley nodded, gnawing his tongue in concentration as he lowered the fat bait into the pool. It lay like a white glob on the dark mud bottom. A tiny, one-inch specimen eased up to it.

"Jiggle the pole, Stanley. You gotta scare that little 'in off so's he can get bigger."

Before the end of an hour, the pail was a scratching mass of crustaceans, striving to climb out of the pail over the bodies of their fellow captives.

"I wanna fish," complained Stanley.

"Ain't no fish. All we got's crawdads."

"Need wiver."

"Huh?"

"Wiver. Pa has wiver."

"Naw. You mean liver. Fish like liver."

"I wanna fish."

"We ain't gonna get fish, so hush up."

"I wanna fish." The lower lip extended into a pout. Stanley sniffed loudly and rubbed his eyes. He peeked through his fingers to see the effect of his performance.

"Now, don't you be bawlin'. We ain't even got no liver. Can't be catchin' fish 'thout no liver."

"Get wiver."

"We can't get no liver. Gotta get it at the store. Or out'a hog."

"I wanna fish."

"Oh, hush up and get more crawdads."

"No."

"I tell mama...."

"No."

"Wait, I got me a idea."

"Huh?"

"We gonna get liver."

"Get wiver," echoed Stanley.

Georgie was galvanized into action. "Grab a'holt onto that pail handle. We gotta take these crawdads to mama."

The boys shouldered their fishing poles and swung the pail between them. Mama was not in the cabin so they set the pail on the kitchen floor. They poked the poles into the mass of crawfish so they would be handy when they got the liver.

"We gotta find a hog."

Stanley agreed. "Find a hog."

"Mama gonna like us when she sees the fish we gonna get. Huh!"

"Yeah, huh!"

The boys peeked through the rails of the hog pen. The fat sow waddled to the fence and snorted her breath at them. She looked eyeball to eyeball with the boys and squealed loudly. Georgie jumped back pulling Stanley with him. It was time for a change of plans.

"Stanley, I reckon they's liver in things 'sides hogs."

"Law, yeah."

"Likely hens."

"Hens?"

"First we gotta catch us a hen. See that'n? Take out after 'im."

The hen ducked and squawked, zigzagging into the woods. They spotted another hen and gave chase with no better success. Just then, InaMae's duck with her freshly hatched babies came waddling by on their way to the crawfish pool for a swim.

Georgie looked at Stanley and grinned. Stanley squealed in anticipation. The mother duck squawked a warning.

Georgie grabbed a baby duck in each hand and Stanley captured one. They turned and ran to the shed with the mama duck close behind. By the time they reached the shed, the mother had given up and returned, scolding, to her remaining brood.

"Wiver," demanded Stanley with extended lower lip.

"Now, Stanley, Pa'd blister me if I was to let you use this here knife, no bigger than you are."

Stanley conceded. He could readily see that he had won the argument for the liver. Georgie pointed the knife at the throat of the baby duck and split it open.

"Law, mama, she gonna be surprised, time she sees what we gonna do."

"Yeah, s'prised," agreed Stanley.

Georgie had seen enough animals butchered to know a liver when he saw one, but he was surprised that this one was so small. It was hardly big enough to bait one hook. That, however, was not a problem. There were more ducks.

Stanley stood holding the ducks while Georgie found a leaf to lay the tiny liver on. "Watch you don't be squeezin' them little ducks and hurtin' 'em, Stanley. We gotta get them back to the mama 'afore she gets any madder."

"Yeah," agreed Stanley, nodding.

"See there, we gonna put these livers here on the milk bench so as we can get to 'em in a hurry once we get these baby ducks back to their mama. Here, gimme two of 'em."

"No."

"Then gimme one."

Stanley handed Georgie a limp, bloody carcass.

"They ain't wigglin'," observed Stanley.

"That'd be 'cause they likely missin' their mama. Hurry up and run. We gotta get 'em back to her."

Georgie and Stanley ran to the crawfish pond. The mama duck saw them coming and quacked loudly to gather her remaining family. She bravely advanced toward the boys.

"Hurry up, Stanley. She gonna pinch us."

The boys put the three tiny mangled bodies down in the path between themselves and the irate mother and ran back to the shed.

"Mama gonna find 'em, now. We gotta get our poles so we can fish. You go get them poles out'a the bucket and I'll be gettin' the liver."

Stanley nodded and ran to the kitchen. In a minute he reappeared emptyhanded. Puzzled, with hands wide-spread, he demanded, "Georgie, come 'ere. The crawdads!"

"No, Stanley, don't be gettin' the crawdads. Get them poles."

"No," insisted Stanley. "Come 'ere."

"Law, sakes," commented Georgie in disgust, "you ain't big enough to do nothin' 'thout me bein' right there by you, sayin' how it gotta be done." He stomped down the path toward the kitchen following his brother. "Just how come is it you ain't pickin' up them poles like you was told?"

Stanley entered the cabin and stood in the middle of the kitchen, pointing to the pail. "See? Come lookie."

Georgie looked into the empty pail, then he glared at Stanley. "How come you to be dumpin' out them crawdads?"

"Didn't. They come walkin'," and Stanley walked his fingers up the fishing pole. "They jumped. I caught one." He reached into the pocket of his shirt and removed a mangled crawfish.

"Huh," commented the puzzled Georgie, looking around. Not another crawfish was in sight. "Reckon we gotta catch 'em again."

"Where at?"

"Law sakes, you don't know nothin'? We gotta catch 'em at the crawfish hole. That'd be the place where a body'd catch crawdads. Here, gimme the fat meat and come on."

They stopped briefly to examine the still motionless bodies of the ducklings.

"Most likely they was tired and they mama said to 'em to take a nap," Georgie decided.

Stanley nodded his agreement. "A nap."

5

Jamie was playing in the dirt just outside the cabin door. Lorena called to him, preparing to return to her cabin. She made one last comment to InaMae, "Not that it'd matter none by now, but a body's not be sayin' you wasn't warned about what raisin' boys was like. You livin' here in the middle of it the last seven years, that'd leave you with no surprises."

InaMae, in a mellow mood, replied, "Aw, them boys never done a bad thing in their whole lives."

Lorena smiled but did not comment as she scooped Jamie into her arms and went home.

Georgie, still with a small concern about the motionless ducks, commented to Stanley, "Likely that mama duck gonna be back to get them babies come time they slept a while."

Stanley nodded agreement. "Slept a while."

And the boys turned again toward the crawfish hole to fish for finny creatures.

Lorena took the long way and walked through her garden. This and that would need to be canned, and the beans could use a bit of weeding. She wondered idly if she could trust the bigger boys with the job.

Finally she entered her kitchen and saw the pail of crawfish. Well, that would take care of supper. Potatoes, carrots, onions, and a few peas could be added to the simmered, peeled crawfish tails, then baked under a flaky crust. Crawfish pie and a bowl of steaming wild greens seasoned with bacon fat. Add a pan of crusty cornbread and she had the perfect late spring supper.

As she reached for the pail, Lorena saw a large, pinchered creature stroll out from under the cook stove and across the kitchen floor.

"Hmmm, where at you come from?" she commented to the creature and tossed him in the pail.

It was later, after she had accidently crunched two of the crustaceans underfoot and had seen another one crawling along the edge of the wall that she became suspicious.

"Georgie! Stanley!"

"How come we got crawdads all over the floor? Why ain't they all in the bucket?"

The boys looked at each other, sober and silent.

"Mama," Georgie hesitated, "them crawdads went walkin' up the fishin' poles." He demonstrated by walking his fingers up an imaginary pole.

Stanley nodded, relieved that the matter was settled. "Law, yeah, mama. They went walkin'."

Lorena looked from one to the other. They stared back at her with wide, unblinking eyes. Lorena knew she would never know the whole of the story, but she also knew they told the absolute truth. The story was much too preposterous to be a lie.

At the foot of the mountain just past the river, the school children were coming home. Junior and Freddie turned off the trail, calling goodbye to their friends, and they began to climb up the hill to their home.

After trudging upward toward the cabin, Freddie sighed over a continuing problem. "Shore wisht we could go huntin' like them Collum boys. Why you think it is that Pa won't let us go? 'Cause we got no good huntin' dogs?"

Junior nodded, wisely. "Been thinkin' on it. Don't reckon that'd be the whole of it. We need to have us a dog, but they's folks'd give us a good trackin' beagle iffen we'd be askin' around."

"Why, then?"

Junior sighed importantly as he launched into his newly arrived at decision. "Likely Pa figures us to be too little to shoot that shotgun."

"But we ain't, are we?"

Junior shook his head. "Nope. Gettin' to practice, that'd be the way to learn shootin'."

A few more steps up the rocky trail as they considered their problem. Junior nodded again.

"We gotta find a way to get practice with that old gun."

"Pa'd likely not let us do that."

"He ain't said we couldn't."

"But...."

"You heard him say we couldn't?"

"No, but...."

"Well, you see there?"

Freddie nodded. They seemed to be making progress. "You figurin' to ask 'im can we use it?"

"Reckon not. Askin' Pa flat out like, that'd be a shore way to get him to say 'no' 'afore he thought it out. We gotta think on just how to do this."

Knowing his brother well, Freddie asked, "You got somethin' thought up already?"

"Purty near. Need to do some talkin' now."

"Yeah, we gotta talk. Pa ever show you how to put them shells in that gun?"

"Nope. Weren't no need in that. I seen how they went in and how they come out." He grinned at Freddie. "I got us four shells hid out I ain't told you about."

"How come?" Freddie asked.

"Figured we'd be wantin' 'em."

"I mean, how come you ain't told me?"

Junior shrugged meaningfully. "Ain't had no chance, dummy. Only done it last night."

"Where you got 'em hid at?"

"Underneath the feather tick. Pa, he gonna be down to the river, givin' us time to get the gun off down the wall and get in four shots 'afore he sees the way the noise is comin' at 'im from."

Freddie nodded his understanding. "Two shots for you and two for me?"

"'Course. But you gotta 'member to hurry with them shots, else we ain't gonna have time."

"We gonna shoot good, ain't we?"

"Reckon so. Ain't no big problem to shootin' a gun. All that's gotta be done is to point and pull the trigger. Figure two shots for you and two shots for me gonna likely give us the practice we gotta have. Then we'd likely be ready to go huntin'."

"Yeah, and we'd be doin' that real good."

The boys quickened their step, the sooner to reach home and the shotgun.

Freddie couldn't resist pointing out, "Ma'll likely be in the house."

"That'd be the reason we'll be real quiet. No reason to be disturbin' Ma."

"Yeah, no need in that."

As Junior and Freddie cleared the crest of the hill, they saw their mother carrying a basket of something and heading down the path toward InaMae's house. The slam-slam of the sledge-hammer against a fence post told the boys where their father was. They broke into a run, reaching the cabin door together.

"Freddie, you reach under the feather tick and get them shells and I'll get up here and get down the gun."

Freddie dashed into the lean-to and felt his arm under the mattress covering their bed. There were the cold, solid shotgun shells. All four of them. He stuffed them into his pocket.

Junior had dragged a cane-bottom chair to the door and eased the shotgun off its pegs above the door. It was amazingly heavy.

"You got 'em?"

"Yeah!"

"Come on."

"What're we gonna shoot at?"

"Whatever we want to. Reckon I'll aim at that pointy rock over through them trees. Here, lemme put in that shell."

Junior shoved the shell in the gun and raised it to his shoulder. The gun barrel was so heavy he could not hold it level.

"Grab a'holt on that barrel, Freddie, and lift up. 'Member to keep your hands away from the end."

Freddie lifted the barrel.

"No, Freddie. I can't see nothin' 'cept your hand. Move your fingers down under."

Freddie readjusted his hand.

"Yeah, that's good. No, wait. See that pointy stick layin' yonder? That'd do better. That's right, now I'm gonna shoot."

A deafening roar boomed out over the mountain, issuing from a gun that suddenly became a living thing filled with rage and vengeance. It slammed Junior back against a tree and Freddie was crumbled into a heap on the dusty ground.

"Freddie? Freddie!" Junior bent down and rolled him over.

"Huh?"

"Freddie, don't you never do me that'a'way no more. I thought you was hit, the way you fell down like that."

"I thought I was hit, too. How come it to knock me down?"

"I don't know but it ain't gonna do it no more. We gonna brace the back against this here little tree and look down it sideways. Hurry up. Pa gonna be here."

"I wanna shoot."

"But I gotta have me another turn."

"But you done had one and Pa's gonna be here. Lemme have it!"

"Shore enough right. You shoot, now."

They braced the stock against the small tree and Junior lifted the barrel. The shot rang out marvelously loud and both boys were still standing.

"I told you we'd get the best of that old gun. I want my other turn," Junior demanded.

"No, I want my other turn," Freddie insisted.

"Well, then, you gotta hurry!"

"Yeah," Freddie adjusted the aim and fired. A small limb broke loose and fell to the ground.

"I hit somethin'. You see that, Junior? I hit me a limb and it broke off!"

"Move over, Freddie, 'cause I gotta get my turn in a hurry."

The gun was reloaded and Junior moved the barrel a little. He took aim at a distant point and fired. The blast rattled their eardrums and echoed across the valley, followed by the loud squawk of a chicken.

"You hit a chicken, Junior."

"Didn't neither."

"Did, too. I heard it out there squawkin'."

"Naw, I only scairt it. See it runnin' yonder?"

"It weren't that one you hit, Junior. Lookie through the trees there. I see it still a'flappin' on the ground."

6

At the first shot, Carl Morgan had become alert.

Someone was hunting on his property without permission. On the second shot, he tossed down his tools. Those shots were entirely too close. The next shot told him that the shooting was done in the vicinity of his cabin site. By the fourth shot, he had no doubts as to who was doing the shooting. He began to run up the hill.

"Junior! Freddie! Where at you shootin? Don't you be pullin' that trigger no more. You hear me? You put that there gun on the ground and call to me where you're at."

Junior lowered the gun to the ground. "Here, Pa. Freddie and me, we're both here."

The bushes parted and Carl Morgan stepped through. He looked from the gun to the two silent boys.

"What you boys think to be doin', shootin' that gun? Who said you could be takin' down that gun?"

"But, Pa, didn't nobody say we couldn't. We was needin' some shootin' practice so as to be ready to go huntin' when you got time, and I reckon we got practice now. I just took the head off that old Shanghi rooster and you didn't even need to take time out'a your work to show us how to shoot. 'Course, that old rooster gonna be so tough, likely he gotta be stewed all night and into tomorrow."

The stunned Carl was still trying to grasp the situation. "What you sayin', boy?"

Freddie chimed in, "He'd be right, Pa. Me and Junior, we both been hungry for dumplins. Speck I better be gettin' that old bird 'afore he flops off in the trees and gets lost." Then Freddie became braver. "And I got me a limb. Lookie right up there. I shot it off the tree and it fell down."

Carl looked from boy to boy. Something had to be done. With growing boys like his, you either stayed ahead of them or they passed you up. A boy as big as Junior should have already been taught to shoot, and Freddie was not too young. It was a sight how youngens shot up. One day they were babies holding to their mother's apron and the next day they were borrowing your shotgun. It was time to take command.

"Freddie, you hightail it down and get that rooster. Junior, you pick up that gun. Now, lookie here, with a heavy gun like this'n, a youngen the size'a you gonna have to prop up the barrel in a tree fork. This here gun's got a mighty kick to it." Junior nodded, knowingly.

Carl adjusted the gun in a fork of a small tree. "Now lean over and tell me what you see in them sights."

"Pa, we gotta move it over a mite."

"No, just leave it there. Tell me, son, what do you see?"

"Pa, I see Freddie a'bendin' over to pick up that chicken."

"JUNIOR! Don't be touchin' that trigger!"

"But, Pa, they ain't no shells in there."

"All the same, we don't be pointin' at no human person even when we know they ain't no shells loaded."

"I was a'tryin' to tell you, Pa. We gotta move it over a mite."

Carl sighed wearily. "Junior, we gonna see about gettin' you boys a gun. A smaller one that's more of size you can use. Time is getting' here for you boys and me to be doin' some huntin'. You boys get on up to the house now, and take that chicken."

The red rooster was indeed through flapping but the blood still dripped. Junior took one of its legs and Freddie took the other, dangling the headless fowl between them.

Late that evening, Carl told Lorena, "Yep, them boys gotta be punished but I ain't decided on how. Would a blisterin' help them boys, and them just tryin' to grow up? Been needin' to get a couple'a beagle pups and a smaller gun. I wasn't no bigger'n Freddie when my Pa took me huntin'. Junior just growed up past me while I was cuttin' hay and beatin' on fence posts and I reckon this was just his way of callin' my attention to the fact."

"But they shot InaMae's rooster," Lorena pointed out.

Carl nodded. "Shame about that, but it'd seem to me that InaMae may well's to get used to boys bein' around, if she ain't already," and he reached for Lorena's hand. "Most likely her boy gonna be a lot like them we got."

7

It was on a Tuesday in late June that Lorena and InaMae prepared to go to the Tuesday Quilting down at the church. The women had decided it was time to make their private arrangement public before Lorena's shape made it unnecessary. They had decided to plunge in with a full explanation at the quilting and let the talk play itself out as it would have to do eventually.

By early afternoon, they sat in the circle of women decorating a quilt pattern with their small, even stitches. The quilt pattern was called "Flower Basket" and consisted of rectangles of a dark color filled with scalloped half circles that created the flowers. They all agreed it was a real pain of a pattern to quilt what with all its whirls and back-tracking.

Mrs. Carmichael, whose daughter-in-law would get the quilt, complained bitterly. "That lazy piece of nuisance ought'a be over a'helpin' to stitch up her own quilt. She been doin' nothin' but standin' on her head over the slopjar for two months. Told that boy of mine 'afore he married her, he was lookin' for trouble and that city girl out'a Jacksonville'd be the one to give it to 'im. Now that boy's learnin' fast what I was gettin' at. He's been havin' to cook up his own meals while that Annalee got herself down to skin and bones not eatin'. She's sayin' she can't stand to look at food. Stays in the bed all hours."

"Yeah," agreed someone else. "And she can get away with it on the first kid but on the next 'ens she'll be havin' the first 'ens to look after while she's bein' sick."

Mrs. Carmichael again, "Annalee done told my boy he better be gettin' whatever kid he gonna want this time, 'cause she ain't fixin' to have no more. Told 'im if he was figgerin' to have another one, he better be plannin' on carryin' it, hisself. Ever hear of a woman talkin' like that?"

"Hmmmm."

"Reckon I'd'a said that, bein' I thought I could make it turn out that'a'way," someone else put in. "I done a lot'a lookin' down the slopjar, myself."

Another one put in, "You know, I was never sick a day in my life on account of carryin' a baby. Ain't even got no notion on my own, what that mornin' sickness'd feel like."

"Be thankful to the good Lord."

InaMae kept on stitching.

"Been so long for me, I 'bout forgot what mornin' sickness was like."

Wrinkled and silver-haired Granny Nelson, usually quiet, spoke up. "Ain't no way I'd ever live long enough for that knowledge to slip out'a my mind. I see them young women with big stomachs and feel a pain in my heart for 'em. It could'a been years, seems like, that I never tasted a bite'a breakfast. Emma Carmichael's Annalee, she likely gonna be the same way. Figure it don't have a great lot to do with bein' a city girl from Jacksonville."

Emma Carmichael became somewhat contrite. "Most likely you'd be right about that, Granny. It was mean-mouthed of me to speak of my

Annalee that away. Should'a tasted my words. Likely she gonna make my boy a good wife, once that youngen gets here."

Maisie Pettengill looked around the circle of faces. "Now, seems to me like Lorena'd be another one that got off light. You weren't never sick with your boys, was you?"

Lorena shook her head and kept on stitching.

"Wouldn't'a minded to have more youngens, myself, sick or no sick," another woman commented. "You figurin' to have yourself another'n, Lorena?"

Lorena paused with her stitching and smiled. Here was the chance she knew would come. "No, I reckon not. Me and Carl figure we got our family. Five boys'd be enough for any family to raise, wouldn't you think?"

There were nods and smiles all around. The knowledge of the Morgan boys' antics was well known about town. Politeness demanded something nice be said.

"Them's good lookin' boys you got, Lorena. Them boys you got, they be enough like your Carl to be slices of bread off the same loaf."

Lorena nudged InaMae with her foot. It was the signal. InaMae responded with a returned nudge. Lorena took a deep breath and looked around the circle.

"InaMae gonna have herself a baby come Christmas," she announced.

Chins dropped and eyes popped open. Motionless needles were poised amid stitch. All eyes turned to InaMae.

"Oh, honey! We're all so proud for you!"

"And after all this time!"

"You been sick? Or be you like Lorena?"

"What you thinkin' to get? Gainin' weight right off means you likely gonna get a boy."

"Spect Marcel'd be happy about that."

Lorena nudged her sister again. InaMae put on a bright smile and looked around the circle of excited faces. "I'm wantin' to say somethin' important to you all. Lorena's gonna carry my baby for me."

The church became quiet as a cave. There was not even the sound of a breath. A pair of bluejays screamed outside the window and a hen began to cackle that she had laid an egg. Sounds of children playing in the churchyard became startlingly clear.

"You sayin' that it ain't you that's got the baby?"

"Lorena said you was carryin'."

InaMae shook her head. "Lorena said I was gonna have a baby. That's the words she said. 'Member?'"

Another spell of silence while the women mentally backtracked to the words that were actually said. InaMae was right, and the comments began.

"Well, I never heard'a such a thing!"

"Sure and givin' up your own flesh and blood'd be sinful, seems to me."

Anger sent tingles down Lorena's arms and she put down her needle. She looked around the circle, pausing a moment at each face.

"You just say to me, if you will, who my sister is if she ain't my own flesh and blood? You thinkin' maybe we ain't real sisters?"

Another pause.

"Yeah, but it's still your baby," one brave woman ventured to say.

Lorena took a deep breath. "You women all listen to me and you listen good 'cause this is gonna be said by me one time and no more."

She drew in a breath and sighed, then began, "If any of you was to say to your mama, 'Come Wednesday, I'll be bringin' over a bushel of snap beans and help you put 'em up,' your mama'd say, 'Thank you.' She'd be knowin' them beans was hers already and she'd not be lookin' out to get some more. She'd wait to get the ones she was promised, and she'd know that you'd not say you might go ahead and put 'em for yourself after bein' promised to your mama."

Lorena paused a moment to let the truth of her words soak in.

"Now this here baby I got in me ain't my baby. I done had my family, like I said. This'n was give to my sister 'afore it was started or it wouldn't'a been started. Listen to it said this'a'way. If my sister was sick, I'd be carin' for her, same as she'd be carin' for me if it was me sick. Same way, if my sister wants a baby and I got it in my power to get her one, it'd be no more'n what she'd do for me."

InaMae kept on stitching.

Grannie Nelson knotted her thread skillfully between thumb and index finger and pulled the knot tight. "It's been done before. They's been times it wasn't even a sister."

"Hmmmmm."

"Well, I never...."

"Reckon so, but...."

"All the same…a baby?"

Lorena cut in, "And I gotta say this, when you get to talkin' about this amongst yourselves, you just 'member about them snap beans. The fact of this baby bein' inside me, 'stead of InaMae, don't have no bearin' on who it's mama gonna be. It was give to InaMae or it wouldn't'a been had."

Her voice was firm and hard, leaving no room for discussion. Then she continued, "And, right now, InaMae and me, we're bein' regretful at havin' to leave early but we gotta get along up the hill. I put me a kettle'a beans on to soak and need to get a fire under 'em." She looked around pleasantly, and added, "Carl and them boys is partial to beans but they don't want no hard cooked beans. They like 'em cooked down thick with gravy to sop a biscuit into.

"Me and InaMae, we just gonna leave our needles right here and we promise to finish up these here blocks next week. Miz. Carmichael, you tell your Annalee we'll all be hopin' she'll be feelin' better real soon. So long, now."

As one person, Lorena and InaMae anchored their needles, stood and walked away, gathering up Lorena's three younger boys on the way to the buggy. As the sisters pulled out of the churchyard, Lorena looked at InaMae and grinned. "Well, we done it."

InaMae grinned back. "We sure did and that ought'a hold 'em a while."

Back in the church building, needles pierced the Flower Garden pattern, and the quilting continued. So did the comments.

"Never seen a thing like that in all my born days."

"How she can stand to do it, is what I want to know? Ain't no way I'd give up my youngen, no matter how many I had."

"Yeah, and likely she had herself an accident and InaMae agreed to take it off her hands."

"Well, we been knowin' InaMae's been wantin a baby...."

"Anyway, it'll most likely be a boy and a right good lookin' one at that. InaMae gonna know what she gonna get, allowin' if Lorena don't change her mind to keep it."

"Still, I never heard of such a thing."

"I just can't be thinkin' how a woman'd feel, doin a thing like that!"

"Well, if one was used to sharin' other things like them girls always done, well, maybe...."

"Could be a good and lovin' thing, seems to me."

"Still and all, I ain't able to calculate how a woman could do a thing like that. Still seems to me to be a sin. Maybe."

Jane Ann McCrey, the young wife of the minister, arose to fill the teacups. "I been busy thinkin', ever since Lorena said what she did. I think I know what kind of woman would do a thing like that."

All eyes turned toward her.

"What kind?"

"I'm thinkin' it'd take one of the most kind, lovin' and carin' kind of a Christian that God ever smiled on to be able to do such a hard and painful thing. Likely I wouldn't be one of them kind and lovin' women, but I consider it to be a fault in me that I couldn't."

Granny Nelson nodded her gray head, "We could all think on that, searchin inside ourselves for how that wouldn't be a good thing."

"Well, I...."

"Sure, and it does seem to be a reasonable idea, right on the surface of it, to be sharin' what you got be it beans or babies."

"Speck InaMae'll be real happy to have her own baby after helpin' out with Lorena's boys all these years. Does seem to be fair when you think on it. I gotta go on home and put on some beans for supper. Lorena just put me in the mind of it."

One by one the women left the church. Finally, it was just Jane Ann McCrey and Granny Nelson. Jane Ann couldn't resist asking, "Granny, I never ever thought of such a thing that just happened."

"Likely none of the others did, neather."

Jane Ann grinned back, her eyes twinkling, "Granny Nelson, I find it amazing, you always havin' the right word at the right time to keep the talk from explodin' into bad feelin's! A word or two from you and their talkin' stops bein' so cross."

Granny's wrinkles deepened and increased in number. Deep lines formed stars around her light blue, twinkling eyes. "Jane Ann, youngen, I don't mind sayin' it takes practice on knowin' when to talk and when to keep your mouth shut and that's the truth."

Granny put down her needle and reached her arms toward Jane Ann for a quick, understanding hug.

"You could see, honey, they was somethin' strong needin' to be said to turn the talk away from the way it was a'goin'."

"Still and all, Granny...."

Granny replied, "Well, honey, it just takes practice and you ain't so bad at it yourself. Times I 'member hearin' you play hopscotch with your words, right through these hen parties, and you keepin' up with the best of 'em. You take right after your grandmama, Esther, her havin' the same job as you when your grandpa started this here church. I credit the Good Lord for makin' you that'a'way so as to be a peacemaker. That'd be one of the first things for a preacher's wife to be. You want help gettin this here quiltin' frame pulled back up to the ceiling 'afore I leave to go home?"

"No, Granny, I can manage and thanks. See you Sunday."

8

Carl Morgan and Marcel McCann were adding a strand of barbed wire to the new fence they had put around the calf pasture. New posts had been set, and the wire stretcher was pulling the kinks out of the four strands of barbed wire to contain the latest crop of calves. It was one of the many jobs that required an extra set of hands, and the two men had worked together closer than brothers from the time they were toddlers.

At the sound of a buggy coming up the hill, they looked up to see Lorena and InaMae ride by on their way home from the Tuesday Sewing Circle. Sounds of their conversation and laughter reached the men as they thought of what their wives would have gone through, only just minutes ago.

Marcel unwound another spool of wire, hesitated and finally said, "Carl?"

"Huh?"

Another hesitation and a sigh. "The words taste strange in my mouth to be thankin' you for what you and Lorena done for InaMae and me, but I got it layin' on my mind to say."

Carl applied the wire stretcher to the strand of wire and tapped it in place with a staple. He did not let his eyes stray to his friend's face. The moment was too emotional. When he was successful with his voice, he responded. "Well, you done said it now, and don't be thinkin' you need to say nothin' more. Tain't no more'n you'd'a done for me, things bein' different. I could be thankin' you for the times you dropped everything to help me outta a tangle…and this here'll just be evenin' things out a mite 'tween the two of us."

He clipped the secured wire and attached it to the post for the next strand. His practiced hands worked without his thoughts for they were with Lorena and what they both had ahead of them. Why did some simple things have to be so hard to do?

9

It was the middle of August, sultry and still with hardly a breath of air to be had, that Lorena tightened the lid on the last jar of hot-water-bath, canned tomatoes and set it on the floor to cool slowly. She heaved herself tiredly into a chair to catch her breath. At that moment, she heard a sound overhead.

Lorena walked tiredly to the door. "Junior! Freddie! You boys get down from there!"

A deep voice answered, "It's ain't the boys."

Her surprised voice asked, "Carl, what you doin' up on the roof?"

"Figurin'."

"On what?"

"I'll say it to you when I get down."

Lorena wiped her aching hands on her apron and walked outside to see her husband descend the pole ladder he had leaned against the end of the cabin.

"I was just figurin' where to tie onto the roof. Gotta do somethin' for space. Them boys is crowdin' us now and it ain't fixin' to be gettin' better any time soon." He grinned at Lorena, "Figure, come layin' by time in the fall, to be cuttin' the timber for the new room."

"Another lean-to?"

"That was my first thought, bein' the easiest way out, but measurin' shows to get a room of any size, it'd butt up agin the hammock tree. Kinda hated to get in the way'a that tree. The only other way'd, be to go out to the back. Trouble there is that the doorway'd be in the way of our bed."

Lorena's weariness melted away with thoughts of this new situation. She walked to the end of the cabin to view it in a new light. New room, huh? They could really use it.

"How big was you figurin' it to be?"

Carl shoved back his mop of black hair that always seemed to be in need of a trimming. "Need to be big enough for a bed and a bureau, I'm thinkin'. Junior and Freddie could go into it, takin' the strain off the lean-to. Big as they're getting, they wouldn't need more'n a bed and a bureau 'afore they'll be on their own."

Lorena nodded agreement as she looked up studying the trees overhead. The massive oaks seemingly towered into the sky. Even the first limbs of the tree were high above the cabin roof.

"Carl, I got me an idea."

"Huh?"

"If you ain't got solid plans, yet, I got an idea."

"Spit it out."

"You know them two floored houses? If we was to make the new room to be two floored, you and me, we could have the high room. Still wouldn't need to be bigger'n a bed and bureau, and maybe a new wardrobe closet."

"Hmmm. Well, I always thought them two floored houses to be a necessity to folks without buildin' land. You don't reckon that'd make a lot of ups and downs for you?"

"Don't reckon. The boys ain't babies no more and they're growing every day. It's little 'ens to see after, that makes the ups and downs be so wearyin' and we ain't plannin' no more. I'd be thinkin' folks wantin' a view might make a two floored house no matter how much buildin' land they got. I've always liked the view'a the valley and the river."

"Hmmmmm. You might have somethin' there."

Lorena continued as thoughts presented themselves. "And the steps up to it could be right where our bed is now. That'd still leave room for the door to the new room."

"Hmmm," Carl stroked his chin as he pictured the change.

"Carl, you gonna start downin' them trees right away, you say? 'Cause I don't want to be hopin' and not havin'…?"

Carl grinned his wide grin. "Done picked out the trees and downed a few of 'em already. Buildin' gonna start right after Christmas less'n you'd be wantin' the logs sawed into lumber. We got money to do that, if it'd be what you want."

Lorena saw no reason to consider the suggestion. "Be no reason for sawin' away good wood. I been all my life with log walls and see no good reason to stop. I'd be wantin' to know the size of the room, though, so as to get started on us a rug."

"The size'd be somethin' to decide together, bein' how big you think you want it to be. I was figurin' to make a trip into Jacksonville to get the window sashes and have 'em here 'afore the rains started. Thought you could go along with me. Just us. Ain't got no calves to be brought back home this time."

Lorena's eyes brightened. "And I was just needin' a piece of dress goods to make up somethin' to wear till Christmas. I was hopin' for somethin' bright like maybe yellow for makin' a Sunday dress."

"Then we'll just make a day of it. We can get ice cream and eat it over at the courthouse yard just like we done when we was courtin'."

Lorena colored slightly behind her smile and Carl winked wickedly at her.

At this moment, a piercing scream cut into their interlude.

"A centipede! He's done run under that rock!"

Junior's voice, "Grab a hoe, Freddie. I'll get the rake."

The interlude was gone, but there would still be the whole day together. A whole, wonderful day. And just the two of them.

10

They started to Jacksonville before daylight. The pony's footsteps clipped along, drumming rhythmically on the gravels of the road drawing the two seated, light wagon carrying the couple. Taking the closed-in buggy would have been nice, but there were the new window sashes to bring home and they needed extra space.

InaMae fed the boys and washed up the dishes. "You boys can crack up some of them hickory nut goodies for your mama. Take this bowl and get the hammer out'a Marcel's shed. That'll make two of you crackin'."

If the boys were given a job early in the day, usually something got done before they branched out into activities of their own. Any energy used in constructive endeavor was energy that was not put to other uses, destructive or otherwise. Junior picked up the bowl.

"Freddie, you go and get Marcel's hammer. Georgie, bring along them nuts in that gunny sack. Here, Stanley, you carry Pa's hammer."

"Me!" complained Jamie.

"Here, Jamie. You take the bowl. No, Stanley, you take the bowl and give Jamie the hammer. Could be he'd drop the bowl and it'd be broke."

Junior led the way to the large flat rock where the official nut cracking was done. There were small dimples in the wide, flat rock and they were beneficial for holding the nuts properly upright so fingers would not be smashed and the kernels would come out in large pieces.

"Now, Stanley, you and Jamie ain't gonna be eatin' them nut goodie fast as we git 'em picked out like you done last time," Junior warned.

"Yeah," agreed Freddie.

Stanley objected, "Georgie ate goodies."

"Didn't neither."

Junior raised his voice to its authoritative level. "Ain't nobody gonna eat no nuts. We all gonna fill that bowl."

Indeed the bowl was full when a flickering, blue-black wasp flew close to Jamie's head.

"Duck down, Jamie!" Freddie commanded. "They's a wasper after you!"

Obediently, Jamie ducked.

"Look at 'im go," observed Georgie, watching the insect. "He's fixin' to come back."

"Back?"

"Duck again, Jamie."

Junior had been observing the activity with concern. "We gotta get that old wasper. He's after Jamie. You go to the house, Jamie."

"No."

"Georgie, take Jamie to the house."

Georgie hesitated deciding whether to re-delegate the chore. "Stanley, take Jamie to the house."

Stanley hesitated, looking around.

Georgie added, "Then you can come back."

With that promise made, Stanley complied, half dragging the protesting Jamie.

Junior and Freddie were already in hot pursuit of the wasp, with Georgie not far behind. The flickering blue-black wings headed toward the cowshed with the loft full of hay.

"There he goes! Hurry!"

"Where's he at?"

"See that crack? He crawled in."

The crack was an opening in a board just above them in the subfloor of the hayloft. The boys stretched their necks to look up at it. It was almost directly over the chicken feed barrel.

"Freddie, hold onto that barrel for me so's I can climb up and take a look."

Freddie obediently held the barrel still while Junior climbed onto it.

"I wanna see," requested Georgie.

"You're too little," announced Freddie, ungraciously.

"Not too little. You could boost me up."

"You don't need to see. Junior's already seein'."

"I'll tell...."

Junior intervened before the threat could actually be voiced. "No, you ain't gonna tell 'cause I got a special job for you."

"What?"

"You'll see. Freddie, go get matches out'a the house. They's a wasper nest in there gettin' real big and we gonna get it out. That'a'way Pa won't be havin' to waste time doin' it."

Freddie hated to leave but realized only he could reach the matches. He disappeared as commanded. Junior took a jug of kerosene carefully down from its high shelf.

"Now, Georgie, you don't want to be doin' this while you're little. Somethin' might happen."

"What?"

Junior thought. "Somethin' bad. You'll see when it does."

Georgie seemed contented to wait until the something bad happened in order to find out. Junior was more than often right when he predicted disaster. Freddie returned with the matches.

"Now lookie here," Junior began. "We gonna take this here little old rag and put it in the kerosene. Pa'd say to pour kerosene on the nest, but we ain't gonna be able to reach it, bein' stuck in 'tween them boards like it is, but this here'll work. We gonna get it wet, like this, and then we gonna poke it up through the hole."

"How?"

"We jab on it with a stick. Freddie can do that. I'll hold the barrel."

"I wanna do it," complained Georgie.

"No. I got somethin' else for you to do."

The rag was duly soaked and the fumes of the kerosene were strong in the shed. Freddie poked the stick with the soaked rag attached through the crack and across the subfloor until it reached the paper nest of the wasps.

"Now we gonna burn 'em out. Freddie gonna hold that barrel and Georgie, you gonna hold the match. I'll be boostin' you up there to the crack and you gonna shove that match in there where we poked that rag. That'll get 'em!"

Georgie was lifted into position. Freddie struck the match and handed it to Georgie. Junior, balancing on the barrel, lifted Georgie toward the crack.

The flame flickered from the shakiness of Georgie's hand but finally regained its blaze. The small boy, with all muscles straining with the importance of the task, moved the match carefully toward the crack. Junior could not hold him very steady but, in spite of that, Georgie was able to poke the burning match through to the area between the floor and the subfloor of the hayloft full of dry hay.

The instant the flame was drawn into the area, it contacted the fumes of the soaked rag and the space between the floors was filled with a sudden burst of fire that shot like a lightning bolt to the other end of the space. It forced tongues of flame out from every crack.

The roar of the combustion and sudden light of the expanding fire startled Junior and set him teetering on the edge of the barrel. Freddie lost his grip and the barrel tipped on its edge and juggled.

Junior loosed his grip on Georgie but jumped clear of the tipping barrel. Georgie fell straight down into the barrel but not before a board from the ceiling was loosened by the explosion and came flying down, grazing his shoulder and arm. He screamed and ducked low into the half-filled barrel of chicken feed.

The flash immediately consumed the available oxygen but left no blaze, and the noise was gone as suddenly as it had come. Junior jumped up off the floor of the shed and looked into the barrel.

"Georgie...?"

"Huh?"

"Freddie...?"

"Huh?"

Junior sighed with relief that his brothers were both alive. Quickly searching for someone to blame for something, he spotted Georgie's arm. "Lookie at your shirt, Georgie! You tore it!"

"The board tore it," Georgie answered, defensively.

Junior ignored the minor technicality. "We gotta get that board fastened back up there. Lookie at the wasper nest! We shore got it! See all them little white wasper babies? We scorched 'em to death."

"Scorched!"

"Yeah, we got 'em!"

"I reckon we fixed him. Pa gonna like that!"

"Yeah, but we gotta fix that board. Georgie, go get the crackin' hammer."

Stanley had returned and was standing in the doorway, reluctant to enter the area of the mysterious blast and roar.

Georgie's eyes fastened on his younger brother, "Stanley, you go get the crackin' hammer."

"Don't know where at?" Stanley objected.

"On the nut crackin' rock where we left it. Hurry."

Unable to think up a quick objection, Stanley left.

Junior and Freddie pulled the loosened board the rest of the way off.

"Them nails gotta come the rest of the way out so as to get pounded back in the right way," Junior decided. "Freddie, you gonna have to do the hammerin' back up, 'cause you can't hold me up, once I got to hammerin'. Georgie, you gotta climb up on them harnesses over there and hold up t'other end'a the board. I'll just scoot this barrel around out'a the way."

Georgie eyed the barrel with apprehension, but Junior's confidence kept him from making an objection. After all, he had not been commanded to climb on it again, and how could a harness wobble and throw you around?

By now, Stanley was back with the hammer. Junior took it from him, "I'll just be gettin' these nails out. Freddie, you got'a help Georgie climb up on them harnesses so he don't slip."

Georgie was accustomed to climbing, and, grabbing a handful of the leather straps, drew himself up toward the heavy iron hook where they hung. With a boost on his rear from Freddie's hand, he was able to reach the hook with his left hand. With a further bit of guidance from Freddie, his right foot found a loop of leather to stand in. The left foot hung loose, ready to catch him if he had to jump. His right hand pushed the loose board securely against the ceiling joist.

Seeing him safely in place, Freddie climbed onto the barrel, planting one foot on each edge and reaching for the hammer. Junior, as promised, wrapped his arms around the barrel to steady it as much as possible.

Freddie, wobbling precariously on the barrel and hammering up toward the ceiling, miraculously bent only three nails. Seemingly the rest of the nails were sufficient to hold as the board appeared to be solid.

"There. Reckin' we done that."

Seeing the board now in place, Georgie felt he could use a little attention. "Lookie at my arm," he pointed out. "My shirt done stuck to it."

"Come on," Junior told him. "We'll go to the pump and wash it a'loose. Freddie, go get them nuts and we'll be takin' 'em on in quick as I get done here."

It was late when Carl and Lorena returned. InaMae had stewed a hen and baked it into a chicken pie with vegetables from the garden. While the oven was hot, she had browned oatmeal cookies with raisins. The tantalizing aroma met the travelers as the wagon entered the yard. The end of a perfect day. The boys were playing noisily in the back yard. All was well.

That evening the boys were washing up for bed.

"Georgie, what you got wrong with your arm?"

Georgie glanced at Junior who quickly explained, "Georgie scraped it on a board."

"Where at?"

"In the cow shed," supplied Freddie.

"Let Georgie talk. What was you doin' in the cow shed?"

"A wasper."

"A wasper was after you?"

Georgie nodded, hesitantly. Actually, it was not true. Technically, the wasp had been after Jamie.

Carl was now interested. "Was they a wasper in the shed?"

Now Georgie could nod enthusiastically.

"Likely got a nest in there. Gonna have to look for it."

Junior now regained control of the explanation and seemingly had permission to speak. "No need, Pa. We got it."

"You did? You got the wasper nest?"

"Yeah, Pa."

"And nobody got hisself stung?"

"Nobody."

"That was a good job you done."

Junior looked at his brothers. "We was glad to do it, Pa. We knowd you didn't have no time to be messin' with a old wasper nest, so we got it."

Junior, Freddie, and Georgie nodded, smiling. The account of the incident had been made truthfully, and no adult was angry. That was the goal of every report.

"Went BOOM!" Stanley reported.

"What went boom?"

Freddie, Stanley, and Georgie looked quickly at Junior.

Junior explained, "Boom happened when Georgie hit the board. You done seen that scratch it made on his arm."

"Yeah, when I hit the board," Georgie quickly agreed.

"Yeah, he whacked it good," Junior elaborated.

Carl looked from boy to boy and was satisfied. They had seen a problem and handled it, and what more could he expect?

It was the week that the field peas from the garden came on with a vengeance. It was a dreaded time, but the nutritions and tasty vegetable could be used in so many ways, and was so easy to grow, that they were planted in abundance. It was because of this that Lorena and InaMae reluctantly decided they could not afford the time to go to the Tuesday Sewing Circle.

Annalee Carmichael, the upchucking expectant mother, managed to keep her head out of the slopjar long enough to attend. She looked around happily and announced, "I shore like not bein' sick. You know what? We gotta think of a baby party for…Lorena? Or who?"

Hmmmm, that required some thought. There had never been a situation like this before, at least in anybody's memory. After a silence, the ideas began to come.

"Well, it'd be winter for it to happen, if we was to wait to be sure she didn't…lose…."

With the confident shake of the head, Jane Ann spoke with assurance. "Oh, remember its Lorena. She'll not have no trouble."

Good point.

Corinne Upchurch considered the point. "You know, on the tail end'a five boys, there's bound to be diapers enough up on that hill for whoever it is that finally gets the baby."

"Yeah, and gowns and wrappers, too."

Annalee Carmichael again. "Reckon we could do somethin' different? Makin' it more like a real party?"

"Yeah, it'll be in the winter, and we'll be wantin' a place to go."

There were nods all around, remembering the dullness of the mountain cabins in cold weather.

"I think Annalee's got a good idea."

"Me, too, but what?"

The cookies were passed around to aid in the thinking. Today, there was a choice of chocolate or peanut butter, and either went well with the peppermint tea.

Essie McGreevy wiped the crumbs from her lips and began, "Well, I'm not sayin' this is what we oughta do, but I did know of somethin' different. There was a baby party in a church over to Jacksonville, and they had somethin' kind'a like we got. That woman had five or six, or more, I forget what. Anyway, the women all got together and made a little quilt and everyone of 'em brought in buttons that they wasn't gonna be able to use on nothin' else. There was big ones and little ones, some fancy and colored and some not. They sewed them buttons all over that quilt pullin' the thread tight so's they'd not pull off. I heard tell it was a sight to see and a surprise to the woman, her not needin' nothin' else. It was talked about a lot, bein' a thing the baby girl liked to play with so she could pat and twist and chew on them buttons and amuse herself."

Essie reached for another cookie, chocolate this time, and looked around the circle to see how her suggestion was taken. There were nods and interested half-smiles as they pictured the button decorated quilt.

Young Annalee was first to speak up. She could see that she, herself, would like such a gift. "You reckon we could get enough buttons to put one in the middle of every block?"

It seemed no more discussion was needed, and the suggestion passed. "I got some buttons," came one quilter, "that're too big and clucky for anything I'd ever have. Been layin' around for years."

"Me, too."

It was time for Jane Ann to pull it together. "You ladies thinkin' a single blanket would be enough for the party? Wouldn't want it to look like we was stingy just cause it was Lorena. Remember, it might be InaMae, like they said. Those girls didn't seem to leave much room for doubt as to how it'd go."

"Yeah, and this'd be her first baby."

There were nods, but someone reminded, "Even so, Lorena'd not need her diapers no more. You heard her say how it was when they shared."

More nods. "Yeah, we heard...."

Jane Ann cast her eyes toward Granny Nelson's silver hair and wrinkly cheeks. "What do you think, Granny?"

The old woman dipped her cookie into her tea, the better for chewing it without teeth. The peanut butter cookie was very tasty, and next to molasses, it was her favorite. She began, "I been runnin' it through my mind. Bein' in her place, and I ain't never heard they was short'a money up on that hill for anything they needed, I think I'd like that kind of a surprise party. Now about that bein' only one thing, I was thinkin' this. With youngens and especially babies, there ain't never too many safety pins in the house. Especially them big diaper pins. I was thinkin' if we was to all get a card'a pins…and…." She paused, giving someone else a chance at part of the wonderful suggestion.

Mrs. Jenkins nodded and clipped her thread, knotting the end, smiled happily, glad to be the one picking up the thought.

"I'm thinkin' I could get Mr. Jenkins to order them pins through the store, there bein' so many, and we'd get 'em at a better price."

Annalee again. Her eyes sparkled at getting so much attention from the older ladies, including her mother-in-law. "How'd it be if we took the pins off the card and fastened 'em all around the edge? Would that be good?"

"Sounds like fun. We could do that."

It was time for Jane Ann to bring the discussion to a close. "So now, who'd it be for, Lorena or InaMae? We'd not want to do the wrong thing, after as much as we already said. This here likely hasn't been easy for either one'a those girls."

Granny Nelson played her part. "Why not make the present for the baby, not the mama. That'a way we'd not make a mistake. Now we need to figure how many pins to let Elsie Jenkins order for us."

While the discussion went on at the church in River Bend, pea shelling and canning was going on up on Rock Mountain at the Morgan cabin. It was a boring, sore-finger sort of a job, and even Carl and Marcel were drawn into it if they paused a moment in the cabin. They tried not to pause.

The boys were set to picking. Armed with baskets, they followed along the rows pulling the purple hulled vegetables. Junior and Freddie were well acquainted with the job and this was Georgie's first serious year. Junior updated him on the rules.

"See here, Georgie, you only gotta pick the ones longer'n your hand. See these little'ns? We got'a let them grow up."

Stanley looked over Georgie's shoulder. "Worms. Bitty worms."

"No, Stanley, them ain't worms. They're baby peas."

"Bitty worms," he repeated.

Junior decided to ignore him. "Georgie, what do you pick?"

"Bigger'n my hand."

"Good. You start right here on my row, and when I pick them this far, I'll see how you done."

The picking proceed for a while with Georgie measuring every bean against his hand before he pulled it. Stanley watched for a minute then left for more interesting things. He crawled over Junior's row into Freddie's row and pulled aside the bushy vines to inspect the crop. "Bitty worms. Bitty worms and bitty worms."

Junior finally had enough. "Hush up, Stanley. Them ain't worms."

Stanley kept still as long as he could. "Worm. Old bigger worm."

Junior warned, "Don't you pull them peas, Stanley. You'll tear up the vines and pa'll get onto you. You let Freddie get it."

"Bigger worm," he repeated.

Sighing with exasperation, Junior finally commanded, "Freddie, step up there and pick that pea so he'll hush. Would you?"

Freddie was getting out of patience, too, so he took a few steps and demanded, "Where at is that bigger worm?"

Stanley leaned forward to point with his finger, so there would be no mistake. That was when Freddie saw the head of the rattler draw back within its coil, preparatory to a strike. Freddie drew in a breath, shoved his brother backward and bravely planted a bare foot firmly behind the creature's head.

Stanley yelled with indignation and screamed, "My old bigger worm!"

Georgie stopped his measuring and stepped over the row of vines. "Where at is that bigger worm?"

The serpent's head moved back and forth but was unable to turn toward Freddie's foot. His other end, however, released from its coil and waved the length of rattles as it twisted up Freddie's other leg.

Georgie stared at the snake and grabbed Stanley's arm, pulling him across the row of vines screaming, "JUNIOR!"

Junior wearily tossed his peas into his basket. "What?"

At last Freddie found a voice. "Junior, come help me! I'm on a snake!"

Leaping across the vines, Junior instructed, "Get off it, Freddie! It's a rattler! I can hear it!"

"I can't step off it! It's tryin' to bite me."

Junior could see at a glance that was the truth. "Wait. I'll get the corn knife."

With a trembling voice, Freddie begged, "Hurry, he's tryin' to squirm out from under my foot."

Wide eyed, Stanley begged, "Lemme see. My bigger worm!"

Georgie, proud of his newly acquired authority, shouted, "It ain't neither your worm. It ain't even a worm. If'n you don't shut up, I'm gonna take you to Mama and you can't even see Junior cut up that old snake."

Stanley sniffed and considered the matter. Being quiet seemed a small price to pay for such an exciting proceeding. He allowed Georgie to hold his arm while he watched the writhing snake winding its body up Freddie's leg.

"Hurry, Junior!"

"I'm a'comin'," Junior promised as he leaped over row after row of pea vines.

Wielding the arm-long corn knife, he reached the scene. "Georgie, pull him back a little more. Freddie, hold steady and don't move your toes. I got'a get this rock and hold down his head so's to get closer. Don't be jigglin'."

"He's 'bout to pull me over."

"Don't let 'im," came the useless comment.

Rocks were abundant on the hillside farm, and Junior located a flat one about the size of a dinner plate. Carefully moving behind Freddie, he instructed, "Now when I put this rock down, don't you move your foot. I got'a cut 'tween your foot and the rock."

"Hurry...."

Junior's steady hand lowered the rock onto the waving head and forking tongue, pressing it to the ground. He planted his foot firmly on the rock and picked up the corn knife. Gregory and Stanley moved to a position of better view. It wasn't often they got to witness an operation as important as this one was about to be.

Junior leaned down with the knife, carefully placing it on the neck of the rattler, sawing back and forth. The writing tail became more active, and Freddy was forced to hold to his brother's back to keep from being pulled down. Blood and gristle appeared and the lashing tail began to relax onto the dusty ground. The tail coiled, then loosened and turned with its pale belly upward. Job well done.

Junior stepped back and calmly cleaned the knife with leaves from the pea vines. Color began to return to Freddie's face, and Georgie stared from brother to brother in rapt admiration.

Stanley pointed his finger toward the dying snake. "Old bigger worm," he repeated, and no one told him to hush.

Freddie stooped and picked up the snake's tail, dragging the reptile to the garden fence, and laying him across the wire.

Junior nodded approval. "We'll cut off them rattles later," he promised.

"Georgie, go on a pick up there and on my row. Stanley, if you see another worm, just call me and don't get close. Do you hear?"

Stanley stared at his bossy brother. "Old bigger worm," he insisted.

The morning sun shone brightly on the garden fence where the sky-blue morning glory blossoms twined. Junior and Freddie stood staring at each other and at the fence where the body of the rattler should be hanging. They sighed and shrugged their sunbrowned shoulders.

"What're ya thinkin'," Freddie opened.

"'Spect it was a 'coon," came the answer from his brother.

A nod from Freddie, "That's what I figgered."

Another sigh and Junior commented, "I was countin' on getting' somethin' made out'a that snake skin."

Freddie brightened. "What was ya thinkin' on?"

Another weary shrug. "I was figgerin' it'd come to me when I looked at it again."

With that, the two boys picked up their baskets and headed down the rows of field peas waiting to be picked.

In due time, Sunday arrived.

Hung on the wall of the Morgan cabin were five crisp cotton shirts of various sizes, starched and ironed to the texture and stiffness of kindling wood. Folded on the top of the bureau was a stack of short pants also in a variety sizes. In the top drawer were five pairs of stockings and underwear, and on the floor beneath the bureau were five pairs of worn but freshly polished shoes. It was a typical Sunday morning.

Breakfast of pancakes and honey was over and sticky fingers had been washed apart. Knobby-kneed legs were enclosed in short stockings and starched pants and the shirts were put on. Black hair was watered down, parted, and plastered back with the comb.

Pennies were handed out. Carl Morgan instructed his sons, "Them pennies better stay in them pockets till the collection plate comes by. You listenin'?"

Five heads nodded rapidly.

Carl continued, "You better be listenin', cause they ain't no reason for one of you not havin' your money ready when the plate comes 'round. Even Jamie. You hear me, Jamie? You got your penny?"

"You gonna lose it?"

Jamie nodded again. His four brothers turned to him, exaggeratedly shaking their heads. Jamie quickly shook his head.

Carl continued, "Show me your penny, Jamie?"

Jamie bent down and pushed his hand deep into his sock, pulling out the penny.

"No, Jamie. Your penny don't belong in your sock. Put it in your pocket."

The small boy opened his pocket with one hand and obediently dropped in the penny with the other. The penny slid through the hole in his pocket and out of his pant leg, rolling across the floor.

"Use the other pocket," instructed Freddie.

Georgie retrieved Jamie's penny and put it in the other pocket. Jamie grinned at the tickle the penny made as it slid through the hole in his other pocket and landed in his sock. Just as it had the first time. The only difference was that his father had been looking away and missed it.

"Now," concluded Carl, "they ain't no reason why you can't hang on to your penny, is there?"

Five heads shook from side to side with deep reassurance.

"Now, go get in the wagon."

The wide, three-seated wagon bumped and skidded down the rutted mountain road to the valley. Without direction, the horse turned east and made its way to the church. In the church yard, the boys were again set free, and they scattered like autumn leaves before the wind. There were a few precious minutes to check out the depth of the river and anything of value that may have been washed ashore. There was also a few minutes to mix with other boys while attempting to avoid parental eyes.

The steeple bell sounded, calling the congregation to worship. The Morgan bench was soon full with all members attentively looking forward.

Georgie whispered to Stanley, "You got'a come with me. I got'a go to the backhouse. You got'a hold the door."

The two boys eased quietly down from the bench, eyeing their parents cautiously. Together they sneaked out to the small building at the back of the church and Stanley stood importantly at the door.

"In due time," Georgie whispered, excitedly.

"Law sakes, Stanley. Somethin' happened."

"You fall in?" Stanley asked, hopefully.

"Nope. I never used the big hole. The little hole ain't big enough to fall through. Somethin' happened, though."

"What?"

"My penny slid out'a my pocket and rolled in."

"In where?"

"In the big hole, dummy. I can't reach it."

"You reach in the hole?"

"Yeah, but my arm ain't long enough. I gotta have a stick."

"I go get one."

"NO! Don't you be leavin' that door! Somebody'd come on in and use the big hole and it'd mess up my penny."

"What you gonna do?"

"You keep holdin' the door. I got'a think."

After a moment, "I know. I can reach it with my shoe."

After a respectful interval, Stanley inquired, "You got your penny now?"

"No. I got'a try again."

"Hurry! I don't see nobody nowhere."

"Law sakes, Stanley. I done dropped in my shoe."

"Law sakes, Georgie!"

"Stanley, you gotta go get Junior and Freddie. Remember, you got'a sneak in under the benches."

"Shore."

Stanley ran to the front door of the church and dropped to his hands and knees. Around the benches he crawled until he could reach Freddie's foot. He grabbed Freddie's ankle and tugged. Freddie bent down.

"What you doin' down there, Stanley?" he whispered.

"You got'a come."

"Huh?"

"Georgie in the backhouse. He lost his penny."

"Oh, law! Go on back."

Heads were bowed as Rev. McCrey asked God's blessing on the service. Freddie looked around. Nobody was looking. He gouged Junior in the ribs.

"Come on," he instructed and, dropping to his knees, he crawled under the bench. Junior was only inches behind him.

Stanley ran ahead to open the door to the backhouse. Tears stained Georgie's face. Junior looked down one hole and Freddie looked down the other.

Freddie shot through the door and across the churchyard. He broke a small limb from a willow tree and stripped its leaves as he ran back.

"Here, Junior."

Junior poked the stick down the hole and easily retrieved the shoe. He handed it to Georgie.

"Go clean the shooey off the side and put it on. Now where at is the penny?"

Georgie pointed.

"How come it to be way over there?"

"It rolled out'a my pocket when I sat down."

"Can you reach it, Junior?" Freddie asked.

"Got to," Junior answered. "Iffen I don't, Pa gonna blister us all."

Junior leaned over the seat, extending his arm into the hole. The end of the stick barely touched the penny but wouldn't pick it up. Freddie watched the operation from the other hole.

"Junior?"

"What?"

"If you was to poke that stick down in the shooey a little bit, likely the penny'd stick on better."

Junior did as suggested. Carefully he eased the stick under the coin. Luck was with them. The penny now adhered to the stick. Slowly, Junior began to lift the stick out of the hole.

Freddie's agile mind saw a possible problem. He pushed the younger boys back. "Get on outside so as not to bump his arm," he directed.

Junior's steady hand guided the stick and the coin out of the hole, extending it toward his brother.

"Take it, Georgie. Wipe it off on the grass over yonder, then come on."

At the front of the church, Junior and Freddie dropped to their knees. As they had just crawled around the bench, Georgie and Stanley reached the door. One by one, they slid under the bench and climbed into their seats.

They bowed their heads as Preacher McCrey concluded, "And we ask that You bless this offering we are about to receive. We know there are many places this money could have gone, but these, thy servants, have brought it to Thee. Amen."

The pump organ played a song as the offering plate was passed. Junior's penny fell into the plate, followed by Stanley's. Freddie dropped his penny and Georgie extended his hand with the penny. The coin had a tendency to stay attached to Georgie's hand. Quick-minded Freddie reached out and rapped sharply on Georgie's wrist. Silently, Georgie's penny unstuck itself from his fingers and joined the others in the plate. Jamie reached solemnly into his sock and withdrew his penny for the collection plate.

Later, at the dinner table, Carl Morgan asked his sons, "Did them pennies all get in the collection plate?"

Five heads nodded quickly and truthfully.

Lorena put Jamie to bed for his afternoon nap and the others slipped out the door.

"Hurry, let's go dig out our cave."

"Yeah, let's dig."

They scrambled up the hillside to a rock outcropping that created a small ledge extending out from a mound of dirt.

"I wanna dig," begged Stanley.

"Naw, you're too little. You got'a watch."

"I tell Pa."

An amended decision was made. "Here, you can dig this side. Push the dirt out over there, see?"

"How far we figure to dig," wondered Freddie.

"Big!" suggested Georgie.

Junior summed it up. "Got'a dig big to get all of us inside of it. Freddie, go get them little 'ens a better stick to dig with."

Freddie re-delegated the assignment, "Georgie, you fellas got'a get better sticks."

Georgie responded, "I got me a good stick. Stanley, you go get that stick over there."

The dirt flew. The flat rock created a solid ceiling over their heads as the cave became larger. Georgie, weary of digging, climbed to the top of the rock.

"I clum up on the roof," he announced.

"You get off the roof," Junior commanded. "You done got to knockin' stuff down on us, jumpin' around like that."

Georgie obligingly moved farther up the hill. "I'm'a gonna jump up and down on the roof," he stated, rebelliously, and began to do just that. In a few minutes, his jumping feet broke through the crust of dirt and he began to fall, slithering into the hole with sticks and leaves trailing afterward.

"Junior! Freddie! I'm'a fallin' through the ground!" His cry for assistance came faintly from a distance.

"Shut up, Georgie."

"Help!" repeated the muffled cry.

"Shut up. We're busy."

Then there was no answer. Apparently Georgie had shut up as he had been told to do. Junior continued to scrape dirt from the cave wall and they all pushed it toward the entrance of the cave and out. He noticed there was more room in the cave than usual, and no noise from overhead.

"Where at is Georgie?"

"I dunno."

"Freddie, look up top for Georgie."

Freddie relayed the command. "Stanley, climb up there and look for Georgie. GEORGIE! Where are you?"

Stanley climbed and looked around, then slid back down the hill. "Ain't no Georgie."

"Call 'im, agin."

"GEORGIE!"

"Huh?" came a faint reply from underfoot.

Stanley, standing on the hill above the ledge, stopped at the caved-in place. Peering down into the loose dirt and rocks he observed, "Georgie fell down into hell."

Junior demanded, "Show me!"

Stanley pointed to a patch of depressed earth.

"Law sakes, we got'a get 'im out. We got'a dig fast in the cave 'till we get to 'im. He likely gonna be dead iffen we don't hurry. You boys got'a help me dig."

Georgie had landed in a dusty pile in a small dark cave. There, under his hand, he could feel warm fur. He moved his hand along a short body and found a tiny mouth and a short, pointed tail. The furry thing had rows of tiny teeth and four little puppy feet. Georgie cuddled the warm furry body to his chest. Then he patted the ground around him and found more puppies. What a wonderful find! He'd go tell Junior and Freddie and they could get the puppies out and play with them.

The cave had a small tunnel leading away from it. In the faint light reflected from the cave opening, Georgie crawled on his hands and knees for a long way. The tiny speck of light was just ahead, so he kept going. He stepped out into the sunlight a half a hundred feet from where his brothers were digging. He walked back to the cave, clawing the loose dirt out of his ears and eyes. The brothers didn't see him because they were busy digging furiously, hand over fist.

"Junior?" Georgie attempted.

"Shut up and dig."

Georgie obediently picked up a stick and began to dig. "I found some puppies."

"Shut up and dig."

Georgie dug some more. "How come we got'a dig so fast?"

"Georgie's in there. We got'a get 'im out."

Georgie looked down at himself and back at Junior. This needed some clarification. "We got two Georgies?" he wondered out loud.

"Shut up and dig," came the repeated command.

Freddie turned around and shoved a rock toward him. "Here, Georgie, push this rock on out."

Junior stopped suddenly. "Georgie? Georgie! How come you ain't inside that mountain?"

Georgie shrugged. How does one answer a question like that when one has such good news? "I found puppies," he ventured.

"Puppies? Real puppies? Where at?"

Georgie's dirt-encrusted arm pointed toward the cave opening.

"Come on! Let's go get 'em!"

"I wanna puppy!"

Junior demanded better directions. "Where at are the puppies you found?"

"Yonder in the mountain. Come on."

Georgie ran to the entrance and began to crawl into the hole. Freddie fell to his knees and followed.

Junior paused to give instructions. "Stanley, you stay here till we get back."

"I tell Pa."

"Ah, you can go on in. I'll be right back of you."

In a line, the boys crawled on their hands and knees until they reached the den.

"Puppies!" Georgie announced, proudly, holding out a squirming ball of fur.

Freddie patted around in the dark and found four more little animals.

"Stanley, I got'a take your puppy till you get back outside. You ain't big enough to hold onto it and crawl at the same time."

"No. I tell Pa."

"You gonna shut up or I'm gonna punch you in the mouth. Now get goin'."

Stanley turned and began to crawl back toward the exit with Junior at his heels, carefully carrying two pups. Next came Georgie with a pup stuffed down his shirt, and Freddie and his pup brought up the rear.

The small animals made tiny, squeaky noises and they were soft and furry.

"Law, Pa, he gonna be glad we got these here puppies. He said he was gonna look for some puppies for us and now we already got 'em," Junior commented excitedly.

"Shore, and he can stop looking."

"I found the puppies!"

"Puppies! Puppies!" agreed Stanley, excitedly.

Carl Morgan was asleep in his hammock in the shade of the tall yard trees. Sundays were meant to be a day of rest. God, Himself, had said so, and nobody had a right to argue with Him. The breeze flowing up the mountain off the river was cool and the songbirds in the trees sang gently. Excited shouts rang out from many young mouths.

"Pa! Lookie, Pa!"

"We found us some puppies!"

"Look, Pa, we got us four puppies. We can get a puppy for Jamie, too."

"Wake up, Pa! Lookie at our puppies!"

Carl Morgan groaned himself awake and set his eyes upon the four wolf pups his sons had deposited on his abdomen. He was instantly fully awake.

"Where at you get them little wolves?" he demanded.

"Wolves? Pa, them's puppies! Ain't they?" Junior suggested, hopefully.

"I want 'em to be puppies, Pa," requested Georgie with eagerness.

Carl Morgan's voice became firm and hard, and just a little concerned. "Them's wolf pups. They ain't dog puppies. You boys show me where at you got them wolves. Pack of wolves'd be just the very thing a cattle raiser'd be wantin' to raise up with his calves." He reluctantly roused himself from his comfortable hammock.

"What you gonna do, Pa?" Junior asked reluctantly.

"Gonna get rid of 'em. That's what I'm gonna do."

"You ain't gonna kill them puppies, Pa. Are you? Please, Pa!"

"Yeah, Pa! These puppies ain't big wolves! They're little bity."

Carl faced them sternly. "Boys, wolf pups grow up to be big, growling wolves. Now let's get goin'."

The dejected boys trudged up the hill, leading the way to the den entrance.

"Gotta crawl way back," advised Georgie.

The man's eyes shot open with horror. "You boys crawled into that hole after them wolves?"

Four heads nodded.

"You boys don't never do that again. Don't you never crawl into no hole that's dark and you can't see the end of."

"How come?"

"Somethin' might be in there."

"But they wasn't, Pa."

"But you didn't know that."

"Yeah, Pa. We knowd."

"How did you know?"

"Georgie crawled out."

"But he crawled in before he crawled out."

"No, Pa," Georgie came to his own defense. "I crawled out first. I was in already."

Carl Morgan drew in a deep breath and looked from one face to the other. Everyone was wide-eyed and truthful. They watched him, unblinkingly. He knew that if he could just think of the right question to ask, they would give him the right answer.

"Georgie, how did you get into the wolf den?"

"Up there. Come on."

Carl followed Georgie up the hill. Georgie pointed to the hole, now filled in with dirt, sticks, and rocks. Carl nodded his understanding. One of the exits must have been concealed by a rock or a bush. The wolf was possibly in the den when Georgie fell through and then it escaped out the other hole. Why, he could easily have landed on the female wolf, itself! Wolves so close to the cabin and his sons!

That settled it. They would get a hunting dog. Carl and Georgie walked down the little hill.

"Boys," Carl began. "I told you boys I was gettin' you a dog. I'm gonna do it."

"When, Pa?"

"Next week. Soon as I can locate a good one."

That evening before the church services, Carl asked a group of men, "I been needin' to find me a dog for my boys. Like to get 'em a beagle if I could. Pup'd be nice."

"Well, Carl," one of the men responded, "We got this little beagle bitch, due real soon. She walked in off the road, not belongin' to nobody here. Likely got herself left behind after a huntin' party, maybe out'a Jacksonville. You'd be doin' us a real favor to take her in."

Carl nodded. "After church, that'd be a good time to get her?"

"Sure, and you're welcome."

Later, as the wagon rolled up the hill, four pairs of hands caressed a little black, brown, and white spotted dog.

"We gonna name her 'Lady.' She gonna have us some puppies," Junior advised his brothers. "It's lady dogs that get to make puppies."

"When?" demanded Georgie.

"Soon, most likely."

"I want puppies now."

"No, Stanley. You gotta wait."

"No. I tell Pa."

"Go ahead. Tell Pa all you want to. Won't do no good."

Georgie lovingly stroked Lady's rounded sides. "She gonna give us puppies for shore?"

"Yeah, for shore."

"Where she got them puppies now?"

"They're in her tummy."

"She ate 'em? Bad doggy!"

Freddie's quick reflex caught the lowering hand as Georgie attempted to administer punishment. "No, Georgie. Don't hit Lady. She didn't eat 'em."

"Get 'em out! Please?"

Junior was exasperated. "We can't get them puppies out till they get big enough, so just shut up. We got'a wait till Lady's ready to make 'em come out."

Freddie backed him up, but attempted to reassure his brother. "We got'a wait but, 'member, this time we gonna get real puppies that we can keep."

At this moment Stanley squealed with delight.

"Hush up, Stanley. What you got wrong with you?" Freddie scolded.

Stanley giggled. "Lady was tastin' my fingers."

Georgie shoved Stanley's hand aside. "Here, Lady, taste'a me."

Carl Morgan guided the horse along the dark road. Shadows from the swinging lantern on the wagon posts made the trees and bushes become creeping, ghostly beasts, reaching their wavering arms toward the wagon. It was a good time for thinking and for regretful recriminations.

"Yep, should'a got them boys a dog long time ago. A farm's got no right to be without a dog for this long."

Lorena cuddled the sleeping Jamie in her lap, allowing Carl's words to pass over her mind. Her eyes lowered to the warm bundle in her lap and the small hand that lay feather light on her arm. Her right hand caressed his soft, chubby fingers. His breath was warm and moist against her arm. He was her last baby. The absolute last.

The decision had been made and it was a good and practical one.

But, Dear God, how could she stand to give up the next one? Of course, it was no longer hers to keep or give, but still....

She felt her tears form, burning, in her eyes. She made no effort to stop them. Who would see them here in the darkness of the mountain road? Who would think of tears with the excited chatter of her sons behind her and the soft-spoked words of Carl beside her? The tears ran down her face and fell on Jamie's now crumpled shirt.

Carl glanced at her. In the faint light of the lantern hanging at the front of the wagon and in the pale light of the new moon, he saw the diamonds clinging to her lashes. He saw the shining trail of moisture across her cheek. Dogs forgotten, he felt his chest constricted painfully in response to her agony.

He put his arm around her and tugged her close.

With the other hand, he tapped reins against the horses' flanks, urging them homeward. Together they'd make it through the next months. There was no other way to go.

Reaching the cabin at last, Carl guided the horses toward the shed.

"Junior, Freddie, you boys make Lady a good place for sleepin'. Rake up some of that straw up back's them feed barrels."

"Likely she'd be hungry, Pa."

"No, she's been fed today. She'll do till mornin'."

Junior took charge. "Freddie, go up in the loft'n pitch down some straw. Stanley, you keep pettin' on her back. Georgie, come help me move this here barrel so's she can get in back of it."

Lady was installed in her new bed. She looked up at the boys with her soft, brown, hound-dog eyes, and the boys melted like dew in the summer sun. Junior and Freddie looked at each other and nodded.

"Pa," Junior called out, "Iffen you was to leave that lantern out here, I'd be gettin' on in with it, directly. Speck we ought'a stay with Lady for a spell, things bein' strange to her."

Carl hesitated. Why not? "You got'a be careful, Junior. That lantern'd have this shed full of hay a'blazin' in no time."

"Shore, Pa. We'll be careful."

Carl left the shed, entrusting the lantern to Junior. Sometimes a father had to go with a gut feeling and trust his son. Sooner or later. But, still...only seven years old? No, he had to do it.

Junior watched his father's departure. He pulled three heads close to his and whispered. Their eyes shone and Stanley giggled, softly.

"You all go first," instructed Junior, "and don't forget washin' up or Ma'll come and make you."

Freddie, Georgie, and Stanley ran to the cabin.

"Where at's Junior and that lantern?" Carl demanded of them.

"He'll be comin' on directly," advised Freddie. "We wasn't wantin' us to leave Lady alone, all of us at once. He was gonna wait and pet her some more."

Carl thought a moment. The explanation made sense.

The three boys washed their hands and faces and went to their lean-to bedroom, carefully drawing the door shut behind them. Freddie gently and quietly raised the window sash as high as possible and stood waiting, listening for footsteps. They were not long in coming.

"Here, Freddie," came the anxious whisper. "Hold 'er careful and put 'er on the bed."

Freddie held out his arms for the little beagle. Georgie and Stanley were ready to help. They drew her in through the window and tiptoed carefully to the bed. Junior ran back to the shed for the lantern.

Moments later Junior and the lantern appeared at the kitchen door. The boy blew out the flame, matter of factly, and hung it on its nail. Carl Morgan relaxed.

"Is Lady happy, now?"

"Huh?"

"Does Lady like her new bed?" Carl rephrased the question.

"Yeah, Pa. I figure she gonna like where she is."

"That's good. Now wash up and get on to bed."

"Yeah, Pa."

Carl Junior washed carefully, then slipped through the door, closing it softly behind him again. Ma didn't seem to notice the closed door. He tiptoed to his side of the double bed.

In the dim moonlight, he could make out Freddie sitting on his accustomed side of the bed, Stanley was at the head planted on the pillows, and Georgie at the foot with a vacancy indicating to Junior where his place would be. In the center of the bed was Lady, being lovingly caressed by six small hands.

Junior took his place and lifted one of Lady's paws. He gently massaged her small, clawed toes and smoothed the fur on her leg. Stanley was first to give up and drop over in contented sleep. Georgie was not far behind. Freddie continued to stroke Lady's side.

"Junior?" he whispered softly.

"Huh?"

"Put your hand here where mine is."

Junior felt for Freddie's hand. Under Lady's short, coarse fur was a slight undulation. A gentle, rolling movement.

"What you figure to be causin' that? You thinkin' she's sick?"

"I ain't for shore, Freddie. I speck it could be the puppies in there."

"The puppies?" was Freddie's excited response.

"Shhhhh!" warned Junior. "'Member the little'ns."

"Oh, yeah," remembered Freddie.

"Let's us lay down next to her so she can go to sleep. Figure them puppies need to be sleepin' 'stead'a squirmin' and rollin' around."

Freddie edged up against Lady's back and Junior scooted his face close to her whiskered muzzle. Lady's tongue lightly touched Junior's ear lobe.

It was past midnight when the squeaky whimper aroused Freddie. He reached over to pat Lady and he felt something moist under his hand.

"Junior, wake up. Lady's sick."

Junior sat up quickly, eyes wide with concern. The moonlight, streaming through the window glistened against a silvery ball lying beside Lady.

"Lookie, Freddie!"

As the boys watched, Lady grasped the silvery ball in her teeth and released a mass of wet, squirming fur. She nuzzled it, licking firmly with an experienced tongue.

"A puppy!" Freddie whispered excitedly. "We got'a wake up Georgie and Stanley so as they can see."

"No, Freddie. Don't be wakin' up Stanley. He won't 'member to whisper. Just wake up Georgie and tell him to shhh."

Georgie sat up, rubbed his eyes and looked at Lady. He drew in a quick breath but Freddie clamped his hand over the excited open mouth.

"Don't say nothin'. You gonna wake up Pa."

Georgie pointed toward Lady and Freddie released his hand from his brother's mouth.

Another silver ball appeared seemingly from nowhere and Lady magically turned it into another puppy. Lady kept smoothing the wet fur with an insistant tongue, nosing them all around. The puppies whimpered and squeaked.

"Shhh, puppies," Freddie cautioned, but the puppies continued to squeak.

"Freddie, we gotta pull the cover up over 'em 'afore they wake up Pa."

In the darkness of the quilt tent held up by the boy's heads, Lady gave birth to the rest of her six puppies. She expertly nudged them toward her bursting nipples and they became quiet.

One by one the heads lowered and the quilt settled around the figures on the bed. Dawn came and the roosters began to crow.

Lorena called out, "Boys! Junior and Freddie! Out'a the bed!"

There was no answer.

Lorena opened the closed door. "Hmmm, be a wonder if them boys ain't smothered, sleepin' under that hot quilt." She lifted one corner of the quilt and tossed it back staring at the scene before her.

"Them boys gonna be the death of me, yet. Carl, come 'ere and look at your boys."

Carl joined her. Stanley was a small ball at the head of the bed. Georgie was spread-eagled at the foot. Freddie's face was against Lady's neck and Junior closed the other side. The puppies were cuddled against Junior's chest.

While Carl and Lorena watched, Lady turned to look at them, rolling her brown eyes contentedly in their direction. She turned to Junior to swipe his cheek gently with her tongue, then she began to rearrange her puppies with her nose.

Carl grinned. "I asked Junior last night iffen that dog was happy with her new bed and he said she was. Reckon he wasn't lyin'."

11

With the help of occasional prompting, Carl Morgan finally remembered to get his sons a gun. At the gun store in Jacksonville, he selected a light-weight rifle and necessary amunition. They'd still have to prop up the barrel but it was something they could grow into and it would be ready when the younger boys put on some years.

"Time them dogs get enough size on 'em, you boys'll be ready to go huntin', for real."

Junior and Freddie jumped up and down on their toes and squealed.

Carl continued, "Now I got a job for you two boys. I got them two calves in the corral that got'a be took down to the pasture. Now, listen to me how you gonna do it.

"You gonna tie two ropes around that calf's neck. Junior hold onto one of 'em on one side and Freddie, you grab a'holt to t'other rope. You got'a make that calf walk in 'tween the two of you. Iffen you don't, him bein' a big, strong calf, he'll likely get a wild notion to run away with you. You hearin' me?"

The boys nodded quickly.

"Now, go get it done."

Off they ran.

"I got me a idea, Junior. Reckon it'd be fun to ride them calves down the hill?"

"They gonna try to scrape us off," objected Junior. "'Member 'em runnin' up agin the shed, draggin' us off?"

"Yeah, but this time they ain't gonna be no shed. In 'tween the corral and the calf pasture there ain't nothin' 'cept trees."

"And InaMae's cabin." Junior was being swayed by the excitement of Freddie's reasoning.

"Yeah, well, we'd just have to keep 'em away from there."

"Pa said tie ropes onto 'em."

"Shore. That'd be the way to guide 'em. Just like horses."

"Yeah, well...." Junior wasn't certain a half-grown calf was the same as a broke horse.

"We could try one," suggested Freddie, hopefully.

Junior thought for a minute. "Likely the two of us ridin', holdin' to the ropes like Pa said...? Likely that'd work."

"Shore, and both us ridin' it'd be easy keepin' 'im guided in the path."

"First off, we got'a find them ropes."

"Ain't they hangin' up there on the shed?"

"One of 'em is."

"Uh...Junior?"

"Huh?

"That other long rope was the one we left still tied to them logs we put up in the treehouse."

"Shore enough."

"It'd be a long job to go and take it down."

"Yeah, and we'd be wantin' to play up there."

"Lookie, Junior. This here rope is real long. Iffen we was to tie one end to one side and t'other end to t'other side, we could still both hold onto 'im. It'd make no difference, seein' we both gonna be up on top of the calf, anyways."

Junior examined the rope and nodded. "Which calf we take first?" he asked. This seemed to be Freddie's venture, so the particulars were up to him.

"Let's get this black 'en with the little horns."

"Well, bring 'im on."

The black calf stared at the boys, tossing his head and rolling his eyes. This might not be as easy as it would seem.

"Junior, let's us be takin' the rope to him. He don't seem to be wantin' to come over here."

The calf snorted at the options, looking from boy to boy and began to walk away.

"Get a pail, Freddie. Make 'im think we got 'im some feed."

Freddie grabbed the feed bucket from the shed and rattled it. Eventually the now-interested calf advanced. He poked his head into the empty bucket and snorted again, irritatedly bucking the empty pail out of Freddie's hand. Then he looked at the boys, again.

"Put some feed in it, Freddie. We got'a get this rope tied onto 'im, somehow."

Freddie ran to the shed, scooped a handful of chopped corn into the bucket and came back. The calf put his head in the bucket and began mouthing the corn, running his tongue noisily around the creases of the pail.

"Hurry up, Junior. He's 'bout to eat it all up."

"I got it tied over here. I'll hold 'im till you tie your end. Bring that loop up around his horn so as he'll know which way we tryin' to guide 'im."

Freddie circled the calf's neck with the rope and tied it on the other side, drawing the loop of the rope between the calf's eye and his small, pointed horns.

"This'll work good. Lookie at that loop'a rope left over 'hind our backs. Most likely it'd be a help for us a'hangin' on to have it back there."

Junior pulled on the pail and the calf followed, reluctant to leave what might be more corn. "I got'a lead 'im over to the gate. You open up the gate and I'll be gettin' 'im on through. Then you close the gate."

The greedy calf followed the pail as he was led through the gate, licking at the empty bottom until Freddie had the gate fastened.

"You get on, Freddie, and hold onto your rope. Scoot up front, so as I can jump on back'a ya. He likely gonna be movin' fast once he gets started."

Freddie tossed his leg over the calf's shoulders, clamping his knees firmly on its neck. The calf shuddered under the unaccustomed weight, but Freddie stayed on.

"Get ready to pull on your rope, Freddie. I'm a'climbin' on."

Freddie squeezed the calf's shoulders with his legs and held his rope with both hands. Junior eased his leg over the calf's stomach and tightened his side of the rope.

The calf angrily drew his head out of the empty bucket and Freddie pulled his rope to the left, jerking the calf's head in that direction. Junior corrected the angle by a jerk to the right.

The confused calf swung his head the other way and knew for certain that right in the middle of his back was something needing to be scraped off. The calf had no shed corner to scrape against so he headed for a fence post.

Junior, seeing the calf's intention, jerked back sharply, sending the animal into the woods again.

Now, filled with unspeakable rage, the calf charged straight into the blackjack trees with their fringe of low hanging branches.

"Pull on it, Freddie! Pull on it!"

"I'm a'pullin', but I'm about to juggle off!"

Eventually the calf's head was turned, and he blindly rammed his head into the low limbs of a cedar tree. He backed out and away from the prickles of the cedar and ran toward the woods. Just before he reached the trees, he turned. He began to gallop down a path just about the time a gust of wind came up from behind him.

The breeze made the freshly washed clothes on InaMae's clothesline billow and whip about, flapping and cracking noisily. The calf reared back at the sight of so much white waving in front of him, and the boys were forced to pull back on the ropes just to stay on. When the calf's front feet came down, he lowered his head to buck, just as another puff of wind opened a pillowcase in front of his nose. Momentum forced the calf's head into the white depth of it. Unable to see, the terrified calf charged dead ahead.

"Duck down, Freddie!" came Junior's unnecessary warning.

Freddie ducked, barely missing the clothesline from catching under his chin. The blinded calf charged angrily toward InaMae's front door, bursting through the screen wire. A sudden arch of its back deposited Freddie inside, crumbled at InaMae's startled feet. The frightened calf retreated back through the screen door with Junior still aboard. The pillowcase was pulled from the calf's head as it withdrew from the screen door and it wheeled and headed for the woods again. Junior slid back off over its tail, landing on his feet.

The loop of the rope at the rear of the calf caught Junior at the waist and pulled him on. Losing his footing, Junior managed to get both hands on the rope as it slid over his head. Now the boy's weight on the rope kept the calf's head pointed straight. The calf galloped on down the hill at breakneck speed. Junior managed to regain his footing and ran with it, trying to keep from being pulled down again.

It was then that a rock rolled under Junior's foot and he fell to his stomach. Over the stony path he slid on his belly. At a momentary halt of indecision of the calf, Junior again regained his footing.

At the bottom of the hill, the calf stopped at the gate of the new pasture. There was nowhere else for it to go. Carl and Marcel were picking up their tools and fence mending equipment preparing to move on to another job.

"Here he is, Pa," Junior called, breathlessly. "I brung you down the first calf."

The men stared at Junior. The pocket and all the buttons were shredded off his shirt. One arm was skinned and bleeding from the wrist to the elbow. One knee was cut and his hair was full of sticks and dirt. Carl stared soberly at his firstborn and stroked his chin. "Son, did that old calf give you any trouble?"

"No, Pa. He come right on along like he was meant to."

"Where at's Freddie?"

"He's a'fixin' to bring down t'other'n. Reckon I'll be goin' on up to help 'im."

"Yeah, son, speck you ought'a do that."

Marcel opened the gate and led the calf inside the new pasture, untying the rope from his horns.

"Here's your rope, Junior. Freddie'll be needin' to use it."

Junior calmly took the rope and started back up the hill. He didn't limp until he was out of sight of the men.

12

Lorena took the bucket of fresh picked garden peas to the deep shade of the backyard trees. She sat down in the sagging wicker rocker and began to shell the peas into her apron.

The noise of sporadic rifle shots from the woods punctuated the drone of the late summer crickets. Carl had taken Junior and Freddie out for shooting practice. Lady had gone with them and the pups were asleep against the gnarled tree roots.

Stanley and Jamie were asleep in the hammock beside her, and, down at her feet, Georgie played in the loose dirt. He had broken up piles of twigs to make a rail fence to keep his pebble cows from straying. He made a road for his wooden-block wagon. His fingers were the "horses" that pulled his wagon currently heavily loaded with "hay" for his cattle.

His strong, capable, little-boy fingers planted "trees" in his pastures and repaired his "fence" where a large, vicious beetle had charged through it. His sturdy, little-boy knees were firmly planted in the dust as he talked to his farm animals.

Lorena watched him, thinking, *My little boy is busy playing 'man'.* She watched him practicing to be daddy, the manager of a thriving farm. From the distant trees came another crack of rifle fire. Junior and Freddie were also practicing to be men. Of course, she wouldn't want it any other way. Little boys always became men if they didn't get themselves killed first.

Stanley was curled up at one end of the hammock. His legs were getting longer and knobby-kneed, in the expected little-boy fashion.

Jamie had one arm hanging over the edge of the hammock. His arm was no longer so soft and round. His dimpled fingers were lengthening. Clearly, he was no longer a baby. The dreaded realization flowed over her in a vicious wave, taking away her breath with the dismay of it all. Little Jamie, her last, was no longer a baby.

The weight of that realization crushed against her heart as an unbearable weight. Tears forced themselves from her eyes. They hung on her lashes, blurring her vision. She leaned forward, burying her face in her hands as Georgie talked to his fence posts and cows. She smothered a sob and tried to swallow the lump in her throat.

Oh, Lord, how can I continue to remember the baby under my heart is not my own? How can I be so selfish? I have five beautiful sons and I sit here begrudging...but, Lord? How can I go on?

Eyes closed in agony, she felt a touch, feather light, on her arm. Small fingers crept along her shoulder.

"Mama?"

"What, Georgie?"

"Do you hurt someplace?"

Lorena straightened up and Georgie worked himself up into her lap, sitting on the shelled peas in her apron. Her arms tightened around him, silently and firmly.

"Mama, you got a hurt someplace?" he insisted.

"Yes, Georgie, I did have a hurt, but only for a minute. It's gone away, now."

Georgie smiled at her and leaned against her breast, the light pressure of his body pressed against her swelling abdomen. He reached up and cupped his small hand against his mother's cheeks. Yes, this one was like Carl, sensitive and intuitive. And always loving.

"Mama?"

"What, Georgie?"

"We could sing that song about the bumble bee. You wanna?" he invited.

Darling Georgie. He had left his play to comfort her from a sorrow he would never understand.

"Yes, Georgie, we gonna do that. Then I got'a teach you a song about numbers. You gonna be gettin' to go to school 'afore you know it."

Shelled peas and pebble cattle were ignored as Lorena and her middle son shared a moment. InaMae came up from her cabin carrying a large kettle. "I did up a batch'a dumplin's, figurin' to bring some of 'em on over."

Lorena's mood lightened. The crisis had passed and she could joke with her sister now. "Come on and tell the truth. You was thinkin' I wasn't feedin' your baby enough, wasn't you?"

InaMae colored slightly. "Well, with you bein' so busy and all...."

Lorena cut in on the apology. "It was good of you. Them dumplin's'll go good with these here peas, if I can get this here youngen out'a my lap so as to start shellin' 'em again." Lorena hugged Georgie a short, hard hug, and he climbed from her lap. He had been excused, now, to return to his play. Sweet Georgie. Like the others, he occupied his own special place.

Junior and Freddie trudged up the hill with their father, their faces flushed and sweaty and their eyes sparkling with excitement.

"Law, Ma, we sure gettin' good on that shootin'. Them pups better hurry up and grow, iffen they'd be wantin' to go huntin' with us."

Lorena smiled. "That's good. Freddie, I want you to go to the shed and shell out some corn for cornmeal. See you don't grind up any sticks or cob in it. Take Georgie with you."

"Take Georgie?"

"Yeah, its bein' time he learned. I got other things for Junior to do."

Georgie jumped up from his pebble cattle and brushed his dusty hands against his pants leg.

"No, Georgie, that won't do. You go be washin' up good like Freddie is. That cornmeal you gonna make is somethin' we eat, and it's got'a stay clean."

Georgie hurried after Freddie.

"Carl?"

"Huh?"

"Way I figure it, any boy big enough to shoot a gun, be big enough to learn milkin'. How you figure it?"

"I figure it 'bout like you do. Come on, Junior."

Carl and Junior left. Lorena returned to her cabin with the shelled peas, and the younger boys slept on.

"Reckon I can make it now, Lord, but I speck I'll be needin' You again from time to time."

13

The lazy summer heat lay spread over the mountain like mist on an April morning. Lady and the pups lounged in the tree shade and the boys were bored. Lorena had a cure for that.

"Junior, you and Freddie get a pail and see if they's enough berries left on them vines to make a cobbler. Take Georgie with you."

"Take Georgie?"

"Yeah, take Georgie and look along the river at them late vines. Georgie, you do like they tell you and don't get it in your head to get into any river water."

Georgie nodded.

Lady watched them leave and she lay back down in her cool place. In the next minute, though, she jumped up and ran after them.

The river was at low water stage, and the berry vines on the bank grew tall and green in the deep, dark soil. The boys had to cover a lot of territory, though, because the berries were mostly gone. Lady stretched out under the vines for a nap but had to keep moving to keep up with the boys.

"Lemme see how many you got, Freddie?"

"We got 'nough?"

"Naw, we ain't got 'nough, but I know where there'd be more."

"Where at?"

"Right past that fence."

"Yeah, but that'd be where that old bull is."

"What bull?" demanded Georgie.

"Big, black one," explained Freddie.

"I don't see 'im," Junior observed, looking over the fence.

"Reckon he'd be hidin'?" Freddie worried.

"Hard to say, but it'd be nice if he'd stay hid a while, givin' us time to get them berries over yonder."

"But Junior...."

"I wanna see the bull," put in Georgie.

"I don't," countered Freddie.

Junior looked through the fence. "Reckon I could take a walk over to see if he's hidin' any place."

"Me, too."

Freddie was quick to cut in, "No, Georgie, you got'a wait with me till Junior can see if it'd be safe."

Junior climbed over the fence and walked out into the pasture. "Ain't seein' 'im nowhere. Bring the buckets and come on," he called back.

The picking was much better in the pasture. No one had picked any of them and the black, sweet berries practically fell into their hands.

Lady sniffed around the berry bushes and found herself a new bed. She had hardly settled down, when a smell wafted past her. She stood up, casting her head from side to side to determine the direction of the smell. She climbed a small hill and looked over. A growl formed deep in her lungs and forced itself past her teeth, rippling her lips.

"What you see, Lady?" Junior asked her, conversationally

Lady growled again.

"You see somethin' over there?"

A hoarse, breathy snort sounded just over the hill, and Lady barked a sharp soprano note, followed by her deep tenor "trailing" bark.

Freddie and Junior looked at each other and Georgie looked from one to the other of his brothers.

"Law sakes, she got a eye on that bull, like as not."

"We got'a run!"

"Yeah, but which way?"

The fence appeared small in the distance. There were two large trees between them and the fence. The nearer tree had limbs that were much too high, but the next one was accessible.

The ground vibrated with angry pawing, and Lady growled again.

"Run to the tree, Georgie. Put the pail down."

"But it's got the berries in it."

"Put it down!"

The bull came charging over the hill between the trees. Freddie had reached the farther tree and grabbed a limb, pulling himself up easily. Georgie, with a full bucket of berries, stood looking at the bull.

"Put 'em down!" commanded Junior.

Lady rushed at the bull's head, barking her "treed" bark. Her high soprano "yip" was followed by a soul-shaking howl and it made the bull turn its head.

Finally, Georgie managed to move his legs and he ran toward the tree with no low limbs with Junior thundering along right behind him.

Safe on his limb, Freddie yelled, "Lady, come back! Lady! That old bull gonna get you!"

Lady paid him no heed. She circled the bull, nipping at his heels as she went by.

Georgie reached the base of the "wrong" tree and looked up.

"JUNIOR!"

"Come on, Georgie. Run to the other tree!"

"I can't."

Lady and the bull were between the trees. The bull was annoyed with the dog and lowered his head, sweeping it from side to side, striking the dog. Lady rolled over and over down a little hill, growling and barking, angrily. She scrambled to her feet and, dashing after the angry bellows, she leaped like a frog, grasping the bull's ear. For a moment, she hung there, growling through her teeth.

The bull tossed his head, flinging her aside. She rolled over once again and began to howl a heart-rending note as though each second was her last. Again the bull turned to look at her. She backed up a few steps away from him, still howling miserably.

"Aw, Lady's got herself hurt!" Georgie wailed. "I got'a get 'er."

"No, you don't!" Junior yelled. "You do what I told you to do!"

"I got'a," Georgie broke loose from Junior's grasp and started for Lady and the bull with Junior close behind.

The bull wagged his head from the advancing boys to the howling dog. Lady rolled over onto her back, howling an octave louder. A dozen feet from the bull, Junior caught up with Georgie and grabbed his arm. Lady's howls went two notes higher.

Junior jerked his brother's arm, causing him to fall down, and he was dragged yelling across the grass and rocks of the pasture to the right tree.

"Freddie?" he called up into the limbs.

"Hand 'im up," Freddie responded.

Junior grabbed Georgie and stood him up. He made a stirrup of his hands for Georgie's foot, tossing him as high as his strength would allow. Freddie caught Georgie's hands and yanked him on up.

Georgie curled his leg around a limb and held on while Junior skinned up the trunk of the tree monkey fashion and sighed with relief, his heart pounding.

Glancing their way, Lady stopped howling and jumped to her feet. She dashed away from the bull and ran lightly to the limbless tree where she stood in the shade, panting. The bull saw her and came charging. Lady dashed toward him, circling and nipping.

Round and around she whirled, each circle drawing the bull a little farther from the tree where the boys watched.

"Hey, lookie! Lady's takin' the bull away!"

"We gonna get ready to run."

"I got'a get them berries."

"No, Georgie, you run. I'll be gettin' them berries. You go first."

Freddie handed Georgie down from the limb and he dropped to the ground. He hit the grass, running toward the fence.

Junior came down next and ran for the bucket. Freddie brought up the rear. Lady came dashing over the hill, her ears flopping. The boys flung themselves to the ground and rolled under the fence with Lady on their heels.

"Good dog, Lady!"

"Lady's a smart dog, ain't she?"

"She shore is. If she wasn't with us, we'd be in that tree till dark and Pa'd be out lookin' for us."

The berries were only slightly damaged from their wild ride to the fence and the boys carried them carefully up the hill.

Lorena looked into the bucket. "My, what a good bunch of berries. Ripe and sweet, just like I like 'em. You boys have any trouble findin' 'em?"

"No, Ma."

"Where at did you find these big 'ens?"

"Down by the river."

"Georgie," Lorena asked her middle son, "what did you do, down there by the river?"

"I picked a lot'a berries and I ate some. And, Mama?"

"What, Georgie?"

"You know what I saw down there?"

Junior and Freddie turned their faces to look full at Georgie. Georgie grinned, mischievously.

"I saw the biggest old...box turtle. He was crawlin' under them vines eatin' up berries that fell down."

Junior and Freddie sighed, relaxed, and glanced at each other, and Georgie grinned again, dimpling his flushed cheeks.

Carl looked down at the boys. "Now, boys, you know to be careful of that old bull down there. I ain't too sure that fence'd hold 'im if he had a mind to be gettin' over. Time you see that old bull over in that pasture, you get goin' and don't be seen by 'im."

"Shore, Pa."

"Did you see him over that fence?"

There was only the slightest hesitation, before Junior answered, truthfully. "No, Pa. We looked over that fence and we didn't see no sign of that old bull."

Georgie echoed, shaking his head, "Looked over and never seen 'im."

"Well, boys, see you don't let him get after you."

"We won't, Pa."

As the August days advanced, Lorena began to think of school clothes. Of what could be handed down and what could be hemmed up.

And then there was the question of Georgie. His early spring birthday meant he could start to school this year or he could wait. He seemed so little. But he would be six next spring. If he stayed home, he could play with Stanley during the winter, but, on the other hand, Jamie was also getting bigger.

"Georgie, stand your back up next to Freddie."

The boys stood back to back. Georgie was a good six inches shorter.

"Ma?" Freddie asked.

"What, Freddie?"

"Georgie gonna get to go to school this year?"

"I wanna go," put in Georgie.

Lorena hesitated. "Well, we...."

"Mary Beth Connelly's little sister gonna go and she's littler than Georgie."

"But...."

"Georgie ain't no trouble, is he, Junior? Me and Junior'd be there, lookin' out after 'im."

Lorena sighed and she felt an invisable weight pull on her shoulders. They sagged forward. There was an insistent movement in her abdomen as InaMae's baby readjusted its position to her new posture.

Some days were just too much to bear, and even the smallest decision seemed impossible to make.

Lorena glanced out the door. "Junior, you and Freddie look after the other'ns for a bit. I'm thinkin' to take myself a little walk."

"Shore, Ma."

Lorena walked to the bluff and sat down on the rock ledge that had been her special place since childhood. There she looked down into the valley and the river, twisting and turning in its rush toward the sea. The light green of sycamore trees bordered its banks. Here and there a sweet gum tree was turning its star-shaped leaves to red and orange.

It was only four months until Christmas.

At Christmas time....*No, Lorena, don't think on it. Just wait. You got no call to put yourself through it now, and then do it again when the time comes. Be bad enough when it happens. You got'a think on other things.*

But the "other things" refused to be thought on. She and InaMae were as close as sisters could be, and not be twins. There was less than a year between them, but InaMae, though younger, was always quicker and stronger.

She had been first to learn to swim in the backwaters of the river, pulling along in the shallows with her strong arms. When playing jump rope, InaMae could always jump more times than Lorena, and most everyone else. Her ivory complexion and butter-colored hair gave her a dainty and feminine look that was totally deceptive.

There was the time that the girls unwisely tried to dislodge a wasp nest from a tree and a cloud of the winged creatures had swarmed out after them. They ran, and InaMae could easily have gotten away, but Lorena had been stung many times, and she tripped and fell.

Seeing her sister was not following, InaMae had circled back and, not pausing to find Lorena's hand, had grabbed a handful of dresstail and dragged to the river backwater.

Swimming with one arm, she had pulled her sister through the water away from the bees.

Lorena remembered her head dipping under the water and out while trying to remember to breathe when she could. She was dragged to a small sandbar and left under water all except for her face.

She seemed to have fainted for a short time but eventually became aware of her sister standing over her with a leafy willow limb in either hand. She was whirling around, waving the willow limbs like a windmill in a storm.

At last, the wasps had given up and left. InaMae had sat down beside her, heaving to catch her breath from all the activity.

When the stinging insects were finally just a remembered nightmare, they had counted attacks. Lorena had forgotten the total of her stings, but her sister had beat her by an even dozen, two of them on her face, and one eye was swelled shut for the next few hours.

As she grew older, it occurred to Lorena that if it had not been for her sister and her quick thinking, she likely would not be here.

Belated attempts to thank her had been shrugged away as nothing. Without a moment's consideration for her own safety and comfort, her sister had pulled her to safety, causing only a few rock scrapes on her back. She had instinctively left her sister in the water to cool against the heat of the stings.

How do women with no sister manage to get along and have a full life?

A slight grin formed on Lorena's lips as she remembered the time of the barbed wire fence. It must have been a cotton-mouth moccasin that seemed to be chasing them, and the fence had three strands of barbed wire. Lorena had reached the fence first and had put a foot on the bottom strand and lifted the second strand for InaMae to crawl through.

InaMae had immediately turned and done the same to her, but Lorena had not taken the time to see where the fence barbs were. After crawling through, she had lifted her leg a bit too high and raked a barb down the backside of her thigh. Blood streamed over her leg at an alarming rate.

Quick thinking InaMae had tossed her dress over her head, following it with her pettislip. Standing buck-naked except for her panties, she had grabbed a mouthful of her pettislip tail and ripped off a wide strip, winding it around and around Lorena's leg, effectively stopping the blood.

Later, their mother had sighed and said, "Did you have to rip the tail off your pettislip? Couldn't you'a thought'a something else to do?"

InaMae had shrugged and admitted, "Might could'a, but I reckoned I didn't have no time to think about it."

Likely she didn't.

There were other times that they had come to the aid of each other, but more times than not, it was herself being helped by InaMae. The memory of it all bowed her head down to her knees in shame.

Here she was, feeling low because the baby she carried was not to belong to her. How utterly selfish could she be? She should be smiling and happy that she could do this wonderful thing for her sister, a thing that no other human could do.

Truly, this was a rare opportunity to repay her to some degree There was no other person who could give her InaMae a child of her own flesh and blood.

What an opportunity, and she should be thankful to the Good Lord for it! And she was…most times.

It was just that…well…when the baby moved, and she could feel that reassurance, that solid evidence of life…that new life that her own body had created. It was…? *Please, Lord, don't let me cry!*

"LORENA!" she shouted loudly and angrily at herself. "Don't start doin' this. You got too many days to go."

She looked around at the trees, the rocks, and the flowing river in the valley below her. "You got no call to have these sinful thoughts. The Good Book says to be a cheerful giver, and you ain't being cheerful at all!"

Having been thoroughly scolded, effectively punished, and loudly shouted at, she forced her mind onto the practical aspects of her life. It wasn't like there were no other aspects of her life that could bear some thought.

She forced thoughts through her mind. She couldn't permit herself to waller around with thoughts like that. Bravely she forced her thoughts onto a different path.

"The boys gonna need new overalls and flannel shirts for school," she told the trees above her head. "Truly amazin' how youngens grow. Here a ma goes thinkin' that youngen ain't hardly gettin' his full height, and then he shoots up toller than his older brother. Seen it happen that way but it won't happen to Georgie. Georgie ain't big enough to wear any of Freddie's clothes, not even his coat. Mr. Jenkins, down at the

Mercantile, he's likely got his school things in. Have to stop in there Tuesday when we go down to the quiltin'."

Lorena sighed and her thought drifted back, in spite of her efforts. Come Christmas InaMae would have her baby. Christmas was for families, or children, and this would be the first year her sister had her own immediate family but it was not without a price.

Conversation was hard, even now, between the sisters, and it could only get harder. So many subjects surrounded family and children, and it was so easy to drift into putting thoughts into words.

InaMae could think only of the baby and that was natural, but she would never speak of it unless Lorena spoke first. Except there was that once.

It was on a Tuesday on the way to the church for the quilting. The ladies had been discussing that there was a need to stop over at the Mercantile for needed items. Making a trip down the hill for just one or two things took a lot of precious time.

"I'll be needin' to get nursin' bottles," InaMae had said, conversationally.

"Bottles?"

InaMae nodded, "For feedin' the baby."

Lorena nodded, trying to understand. "Even from the first?"

InaMae looked out the window and swallowed twice. "Reckon we'd be needin' to use 'em soon as we could. The baby'd need to be clear in his mind who his mama was."

The words had been spoken of necessity, softly, gently, and with understanding, but they had cut through to the quick of Lorena's heart. It was just another facet of motherhood she had not thought on. Another one she would not have. Holding the baby close as he nursed…savoring the precious weight of him against her arm.

She had bowed her head and when she looked up to speak, InaMae was staring out of the buggy with such pretend interest one would think she had never seen a bluebird next.

After that had happened, they were both very careful of the words they spoke.

Lorena had mentioned, however, that she regretted the necessity of going to the "laying in" hospital in Jacksonville.

"Don't seem fittin', somehow, to be goin' to a hospital and not bein' sick. Seemed to me like home was the place to be birthin' a baby."

InaMae had understood. "It'd be fine with me, Lorena, iffen you was to decide not to go. That'd be somethin' I'd understand, right off, and we'd find a way to fix the papers."

But that day Lorena had bravely answered. "No. We done reasoned it out, and it was good thinkin'. This'a'way the birth papers gonna be made out by someone else, and gonna say the right names and they'll be no question in nobody's mind who that baby gonna belong to."

InaMae had looked relieved, but she had repeated, "That'd be for you to decide."

Don't be thinkin' about that, Lorena told herself. *They's other things that gotta be thought on. You best be goin' back to 'em.*

The boys would need a larger school lunch bucket with Georgie starting this year. Or likely, two buckets would be better.

And there was no reason why Georgie couldn't climb the hill every day. He'd be doing something just as active if he was at home, and there was the promise of Freddie to look after him.

Quick-thinking Freddie would do a good job. Of the five boys, Lorena knew that it was Freddie who was most like his Aunt InaMae.

Like her, he was quick to see the needs of others and ready to help. The world needed more people like her and Freddie. Maybe this baby...?

The baby moved again. Softly, meaningfully. *You gonna just have to get used to it*, Lorena told herself, sternly. *Ain't no way you gonna be runnin' out here to the ledge to feel sorry for yourself every time InaMae's baby turns hisself over.*

Lady came trotting out to the ledge and flopped down beside her. A silky ear fell against Lorena's hand and she caressed the dog's soft neck fur.

"Good dog," she told Lady. "Come on, we got'a go back, now. I done used up enough time."

Lady trotted ahead of her back to the cabin. The boys were playing "drop the handkerchief" when she returned. Even Jamie was a part of the circle, squealing with delight when the hanky was dropped behind him. He toddled after Junior and almost "caught" him.

The boys didn't even see their mother as she went past them into the cabin.

Picking up her kitchen duties, Lorena struggled her thoughts together. Sure, and she was having a hard time... *but just think of InaMae for a minute.*

Just think on never havin' a baby that was your own...? Not a borrowed nephew for a time...? Think on never getting' to make a decision concerning him...?

She groaned inwardly. The thought was just too heavy to wrap her mind around. She gazed out of the window, seeing nothing. "Like I said to you, Lord. I'm gonna need all the help you got layin' around up there."

One last sign, and she picked up a stick of stovewood and put it in the firebox. Always a next meal facing her. Time to get at it.

14

It was a Sunday evening in late September that the Morgan family arrived, as usual, a little early for the evening church service. Freddie and Junior slipped down to the riverbank behind the church to get a last moment away from adult surveillance.

"Lookie down there," Junior pointed.

"Where?"

"Right there! See them rattlers? That there's a snake tail. Hand me a stick."

Junior watched the tail, unblinkingly, until Freddie thrust a stick into his hand. He reached out with the stick and poked the tail. Nothing happened. He poked it, again. Still nothing.

"It's dead," pronounced Junior.

He poked it once more, and then eased silently down over the bank. He bravely grasped the rattles and tugged, jumping back.

"See, it's dead."

"How come?"

Junior grasped the rattles again, dragging it from its hiding place behind a bush. "Law sakes, this'n here shore is long. Lookie at that, Freddie!"

Stretched out flat, the snake was a good four feet long. Where its head should have been there was a mass of bloody gristle.

Junior gave a knowing nod. "That old yeller cat of the preacher's must'a got at it. He's a snake cat, ya know. Done gnawed the head plumb off. Lookie there where his tooth marks show."

The boys leaned down to examine the carcass.

"Freddie, we got'a take this old snake home."

"Home? How come?"

"I can tell you how come. You 'member that belt Mr. Jenkins wears that looks like a snake skin?"

Freddie nodded.

"We got us a real snake skin right here, bein' long enough to make two belts and we got'a get it home."

"What'll we do 'bout the guts? Likely they'll get to smellin' real bad."

Junior stroked his chin. "Figure they's a way to turn 'im inside out so as to get to the guts with a knife. Then it'd just be a trick to cut out them belts."

Freddie nodded. "First, we got'a put it in the wagon."

"Yeah. No, we don't! Happen we put that old snake in the wagon, Ma'd for shore put her hand on it and scream, likely droppin' Jamie, or somethin'."

"What'll we do?"

"We got'a have it where we can keep our hands on it and know where it's at all the time."

"Jamie's pallet?"

Junior considered the suggestion. "Yeah! That'd be best. We got'a catch Ma talkin' and sneak it in. Then, after church, we can reach under and get it."

"You thinkin' I ought'a get ready to take it in now?"

"Yeah. I can stand at the door and watch Ma. Go ahead and wind it up little as you can, and when I wave my hand, you come on with it."

Junior ran to station himself at the church door while Freddie wound the snake's body around his arm. The rattles on the tail whispered their papery sound.

Junior watched carefully. When he waved his arm, Freddie came in, walking fast. He marched quickly through the door and around the benches. He dropped to his knees and peeled the snake off his arm, pushing it under Jamie's quilt pallet that was always spread under the family bench. No one looked his way.

Freddie nonchalantly left the church. Junior joined him in the yard.

"Law, we shore done that good!" Freddie complimented.

"Yeah. Ain't nobody saw nothin'."

The church service started and the choir sang their three songs. Junior and Freddie gouged each other with their elbows and tried to keep from whispering about their valuable find. Jamie dozed off to sleep and Lorena put him to bed on the pallet without incident.

Stanley began to nod and Lorena whispered in his ear. Stanley lowered to his knees and crawled onto the pallet. He lay down and pulled a corner of it up over his shoulders.

The release of pressure when the pallet corner was lifted off the coiled snake carcass caused the snake's body to slither into a new position. Stanley shut his eyes and was instantly asleep.

Mrs. McGruder, who sat across the aisle, saw the movement and looked closer. Her eyesight was not what it used to be but not so dim that she did not recognize a snake when she saw one. Or did she? She searched her purse for her reading glasses. The strong lens magnified the outline of the snake and it was now unmistakable. She whispered to Mr. McGruder, who had a little trouble hearing.

"See that snake?"

"Rake?"

"No, snake!"

He shook his head. "Ain't no snake in here. We're in the churchhouse."

"Likely not, but lookie there," she suggested. "What're you thinkin' that is?"

Mr. McGruder cleared his throat loudly, thereby dismissing his wife and her foolish notion of seeing a snake in the Lord's House.

There was no use in trying to change the McGruder mind once it was set, but she couldn't take her eyes off those rattles.

Stanley shifted in his sleep, and the snake moved again. Somebody had to do something, she decided, before that little Morgan boy got himself bit. So Mrs. McGruder tapped the shoulder of the boy on the bench in front of her, and little Billy Tucker turned around.

"Billy, you go say to your papa that a snake got in the church."

"Where at?"

Mrs. McGruder pointed.

Billy's sisters, Janet and Alicia, noted Mrs. McGruder's pointing finger. They clamped their hands over their mouths and stared, wide eyed at the reptile. Alicia whispered to her mother, "Mama, they's a snake over there."

Louise Tucker, Alicia's mother, told her, "Hush up, Alicia, and pay attention to the preacher."

Aaron Scott heard Alicia and saw the snake. He poked Donald Barker and pointed. Meanwhile, Billy Tucker had gone to his father who sat on the deacon's bench.

"Pa, they's a snake back there."

Dave Tucker dismissed him. "Reckon you saw a shadow."

"No, Pa...."

"Go sit down, Billy."

Junior and Freddie Morgan stared straight ahead.

Billy came back to his seat and sat watching the now motionless snake. Donald Barker eased off his seat and joined Billy. "We gotta get that thing out'a here ourselves. My Pa wouldn't believe there was no snake."

Donald leaned over, studying the problem. Three Scott children and Billy's two sisters also leaned over to see.

By now, Dave Tucker, Billy's father, began to have second thoughts. Perhaps he had been too hasty. Billy was not one to be imagining things. He stood up quietly and walked to the back of the church.

Billy Tucker and Donald Barker dropped to their knees in the aisle. Rev. McCrey, sensing a restlessness among the children, paused a moment to determine the cause. As most commotion originated around the Morgan bench, he looked there first.

Junior and Freddie sat like carved stone statues, staring at him. There was, however, curled around the leg of their bench, a rattlesnake. It was practically crawling over the baby. He stared, wordlessly, his feet frozen in their position.

Billy and Donald were advancing stealthily toward the snake.

Rev. McCrey could say no more, all his words having fled his mind. The church became deathly silent as Donald reached for the snake's tail and yanked, yelling, "I got it! Get out'a my way!"

With Billy running interference down the aisle, Donald ran to the door and flung the snake as far as he could.

Donald and Billy returned to their benches, wiping their hands on their overalls with the righteous pride of conquering heroes returning from the war.

Junior and Freddie saw their snake being carried to the door. They looked at each other without expression. Finally Rev. McCrey retrieved his train of thought and the service continued.

At the last "Amen" of the dismissal, Freddie shouldered his way to the church door with Junior close behind. In the darkness of the churchyard, the boys patted the ground, earnestly.

"I got it!" Junior announced, in a coarse whisper.

"Sneak it in the wagon," Freddie advised him.

"But I got'a get in with it so Ma won't see it."

Lorena listened to the account of the heroic rescue that went on behind her bench. She listened to statements that the church must take steps to see that no more snakes crawled into the building. She did not seem unduly concerned about the safety of her younger children. She looked around for Junior and Freddie and was not surprised that they were not nearby.

Donald and Billy, however, were there, and they glowed under the warmth of adult approval and praise.

Junior and Freddie sat in the wagon, leaning against the endgate. The snake carcass was imprisoned between their backs and the endgate board.

"You really, for shore, think they's enough snake skin for two belts?"

"Law, yeah! You saw how long that snake was, flyin' out 'hind Donald, him runnin' for the door!"

In November, the rains came and with them came the lowered spirits and general irritations. Jamie and Stanley fought over the toys and begged to be let out to play in the cold rain. Water streamed off the eaves of the cabin, and the inside was steamy from drying necessary clothing over the stove. Bedding felt damp and clammy. The walls seemed to close in and there was no escape. It was one of those impossible days.

Carl slogged to the shed, spending his time on winter activities, repairing tools and pitching hay to the soaked animals. Water streamed over the hill, and the wet and smelly pups were allowed into the cabin to keep the boys from killing each other in their boredom.

Lorena could not face the day and had stayed in bed. It was the fourth day of the rain, and she could not make herself arise. Arms and legs pressed themselves down on the mattress, much too heavy to move.

Junior, Freddie, and Georgie prepared their own lunches and walked out in the rain. They were drenched before they left the yard, and by the time they reached the foot of the hill, they had not a dry inch from the knees down. Oiled slickers funneled streams of water into their gumboots.

Carl had made the coffee and fried their eggs. Stanley and Jamie fought over the dominoes as they built houses on the table.

Heavy and tired, Lorena huddled under the quilts, mired in dejection. Her limp hair fell around her neck and she had no strength to comb and braid it. Her head ached. She lay beneath the quilts in a stupor until noon.

For lunch, Carl fed the boys whatever he could find and took them to the shed with him.

Got to fix up somethin' for supper, Lorena told herself, but still she did not move. Her arms still weighed a ton with a pain that would not get eased. She was clearly too old and tired to birth a baby. What had ever given her the fool idea that she could go through with this? Why, she might not even live, being as old as she was!

The door opened and she did not move. Carl would have to handle whatever needed handling. She didn't even open her eyes. Someone sat on her bed and she heard her sister's voice.

"I brung up some 'tater salad and cold fried chicken."

Lorena didn't answer. InaMae went on, softly, "Carl said you was feelin' poorly."

It was then that Lorena turned to look at InaMae. There she sat, tall and slim with her pink and white skin. Her shiny yellow hair had been combed and her dress was crisp and clean and fitted her the way it should. Of course she could look that way. What else did she have to do? Her kitchen stove was not draped with soggy, wet overalls. Her eyes were not dull from sleeplessness. Her smile and fresh cheerfulness grated on Lorena's nerves.

"Did my Carl come down there bellyachin' on how bad things was up here? That his fat, old, ugly wife wasn't cookin' up nothin' fit to eat?"

Before InaMae could answer, Lorena continued, "Reckon he said how purty you looked, not havin' to figure out how to dry out clothes for five boys? Sure was glad to have you close there so as he'd have someone to go cryin' to."

InaMae stared in amazed silence at the unexpected attack. Lorena continued, "I allow I ain't so far gone I can't fix my own family their food. Screamin' boys and the rain and wet clothes ain't gonna stop me, and you can say that to him, happen he comes over to cry on you later. Ain't never yet left 'em to starve."

InaMae sought words. "But, Lorena, I just...."

But Lorena was not finished. "And you know what else? You can be pickin' up them dishes of whatever you brung and take 'em right on back. I don't have no hankerin' for no 'taters nor chicken."

Lorena turned over, heavily, and dismissed her sister by pulling the quilt over her head.

After a stunned pause, InaMae went to the kitchen and left the cabin through the side door without a word.

The door had hardly closed behind her when Lorena regretted her words. She had never before spoken to anyone like that and certainly not her sister. InaMae often brought food, both fresh cooked and left over, and it had always been welcome. Not only that, the way she felt today, any food should have been considered a godsend. But now she had sent InaMae and the food away. Whatever had gotten into her? And she still had the fierce headache. The pillow seemed suddenly hard, and it seemed to push up against her sore scalp.

The door opened again and Carl deposited Jamie inside and left. In a few minutes he was back with Stanley. He had carried the boys through the muddy yard to keep them from tracking into the cabin. Lorena sat up on the bed.

"Carl, you bein' already wet, would you mind to get a jar'a apples out'a the cellar? Might get a jar'a corn while you're down there."

Carl left again. The little boys were inside now, and she really needed to get up and do something. Life, however miserable, still went on. Her mind moved forward to the next meal. She would bake apple cake and make corn fritters. The boys always liked the crusty fritters and they were bound to be cold and soaked when they got in from school. Then there would be more wet clothes and shoes that needed drying over the stove.

Oh, how her head hurt! She lay back down just for a minute. It didn't help.

Carl slogged back up to the door and, kicking the clay from his boots, he came inside. He put the jars of apples and corn on the table.

"Lorena?"

"Huh?"

"Don't need to be botherin' to fix nothin' for me. I ain't gonna be here, come supper time."

"Huh?"

"I got me business in town."

"You ain't wantin' no supper?"

"Reckon not."

"Where at you gonna eat?"

"Down at the cafe in River Bend."

"My cookin' ain't good enough all of a sudden?" Lorena asked, resentfully.

"What'd be different tonight?"

"I got someone I got'a eat with."

Lorena sighed. Someone else for supper. Oh well, how much trouble could one more person be? "Bring 'im on. We gonna have corn fritters and they's always more'n enough."

Carl seemed to consider the offer, then shook his head. "Reckon not, Lorena, this here person bein' a woman."

Lorena felt her heart shrivel within her. Fat and lazy she was, with ragged, greasy hair, and she had spent the day in bed when she was not even sick. For shame, Lorena! What she had done had forced her Carl to say such a nonsensical thing! Well, anyway it got her attention.

Without another word, Carl left again. Lorena went to the kitchen and poked at the dying coals of fire in the stove. She put a stick on the glowing embers and blew them into a blaze. The stove reservoir held enough warm water to wash her hair.

Why would Carl say a thing like that? Of course, he was just joking but the sound of it wasn't the same as his usual jokes.

She opened the cupboard to get the flour for the cake and saw the potato salad and the platter heaped with cold fried chicken. Good old InaMae. She had known Lorena had not meant those cruel things she said. So now, a cake, along with the chicken and potato salad, would make a fine supper good enough for whoever Carl brought in. This would make up for Carl having to fix his own dinner.

Massaging the lather of the lye soap on her hair made her head feel a surprising lot better. There was nothing better than the thick, white bar of lye soap for cutting the grease from winter hair. In fact, the headache had almost stopped. She brushed her hair in long, even strokes in front of the open oven door. It dried into its natural waves, glistening and shining, and she suddenly realized the ache was completely gone.

She closed the door of the oven so it would heat up for the cake. She broke six eggs into the bowl and added a cup of flour and three cups of rolled oats to make it chewy. She put in the dried persimmons that had been put through the grinder. They would make it spicy sweet. And finally, in went some soda and a glob of lard. Apple cakes were easy and delicious, good for filling up hungry men and boys.

She poured the batter into the pan and spread the apples on top, poking the chunks down into the batter. A sprinkling of sugar on top made it perfect.

The sweet spicy smell of the cake was filling the cabin when Carl came back.

"I need me some dry clothes," he announced without explanation. "I want my good ones."

"Huh?"

"My good pants. You 'member? The ones I wear to church."

"But Carl?"

"I told ya I was a'goin' down to River Bend."

Lorena was puzzled. "I got apple cake a'bakin' in the oven."

Carl nodded agreeably. "The boys'll like that. 'Course, I ain't gonna be here."

This was too much. No joke should be carried this far.

"Carl Morgan, you say to me what's got into you? Tell me, flat out, no chasin' 'round the bush. What you got goin' on?"

"'Bout what?"

"'Bout you eatin' in the cafe with some woman. Be speakin' up, now."

"Sure, Lorena. They's a lady I've knowed for a long time, a bunch of years, and her bein' a favorite of mine. I ain't seen her around in a month or two and I was a'figurin' that she might show up down at the cafe. I seen her there lots'a times, long years ago. I got a thought that I wasn't sayin' things to her to make 'er come around anymore so I needed to be changin'. I been missin' her."

Lorena stared at her handsome husband, unable to command her tongue to function.

Carl continued his explanation. "Figured to try to look good tonight for her, not havin' hay in my hair and manure on my boots. Knowd I'd have to clean up some. They any hot water left? And don't you be botherin' to lay out them clothes. I wouldn't want to be puttin' more on you than you done been put through."

Carl checked the stove reservoir. A little water was left. Lorena decided she was having a dream. The cake began to smell "done" so she took it from the oven. Carl sniffed appreciatively.

"Them boys gonna get themselves a good supper."

Lorena sat down at the kitchen table and watched Carl as he put on his Sunday clothes. She watched him go to the closet and look through her clothes. He selected her good, yellow dress.

"Iffen I got me the right to choose, I'd want that lady to be wearin' this here dress."

Lorena kept watching him. Clearly the dream should end by now. She sliced the cake, releasing fragrant steam along the knife blade. The cake did not seem to be part of the dream.

Carl put the yellow dress on the bed. He took Lorena's Sunday shoes from their drawer and put them on the bed beside the dress, then he came to the table and, guiding her gently, led her to the bed.

"I'd be pleased to have you put on these things, Miss Lorena, 'cause we goin' in to town, tonight. We leavin' here quick as them boys get home."

"But they...." Automatic objections arose in her mouth.

Carl's words stopped her. "InaMae gonna come up here with the boys and she gonna dry 'em out and feed 'em 'cause you and me, we ain't gonna be here."

"But the rain, Carl?"

Carl grinned his handsome grin. "You think I forgot how to drive that courtin' buggy through the rain? You forget all them times I come up that clay hill and the weather pourin' down? You forget them times I courted you and the rain didn't never come down too hard for me to make it up that hill? Reckon you think I got so old them horses don't mind me no more?

"Now I'm sayin', you put on them clothes, purty woman, and you be quick about it. I aim to show you who can still court a lady and who can still get that buggy up and down the hill in the rain."

Lorena finally began to realize she was not asleep. "Carl, you don't got'a do this. They ain't nothin' to worry about with me no more."

"Yeah, but they's somethin' to worry about with me. I ain't been out sparkin' with a purty woman for more'n eight years and that'd be a mite too long. Get movin' now. I see InaMae comin' up the road this minute."

Lorena slipped into the yellow Sunday dress and the shiny black patent leather Sunday shoes, which seemed a ridiculously frivilous thing to do on a rainy, mid-week night.

There was a sound at the side door as InaMae stomped the mud from her feet and came in, holding her coat over her head to keep dry. She put the coat on a chair and looked at Lorena.

Lorena looked at the floor. "InaMae…?"

InaMae touched her sister's arm and Lorena looked up. She smiled and shook her head, gently. "No need to explain," the look was plainly saying.

There came another sound of stomping at the south door and three soaked boys burst dripping into the cabin. They stood, water puddling wetly at their feet, and stared at their parents clad in Sunday clothes. InaMae explained, "Your ma and pa got somethin' they got'a do but we gonna have us a picnic. We got fried chicken and 'tater salad."

"Picnic?"

"In the rain?"

InaMae grinned, reassuringly, "We gonna have our picnic in here. Lookie at what your mama made us? Apple cake!"

Carl had gone out, but now he was back.

"Got the buggy pulled up just outside," he told Lorena as he scooped her up in his arms and carried her through the door and over the muddy ground. The boys watched through the window, rolling with laughter at the strange antics of their parents.

The storm-flaps had been snapped onto the buggy, and Carl zipped them up snuggly, leaving only enough room for the reins. The raindrops spattered on the buggy roof and whispered down across the small isinglass windows.

Carl tucked the lap robe warmly around Lorena's feet and legs. He winked a dark eye wickedly at her and they started down the slick, clay hill, avoiding, when possible, the deep ruts flowing full with muddy water. Lorena could think of nothing to say, and Carl sat smugly content and didn't even try to talk.

Once down the hill and the horse clomped solidly on the gravel, he reached for her hand and held it, expertly guiding the horses along the river road with the other hand.

In the town of River Bend, he stopped in front of the Mercantile. Without an explanation, he left her in the buggy, promising to be right back. And sure to his word, he was back in ten minutes with a wide smile. Clicking to the horse, he moved the buggy onto the road. In front of the Main Street Cafe, Carl tied the horses to the post and again picked up Lorena in his arms and carried her to the door. Several people put down their forks and coffee cups to enjoy the show.

Carl selected a center table. The girl in the apron came with her order pad, and Carl told her, "My girl, here, she gonna want a cup'a hot chocolate right off to warm 'er up. Gonna want extra marshmellers in it. I'll be wantin' one, too. Now, Lorena, honey, what you feelin' like eatin'? Chicken? Ham?"

The girl with the order pad chuckled with merriment at the old married couple pretending to be courting. Ready to go along with the fun, she offered, "We got us some real good chicken fried steak and we got deer meat stew. That sound good?"

Lorena considered and nodded. "That stew'd be the very thing I'd want, bein' out in that cold rain."

Carl smilingly added, "Bring 'er extra crackers, would ya? I'll take that steak and we gonna want pie. You got mincemeat?"

The girl nodded, her eyes twinkling. Mincemeat was a favorite and was always on the menu.

Food came quickly. The chocolate was steaming and frothy with marshmallows. It was dark, rich, and sweet, driving away the bone chill of the November rain. The stew was thick with chunks of meat, hunted and prepared from animals that had climbed the mountains around River Bend. It was colorful with vegetables preserved at their time of freshness in glass Mason jars. They were vegetables that Lorena had not peeled and scraped and the stew was seasoned with flavors different from hers. The mincemeat pie was tasty and rich, but the crust was not quite so flaky and tender as her own. All in all, it was a perfect meal.

"Carl, this was real good for me but you hadn't ought'a let InaMae put you up to it."

Carl raised surprised eyebrows. "InaMae? She never said to do this."

"But, she...."

"She was a'bringin' up the chicken 'cause I asked her to and you wouldn't let her say what it was for. I asked her to do that so we could get away, just you and me. She's been knowin' for a couple'a weeks I wanted 'er to do this. They was somethin' I was wantin' to say that was hard to say 'round five noisy boys, and I was sure this here rain wasn't gonna stop me."

Carl reached into his pocket and brought out a tiny box covered in shiny blue paper covered with silver stars. He cleared his throat loudly, and a number of people looked their way. Carl opened the box with a flourish and took out a ring with a large pearl set. He held up the small circle in his large, work-calloused hands. The pearl was surrounded with tiny, sparkly yellow stones that glistened and flashed in the soft light of the wall lamps. The lamplight on the pearl glowed warmly.

Carl reached across the table and took Lorena's hand. He slipped the ring on her finger and questioned earnestly, "Lorena, honey, will you marry me?"

"Carl! What you talkin' 'bout? You out'a your mind…or what?" She grinned and lowered her head. The lamplight shone on the shiny waves of her hair and on the thick, coiled braids. Even the tucking of her head could not hide the flush of pink on her cheeks.

Carl shook his head. "Ain't nothin' wrong with my head. I got me eyes to know a good thing when it passes in front of me. It was nine years ago tonight, if I'm countin' right, when I asked for you that other time, and I didn't have no purty ring to give you that time. Them was nine good years you give me, so I felt like it was time I ought'a put in a word for the next nine. That bein' if you'd have me."

The other customers in the cafe ate quietly with silent silverware, straining to hear their words, but now Carl lowered his voice.

"They's somethin' I want to tell you, Lorena, and maybe it'd be a thing you'd be wantin' to know. It'd be about InaMae and Marcel."

"Huh?"

"I never told you how I had'a give Marcel my triple bladed knife to get him to court InaMae so as I could have you."

"Huh?" she repeated in puzzlement.

"Well, you 'member Marcel and me bein' friends and growin' up together, we was what you might 'member as bein' a mite slow in our thinkin'. We spent our time not seein' nothin' till it hit us on the head a few times. We knowd you girls all our lives, but then one day, all of a sudden, we saw what you both was and how you was bein' looked at by other fellows. We saw you and InaMae was purty and smart and all them other things. We commenced tellin' ourselves we better get a move on, else somebody'd be carryin' you both off and we'd get no chance at you, even to get turned down. We talked it over and we was both wantin' to court you, but I swapped him my triple bladed knife for the first chance to ask you. 'Course, it turned out that he liked InaMae, and likely it'd turned out that way from the start, 'thout the help of the knife, but I wasn't wantin' to chance it."

Lorena looked down at the ring on her finger. "Carl, you tellin' me the truth?"

"Shore, it's the truth. You could even ask Marcel and he'd say it. Reckon he must remember."

"Aw, I couldn't never do that. I couldn't say that to him."

Carl sipped his chocolate and watched her. Lorena felt herself blush like a bride.

"Lorena, honey, I know what you could do. You'd be somewhere and need to get a wood sliver out'a your finger, or somethin', and ask Marcel for the us'a his knife. See if it ain't the triple bladed, pearl handle knife my Pa give me. You'd see it and remember what I'm sayin' when that was the knife he'd hand you."

Lorena studied the ring on her finger, turning her hand slowly this way and that to admire the sparkle. Carl reached for the hand, enclosing her fingers protectively inside his palm. "I figure to get me another piece of that pie 'afore we head on up the hill. They likely gonna have trouble gettin' rid of a pie with a crust tough like that'ns got. You ought'a stop in here sometime and tell 'em how the crust ought'a be done so as it'd come out like yours. You want more pie?"

Lorena shook her head. "I'd be likin' another chocolate, though."

It was still raining when Carl and Lorena headed the rain-soaked horse up the hill toward home. Carl held Lorena's hand, gently turning the ring on her finger.

"Carl?"

"Huh?"

"How was it you was able to get my right ring size in such of a hurry? You weren't in the Mercantile more'n ten minutes."

"Law, honey, I had me that ring picked out'a the catalog since summer. Had'a wait 'til the salesman brought it out to the Mercantile to see it for real. The size of it was a mite chancy and they was some guessin' done. I did a lot'a lookin' and studyin' on them little hoops Mr. Jenkins' got, 'afore I could be sure I had the right memory of your finger size. Mr. Jenkins been savin' it for me down at the store."

"Savin' it?"

"Shore, 'cause I knowd iffen I was to take it home, they weren't no place in that house where I could put it where you'd not run on to it."

Lorena turned her face toward him in the darkness of the buggy. "You knowd since summer you was gonna do this?"

"Shore thing."

"But, Carl, I talked so mean and I felt so ugly today. There weren't no time that I ever felt this'a'way with the other'ns. I didn't never feel like this when I was carryin' them."

Carl squeezed her hand. "Yep, but they's a difference. Them other times you was knowin' you'd get yourself a baby when it was over and this time you know you ain't. Seems reasonable to me you'd be feelin' down. Marcel says InaMae been feelin' down for years, watchin' you have a baby every spring and her havin' nothin' but a hope to hang onto. Then finally she didn't even have that. Only other good thing she got was a little time to hold your baby."

Lorena sighed and leaned against Carl's broad comfortable shoulder.

The horses cleared the top of the hill, anxiously pulling for the dry shed. A sheet of muddy water flowed across the yard and the sodden animals splashed through it.

"You sit right there," Carl told Lorena. "I want you to wait in the buggy till I get these horses took care of."

Lorena waited.

Carl finished and came to the buggy. He lifted her as he had lifted Stanley and Jamie and splashed through the puddles to the cabin. He set her down in the empty kitchen.

Empty! "Carl! The boys! They ain't here!"

Carl reached for her hand. "InaMae got 'em down to her house. They ain't nobody here but us. Just you and me."

"But...."

"It was her idea. She made me promise to let her keep 'em. Come, Lorena, honey. It's just you and me, all night long. Just us two."

15

The next day the kitchens of River Bend buzzed with the gossip.

"You know what happened down at the cafe last night? I wasn't there but I heard it from Bessie, and she was."

"What're you talkin' about?"

"Well, it was rainin' pitchforks, you 'member, weather you wouldn't kick a dog out into, and who'd you think came down that muddy clay hill but Carl and Lorena Morgan without them boys."

"I can't be faultin' her for that. Them boys, they...."

"That ain't it."

"I'm a'tryin' to tell ya. Well, that Carl picked Lorena up from the buggy and carried her to the door, careful as a crate'a eggs, and her big as the side of a barn with that baby."

"Reckon that'd not be much of a load for that Carl. He'd have the size for it, I speck."

"Yeah, and they sat down right there in the cafe like they was courtin'. 'Course, back when we was all a'courtin', she'd'a had her sister along. Well, they sat there and had chocolate and she ate stew and pie like she didn't have a kitchen full of food at home. For free."

"Wisht Harvey'd do me that'a'way, one time." The neglected housewife sighed with envy.

"You keep buttin' in. I got'a tell you about the ring."

"What ring?"

"The one I'm a'gonna tell you about, chance you let me. It was a ring that Carl had in his pocket. Had a stone in it the size to choke a horse. And shiny. Bessie was a'sittin' close and she said that ring was fit to blind a body with the light flashin' off it."

"That big!"

"Yeah, and that Carl, he just sat there and put that ring on her finger like he was proposin' to her right there in front'a God and everybody. And her with five down and one a'comin'."

"Hmmm. Imagine such a thing!"

"Yeah, and her a'duckin' and a'colorin' up like she was a bride on her weddin' night."

There was silence.

"You 'member she said this youngen was gonna be give to her sister? Don't reckon I know how she could do that after carryin' it for nine months and then to have it right next door where she'd have to look at it all the time. We all know how Lorena always liked babies."

The two women were in agreement. "Don't know as I could, neither. It'd shore be a thoughtful thing to do, though, if it works out that'a'way."

"Hafta say, they got 'em a good lookin' bunch'a boys."

"Yeah, be interesting to see how all this is gonna go."

There was also talk down at the livery stable. Men gathered there to whittle, mend harnesses, and forge wagon axels. Winter work. And they gathered to find out what was being talked about.

"Hope it don't get around that Carl Morgan give his woman a ring. Every woman in the county gonna get herself in a family way just to get herself a ring."

But someone else said, "They's two ways to look at that. Likely that Lorena deserves whatever she gets. Woman able to shell out sons like she done for Carl, she ought'a get somethin' for her effort."

"Yeah, still hear they gonna give the next baby to Marcel McCann and his wife. That'd be somethin' out'a the usual."

"Be purty hard on Lorena, I'd say."

"Don't figure it was no trouble to Carl, though, with them five boys he got. He got plenty to keep him busy."

"Yeah, them boys of his'n gonna be a fist full when they get some size on 'em and go to courtin' all at the same time. Look enough alike to be chopped out with the same biscuit cutter. Gonna be strange lookin', though, havin' one of 'em livin' next door."

The November rain finally stopped for a few days. It was Tuesday, but Lorena couldn't bring herself to get ready to go to the Sewing Circle, though she was fairly suffering to see a few different faces and voices. If she could have heard the conversation, she might have found something for a smile or two.

The weather kept away some of the women who lived up in the mountains, and those a long way up the valley, but the ladies from town happily gathered around. Once more Annalee Carmichael managed to leave the slopjar long enough to come. She had been attending to the annual job of sorting, packaging, and inventorying the flower seeds collected as the yard blossoms faded in the fall and an idea had occurred to her.

Eyes sparkling, she had said to her mother-in-law, "Miz Carmichael, you see how many'a these sweet clover seeds we got. I sifted 'em and filled up that oatmeal box, and I still got seeds. We got enough seeds to plant sweet clover for all the bees in River Bend, I'd wager. Shame we don't know who'd be needin' some."

Whereupon her mother-in-law had responded. "Yeah, it'd be good. Don't know how we'd know, though, less'n we spoke up at the Tuesday Sewin'. Don't seem like the seeds and the needs ever come out even. Some years the birds and varmints leave us with not more'n a cup'a sweet clover blooms, and nothing else makes honey that good."

Annalee sifted the remaining seeds and funneled them into a quart Mason jar. "You know, if we was to take this here jar with us, likely we'd find…." She hesitated and concluded, "No that wouldn't work. We'd not want to let our jar get away."

There was truth in that, the glass Mason jars being almost as valuable as what went into them. Emma, the senior Mrs. Carmichael, nodded thoughtfully, allowing an idea to form in her head. "Now, Annalee, think on this. If we was to leave the seeds at home and just say who needed seeds, likely they'd bring something the next week to take 'em home in. We could do that. You know, Annalee, I sure wish Maisie Pettingill would do that with her teacup zinnias. Them big old flowers had the best colors I ever saw in zinnias and everyone knows zinnias are about the easiest flowers for a busy woman to grow."

Annalee considered her mother-in-law's words while patting her rounding abdomen with one hand and tapping her finger in her own chin dimple, a habit she had when she was deep in thought.

"You know, Miz Carmichael, if we was to just say to all the ladies they could look at their seeds and whatever they had too many of, they could bring, and we could all swap and take a start of what we didn't have none of. You think that'd work?" Annalee really liked her mother-in-law, and she loved to please. She hoped this was a really good, grownup lady suggestion.

"Why, Annalee! You just had the very best idea! I'm thinkin' that'd be a good thing to add to our baby party and the button blanket. That'd be somethin' we could say to Lorena and InaMae, that we was havin' a seed-swappin' party. Thataway it'd be a surprise, and by that time we'd be knowin' which way the baby went. What'd you think of that?"

Annalee amazed herself by jumping up and joyfully hugging her mother-in-law, just before the sudden movement within sent her to the slopjar once more.

The idea was an instant success, and as it happened, it was a Tuesday Lorena was too exhausted to think of coming down the hill.

Carrie Woodward allowed she could use some of the sweet clover seed, and she had rose moss seed she'd bring. Mrs. Jenkins from the Mercantile offered to bring some seeds from her giant sunflowers that made seeds big enough to roast and eat. They were something new that the seed catalog had, but it was hard to keep the birds away until the seeds got ripe.

There was a promise of cosmos and verbenias and a lot of coreopsis seeds. Sadie Basham wondered if anyone could use little two-inch-high althea plants.

"You mean them white ones that grow into a tree and make double flowers? I'd sure like them but I thought they didn't make good seeds."

"They don't," came the reply. "But sometimes they come up all over. Clyde turns the goats in on 'em in the spring, or we'd not be able to get out the door come summer. Them goats make short work'a everything they can reach. I'll just bring them little trees in a wet cloth and anyone that wanted some could bring a cloth to get 'em in."

"Well, I want some."

"Me, too."

And then there was talk of when the party would be. Why not wait till up in January when everyone was let down after Christmas and wanting something to do? It wasn't like the baby would need a blanket right off at the beginning, being there had been recent babies on the hill. It had been a lot of fun, though, passing the small quilt quietly from woman to woman at the church services, for each to sew on her own buttons and attach her diaper pins to the edge.

It was going to be a fun surprise tucked in among the seed swap, and it made a thing to look forward to.

Winter dullness continued on the hill as InaMae hemmed diapers and stitched flannel gowns while Lorena pieced a quilt top. They worked in InaMae's house because of the bulk of the diapers. A huge kettle of field peas stewed in ham and ham hocks and a jar of tomatoes stood ready to become stewed tomatoes with onions and broken-up, left-over biscuits. The fireplace at the other cabin had been allowed to die out. There was no use wasting wood that took a lot of effort to saw into chunks. It had been a relaxed and pleasant day.

The boys were playing at something in the shed, and it was not likely to hear anything from them until someone got hurt or hungry.

Freddie had been pitching his rubber ball against the wall of the shed to practice his catching skills when an idea struck him full in the face.

"Hey, Junior, 'member that story in the book that Mr. Wilson brought? That one about a man in a red suit bringing toys for Christmas?"

"Yeah, kind of a strange story. Folks wouldn't even let 'im in so he had to come down the stovepipe chimney. Still yet, he was good enough to give out presents."

"And candy!" added Georgie, eager to remind the big boys he had also heard the story.

"What was makin' you think on that story?"

Freddie thought a minute. "Well, I was a'thinkin' how it'd been if there was a fire in the fireplace and he was to land in it in his shoes. The story said he got black ashes all over 'im, but it did't say nothin' about his shoes. I was thinkin' if he came down the chimney in every house, he'd need a new pair'a shoes every time. He couldn't be goin' without no shoes 'cause there was snow on the ground."

Stanley stared enviously from one to the other of his older brothers. To be big enough to attend school, in the wide, excitingly wonderful world outside of their farm must be the most marvelous thing that could be imagined.

Wishing to add something to the story, he observed, "That man couldn't come down our chimney 'cause we ain't got no snow."

"Sure enough, Stanley. But that was just a story you never seen. We could play Santa Claus and you could see how the story was, seein' you wasn't there to hear it."

Freddie was doubtful. "You 'memberin' all them rhymes that the words made?"

Junior lightly dismissed the problem. "Naw, we ain't needin' them words. What we need is just the story so them little'ns can know what we're talkin' about."

Georgie's eyes brightened with interest. "I could be the man in the red clothes that had ashes all over it. I could get ashes out'a the fireplace."

Junior shook his head. "No, Georgie, that wasn't the way it was. The ashes got on 'im when he was a'comin' down the chimney with his sack full'a toys. We'd need to figure a way to do that."

Freddie frowned, thoughtfully. "How big is that chimney hole anyway?"

"I never thought to notice," Junior admitted. "We could go look."

"Go look," decided Stanley, and he took off toward the house, the others following.

The big fireplace occupied a space between the wall of the kitchen and the sitting room, rocked up with large stones brought in from around the farm. The foot-high hearth on both sides kept the logs and ashes in place and made a spacious firebox that heated two rooms.

Within minutes the boys were lined up on the hearth, leaning over the cool ashes peering up into the dark depth of the chimney.

The three younger boys turned expectantly toward Junior. In due time the serious decision was made and he nodded his head. "Yep." Then he paused, chewing his lip importantly. Another nod, and then, "Yep,

I'm thinkin' we could do it. Georgie sayin' he'd be that man was likely the best thing, him bein' littler'n me and Freddie and that chimney hole bein' not overmuch wide. That chimney don't look big 'nuff to let a full grown man slide down. Likely the chimneys were bigger when they wrote that book."

Georgie's smile spread across his face. His head bobbed up and down in a nod. "Yep," he said solemnly. Another nod, and, "Yep, I could come down that old chimney." Then a thought struck him, "But I ain't got no toys to be in the pack on my back."

Freddie took that problem away. "We'd not be needin' real toys. We're just doin' this so Stanley can see how it went, weren't we, Junior."

Junior, who had also begun to be concerned about the lack of toys, was relieved to see the problem disappear so easily. "Freddie's right. We ain't needin' no toys. We'll get us a sack and put in sticks and a couple'a little rocks."

That problem taken away, the next thing was to put it in action. Dragging the ladder to the edge of the cabin, the four boys climbed to the roof.

"Now, Stanley, I let you come up here, but after you look down the chimney hole, then you got'a go back down so's you can see the Santa Claus when he comes down."

Stanley nodded in agreement. It was very flattering to have his three brothers creating a show just for him, and it was best he agree to anything they wanted, otherwise they might change their minds.

The chimney bucket that was used to put over the hole to keep out the rain was lifted off. Georgie leaned over and looked down. "It's dark down there," he observed in a shaky voice.

Junior was quick with his response. "Yeah, and that's why we can do that. If it was light in that hole, it'd mean there was fire down there, and then we couldn't play this game."

Georgie saw the truth in that and nodded slowly, his face sober and his mouth a firm, tense line. This could possibly be a time when he should have waited before offering to be the star of the play, but having offered, he could not conveniently back down.

Stanley was lifted up to look down the hole, and he shivered in anticipation at the wonders that would soon be presented to him.

"Now, Stanley, you got'a go on down, 'cause we're gonna go down and I can't let you stay up here and fall off."

Stanley, not wanting to upset his brothers in any way, allowed himself to be led to the ladder and helped down.

In time, a suitable bag was found for the toys. When salt was purchased for the cattle, the small cloth bags were washed and stacked in the barn for whatever use came up. The small sack was just the right size.

"I know what we could use for toys," decided Freddie, picking up a handful of the cobs that had been shelled of corn. After the corn was removed from the cobs, they were kept in a barrel to be available for their multiple uses on the farm, all the way from being turned into handles to anything, scrubbers when needed, and fire starters if nothing else was handy.

Corncobs were handy and lightweight and the small cloth sack soon had its "toys." The three older boys climbed the ladder once more, and Stanley was stationed inside the cabin to be the audience.

The time had come. Georgie walked slowly toward the chimney hole and was helped to stand while he positioned himself straight with the stone-lined tunnel extending down to the firebox. He peered once more into the darkness and deemed the Santa Claus person to be very brave to go sliding down the scary tunnel into everyone's house.

Then a thought crossed his mind. "Junior, how is it I'm gonna get back out? That man went zooming back up after he emptied his toys. Am I gonna zoom back up?"

That was a new thought. Junior and Freddie looked at each other. Getting down would be easy, because where else could he go but down? Georgie had put his words on the real problem, though, so something else had to be done.

About this time, a petulant voice came up from below. "I don't see no sandman a'comin' down!"

Junior was a bit irritated with this hitch in their plans and he called down to the voice from below. "Just hold your horses down there. 'Sides, it ain't no sandman, it's a Santa Claus man, anyway, we still got somethin' to do to make it work." Then he turned to his next in command, "Freddie, go get the rope and we can tie it around him. That'a'way, we can pull 'im right back up when he empties the toys."

Freddie was not particularly pleased, but he could see he would be the logical one to take care of the errand so he headed for the ladder. Georgie, however, was more than a little happier at the thought of a rope around himself with his trusted brothers on the end. He also added a small twist to the story.

"When I get down there, I can empty them corncobs into the woodbox."

Junior nodded as he considered the matter. "Good thought. You can do that." He bent importantly over the hole. It was a long way down, and it was, indeed, dark. A part of him wished, sincerely, that he had not gone along with the plan. It was too late to back out now and risk losing face. In fact, here was Freddie with the rope.

The rope of many uses was tied securely around Georgie and positioned snuggly under his arms. The small boy licked his lips nervously and allowed himself to be helped onto the chimney once more and stationed over the hole.

"Now, you got'a sit down and put your feet in the hole," Junior instructed. "Then me and Freddie, we'll help you slide down."

Freddie picked up the loose end of the rope and tapped Junior's arm, questioningly. Junior nodded. "Yeah, you're right. I gotta tie that end around my stomach, so he don't go down too fast."

That done, Georgie began to scoot on his bottom toward the seemingly endless hole. With his brothers holding one hand, and the other hand holding the bag of toys over his head, Georgie took a deep breath, straightened his legs, and slid into the hole.

It was only seconds until the rope tightened alarmingly on Junior's middle. "Leggo that rope," he yelled down to Georgie.

Georgie yelled back, "I can't it's a'squeezin' me and it won't let me fall on down."

At that moment it dawned upon Junior that they had not checked the length of the rope. Georgie was now suspended inside the chimney with his hands over his head, and his entire weight was pulling against the knot in the rope around his own stomach, drawing him roughly against the stonewalls of the chimney.

He looked in despair toward Freddie. "Oh, Law, we done it now. This here rope we got is too short and it ain't lettin' him down."

Wide-eyed, Freddie suggested, "Untie it and we'll hand 'im down."

Junior shook his head. "Can't. Him hangin' down got to pullin' th' knot too tight. Ain't no way we could untie it."

Freddie had another suggestion. "Cut the rope?"

Junior thought a minute.

A muffled voice came from the chimney hole. "Hey, somebody get me out'a here!"

Junior called back, "We're a'tryin'. You just hold your horses."

"I ain't got no horses. My arms are stuck and they hurt. The corncobs are'a itchin' my head."

Another irritated voice came up from the dark depth. "There ain't no man a'comin' down the chimney. How come there ain't no man?"

The two on the roof ignored the second voice. "Junior, I could step up on the chimney and try to pull 'im back up?"

"Yeah, try it!" was Junior's enthusiastic encouragement.

Gingerly, Freddie stepped up on the stones. A small chunk of stone crumbled off and went clattering down the shingles and bounced off to the ground.

"Freddie," Junior whispered, "You got'a be extra careful you don't go down that hole after 'im."

Freddie nodded. "I'm a'tryin'. I'm a'thinkin' I could sit down, and then I wouldn't fall."

"Yeah, man! Sit down."

Freddie spread his legs, one on either side of the chimney hole, and dangled his feet over the outside edge. Gripping the rope with both hands, he pulled, lifting Georgie a few inches.

A sound came up from within the pipe. "Ouch. It's a rubbin' the skin off my elbows."

Freddie sighed, "I can't pull no more. He's too heavy."

Junior replied, breathlessly, "No, he ain't too heavy. You got'a pull 'im up. Get this rope to loosen up and I'll help."

"SOMEBODY HELP ME!"

"Hush up, Georgie. We're tryin'."

Freddie took a new hold onto the rope, but his sweaty hands slipped. Dropping the rope, he stripped off his shirt.

"What're you a'doin'?"

"The rope's a hurtin' my hands! I'm a makin' me a handhold outta my shirt."

"SOMEBODY GET ME OUT'A HERE!"

Junior tested the small amount of slack in the rope. "Wait, Freddie. I think I can reach 'im, now."

Four hands clutched the rope and pulled. Georgie was lifted another few inches. Then a scream. "Stop it! Don't pull me no more! Somethin' got a hold'a me! It's a'bitin' me in the back side!"

"Naw, you're just bein' scared!"

"No, I ain't. Somethin' diggin' into my back side'n I ain't lyin'. I think it's a nail."

"Naw, there ain't no nails in there."

"Yes, there is. I know there's something' pokin' at me."

Freddie stepped closer to the chimney to get a better grip and was punched by a metal bar protruding from the stones. "Look, Junior. I know what's got 'im. That bar sticks all the way through them rocks."

Junior wearily nodded his head with recognition. They couldn't pull him up because the bar that held the chimney bucket in place was stuck in his clothes. He yelled down the hole, "What's the nail stuck on?"

"I mean…oh, Law…he don't know 'cause it's in back of 'im."

"Now what?"

"Uh, Freddie, you go down in the house and see can you get 'im a'loose."

Obediently, Freddie descended the ladder, sincerely wishing he had never heard of the Christmas man and the toys…and most of all, the chimney.

A very irritated Stanley still stared up from below, expecting the "man" to come down into the firebox.

Freddie had no patience with his brother's disappointment. "Get out'a the way, Stanley. I got'a get up in there."

"NO!" screamed Stanley. "We got'a wait!"

Freddie ignored him. Stepping into the ashes, he lifted his head into the blackness above him. Two dangling feet were hanging down just out of his reach. As his eyes accustomed themselves to the darkness, he saw the problem. It was what he had thought.

The metal rod extended through the stonework, just as he has guessed, and the end of it was stuck into Georgie's rear pocket holding him down when the rope pulled him up and keeping him from coming any farther down. In addition, the pocket was much too high to reach. He spent a moment in contemplation, and an idea struck him.

Ducking back out of the chimney, he dashed across the room and lifted his grandpa's old walking cane from its place. Resuming his position in the firebox, he thrust the cane up toward Georgie, who was now crying dismally.

Hooking the cane into first the right pocket and then the left pocket, he worked the britches down a fraction of an inch at a time.

Georgie, realizing something was being done, hushed his crying, but Stanley took it up, demanding the man had to come down and Freddie must get out of the way. When the pant legs came within reach of Freddie's hands, he took a good hold and slid them off. Calling up the chimney pipe, he instructed, "Junior, try and pull 'im up."

Georgie was lifted a few inches. "Got'a have help!"

Freddie fairly flew from the room, skittered up the ladder and, with one foot on either side of the chimney hole, he joined Junior on the rope. Inch by painful inch, the weight was lifted.

First the bag of corncobs appeared. Junior grabbed them and tossed them away. Next came the hands and they were clasped by his brothers. Walking his toes up the inside of the rockwork, Georgie now helped them pull him out.

When he was again sitting on the chimney, the three brothers looked at each other with profound relief. Freddie stared at his skinned hands and nodded toward Junior whose hands were also blood stained. Junior had a band of rope-burn around his waist. Together they lifted Georgie off the rockwork and turned him around. Lowering his underpants, they saw a two-inch long scrape, still oozing blood. The underpants were well stained. Around his chest just under his arms, he had a rope burn that out-matched Junior's.

They would have said something to each other, if there had been any words to say, but there were none. First Georgie, then Freddie, and lastly came Junior, carefully descended the ladder on shaky feet.

Freddie ventured, "Junior, we got'a get this ladder back."

Junior agreed, "But first we got'a wash the blood off Georgie's underpants."

"Yeah, that'd be first."

The three older brothers were sworn to secrecy by their involvement in the caper, but there remained Stanley who was sure to complain to the parents. This would take some thought.

They stood looking at each other, searching their minds for words. Georgie volunteered, "Well, I got half way down."

His brothers nodded. He had gotten halfway, and the Christmas man was a whole big man. Of course he could get all the way down the chimney whole. That story would work and Stanley would believe it. The trio turned toward their younger brother.

"Now, Stanley, what you got to see today was part of the story. That Santa man was a lot bigger, and he could come all the way down to the floor. If you don't tell nobody about that story, then when Georgie gets bigger, you'll get to see him come all the way down. That be all right with you?"

Stanley ducked his head sideways to think. It really wasn't all right, but he could see that he might wheedle some other immediate favor out of the brothers. "I want'a climb back up and look down that hole again."

Freddie and Junior cast concerned looks at each other. Georgie looked from one to the other and saw that they had the answer to his fears. Staring into his brother's eyes, he explained, "Yeah, Stanley, we can take you up there and let you look. You'd like that. 'Course, if you did, then you'd not get to see me come all the way down when I get to be a growed up man."

The three brothers looked at Stanley while he decided. Delayed gratification had never held any satisfaction to the smaller boy. "Yeah, I want to climb up now."

Smiling, the older brothers again leaned the ladder against the cabin and helped him up. Junior held him while he peered down the dark hole and hollered a few times, listening to his strange sounding echoing voice. Then he was ready to come down. The protective chimney bucket was replaced and soot dusted off hands.

The ladder was again put away, and Junior whispered to Freddie, "Where at did you put them wet underpants?"

Freddie whispered back, "Under the bed ta dry." And his brother nodded approval.

At the supper table, Carl frowned at Freddie as he passed the biscuits. "Son, what's the matter with your hands?"

Whereupon Freddie shrugged, indifferently. "Rope burn."

Stanley spoke up. "Junior got rope burn."

Junior displayed his own hands, momentarily, and continued eating. Their father nodded, "Tug-o-war, I'd wager. It'll burn the skin every time."

The boys continued to eat. Their father had a right to believe whatever he wanted to believe, and no one had a chance to examine Georgie's raw bottom.

Stanley nodded a smile of satisfaction. Twice he had been permitted on the cabin roof and he had even gotten to hollar down the dark hole. Who cared about the old sandman, anyway?

Winter had its problems. The chopping axes were busy providing cabin wood, fresh hay was tossed down for the calves, and a myriad of small concerns were appearing hourly to plague them.

Just last month the men lost a calf to the wolves and a week later they lost another one. Lady had been doing a lot of nervous barking and the pups had joined their mother in setting up a continuous howl and outcry. Clearly something had to be done.

In desperation, Carl and Marcel shouldered their guns and Junior and Freddie were permitted to go along. The excursion would add to their experience with the gun.

The inexperienced pups were locked up, but Lady was permitted to accompany them. The animal trails criss-crossed and overlapped from the top of the mountain to the bench land where the cabins were, indicating a frightening overpopulation of wolves. The gray-furred animals were wary and shy, and when one was sighted, the thick grayness of the November day would seem to swallow up the shape of it as though it had been a ghost.

Their furry hulks stared at the men for an instant and Lady would freeze into position, but the wolf would be gone before a gun could be sighted.

Junior was carrying the light gun when Lady stopped, holding her head high. The hair arose on her hackles as she stared, her lips rippling with irritated, rumbling growls. Standing there, just up the hill from the hunters and silhouetted against the sky, was a full grown wolf. It stood its ground, its yellow eyes trained on the hunting party, not melting away like the others.

Junior raised his gun and sighted.

"Shoot, son," Carl instructed.

Junior held the rifle steady and firm and the wolf stood still. Junior pulled the trigger and the furry form crumbled. Junior and Freddie began to run toward the animal.

"Get back here!" ordered Carl. "Don't you never run up on a animal just been shot like that'n. 'Specially a wolf. That varmint possibly got one last bite in 'im."

They advanced cautiously. The wolf was indeed dead, the bullet hitting him squarely in the head. Its blood stained the gray fur.

Marcel leaned over the wolf's head and motioned for Carl to come and look. Dreaded flecks of white foam dotted the fur of the wolf's muzzle.

"Hmmm. Yeah, that'd be why that thing stood there lettin' hisself get shot."

Marcel nodded. Junior and Freddie looked from father to uncle, needing an explanation.

"Gone mad," Carl said to them.

"That'd be bad, huh, Pa?"

Carl nodded. "Real bad. Mad wolves mean mad skunks, 'coons, and dogs. Them mad animals got no sense in 'em. It's a sickness in their brains. They don't run like they'd ordinarily do."

Out of concern, Marcel added, "Them boys gonna have to watch out close, comin' and goin' to school."

Carl nodded agreement. "Boys, you be lookin' every way at the same time while you be goin' and comin from school. Iffen you see a wolf that don't run like you'd think, you shinny up the first tree you reach. See Georgie gets up there with you if you got 'im along. Don't you come down out'a that tree even if the wolf goes away. You STAY in that tree. Now what you gonna do, Freddie?"

"STAY in that tree!" the wide-eyed boy repeated with the required emphasis.

Carl nodded. "Then, iffen you ain't home on time, I'd be comin' by to find you. Hear?"

The boys nodded.

"We got'a set traps, Carl. We ain't doin' no good like this. Walkin' this much land's takin' time we ain't got."

Carl nodded. "You sayin' right. Law, I hate them traps. Seems somethin' always gets in them traps that they ain't been set for. 'Course, after we catch a wolf or two and spread the meat around, likely they'll back off and let us be. Let's be goin' on home, boys."

The silent quartette made their way through the leafless trees, Lady leading the way. She flung her head from side to side, casting for a scent. Stepping up on a pointed rock, she stopped mid-step, looking this way and that, and whispered a growl. Another wolf materialized directly ahead. The foam on his muzzle was visible even at thirty feet.

Carl swung his gun to his shoulders, but, faster than a shot, Lady sprang into the mist and leaped at the wolf's throat. The wolf shook her off and lunged toward her, gashing Lady's leg with his fangs.

Lady yelped once, wheeled around and went for the throat again. The weakened and wounded wolf had no fight left in him. He rocked forward and toppled onto the pile of leaves that had accumulated under the trees. Lady, her leg bleeding, held her grip on the wolf's throat until the animal was motionless.

"Shoot it, Pa," whispered Freddie.

But Junior answered, "It's done dead, Freddie."

Lady turned from the wolf and strutted back toward them, unmindful of her bleeding leg. Her tail wagged a brown arc of pleasure and pride.

Carl watched her and made a necessary decision. He leveled his gun. "Junior, Freddie, turn yourselves around and look behind us."

The boys turned to step back and Carl put a bullet between Lady's soft, brown eyes. She crumbled to the ground, a heap of white and brown fur, glossy against the dull brown of the fallen leaves.

At the sound of the bullet, the boys turned and gasped.

"Pa, you shot Lady!"

"Oh, Pa, she's hurt. She's DEAD! Oh, Pa, PA!"

As the boys turned to run to the dog, Carl caught Junior and Marcel pulled Freddie back.

"Pa, happen she ain't really dead!"

"Please, Pa!"

The boys looked at their father, tears streaming down their faces.

"Pa? Marcel?"

Marcel was crying, too.

Finally, Carl cleared his throat and found words.

Sniffing loudly, he began, "Lady was a good dog. She died thinkin' she protected us from that wolf. In a dog's mind, that'd be just about the best thing it could do. She was willin' to die for us when she lunged at that wolf. She loved us and she thought that was her duty."

"But, Pa, you shot her?" Freddie accused.

A sigh and a hesitation, then, "Boys, I know you're hurtin' more'n you can stand, but happen there'll be a day you'll be knowin' it was out'a love for Lady that I shot her. This way was quick and easy. Fact was, she got that madness the very minute when she bit into that wolf, and after that there weren't no way to get 'er well. She was runnin' to you, glad and happy, and she would'a give the sickness to you boys. She was gonna die, no matter what we tried to do for her. This way was best."

"She could'a give it to us?"

Carl nodded. "Yes, she would'a and then you could die. That'd be why you boys got'a watch every minute while we got rabies on the farm. Any animal you see doin' somethin' different from usual, you get away from it. Even squirrels and such."

They nodded, sniffing and red-eyed from grief.

Marcel turned over a large rock and began to dig with his hands in the soft dirt. Lady was gently slid into the hole and covered up with the large rock. No wild animal would ever dig into Lady's grave and ruin her.

The November wind cut through the damp woods, tugging at sleeves and coat tails and reddening cheeks, still wet with tears. Icy fingers held to cold gunstocks, and cold, wet feet trudged over the deep carpet of damp leaves. The joy of the hunt was no longer even a memory. They went back to Marcel's cabin, and in the warmth of the wood fire, the boys looked up at Carl with pleading, glistening eyes. The hurt was too great to bear.

From the depth of his bleeding heart, Freddie voiced softly, "I want Lady."

Carl reached out to the boys and they buried their faces against him and sobbed.

"Boys," Carl said, after a minute. "I got'a say somethin' more to ya."

"Huh, Pa?"

"They's somethin' about this day you got'a remember. You be 'memberin' that some boys didn't never have a good dog like Lady and you had her for a good little while. She was a dog better'n a lot'a others and you got all them good memories of bein' with her. She was with you when you two was learnin' to shoot. But that little dog, she knowd that wolf was more'n a little dangerous, and likely was afraid you'd not be able to kill it with your gun. She knew she could. There'll come a time when your sadness dies down a little that you'll like thinkin' on that. It'll be somethin' that'll make the memory'a her more easy, and there'll be stories you'll tell your sons about it. And that Lady, she left you the pups and they'll bring you a lot of fun and more memories…." Carl stared at the reddened and wet faces of his sons and had no more words.

Junior and Freddie looked at each other, remembering the bull chase. Lady could have been killed then. She had left them with memories that no one else knew of.

Finally, Carl found words and continued, "We can cry and that's all right, but we gota 'member, we was lucky to have a dog like Lady, even just for a little while."

The boys sniffed and rubbed their eyes and followed their father on up the hill to their cabin.

The next day Carl kept the boys home from school. It seemed too soon to let them go, after their devastating loss, and he had a job for them that would help occupy their thoughts.

An ice storm, caused by a cold snap after the rain had frozen the puddles and the ditch water. Stones were glazed with a layer of clear ice and tree twigs were encased with tubes of frozen moisture. He could have taken the boys to school in the wagon but he really needed Junior and Freddie to help with the wolf traps and thought they needed something important to do.

The traps and the bait they had cut from the last wolf-killed calf had to be carried to areas frequented by the wolves. A good tracking dog would have been a help to find the most frequented trails, but no one mentioned it.

The two men and the two boys trudged to the far corners of their property with the steel traps slung over their shoulders. They baited the snapping jaws of metal with the meat and covered the traps and the holding chains with dead leaves, marking a hand-drawn map with the location of each trap so they could be retrieved.

Junior and Freddie walked on stumpy feet, wooden with numbness, their white-knuckled hands carrying their loads. The frozen leaves crackled crisply underfoot. It should have been a fun day of hunting. The whole mountain was an ice sculpture and the valley was a crystal wonderland, but there was no happiness. The boys were silent, searching with their feet for solid footing, breathing deeply, and thinking their own thoughts.

Lorena and InaMae sewed and tried to keep from talking about babies. A kettle of beans simmered on the stove, the chunks of ham releasing their flavor and aroma into the steam. The cornbread would be put in the oven when the men came in. InaMae had brought up a platter of sugar cookies. The best spirit lifter was good food and warmth, and the men and boys would need any lifting that could be given them.

Stanley and Georgie had teased to be permitted to go play on the ice, and finally their exasperated mother relented. Bundled from head to foot, they were pushed through the door. Jamie finally won his own plea and was allowed to go with them.

Georgie picked a twig from the bush and nibbled the ice off it. Stanley shook a small shrub, marveling at the glassy rattle of ice on its branches, which sounded like a pocket full of marbles. Jamie stepped on a slick rock and slid down, landing on his well-padded bottom.

"I wanna go to the crawdad hole," announced Georgie.

"Me, too."

"Me, too."

The ice cover on the crawdad hole was very satisfying. It was frozen smooth and shiny from one edge to the other, a condition happening only once or twice a season in the usually mild Arkansas winters.

Georgie slid icy pebbles across the frozen surface. He pressed his face against the ice to check on the condition of the crawfish.

Stanley stepped carefully onto the edge of the ice and it held his weight.

"Lookie at me!" he called.

"Comin' out," Jamie promised.

"Don't you be goin' out there, Jamie. That'll break. Stanley, you come back."

Stanley shook his head. "Ain't gonna break."

"Gonna break," echoed Jamie.

Georgie tested with his toe and it felt firm. "Stay over to the edge," he ordered.

Stanley walked carefully around the edge, but Jamie started across the pond. Georgie reached for him but Jamie ducked away from his brother's grasp. His feet slid out from under him, and his bottom collided sharply with the thinner ice in the center of the shallow pond, sending crackling fissures in all directions.

"You broke it," accused Stanley, resentfully.

"You gotta come back now," Georgie told him. "You done broke the ice."

Jamie's hands were cold from being placed flat on the ice, and his brothers' accusations and disapproval began to concern him. He leaned forward to get onto his knees, and a fresh wreath of crackles surrounded him.

"Hurry up!" urged Georgie. "Here, gimme your hand."

Jamie shifted his weight to extend his hand to Georgie, and the crackles sounded again as a section of ice broke away and sank, lowering Jamie into the icy water. His large, chocolate eyes became saucers of surprise as the freezing water seeped through his multiple layers of clothing.

Without fanfare, Georgie tromped through the floating chunks of ice and grasped Jamie's hand, pulling him to the bank, scooting on his bottom.

"Law sakes, we done it now! We let Jamie get wet clothes," sighed Georgie.

"We didn't do it," hedged Stanley. "He was standin' in the water and the water got him wet."

"Yeah, but Ma said it was stayin' in wet clothes what makes folks sick."

"He shore got wet."

"Yes, and he gonna be sick."

Georgie began to unbutton Jamie's coat. "Don't you cry none, Jamie. We gonna get you out'a them wet clothes so as you won't be gettin' sick. Stanley, you untie Jamie's shoes."

Georgie drew the coat off Jamie's arms. The wet cloth of the sleeve clung to the wet flannel of his shirt, but Georgie managed to get them separated. The coat was now turned inside out.

"Them shoes is untied now," Stanley reported. "Lift your foot, Jamie."

Jamie obediently lifted his foot and Stanley eased off the wet shoe and stripped away the sock. Jamie put his bare foot on the frozen gravel.

"Look out, Stanley. His overhalls is comin' down."

Stanley, seated on the ground in front of Jamie, leaned back to allow the overalls to fall.

"Now lift up t'other foot, Jamie."

Georgie was struggling with the buttons on the wet flannel of the shirt, hardly able to manipulate them with his own frozen fingers. Jamie was sobbing, dismally, both bare feet on the ground, and the wet flannel shirt was stripped from his arms.

"Now get his underwear."

"Cold," complained Jamie.

"Yeah, I reckon you are, but you ain't wantin' to be sick, are ya? Ma says them wet clothes'd do it. Stanley and me, we're cold, too, and we ain't bellerin' about it. Step your foot out'a there."

Jamie lifted his foot to allow his last stitch of clothing to be taken away.

"See? Now you ain't gonna be sick. We got off all them wet clothes."

Back at the cabin, Lorena dragged the wooden spoon through the simmering beans and mashed one bean against the side of the pan to test for tenderness. Perfect. She put another stick of wood in the firebox so the oven would heat for the cornbread. The men would be in soon, probably frozen stiff.

She glanced out the window and down the trail to see if the men were coming and saw Jamie step out of his underwear, aided by Georgie.

"Merciful heaven! That child ain't got a stitch of clothes on him!"

InaMae tossed her sewing aside and ran to the window. Lorena was reaching for a coat with one hand and the door handle with the other. InaMae grabbed the coat away from her.

"I'll get 'im," she promised, running nimbly down the icy road to the crawfish pond. She grabbed up Jamie, tucked him inside the coat, and turned to run back.

"Come on, you boys. Hurry!"

Georgie and Stanley hesitated just long enough to gather up Jamie's wet clothing, then ran after her.

Lorena had the oven door open and hot air streamed out into the cabin as InaMae opened the coat to let the warmth reach Jamie's trembling body.

Stanley burst through the door and Georgie brought up the rear, slamming the door soundly behind him.

"Jamie ain't gonna have to be sick, Ma," he announced. "You glad'a that?"

"Huh?"

"Jamie ain't gonna be sick. We made 'im let us take off them wet clothes after he fell in the water. We knowd it was wet clothes what made folks sick, just like you said. Me and Stanley, we like to'a froze our fingers off, but we done it!"

Georgie grinned proudly up at his mother. Stanley edged closer for his share of the thanks, for the task earned with tingling, frozen fingers.

Lorena patted their heads. Like Carl says, who do you punish? Which one do you scold? And what do you say to the faces looking up proudly at you? Knowing for certain they'd done the right thing?

The men came in, silently taking off their coats and caps. Junior and Freddie sat down heavily at the table at their accustomed eating places, chin in hand, and waited.

Lorena poked up the coals to hurry the cornbread along. Everyone would feel better after they were warm and full. Food was the world's best mood-changer for man and boy.

The ice storm melted away suddenly and the winter sun brought rabbits and field mice out of their holes in search of food. The wolves caught the rodents and stayed away from the calves. The traps yielded only two wolves and a nosy 'possum, and the wolf carcasses were chopped apart and distributed over the land. Live wolves did not like to come where one of their number had been slain and their meat lay rotting, so they found other places to hunt.

Lorena began to think of Christmas. There would be a number of chores to attend to and she would have to get at them early this year. There was no way to know when she would have to leave for the laying in hospital, so the baking and cookie making needed to be started.

Apple cake, of course, and this time it would be festive with raisins and hickory nuts. The boys would like that. There would be oranges if she could get some in River Bend. She would make candy and there would be popcorn balls. If the baby was on time, however, she, herself, might not be at home. The thought was distressing. How could her sons possibly have Christmas without her?

By the fifteenth of December, she had felt several small reminders of the coming event. By the eighteenth, she was becoming concerned, also relieved. If the baby was early, she might be back home for the festivities.

By the morning of the nineteenth, she knew she should make immediate plans to leave. Jacksonville was a three-hour ride away, no matter how one looked at it. She opened a half-gallon jar of canned blackberries and made a kettle of dumplings, rich and nourishing. She made an extra pan of cornbread.

The buggy was made ready to leave at a moment's notice. Marcel moved in with the boys. InaMae brought along her newly made quilts and a warm, flannel gown for the baby. She added a jar of milk and the new nursing bottle and packed it in with the cookies and sandwiches in the picnic basket. Who could know where or when the next food would be available and it was best to be prepared.

By noon, the three were riding down the hill in the buggy. The only sound was that of the iron-rimmed wheels against the gravel and Carl's voice directing the horses. Then followed a three-hour ride of almost total silence. Carl stared ahead, occupied with his own thoughts.

Lorena was very uncomfortable in the constant sway and jostle of the buggy on the gravel road, and the strengthening contractions were becoming a concern about the time. InaMae studied the winter-brown scenery along the roadside as though it was her first trip along this road. She concentrated on forcing herself to breathe normally.

The day turned gray and cloud banks heaped in the northern sky, while a bone-chilling wind whipped through the valley. At the edge of

Jacksonville, the horses were directed down the back streets toward the laying in hospital.

Two sisters operated this hospital in response to the need of city women who thought they could not birth a baby without help other than their own kinfolks. Mrs. Connelly and Mrs. Olmer were both widows and highly experienced in these matters. The hospital was roomy and convenient—still, it was a hospital.

At the entrance, Carl lifted Lorena down from the buggy and InaMae went with her into the building while Carl put up the horses in the hospital livery.

A questionnaire was thrust at Lorena and her hand shook as she wrote. Name: *InaMae McCann*........ Father's name: *Marcel McCann*........ Number of living children: *None*........ Number of stillborn children: *None*........ and on it went. Name of mother's parents, name of father's parents....The questions seemed to have no end. InaMae paced the length of the room, clenching and unclenching her fists.

Carl came in and stood beside Lorena as she wrote. The sheet, finally completed, was handed to the attendant.

The white uniformed assistant looked at the sheet and then at Lorena.

"First baby, huh?" Obviously, Lorena was well past the median age for first babies. Likely she didn't even know if she was in hard labor or not, having no remembered experience of the way it felt. "You just sit there for a minute, Miz McCann, while we make up a room fresh for you."

"Ma'am, please hurry."

"Just how close are you?"

"Two minutes."

The attendant smiled reassurance. "Law, ma'am, you got yourself lots of time. Them first babies seem like they take forever with their startin' and stoppin', 'afore they finally decide to come on." She glanced up at Carl. "Reckon you're the daddy?"

Not knowing what else to do, Carl nodded, truthfully.

"Well, now, Mr. McCann, you just find yourself a comfortable chair over there, or go in town and do come lookin' around, and we gonna get you a big, fat son. Reckon you'd be wantin' a son first?"

Carl squirmed, uncomfortably.

"No need to be denyin' it or bein' ashamed to say it, Mr. McCann. All men be alike in wantin' a son to follow after 'im."

Lorena shifted, bracing herself against the next pain. "Ma'am, please hurry."

"Shore, iffen you'd feel better on a bed. Some of 'em likes to walk around a bit, just to get things started. Likely they got you a bed ready by now. Just come on along."

Lorena hesitated until the current pain passed over. InaMae grasped her arm firmly, assisting her down the white-painted hall.

The attendant turned to InaMae, "Who are you?"

"I'm her sister, uh, Lorena. She'd want me to be with her."

"You had any babies?"

Instinctively, InaMae shook her head.

"Then I can't see how you'd be no help to her. She come here payin' her money for help from us. Best leave the helpin' to those as knows how. Iffen you'd just stay back there with her husband...."

Lorena stopped in the hall and turned to face the girl. She stared meaningfully at the uniformed girl and spaced her words so there would be no misunderstanding. "I...want...her...to...come...with...me." Her firm voice left no room for discussion.

"Huh?"

"I WANT MY SISTER TO COME WITH ME!"

"Well, ma'am, I'd have to see if that was allowed."

Lorena clutched at InaMae as a pain passed through her. "You listen here to me. I want my sister and iffen she ain't let to come in with me, I'll be goin' right out to my buggy, that we come here in, and I'll have this baby right out there in the winter wind!"

"Uh, well, you just go right on in with her Miz...Lorena. Reckon it'd be allowed."

They were herded into a room with a narrow, white-sheeted bed. The room had chilly, white walls and high, white-painted windows, bare of curtains. There was no heat in the room and the December chill had permeated every crevasse. A distinct draft seeped up through the floor.

Lorena shivered as she slipped off her shoes and stockings. InaMae helped her remove her dress. Twice they had to pause for a pain to pass over. The furnished gown was a cold, starched white thing that rasped against her trembling skin. InaMae drew back the thin quilt for her.

"Reckon you can get under here and get warm, Lorena?" InaMae whispered. "I wisht we hadn't'a come. This is gettin to be a misery to you. You ain't likin' what you gotta do in this awful room. On top'a that, they tryin' to freeze you to death."

Lorena took a deep breath. A fierce pain swept over her as she sat down heavily on the bed. InaMae ran down the hall, "Ma'am, you gotta get someone to attend to my sister."

"Shore, and Miz Olman be washin' up right now. She gonna be in there, directly. I wouldn't be worryin' none iffen it was me."

"But it ain't you," InaMae retorted, sarcastically. "That woman better git herself on down here, happen you ain't wantin' to hear some real yellin'. 'Nother thing, you take note'a of the size of her husband, sittin' out there? Iffen I start yellin' out on how his wife's bein' treated, he gonna be back here, fit to send someone on to the Promised Land!"

InaMae ran back up the hall to the ghostly room. Lorena was staring at the upper corner of the room with her lips firmly clenched in her teeth. The pain passed and she sighed. "This here place ain't even got no pullin' rag on this here bed."

InaMae grabbed up the pillow Lorena had shoved onto the floor. She shook the feathered bag from the case and tied the crisp linen of it to the metal headboard. She closed Lorena's hand over it for something to strain against when the pains were at their worse. Still no one came.

InaMae placed her hand on Lorena's abdomen, feeling the tightening of flesh under her fingers. This contraction did not fade away. Lorena gripped the pillowcase with both hands and squeezed her eyes shut. The pain had forced her breath away. InaMae knew there was no time for anyone to come to help.

She threw back the flimsy quilt. She grasped Lorena's right knee and held it up, massaging the straining abdomen. She heard her sister sigh, releasing a long-held breath. Relief. The pain backed away. Lorena gathered her strength for the next on-slaught of agony and met it head on. Breathe. Hold it! Breathe, again. One more time…? She felt the pain gathering and knew this was the last one.

The pillowcase limp from her grasp held firmly to the bedframe and the pain tore through her body…then the expected relief.

Black hair appeared. Then a tiny, wrinkled face. Then soft-skinned, rounded shoulders. Slippery arms….

Lorena breathed long and deep. Experience told her that the worst was over. She could make it, now. She looked up into InaMae's face, eager to see her sister's pleasure…to see her sister's smile of greeting to this new person. That sight would make this agony worthwhile.

But InaMae was not smiling. Her mouth was open in an expression of horror and anguish. She stared, speechless, at the baby bunched on her out-spread palms.

"Is he...? Is he all right?"

InaMae lowered the baby to the bed and made no further move to touch the tiny infant. Long silence. Neither sister breathing.

Neither sister saw the attendant and midwife approach the door where they had stopped, startled, and were staring.

InaMae dropped to her knees beside the bed and threw her arms around Lorena, sobbing. Tears coursed down her face, dropping on the crisply starched gown. Her agonized whisper was inches from her sister's ear.

"Oh, Lorena! Lorena! I feel so bad to be cryin' on you, knowin' what you been through, but I just can't stop myself. I been knowin' all these months you was tryin' to be ready to give up your little boy but I can't take this here baby."

The midwife and the attendant stared at each other, open-mouthed. The baby, ignored, yelled a loud, protesting objection.

Lorena spoke sternly, "InaMae! Listen to me, you gotta tell me what this baby got wrong with 'im. Say it, flat out!"

InaMae shook her head, still sobbing, "I ain't holdin' you to nothin' you said. It ain't right, what we done."

She raised her quivering voice. "You gonna tell me what you see wrong with that baby?"

InaMae shook her head. "They ain't nothin' wrong. It be just that it's...Lorena, you had a little girl!"

Lorena's sharp intake of breath was a startled gasp. "A girl!" Her eyes were wide with acute agony, then they closed with numbness.

InaMae now noticed the women in the doorway. She arose with dignity and shook out the soft, flannel square she had lovingly hemmed and wrapped it around the screaming baby. She turned to the two women with a look of dripping sarcasm.

"Iffen one of you bumps-on-a-log'd be kind enough to bring scissors and thread and if the other'n'd bring me some warm water, I'd be finishin' up this here job I just done." Her voice had the brittleness of crunching icicles.

The requested articles appeared. The midwife reached out for the baby but InaMae's stare stopped her. "Happen you so much as breathe on this here baby, I'll be obliged to put a dent in your head with my shoe heel!" She cuddled the baby with one arm and reached toward Lorena's shoe lying beside the bed. The women, convinced this person had gone mad, backed out of the room.

Cauterized by her anger, InaMae again had control. "Lorena, you had yourself a little girl. Black hair all over her head, just like you wanted. Listen to me, I'd be happy to wait. You just say the word."

Lorena had no words.

Ina Mae continued, "Shore, and it'd be a disappointment but I done had a'plenty'a them. You was always wantin' a girl. I'd been pleased to have any of them boys you got. You take this'n. I can wait. We'll say no more."

Lorena bit her bruised lip. *Oh, Lord, do I gotta go through all this givin' over and over again? How many times do I gotta go through all this?*

She drew in a breath and let it out, slowly. "InaMae, this here baby got itself born to InaMae and Marcel McCann. We done got papers that says that. I got no rights to be decidin' 'bout nothin'. You speck you could be lettin' me see my little niece any time soon?" The words had been firmly and clearly said for the last time and relief flooded over her like a summer shower.

InaMae held the bundle of soft flannel down so Lorena could see the baby girl. The pugged button of a nose and the creased chin could have been Jamie's or Junior's. The smooth brow and mop of hair could have belonged to Stanley. Or Georgie or Freddie. A tiny fist closed and an arm extended from the folds of the blanket, reaching waveringly toward her. Lorena's heart ached with love. The tiny girl's eyes were tightly squenched, but Lorena knew they were chocolate ice cream brown.

Lorena knew InaMae was watching her face. Hoping. Regretting. Wishing the baby had been a boy so the gift would not have seemed so great. Wishing some of Lorena's pain could be tempered by her own joy.

Lorena knew these things because she knew InaMae so well. She could not bear to look up at her. But if the baby had been a boy, would this gift have been any easier to give? Would that have made this moment set more lightly in her mind? Not likely. What had to be done was now done.

"Carl?" she finally asked.

"He don't know nothin', yet. I was wantin' you to give it last thoughts."

"Well, now I've had 'em. You go in and tell him, InaMae. Show 'im your baby and then tell 'im I need to see 'im."

Swallowing hard, InaMae left. Lorena told the white walls, "She never was my baby, that little girl weren't. There weren't no minute her mama wasn't InaMae. It was truly fittin' that it was InaMae, bringin' her out. Her mama was InaMae and there weren't no doubt 'bout that."

Carl's footsteps were in the hall and Lorena made her mouth smile as he knelt beside her bed. Carl spoke first.

"Lorena, honey, we gave them a little old girl and they'll just have to make the best'a what they got. They gonna just have'ta learn to get by with it!" He smiled his special smile, wrapped lovingly around his teasing words. His large, warm, comforting hands closed on both of hers.

"I wanna go home, Carl."

He shook his head. "There's three hours'a rough and cold out there. You gotta rest here the night."

"No, Carl. We gonna go home."

"But...?"

"Carl, listen at me. I can lay on the floorboard of the buggy, same as here in this rock-hard bed. The cold outside won't be different than the cold in here. Won't be no harder on me. That cold won't be no worse'n this awful room. We gonna go." She nodded her head with uncontestable finality.

Carl made another attempt. "But, Lorena, it's almost dark out there."

"You didn't bring along no lanterns for that buggy?"

"Yeah, but...."

"You go get the buggy. InaMae gonna pay the bill and help me into my dress."

Carl left the room and InaMae came back. The midwife followed her to the door.

"Miz McCann, do you got a name for the baby? We need to be puttin' it here on this registration."

Lorena looked her questioning eyes toward InaMae. InaMae answered, "The baby's name is Marcelene McCann. Spell it M-A-R-C-E-L-E-N-E."

The midwife wrote it down, carefully, and looked at the ten dollar bill InaMae offered. She shook her head.

"You ain't owin' us no money. You did all the takin' care of the baby."

InaMae's face was sober and firm. "But we payin', all the same. Ain't never made no bill we wasn't figurin' to pay, but I feel like sayin' this to you. Come time a woman be in here sayin' to you to hurry up, you'd do well to give her an ear. Happen she won't have no sister along to help her like my sister had." Instructions and advice clearly given, she turned and walked away.

Carl carried Lorena to the buggy. The lap robe had been spread on the floorboard and a brand new, store bought blanket was tucked around her. *Where did that blanket come from*, she wondered faintly.

Quilts were spread on top.

The street lamps had been lighted by the time the buggy turned east toward River Bend. Marcelene McCann whimpered a little but was comforted by the nursing bottle and loving pats from her mother. Lorena forced herself to concentrate on the grinding crunch of the buggy wheels on the gravel beneath her. All other thoughts were mercifully ground away by the wheel noise.

For three hours, the December wind tore at the buggy and its cold fingers seeped into their bones. No words were said. Each of the three adults rode along, huddled inside of their private thoughts, trying to gather strength for the hours ahead. Tiny Marcelene slept, her miniature tummy comforted by the few drops of milk.

They began to climb the last hill and Lorena felt a painful loneliness settle over her. She longed for Georgie's loving arms and Freddie's grin. For Junior's clumsy feet and his independence… and for Jamie's pout. She saw Stanley's intense look, trying to learn everything from his brothers at once. She smiled in the darkness of the buggy floor. She was so lucky! Who did she ever know who had so much joy for herself and was still able to give a gift so precious as little Marcelene to the sister who seemed to be an actual, physical part of herself?

And now she would be home with her family for Christmas! Both families would be together and complete, hers and InaMae's.

At the cabin, Carl carried Lorena to the door while InaMae waited quietly in the buggy. It was a homecoming for Carl and Lorena, and they should have their moment.

With new eyes, Lorena looked around her home. The soft light of the oil lamp illuminated her familiar kitchen, but the table was decorated by a small cedar tree set in a bucket of sand. Paper candy canes and lopsided chains festooned its branches. Popcorn balls were on the table. Marcel and the boys had been very busy.

A sign made with red paper cut-out letters said, "MERRY CHRISTMAS MAMA." Pictures of animals and of houses with smoking chimneys decorated the entire room. She had been gone from home for less than twelve hours. Why, they must have been busy every minute!

Junior and Freddie were asleep in the lean-to and the other three were draped over Marcel on the other bed, snoring softly. Marcel opened his eyes and eased himself out from under the small bodies.

Carl still held Lorena in his arms and the door opened behind them. InaMae came in and walked toward Marcel, almost shyly. "We got us a little girl, Marcel."

"A girl?" Marcel cast a quick look at Carl. Carl shrugged his shoulders, meaningfully.

Jamie sat up, rubbing his eyes.

"Mama? MAMA!"

Lorena lost interest in the baby in her sister's arms and in the happenings of the day. She reached her hand to Jamie and he stumbled toward her, pointing a wavering, sleepy hand toward the decoration.

"For mama. 'Unior, Reddie, Anley, Gordie," and pointing to himself, "Aimie." He grinned again. "For Mama."

InaMae touched Lorena's arm, whispering, "See you in the morning," and she and Marcel were gone.

Carl placed Lorena in the chair beside the stove, and Jamie climbed into her lap. "For Mama," he repeated as he snuggled against her.

Carl carried Georgie and Stanley to their bed in the lean-to, and Lorena held Jamie and looked around their cabin. Comforting heat seemed to radiate from the wood walls, polished to satin softness from contact with human skin. The massive woodstove was a friendly invitation to draw a chair closer. It was so different from the ghostly white of that hospital room, so long, long ago and such a blessed distance from her.

Carl was back and he slipped Jamie's arms from her neck and put him in bed with his brothers.

The old coffee pot steamed with the potent remains of Marcel's evening refreshment. Carl lifted Lorena and carried her to the table. From the cupboard, he took down the pan containing the last of the blackberry dumplings. He dipped the dessert into two soup bowls and poured top milk over them. He set cups of coffee and the dessert on the table for himself and Lorena.

"'Bout time we had us somethin' decent to eat," Carl commented, lightly.

Lorena looked at the food and was suddenly hungry. She picked up the spoon but hesitated, turning full-face toward him. "But, Carl, did we...?"

"Lorena, we done a good thing. We done what we wanted to do and we done a good job of it. Now we got us five boys to raise. You eat them dumplin's 'cause them boys is gonna take all the strength we can muster up."

The door opened softly. Jamie's bare feet padded across the floor. "For Mama," he repeated, sleepily.

Lorena drew Jamie into her lap and again picked up her spoon. Jamie sighed and cuddled against her once more. She sipped the strong coffee and felt relief and energy flow through her body.

Five sons. Her sons. Carl's sons. Her mind extended into the future. Sons. She would need a lot of quilts to give her daughters-in-law when the boys made their choices. How long would that be? Junior was almost eight, so maybe, ten or twelve years? She had better get busy because there were only ten winters to work on them, and once Junior got it started, the others would follow on quickly. Just like they did now.

Yes, she'd get busy with them quilts, but first there was the rug for the new room Carl would be constructing for her. A high room, and it would have windows in every direction. Her many trips to the bluff to relax and gaze out over the river were good, but a plate glass window in her bedroom could be used anytime and in any weather. She could sit there and piece the quilts.

She and InaMae would take the quilt tops and THEIR children down to the church on Tuesdays to get them quilted by the church quilters. The Tuesday quilting was such a pleasant break in the week, and who knew what interesting thing one might hear?

She smiled as Carl once more carried the sleeping Jamie back to bed. Yes, she'd have to get out them quilt-piece patterns and get busy. It didn't pay to put things off.

And she was home for Christmas. She and Carl and their boys, they were all together and it was almost Christmas. What else could she need?

Carl was back. He picked up the dishes and cups and set them on her work table. He held a hand toward her, and she met it with her own.

What else could she need? Nothing!

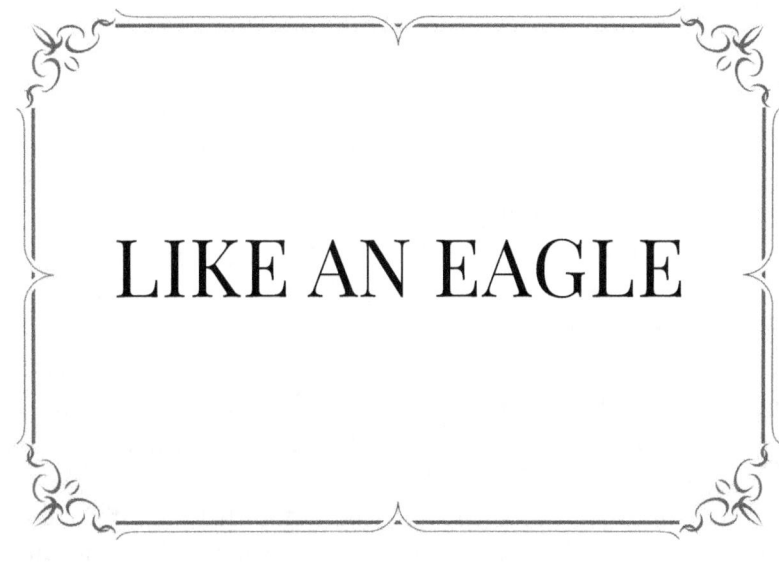

LIKE AN EAGLE

1

This was the day of her husband's funeral. The weather was windy, and the biting, bone-chilling cold had settled like a mist on the huddled group of people standing on the mountainside.

Floralee Baker stood with her black shawl over her hair and looked down at the freshly dug hole in the ground. The hole that would soon accept the body of her slain husband. She was dry-eyed as she waited for the terrible current of present events to sweep past her and permit her to walk away.

The voice of Rev. McCrey droned on: "It is written that from dust we came, and to dust we shall surely return, and it is with sorrow we commit the body of our friend and neighbor to the ground.

"But as we perform this duty, it is important that we look upon the living he left behind. To his good wife and lovely children, we repeat the promise that God will not leave them comfortless. In addition to that promise, we may claim the greater promise that if we trust in Him, we may mount up with wings as the eagles, we can walk and not be weary, and we can run and not faint...."

Weariness settled over Floralee like a garment, numbing her to the cut of the winter wind. Toddling Naomi snuggled against her mother's swelling abdomen, seeking shelter from the wind. Her seven-year-old sister, Charity, knelt down and opened her coat to her little sister, then she closed it around both of them. The closeness of their bodies made up, partially, for the thin raggedness of the coat.

Floralee stared at the hole in the ground and at the pine box within it. Then she looked up at the gathering of people, seen from the mist of the unreality that surrounded her. This box surely could not contain the man with whom she had spent almost eighteen of her thirty-four years of life. Why was she standing here?

The last few days disjointedly refused to be connected. She could still hear the whine of the bullets and the ping of their ricochet against the granite boulders of the valley. She heard her own screams as she shouted a warning to him, a warning that came seconds too late. She should have run faster, but her six-month pregnant body had refused to obey her commands. So now Nathan Baker was being lowered into the cold clay.

Also now, today, Nathan Junior, her first-born, moved closer to her so that his elbow nudged protectively against hers. Their shoulders, his now above hers after his sudden growth, provided a little warmth for each of them.

Sarah, age fourteen, and Betty Lou, now eleven, stood apart from the others, heads bowed respectfully but glancing at their mother for a clue as to the behavior expected of them. How does one act at the funeral of one's father?

Nine-year-old Donald also stood apart, solid as a rock, with a dry, impassive face. On the toes of his slightly too large shoes, sat Henry, five years old, leaning against his brother's legs. Clad in their thin clothes, they shared a small ray of warmth in this way.

A blood-red leaf from a maple tree dislodged from its twig and blew past Floralee's face, its dry points catching briefly on the folds of her shawl. Then, pulled free by the wind, it was carried to the pine box. Slowly, the box and the leaf were lowered together into the grave. Floralee waited, not breathing, for she knew what painful penalty would be extracted from her in a short minute.

When the pine box settled at last on the floor of the grave, she stepped firmly forward, holding to Nate's arm. She picked up a handful of the cold, crumbled clay. Extending her arm, she dropped the dirt onto the pine box in the hole. She noted with strange clarity of detail how the red maple leaf lay lightly, delicately, on the new wood of the box.

The crumbled clay fell from her hand, signifying that she was conscious of his departure and that she willed him to be committed to the ground. Then she stepped back to her other children, with Nate still by her side as a son should be.

Neighbors gathered about the family, easing them away from the grave, blocking the view as shovels were pushed into the rocky clay to lift it into the gaping hole. No number of concerned neighbors, however, could block out the sound of the chunk and clatter of dirt and stone against the lid of the pine box.

Charity stood up, removing her coat from around her sister, and little Naomi began to cry silent tears. Miserable tears flowed coldly down the little girl's face. Charity looked quickly toward her mother and saw she was occupied, so she scooped up her little sister into her own small arms. Perhaps mother was right and Naomi was too heavy for a seven year old to carry, but the girl also sensed that today, at least, mother would not care.

The smaller girl's sobbing stopped, but the wet face was red in the biting wind. Charity put Naomi down and wiped the small cheeks with the corner of her own scarf, then picked her up again and stumbled across the rocky cemetery toward the dilapidated family wagon.

Sarah and Betty Lou raised their bowed heads and began to follow their mother to the wagon. Sarah noticed the stumbling Charity and gently took Naomi from her.

The ancient mule leaned into its traces and the wagon moved slowly onto the rutted road. The uneven and wobbly wheels were caked with the clay that had been picked up on the road, and as chunks of it became too massive to adhere to the wheel, they fell away, leaving gaps of height that caused the rickety old wagon to rock precariously as it traveled the rutted road. The wheels screeched and whined as they turned, rubbing rusted metal against rotted wood. The wheel brake, which would have helped the mule to slow the wagon as it rolled downhill, had long since been warped out of usefulness.

Other wagons and buggies followed. Folks who had not been able to climb up to the mountain cabin for the "laying out" had now brought containers of food that they had graciously placed in the old wagon and slipped away. Personal sympathy could be extended later.

"Ma?" Nate whispered.

Floralee heard her son but could not respond.

"Ma, they gonna be waitin' to get me," Nate told her in a low voice.

Floralee looked at her son, her mind refusing to focus on his words.

"They made me to promise, iffen I got to come to Pa's funeral, I'd be ready to let 'em get me. I wasn't wantin' to tell you sooner, Ma, you havin' enough on you. But I got'a tell you now."

"Nate…?"

"I know, Ma, but I done what I had'a do. A son got'a stay 'side his pa, helpin' and protectin'. I always knowd that. I wasn't aimin' to wing that revenuer with the rifle. I was just aimin' to skeer 'im off till Pa got away."

His voice was a whisper, barely audible over the squeak of the wheels. "I made me a deal with 'em, Ma, so as the little'ns wouldn't be slapped in the face with it all. Once we turn to go uphill, I'll be jumpin' off the wagon whilst you go on home. That'a'way the youngens and the neighbors ain't gonna see 'em take me off."

"How long, Nate? Did they say how long?"

Nate shook his head slowly. "Reckon what I done was real bad, putting a bullet in that revenuer, like I done. Likely I'll be doin' time at county. Chance they'll turn me loose come spring plowin' but they didn't give me no promise."

Floralee straightened her back and flexed her shoulders. *Spring plowing* on her hill was a season of the year, not an occasion of work. The Baker property had hardly a square yard of soil that was flat enough to plow. She lifted her chin and managed a small smile. "You done what you had'a do. Now we all gonna do what we got'a do."

At the foot of the hill, the wagon hesitated before the mule turned toward the mountain, its wheels sliding and scraping. The wet clay ruts of the mountain road were red gashes extending into the trees, before completely disappearing as the road turned.

Nate whispered, "Here, Ma."

Floralee took the reins from her son and watched as he nimbly leaped from the wagon to the ground. She forced herself to look through the leafless tree trunks, and in the faint distance she saw the county sheriff on horseback with another horse standing beside him. She refused to allow her eyes to linger on the view, so the younger children would not follow her gaze.

"Reckon where at Nate'd be goin'?" Donald wondered.

Sarah was quick with an answer. "Likely thought he saw a squirrel." Sarah didn't miss much.

The mule struggled against the pull of the red gumbo clay on its wheels and the wagon inched slowly forward.

Little Henry lifted the cloth cover and looked into one of the bowls of food. The potato salad was yellow with chopped up egg yolks. He licked his lips and poked an exploring finger into the food, then into his mouth.

Betty Lou wordlessly pulled the cloth back over the bowl and moved it a meaningful inch away from Henry's foot. He looked at his sister for a moment as their eyes met, then he turned to watch the leafless gum trees and chestnuts along the side of the road. Betty Lou put out an arm to surround him and ease him closer to her. He leaned against her and raised his thumb to his mouth for the small comfort it brought.

The mule did not stop until it had pulled the wagon into the sadly leaning shed of a barn and thrust its head into the hay manger. He chewed a wispy mouthful as the children jumped off the wagon, the older ones carefully picking up the bowls of food to carry into the cabin.

Floralee handed the reins to Donald and he went about unhitching the mule. She stepped out of the shed and turned her face into the bitter north wind. She lifted her chin and drew a breath of icy air into her lungs, squared her shoulders, and turned to face the cabin. Someone had lighted the lamp against the early winter dark. That was an extravagance that must be foregone, but tonight? Yes, tonight, there would be lamplight.

Floralee set aside the potato salad (with eggs) because just now they needed something hot to warm them. She set aside the chicken dumplings because they took too long to heat and something nourishing would be needed tomorrow. There was a pound cake and a crock of butter. A quart Mason jar of sand plums and another of apple butter. There was a quart jar of thick, dark substance. Ahh! Fresh, thick sorghum molasses! There was strength and comfort in the rich sweetness of molasses.

Floralee took the large iron skillet, almost a foot and a half in diameter, and set it on the wood-burning cookstove, then poked the dying embers into a blaze.

In the large bowl, she mixed cornmeal, salt, and baking powder. She added a glob of bacon grease and stirred in a quantity of fluffy, clabbered goat milk. With practiced vigor, she whipped lightness into the mixture.

The skillet was now hot and smoking, causing the batter to sizzle and whisper as it came in contact with the hot bacon grease. Floralee ran the edge of the spatula around the edges of the cornpone to loosen it. She shook the skillet lightly to level the batter.

The minister's words came to her. "Mount up with wings as the eagle...."

The cornbread began to rise. She slid a flat lid under the cornmeal cake and flipped the whole creation over in one smooth movement. The bottom was now the top and it was smooth, crusty, and golden brown. It arose, slowly, in the pan, urged upward by the heat and the baking powder.

To "rise up with wings as the eagle" was, of course, too much to ask for. That would be too difficult, possibly, even for God. But as she looked at the flat, brown, nourishing bread, she knew she would rise. She would rise up like a pan of cornbread. There was no doubt of it.

She felt a flow of sensation from her neck, through her arms and down to her feet. It was a momentary feeling of power and strength. She would now be in position to make decisions for herself and her children and have them carried out. She could make plans. The fortunes and future of herself and her children would depend solely upon her. *And God*, she hastily added.

She would rise, she knew, and her seven, no, eight, children would rise with her. Excitement prickled the skin on her arms and on the back of her neck. Just like this pan of cornbread, she would rise. Just watch her!

Floralee slid the massive cornpone onto the large pewter platter and set it on the table. Beside it, she placed the crock of butter and the jar of molasses. Cups or Mason jars of goat milk were at each place.

She bowed her head and the children bowed with her. The only words her mouth would form were, "Help us, Lord. Amen."

Sarah and Betty Lou began to cut wedges of the fragrant bread. They slathered the wedges with butter and a generous dollop of molasses to hand to the younger children. The wedges were lifted to hungry mouths, and Floralee watched as her children ate their supper.

The early winter darkness settled in and the cabin became a part of the blackness of the mountain. The wind huffed against the logs and found holes in the chinking between them in which to insert its icy fingers.

The small lean-to at the rear of the cabin contained a double bed with a solid iron head and foot and was covered with a feather tick mattress. The four girls shared this bed, combining their body warmth under thin, ragged quilts. Heat from the potbelly stove did not reach into the lean-to, leaving it to the fingers of icy air creeping in around the loose-fitting door and window.

The sleeping loft above the other room extended over half the length of the room and was floored with pallets for the three, now two, boys. Floralee and Nathan had shared the bed beneath the sleeping loft. It was made of planks under which the winter store of canned foods was kept. A feather tick over the planks of the bed served as a mattress.

Sarah had held a blanket before the blazing cookstove to absorb the last of its warmth. The blanket was then spread on the bed in the frigid lean-to, and the four girls jumped in and covered themselves quickly to retain as much of the heat as possible. Sarah and Betty Lou took the outsides of the bed, and Charity and Naomi were tucked snuggly between them.

The boys, Donald and small Henry, wandered about until their mother directed Donald, "Wash up Henry's face and get 'im on up in the bed, will you, son?"

Donald quickly complied, grateful to have a bit of direction and to be relieved of thought.

Floralee carefully closed the sagging door between the two rooms. The leather hinges were weak from years of use. She drew a rope-bottom chair close to the heavy table constructed from rough-sawn sweet gum slabs. The slabs were now worn smooth from use. Plates and bowls, hands, many activities, and much scrubbing had all done their part.

Then Floralee resolutely lit a candle and its flame flickered from the draft coming around the ill-fitting window. With a puff of breath, she extinguished the soft, yellow glow of the coal oil lamp. Oil was too precious to burn. At least, just yet.

From a high shelf, she took down a stub of a pencil and sharpened its lead with the paring knife. She took a scrap of paper from her stash, hoarded for moments such as this. Down the center of the page she drew a line. One side of the page was headed, "Things I have," and the other side proclaimed, "Things I need."

She planted her elbows on the solid planks of the table and cupped her hands around her chin. There was planning to be done, now that the funeral was past, and it was none too soon to begin it.

She stared into the candle flame, watching the tallow melt at the base of the flickering blaze. A pool of liquid wax formed, and then, like a teardrop, the wax spilled over the edge of the candle and slid down its side. Midway down the shank of the candle, the drop of wax solidified and it clung there, firm and hard. Just like her own tears, it could not fall...like her own tears that stubbornly clung painfully inside her eyes, bringing her no relief.

Her mother had lovingly advised her, "Floralee, you got'a cry. Loosing' a man'd just naturally bring out the tears. Keepin' 'em inside gonna draw the pain out longer. It ain't natural, not to be cryin'!"

"But, Mama, I got no tears."

Mama had been scandalized by her words. "Shore, you got tears, Floralee, loosin' your man like you just done."

But Floralee had shaken her head, sadly. "No, Mama. I reckon a man's got just so many tears allotted to him in his lifetime. Happen he don't make his woman cry, them tears gonna fall when he gets taken away from her. But iffen them tears be shed all along, and him causin' the biggest part of 'em, what's left to be shed at his passin'?"

After a brief pause, Floralee answered her own question. "None, Mama. I can't shed no tears that ain't there."

"Floralee!"

"Mama, we ain't talkin about lovin'. We talkin' about cryin' tears. I reckon I got no tears left. I got pain and heaviness, him bein' my man, but I just ain't got no tears. I got sadness, for sure, but no tears. That's how it is, Mama, and talkin' don't change it none."

2

And tonight on the dark mountain in the small cabin, Floralee still had no tears. She looked at the paper before her, picked up her pencil, and wrote. The words flowed with determination from thoughts long held within her mind and stifled by her life's mate. The words she would have said and the thoughts she would have expressed to him, now crowded into her mind as solid and well-formed as the stones around her hillside cabin.

THINGS I HAVE:

1. 13 acres of land

2. Cabin, needs work

3. 5 goats

4. 2 cows, 1 coming due

5. 3 bushels of corn. It is down under the hill at the still. Donald can carry it up.

6. Firewood. Rick and a half, maybe. Need Nate but I don't got him.

7. 2 bushels of sweet potatoes

8. Mule, too old

9. Chestnut trees and acorn trees. Nathan never listened when I talked about them trees. I always thought they could be the answer.

Floralee thought for a moment, but no other possession of value came to mind. She started on the other list.

THINGS I NEED:

1. Nate, maybe come plowing time

2. Warm clothes

3. Pigs. Nathan never listened to me on that, neither. Hated pigs. I was always thinking they were part of the answer, but Nathan didn't think there was no question that needed an answer. At least from me.

4. More firewood. Hate to ask Sarah to help on that but maybe have to.

5. Money. Not got enough for youngens clothes and pigs both.

Floralee turned the paper over and wrote,

IDEAS:

1. Chestnuts and acorns make pigs fat, maybe they fill children's stomachs.

2. Rail fence might make a pen hog tight. Got that spring of mineral water down at the still. Needs more thinking.

She had ample room for many more ideas on the paper but she could think of no more of them at the moment. She chewed her pencil thoughtfully and turned back to the list of "Things I have." She added one last item to the list:

10. Eight babies and no more.

She contemplated this last entry and nodded her head. Yes, that was one of the "plus" items, so it was in the right column. Floralee had produced a child approximately every two years of her married life, except between Sarah and Betty Lou. That was the year Nathan spent time in the county jail. He had said, then, that they'd never take him alive, and he had been right. They hadn't. The baby she now carried was due in February and then there would be no more.

Three more drops of liquid tallow had spilled over the edge of the candle and now adhered to the side of it like frozen teardrops, heavy and painful and still refusing to fall. The clock on the high shelf said it was almost two o'clock in the morning. Floralee went to her bed and reached far under the feather tick for the sock, worn and faded. She untied the knot and spread the coins out on the planks of the table. She placed the shiny metal disks in stacks of like denomination.

The small stacks of silver and copper totaled seventeen dollars and thirty-seven cents, and it was now November, fast going into the dark and moist cold of an Arkansas winter.

Nathan had not known about the sock. Its existence had become necessary when Sarah was a baby, that being the year Floralee realized her husband would never provide clothes for his family. He bought food, after a fashion, but not clothes. If there was a rag covering their nakedness, it was enough for him.

Her own hoarded pennies, taken to the secondhand store in Jacksonville, had provided dresses, overalls, and coats. Never being one to notice the details of his children's lives, he never noticed the "new" used clothes…the children's or even his own.

Seventeen dollars and thirty-seven cents, previously earmarked for clothing purchases, must now be re-evaluated. A young pig could possibly be bought for fifty cents, maybe less, going into winter like they were.

Floralee glanced at the clock on the high shelf. It was now past three. The winter chill had seeped through the logs and frost formed inside the plate glass window that looked out over the valley. Before the winter came again, there would be some changes. Many changes. That was one thing she promised herself.

She selected a medium-sized stick of precious firewood and put it in the cookstove, stirring the coals to a blaze. The cross-cut saw was fairly sharp, so maybe Sarah and Betty Lou could work together to saw up some logs into chunks. Or perhaps Sarah and Donald. Betty Lou was such a tiny thing to be handling a two-man saw…for that matter, they all were.

Donald could bring the corn up from the cave containing the "still" and Charity could look for chestnuts and persimmons still under the trees. Ones that might have escaped the 'possums.

Little Henry could amuse Naomi for her and Floralee would be free to make plans. This would be the day for plans to be made. Perhaps Donald should be making the pen for the pigs and leave the corn till later.

If Nate was only here! Poor Nate! Doing what he thought was the right thing to do. Following the example of a father who was only teaching him to bring more trouble down on himself. But Nate was young, and there was still time…wasn't there?

Perhaps she should forget about cutting the wood. They could scrounge up dry sticks and logs, maybe from the plot next door belonging to Nathan's brother, Dwight. He had given up his part of the mountain acreage and moved his family into River Bend.

Yes, that would be the way to go. The pigpens were more important. It was past time to be putting her plan into action. Sarah and Betty Lou could bring up the corn and she could help Donald with the pigpens.

Pigs were the answer, of course. Nathan would never hear to having hogs on the place. "Dang, smelly beasts, snortin' and grubbin', messin' up the taste of the squeezin's, likely bringin' down the price of 'em. Iffen a body'd get the hankerin' for ham or bacon, they's pigs a'plenty runnin' loose in the woods." And he had brought in a dressed-out hog fairly frequently. Floralee never asked about its origin. Though she sometimes suspected, she really didn't want to know.

The clock now indicated five-thirty. She would let the children sleep as long as they wanted to on this day. Yesterday had been hard on them. Floralee blew out the candle and sat in the darkness. It would be a while, yet, before it came daylight. Sunrise was late at her cabin, situated as it was on the afternoon side of the hill.

She heard a whimper from the lean-to and she slipped through the sagging door. She drew tiny Naomi out from under the quilts. She was wet. Emotional days always seemed to affect her bladder. The girls' whole bed would now be wet and it would be hard to dry it out in the winter.

Extra bedding would have been nice, but it did not occur to Floralee to wish for it.

Perhaps she should take Naomi into her bed from now on, now that Nathan was gone. It would help even things out. The girls' bed was becoming crowded as they continued to grow.

Or should she give that privilege to Sarah? Her oldest daughter would be very important to the future to the family and perhaps deserving of a special consideration. It was something to think on.

Floralee put dry clothes on Naomi and opened the stove door, stirring the coals into a blaze. She cuddled the little girl as well as her expanding abdomen would permit, and Naomi drowsed back to sleep. Floralee put her under the quilts on the plank bed, and by now the fingers of light signaling the dawn had found the kitchen window.

Floralee opened the flour bin and estimated the number of breakfasts left. Maybe two weeks more. She contemplated the apple butter for breakfast. Why not? She pried up the metal lid and poured half of it into a bowl, then recapped the jar. What was left in the jar would make another breakfast. She measured the flour into the biscuit pan and began to stir in the clabbered goat milk and baking powder.

The cookstove crackled and popped as it devoured sticks of wood, warming the tiny kitchen and heating the oven.

Sarah came in first, then Betty Lou, and before the sun cleared the mountain, six children sat around the plank table, anticipating the fragrant biscuits.

Floralee told them, "Donald and me, we gonna make a pigpen today."

Donald looked up at her, wide-eyed and surprised. "But Pa said we..." and he paused, looking down at his knuckles.

His mother did not react to his words and continued, "We gonna put it 'neath them acorn trees, aimin' to move it when the acorns are ate up from under that tree." She nodded firmly and smiled brightly, thereby putting the first plan into place.

No one asked about Nate. Floralee was continuously amazed that information possessed by one of the children seemed to flow into all of them without benefit of words. Perhaps living so closely together on the isolated hillside had helped to create their common mind. It was a relief, most times.

On second thought, however, though it was good it was also bad. Painful talking was avoided in this way, but there were times that things needed talking out. The talking this time, however, would have to wait.

3

Abe McCullough stood in the grove of wild chestnuts with his back to the biting wind and waited. In his imagination, he toyed with thoughts of young Nate Baker. Would he come walking over to the law to be taken into custody as he had promised? Abe had staked his word as a lawman that Nate would do just that. He didn't often go that far out on a limb for anyone.

There was a sound of crackling leaves behind him, and reflex, born of experience, made Abe reach for his gun as he pivoted toward the noise. His instant, wide-angled gaze, common to a native hill man, observed a flash of a bushy tail disappear around a tree trunk. No doubt the squirrel had dropped a nut, but more likely, the animal had thrown the nut at him to drive him away. Abe was the invader of this woodland.

He placed his gun into the holster once more and turned his back again toward the wind and waited.

His thoughts returned to Nate. Tall and rail-thin, he was acquiring the raw-boned good looks of his father. Abe remembered when Nate had been born. That baby boy had sealed the death of Abe's own dream that Floralee might get the handsome stranger out of her system and become his.

Beautiful, beautiful Floralee. She had risen gracefully up out of the freckled, knobby-kneed child with flaming red hair into an ivory skinned beauty who had filled Abe's dreams at night. Just when he thought he might have the courage to talk her into seeing him, the handsome outlander had moved in and taken her.

Abe had accepted his loss, being a sensible person, and had turned to Louisa. And they had a good marriage. If Louisa ever suspected his feelings for Floralee Callahan, it would be because she could read his mind, as in occasional nighttime dreams he still had of the young Floralee. Dreams of the times they were both young. Dreams and hopes....Oh, well, that was a long time ago.

He stomped his feet to encourage circulation and possible warmth. What he wouldn't give for a cup of hot coffee or chocolate served in the heavy earthenware cup Louisa always used to serve him. It was a large cup to hold in the circle of two of a man's hands and warm the outside of a man as well as the inside.

Abe grinned. Just look at him and think of the stupidity of it all! Standing on this hillside in the bitter wind, thinking thoughts of love directed toward a coffee cup!

A faint noise, alien to the elements of the mountain, alerted him. A distant wagon sound and the plodding of a horse over frozen, rutted roads. Through the curtain of tree trunks, he could see glimpses of the wagon full of people, but there were no shouts of laughter usually expected with children. He could see them now, hunched together against the cold, riding behind the ancient mule.

Gloom settled dismally over him. Here he, the law, stood waiting to take away the only one of Floralee's children who might mean the difference between meager subsistence and starvation. God only knew what would happen now. It was at times like these that he most hated his job.

The wagon did not pause but turned toward the mountain for the straight climb to Nathan's...no, Floralee's farm. He could see the boy, dwarfed by the tall trees as he was making his way toward him. The wagon continued slowly, still silent of human sound, up the frozen trail to the cabin above the still.

"Hello, son," Abe McCullough greeted Nate Baker. *Well, he should have been my son,* Abe rationalized. *Life should not have turned out the way it did.*

Nate nodded his head respectfully to the law but said nothing.

"You can ride that'n," Abe indicated with his elbow, and Nate swung onto the waiting horse as Abe leaped astride the other animal. They worked their way through the trees to the main road into Jacksonville. The horses' hoofs made musical notes as they trotted along the cold-hardened stones of the road.

"We gonna stop over to my place up the road. I ain't had a bite since early today. Seems like I maybe got a echo in my guts." Abe's attempt at humor went by unnoticed, but Abe was used to that. He had never been known as a wit. He was more of a practical person. Before he had left his house, he had told Louisa that, if she could manage it, he'd like to have fried chicken and gravy ready. Likely the boy would be able to eat most of the chicken himself.

A half a mile down the road, Nate spoke his first words to the law. "Won't be no hardship on me, stoppin' over. I ain't what you'd call in no big hurry to go where I reckon I got'a go."

Abe nodded to himself. At least the boy was talking. "Where at you reckonin' you got'a go?" Abe asked, attempting to prolong the friendly attitude.

It was another quarter of a mile before Nate answered. "I speck to be lookin' at the world through bars, Mr. McCullough."

"What you say, son?"

"Speck bars is what they got waitin' for me. You figure they'd be a way they'd let me have a couple'a weeks 'afore they send me up? My ma, she shore gonna have herself a time with all them little'ns, gettin' in the wood. 'Member, Donald'd be barely goin' onto nine, hisself."

Abe sighed. "Don't reckon so, son. They done stretched a point so as you could be with your ma at the funeral. Took some tall talkin' to get that for ya. Iffen I hadn't been right confident of you bein' a man of your word, I'd'a never put my name on the line for you like I did. But I reckon I can set your mind to rest about one thing. You ain't gonna be back of no bars for a long time."

"How come, you say?"

"'Cause you ain't had your sixteenth birthday yet, have you?" Abe knew exactly when Nate's birthday was. It was the day he had asked Louisa to marry him.

Nate shook his head. "That day ain't till spring."

Abe nodded reassuringly. "All to the good. The law gonna say you was a child, not knowin' what you was doin'. They don't put no youngens 'hind bars, no more. They gonna, most likely, send you to some school."

"School? But, Mr. McCullough, I knowd what I was doin'! Reckon I didn't aim to hurt nobody, but I knowd the revenuer was out there where that bullet was aimed."

Abe nodded. "I know that and you know that, but them men that'll be talkin' with you, like they gonna be real soon, they ain't gonna know that, less'n you or I tell 'em."

"You don't reckon they gonna ask?"

"Yeah, they gonna ask lots of things. What you say back to 'em when they ask, that'd be your business."

"Mr. McCullough, you worried I ain't gonna be truthful? I'm sayin' to ya I ain't never been no liar. They get to askin' me things, I'd be givin' 'em the truth. Don't you be thinkin' I won't, Mr. McCullough."

Abe McCullough sighed. How should he say this? "But you won't need to give no answers to questions they don't ask, Nate. Just say what you got'a say and no more. They's times when a lot'a talk just confuses folks."

Nate nodded his understanding. "You can count on me, Sir. I aim to be plain in my talking' so's they be no chance they gonna get mixed up."

Abe McCullough sighed again, long and wearily. This was one of the many times when he felt as though he was a human bridge between the legal system and his own mountain people. He could talk with and understand each group of people, but they would never understand each other. It was very hard to sort out the reasons, but the basic problem seemed to be that the words did not have the same meaning to both groups. It was like two languages in which the words sounded the same but the meanings were entirely different.

"Nate?"

"Yes, Sir?"

"Tell me, flat out. Why was it you shot the revenuer?"

The boy turned to him and Abe saw a man's sadness looking out at him from a boy's face. "I had'a shoot 'cause they shot my pa. Mr. McCullough, what kind of a son'd see his pa fall and not stand up for 'im? It'd be a shame for a son to run off, seein' his pa fall down the way I saw mine fall. I never meant to hurt nobody and that's the honest truth."

"But you knew the revenuer was there and that you, bein' a good shot, stood the risk of hittin' 'im?"

"Yes, Sir."

"Iffen you didn't aim to hit 'im, how come you to pull on the trigger?"

"I done told you, Mr. McCullough. A son got'a stand up for his pa or he got no right to hold his head up around folks. I done what I had'a do. Ain't that what you'd'a done, you bein' me and your ma standin' there, lookin' on?"

Abe nodded. Likely, he would have done the same thing if he had not chosen to become the law. Both sides were so clear and easy for each to understand, but not to each other. Young Nate Baker's words would likely give those college-educated lawmen a run for their money. If Nate just held to the truth, strange sounding though it was, and if he didn't go and get himself mad and get the lawmen riled up, maybe...? If, if, if....

They were now approaching the white picket fence around his own comfortable cabin. Smoke, punctuated with plumes of sparks, billowed from the chimney. Louisa had obviously been watching for him and was now stoking the fire with seasoned hickory to drive the chill out of his bones. And it was going to take some tall driving.

The fragrance of fried chicken met them at the door. Louisa took Nate's skimpy jacket and Abe's sheep-lined coat and urged them both to back up to the fireplace. Gracious, comfortable Louisa, and Abe knew he was lucky to have her, still....

The crust on the chicken was crisp and browned, and the small, boiled potatoes swam in rich cream gravy. The biscuits were thick and filling.

"Son, you may as well find somethin' you can eat 'cause you gonna have to wait on me, anyways." Abe didn't add that there was no telling when the next meal would be or what it would consist of. The sooner he was sent on up to Benton, the better for Nate it would be. Once again, he was grateful that Nate was not yet sixteen. Only a few months, it was, but they could make a sight of difference in the rest of his life.

Finally Nate began to eat. Youthful appetite and borderline malnutrition gave him room for biscuit after biscuit and he continued to eat until the plate of chicken was as empty as the gravy bowl. Here he was, forced to make a choice between nutcake and rhubarb pie, when just his fill of biscuits with butter and strawberry jam would have been a treat.

Abe told Louisa, "That wind out there's fair blustery enough to cut through a body's ribs and whistle a tune on 'em. Reckon an old man like me ought'a hitch up the buggy for warmer ridin' and put on them storm flaps."

Louisa nodded agreement and they both knew it was either that or risk an affront to Nate's pride by insisting that he wear one of Abe's heavy coats. Pride was not a thing to injure needlessly and Nate's had been wounded enough already. The boy would need all the pride he had left.

Louisa broke open the remaining biscuits, spooning in butter and jam. She winked at Nate. "That Abe, like as not, he gonna be hungry again by the time he gets to the city. Likely he'll be wantin' a little somethin' to nibble on. You just sit here in the warm till I take this here basket out to the buggy, else'n he'd likely walk off without it."

At the shed, she told Abe, "See you get that boy to eat these 'afore you let him out. Even if you got'a eat one yourself on top'a that dinner you stuffed yourself on."

Abe took the basket and affectionately patted Louisa's ample rear as she departed. Yessiirree, life would have been hard without Louisa. He was a most fortunate man to have her.

4

The trip to Jacksonville was distressingly quiet. What was there to say? At the edge of town, Abe told Nate, "Boy, I got a favor to ask. Louise always makes me a picnic to nibble on whilst I'm on the road, and I just ain't findin' myself too hungry today. But knowin' how women are, I ain't wantin' to take them jelly biscuits back home, not bein' eaten. Iffen I did, they's no tellin' when I'd get more, women bein' sensitive the way they are. Reckon you could do me a favor and eat some of 'em? Many's you can. I'd consider it a good deed from you so as I could stay in favor with Louisa."

Nate lifted the cloth from the basket and peered in. The biscuits had jiggled this way and that and the lovely red jam was oozing out. Abe McCullough had been so nice to him and this was a way he could do a favor in return. He carefully lifted the top biscuit and caught the dripping jam from the edge with his tongue before he bit into it. As the horse ambled slowly to the police headquarters, Nate finished the biscuits and licked the sticky jam from his fingers.

Abe and Nate walked to the police headquarters. "Brung 'im in jist like I said'd happen," Abe told them. "This here boy be good on his word. Ain't many I'd be trustin' like I trust this here boy."

Nate was taken away to a room by himself and left alone. It was a warm, quiet room, and Nate sat down on a soft chair, along with his thoughts and his agony.

Pa, what'll I do now? You be somewhere out there that you can see things goin' on here? Somehow, the thought was not comforting. *But, Pa, Ma, and them little'ns got nobody and I ain't even knowin' what'll happen to me. Pa! Oh, Pa! How come this to happen?*

Tears oozed from his eyes and flowed down his bony cheeks. *What'll I do, Pa? What'll I do now?* he pled of the white walls that surrounded him.

In another room, Abe McCullough was also pleading, "Reckon you could bend a rule and let that boy go in a week or two? It ain't like as though makin' 'im suffer was a'gonna make that revenuer's arm hurt less."

But the answer was firm. "No, we have to keep him. There has to be an example made."

"To who?"

"Why, to the county, of course, and to the state."

Abe looked out the window. "I ain't seein' no county nor no state out here watchin'. How many folks you reckon even knows we got him, outside'a you and me and his family?"

The officer shrugged. Rules were rules, and they were the fabric and structure of the law. They gave direction and removed any feeling of indecision. The law would be obeyed.

Abe continued, "The next boy they got at his house is nine years old. That woman and all them girl children is alone on that mountain."

The officer looked out the same window. What Abe said was true, but he answered, "This here's November. If that boy was at home, he'd be another mouth eating. Here, we'll feed him. Do they have a farm out there where they can grow anything?"

"Shucks!" scoffed Abe. "That land of their'n is so straight up and down and so full of trees, you couldn't find a patch'a ground level enough to raise a fuss on."

The officer nodded. "Then how do you think that boy would be a help if we let him go? By running off another batch of moonshine? Then we'd be after him for another reason."

Abe sighed. He should have known better than to attempt verbal logic with an educated lawman. The state lawmen just did not understand a man's rightful place in a hill household. Hunting and woodcutting should not be done by women and girl children and nine-year-old little boys. God only knew how Floralee would make it through the winter.

The man behind the desk continued, "Abe, has that boy got himself an education? Has he completed the sixth grade?"

Abe shook his head. "Likely not more'n the third grade. The first son of a big family don't hardly have hisself much of a chance."

The officer nodded and smiled, faintly. "This one is going to get his chance. I'd not be doing my duty if I didn't hold him until he got an education...the one he missed by being born first. Somehow, that family will make it. It's my duty to see that this boy has a chance to make it, too."

It was then Abe knew he had lost. All the good sounding words he had in his head were crowded out by the officer's logic. He made one final attempt. "They gonna 'member it in his favor that he come on like he promised to do, 'stead'a cuttin' out the other way? He done just like he said he'd do."

Now the officer smiled. "Do you think we put boys behind bars for life just for the fun of it? Believe it or not, we're hoping to help that boy so we don't have to give his mother another man to bury. Sure, him being good to his word is going to be in his favor, and you've done your part. Your opinion carries a lot of weight."

So Abe was content that he had done his best for Nate. "Then I reckon I got'a go on back home. Figure to step down the hall and say a word to him, 'afore I leave."

At the door, Abe stopped with his hand on the knob. Sounds of sobbing came from the room. "Pa? How come it to happen like this, Pa?"

Abe rattled the doorknob and then paused. All became quiet inside the room. He stepped inside and Nate drew a sleeve across his eyes and looked up.

"Son?"

"Yes, Sir?"

"I got'a be runnin' on now, but I wanted you to know. I aim to be askin' about your ma and seein' to it that things ain't too bad. They gonna be sendin' you upstate to a school for a while. It'll not be too bad, and you got'a just do what you're told. That school gonna be a good thing for you."

"School...?"

"Yep, but don't you be worryin'. Things look tore up now, but they gonna come together. You gonna see."

Abe nodded encouragement and left quickly. It was a long ride home, and Nate's tears were close to his eyes. Likely he had not even had time, as yet, to mourn his pa's death. Tears were there and they must be shed, no matter what the age or relationship. Nate, trying to be a grown-up man, could not change that.

It was dark when Abe McCullough reached his home. The white picket fence stood out in bold relief from the dark landscape, and a shower of hickory sparks plumed into the dark sky. Somehow Louisa knew he was coming. Likely, she had been at the window, watching for the buggy lantern.

"I'm comin', Louisa. I'm'a comin' home," he told the wind that whistled coldly through the gum trees.

5

The kitchens of River Bend buzzed with speculation. The funeral of Nathan Baker gave rise to a new subject of conversation. Floralee Baker, who hardly ever got to come to town, would have been amazed to know she was the chief topic of conversation for a week or more.

"What you reckon she'll be doin', losin' her man like she done?"

"Likely she'll be doin' 'thout, same as any woman left alone."

"How many youngens she got now? A dozen?"

"Not yet, but I'd be layin' odds she would'a had iffen old Nathan hadn't got hisself picked off."

"Reckon the revenuer done her a blessin'?"

"Possible."

"She seemed heavy hearted at the funeral, but I didn't lay eyes on a tear comin' down her face. Hafta say, them is well mannered youngens she got. Never seen a questionable thing out'a any of 'em."

"No, 'cept that one that winged the revenuer. That boy likely aimed to miss hittin' the lawman and couldn't for bein' mad and scairt."

"How you reckon she'll feed them youngens off'a that rocky hillside? It ain't flat enough to place a garden nowhere. Likely have to shoot the seeds in the rows from the hill back of it. A kid loosin' a footin' on that hillside'd likely be landin' up in the valley."

"She's got goats, ain't she? Goat milk and cheese is good for youngens. Them goats can be ate iffen a body got hisself strong teeth and a mind to do it. My ma'd cook up one of them young ones from time to time, stewin' it a day or more, throwin' in peppers and onions and some stewed tomatoes. Tweren't bad, dependin' on how hungry you found yourself."

"She got that one girl comin' on to marriage age, ain't she? Reckon she'll be a help. Could even send her to town to do kitchen work, iffen she could be spared better'n they could do without cash money."

"I got a thought that Floralee'll be the one as'll keep things together, 'stead of the other way around, Nathan Baker bein' one for big talk and no do. I figure, 'cept for the cash money brought in by the moonshine, she'll likely be better off."

"Yeah, and that brother of Nathan's livin' down here in town, likely he'd be a help to her iffen things get bad enough. Sure couldn't count on nothin' from that'n living up on the mountain 'long side'a her. He'll be nothin' but trouble, and her not needin' any more of that."

The talk in the livery stable was also of Floralee, but mostly of the deceased Nathan. They stood among the feed bins, spitting, whittling, and surmising.

"Where you reckon we gonna find somethin' to quench the thirst? Nathan bein' gone and the squeezin's likely gone with 'im."

"Happen that brother of his'n'll take over the still? That mineral spring there at the foot of that hill be 'bout the best for makin' likker I ever witnessed. Nathan's pa 'afore 'im, he ran off a good tastin' batch, nigh as good as Nathan's."

The voices were lowered. "Would ya 'speck that boy of his'n'd be aimin' on carryin' on after his pa, do ya? Him bein' growed, like as not he knows the secrets of his pa, like any man'd pass onto his son."

"Ain't gonna know for a while, yet. The law got 'im."

"The law? You mean Abe picked 'im up?"

"Yep, got 'im and took 'im off."

"Naw! I seen 'im at the buryin', big as life, standin' there next to his ma, holdin' onto her."

"That was for show, the law lettin' him stand with her. They got 'im all right, and him not even gettin' home. Nathan's wife and that passel of youngens are left perched on the side of that hill, hand to mouth for somethin' to eat. The law could'a let her keep that boy, her needin' 'im more'n they did."

"Yep, and iffen that youngen 'membered any of his pa's secrets, and him livin' there by that good water, he'd be able to help right smart with their livin'. I for one'd be willin' to pay cash money and pick up a jug or two extra, just be helpin' 'im out in his hard time."

"And I'd pick up a extra jug, myself. Been aimin' to lay in a supply for when the weather sets in. Likker brewed in the winter storm just don't have the smooth body, flowin' 'cross the tongue, like when it'd be a clear day and sun comin' out."

"Likely, they'd be just holdin' that boy a month, maybe, to put some fears in 'im. Come spring plowin', chance they'll be listenin' to a letter from his ma, sayin' how bad they was needin' him t'home."

"Yeah, and I'd be willin' to take a day out and run that letter over to the law myself."

"Reckon you would if that'd mean the booze'd commence to flow agin."

"Been thinkin' on it, and it'd be a clear thought of mine. That boy'll foller after his pa, him feelin' free to take a pot shot at the law like he done. Winged 'im right in his shootin' arm. Reckon that law man gonna have a painful time of gettin' a cup'a coffee up to his mouth come the next week or two."

"Hard thinkin' is still in the front of us. What we gonna do till spring gets here and the next batch be run off?"

"I'm in the 'memberance of a place over the ridge near Piney, it not bein' shut down as of a year back. Squeezin's from over there ain't got the smooth flow of the way Nathan's done, but likely be good enough, a body be dry enough. Purty high ridge to wag the jugs over, owin' to there not bein' no road up to it. A pack mule and a man on foot'd be the way to go."

"Happen the trip'd be easier, there bein' more'n one of us makin' it. Be good to have someone along for talk, on the climb."

"We could set us a day, bein' convenient for all, and head on over that'a'way. Hate to risk gettin' too low, myself, not knowin' where the next jug'd be comin' from."

6

Breakfast was being prepared in the hillside cabin. The fragrance of the baking bread filled the tiny room, and there was no comment about the bowl of spicy apple butter setting in the center of the table, but each child was enjoying the knowledge of its presence.

Little Henry stretched his arm toward the bowl, slowly, carefully, with an exploring finger extended. Slowly, gently, Betty Lou extended her arm alongside his and clasped his hand in hers.

He looked up at his sister who smiled down at him. Slowly she drew his arm back to the edge of the table. Henry withdrew his hand from Betty Lou's and clasped it with the other hand in his lap, his gaze still fastened on the apple butter.

Their mother checked the biscuits in the oven. They had risen to golden perfection, so she set the steaming pan on the wooden trivet in the center of the table and put the crock of butter beside it. The hungry children made no move toward the food.

Floralee bowed her head. "Lord, we bein' still thankful for these biscuits. And, 'member, we gonna need a lot'a out'a You in the next few months." Thus warned, God was released to go on about His business, and the children reached for the steaming biscuits. Floralee broke open a biscuit, put in butter and apple butter, and handed it to Naomi.

The bone-weary mother was watching the children and collecting her thoughts to make the day's assignments when Sarah asked, "Ma, why was you settin' up all night, and you carryin' a baby?"

Floralee was startled at the direct question but decided it needed a direct answer. "Likely, I had me thinkin' to be done as couldn't stand the light'a day."

Donald asked, "Ma, you get it done?"

"What done?"

"That thinkin'."

"Reckon I must'a."

Floralee instructed the older girls to begin to carry up the corn in small containers and dump it on the bed quilt. Then they were to bring up the heavy barrel. It was to be placed in the kitchen, safe from raccoons and possums and from spoilage. Then she took Donald tramping through the ankle-deep leaves toward the chestnut trees.

"How many pigs we thinkin' on buyin'?"

Floralee sighed, thinking of the money shortage. "Reckon to be startin' with a brood sow or a litter of six or seven, that bein' most likely what we'd have money for."

They walked on.

"Son, to tell the truth, I ain't really thought on how many. Today we gonna start that pigpen and tomorrow you gonna finish it up while I'll be goin' after the pigs."

Donald glanced up at his mother through his red-blond lashes. This confident voice could hardly belong to the mother he knew and loved. The first part of last night had weighed heavily on his mind, him being the oldest male at home. Who knew what tremendous adult responsibility was about to be thrust upon his shoulders? Now it seemed a fair bet that at least some of that worry was wasted.

Another thought entered Donald's head on the heels of that one. "Reckon I'd be needin' to quit goin' down to school, you needin' me here, like you'll be."

A faint smile played at the corner of his mother's mouth. "Reckon you to be back in school in a week, and then havin' to make up what you'll be missin' today."

The boy's frustration gathered into the toe of his too-large shoe, and he kicked a small stone sending it spinning out over the bluff and on past the mineral spring.

The wind was not so fierce today and the sun finally broke through the cloudbank. The leafless limbs of the massive oaks arose above mother and son like woody skeletons, last year's bird nests starkly evident. A pile of split rails lay near the fence line, evidence of a fence that did not materialize. The termites and beetles had made their presence known, but most of the rails were still fairly sound.

"Donald, grab up two'a them rails and let's drag 'em over to the chestnut trees."

The prickly chestnut burrs had opened, dropping the tiny, wild nuts into the dry leaves beneath the trees. Squirrels scurried through the limbs, making use of this warmer day for storing a bit more food against a storm.

Floralee selected a group of three nut trees and marked out a circle around them by dragging a stick through the leaves. "Donald, we're aimin' to make a rail fence settin' on that line, usin' them rails as far as we can stretch 'em."

She had another thought, "Gonna have to be sinkin' that first rail 'neath the dirt, agin the rootin' and grubbin' of them pig snouts."

Donald pondered, scratching his head full of red curly hair. "Ma, you been lookin' at that pile? Reckon they gonna be enough rails, big as you drawed that line?"

"Likely not, son, and that'd be where the sweat gonna start. Little trees got'a be cut down, you bein' too little to split them big 'ens. Got'a make enough rails so's we can finish out."

Donald studied the pile with new interest as his mother continued.

"Happen I get us a litter 'stead'a a brood sow, we'd have us more time, them bein' too little to push over the fence right off."

They carried rails until lunch time. Floralee stopped often to look up the hill, then down. The thirteen acres of the farm stretched a half a mile from the top to the bottom of the hill, the only level place being used for the cabin and the tiny barn. Her husband's father had divided his land among his three sons by cutting it into strips from the top of the hill to the valley, his idea of fairness. The resulting third was a half a mile long and 200 feet wide, creating a narrow ribbon of land almost totally covered with trees.

The sons had drawn lots for the strip with the mineral spring in the valley, and Nathan had won it. This was construed to mean that he would also be the rightful heir to their father's business, so he proceeded to carry on in the tradition of his father, producing unsurpassed moonshine liquor from the mineral water.

Nathan's older brother had moved to River Bend, leaving his strip of land to the chestnuts and gums.

Floralee's thirteen acres were fenced, due entirely to the efforts of the adjoining property owners. A fence had not been necessary to Nathan's business...only a good rifle and careful watchfulness.

The crunch of the ankle-deep dry leaves and the wine-sharpness of the air cleared Floralee's mind and sharpened her senses. She rested briefly, drawing deep breaths. The baby changed positions, settling heavily against her rib cage. She pushed her hand against the pressure on her rib cage and the baby obligingly moved into a more comfortable position.

Donald paused beside her. "What you thinkin' on, Ma?"

"I been thinkin' on the good things we got, like this farm and the mule and the goats and cows and each other. But mostly, I was thinkin' we got lots to do. Land like this, straight up and down, it ain't gonna be fit for much, but we gonna find out what."

Donald, wielding the grubbing hoe, had the first layer of rails lowered into the ground, and he and his mother had carried and placed two more layers above it. The enclosure was now almost knee high.

"We gotta start leanin' them rails in toward the middle now, Donald. Got'a make it so them pig snouts'll not be pushin' it down."

At noon she called the children in to eat. There were fried corn cakes, and the potato salad with chopped eggs was divided onto the plates. A quart of pickled beets finished the meal. They'd have to eat good and work hard and that would help to keep them from thinking. Maybe.

Floralee wearily leaned her head against her forearm on the table, just for a second. The next sound she heard was a bump and a grind as the heavy wooden barrel slipped from Betty Lou's grasp.

"Shhh, you wakin' Ma up!" Sarah warned in a loud whisper.

"I didn't go to do it! Wasn't wantin' to wake her up, neither," was the answering whisper.

Floralee raised her eyes to the clock on the high shelf. Half past five and she had slept for more than four hours, leaning forward on the table.

"Lord'a'mercy, how come you girls to let me sleep, bein' so much to get done?"

Sarah touched her mother's arm, gently. "You was needin' to sleep, Ma. See, we brung up the corn and we was just havin' a little trouble with that old heavy barrel."

"I smashed my finger," Betty Lou complained, amiably.

"Where at is the little 'ens?"

"Charity got 'em out pickin' up nuts like you told her."

Floralee sighed, "Sure didn't aim for her to have both of 'em out on that bluff alone. You girls should'a woke me."

"Ain't nothin' happened, Ma. We been watchin'."

The barrel had now been worked into the corner beside the woodbox, and the corn was being transferred to the barrel from the quilt. The sound of the hard, nutritious kernels falling into the barrel was akin to the sound of clinking coins, or possibly even better, since money could not be eaten. The only problem with the corn was that it would not last until the next growing season.

Oh, yes, the pigpen! Floralee stood and looked out the kitchen window. In the distance, the tiny figure of Donald could be seen between the tree trunks. She walked out to him and he stood back, his eyes shining and his face damp and rosy from energetic activity. She saw the fence was now five rows high.

"Donald, honey, you done a good job!"

"But, Ma, they ain't rails to make another round. Gonna be havin' to start in the cuttin'." He nodded his head wisely and repeated, "Yep, gonna be havin' to start cuttin'."

And there was Charity with Henry and Naomi. "Lookie, Ma, we got us a whole pail 'a chinky pins!"

Floralee looked at the bucket of wild chestnuts. Charity's "full" pail was actually a little over half full, but represented a lot of work for small fingers, nevertheless.

"You a good girl, but I wasn't aimin' for you to be seein' after both them little 'ens out here on the bluff. One of 'em could'a run to edge, you lookin' at the other'n."

Charity lowered her head. "Then I reckon I'll not be doin' that no more. Sarah was thinkin' you was to be let sleep and she didn't want no noise. What was we gonna do with them chinky pins?" Charity's earnest, up-turned face was splotched with freckles and the sky blue eyes, fringed with red-gold lashes, were unblinking. Floralee smoothed her daughter's curly red hair.

"Come time we get the shells off a them chinky pins, we'll be figurin' on what to do with 'em. You just keep on gatherin' 'em into your pail and I'll be takin' the little'ens on in. We'll be havin' supper in a little bit."

The tinkling sound from the shed indicated that Betty Lou had brought in the goats to be milked. Floralee went back to the cabin and stirred up a pan of cornbread to eat warm with the fresh goat's milk. No one asked about the butter and molasses.

After supper, Floralee began to stir up a batch of biscuits. "Gather 'round, we got'a talk. I'll be makin' biscuits tonight, there not bein' time in the morning."

All eyes studied their mother's face.

"Way 'afore daylight, I got'a be on my way to Jacksonville. Gonna take Sarah and Betty Lou along with me."

The two girls tried to look at each other without moving, cutting their eyes sideways. This was an unexpected treat. Charity's chin began to pucker.

"Don't be cryin', darlin', next time'll be your time. Yours and Donald's. Tomorrow, you gonna take the hulls off a them chinky pins and watch the little 'ens while Donald got'a milk the goats and work on that pig pen."

Floralee looked at the sad face of her daughter. "Charity, darlin', I'll be countin' on you not to let the little'ens past the house. Happen you got'a get water from the spring, make Henry go stay with Donald and you put the table leg on Naomi's skirt tail, keepin' her put till you get back."

Charity's eyes were still downcast but they were dry of tears.

"Donald, you be careful stokin' up that fire, like I know you'll be. They's that big tin can'a pork and beans that they give us, that you can eat for your dinner."

Charity's eyes brightened and she stole a look at Donald. The day would not be all bad. Store-bought pork and beans was always a treat.

With a weary sigh, Floralee blew out the candle and went to bed.

7

It seemed she had hardly settled down when she heard, again, the tromping and snorting of horses and the loud, commanding sound of male voices. She heard the exchange of gunfire and the sickening whine of the bullets.

She could hear feet running through the dry leaves and loud yelling. She ran to the cabin door and looked down the hill toward the valley.

There she saw Nathan, standing with the rifle cocked. "Get back, Floralee," he yelled, but her feet had a mind of their own.

She heard the shot and she saw him fall, the gun barrel glinting in the afternoon sun. Like a flash of lightning, she saw her handsome, red-haired son rise up from his crouched position, shoulder his father's rifle, and fire, all in one fluid movement.

Floralee screamed. Nate dropped the rifle and raised his hands over his head.

Then Floralee heard a voice say, "Ma? What's wrong, Ma?"

She stared into the cold darkness. She was sitting up in her bed and tiny Naomi was curled into a ball beside her. The voice belonged to Sarah, calling from the lean-to.

It was a dream. Only a dream. Must she live through that terrible day, yet again? How many times…?

"Just a dream I had, Sarah, darlin'. You go back to sleep."

"Ma?"

"What, Sarah?"

"You want I come in there, you bein' lonely like?"

While Floralee hesitated, Sarah made the decision.

"Wait, Ma. I'll come in there."

Sarah gently moved aside the warm little ball that was Naomi and snuggled under the quilt that covered the plank bed.

"Now you can go back to sleep, Ma, not needin' to dream about Pa no more tonight. I'm gonna be right here 'side you to keep you from dreamin'."

When the alarm went off, Naomi had been returned to the lean-to and Sarah and Betty Lou were in the kitchen, dressed and ready. In the light of the lantern, Floralee harnessed the old mule to the wagon and they started down the steep, rutted trail toward the river road that would take them into Jacksonville.

8

The boy in the reformatory at Benton, Arkansas, spread the paper before him and tapped the pencil against his teeth, thoughtfully.

Dear Ma,

How are you doing? I keep thinking on you and the little ones. And if you got food and chopped wood.

They are good to me and I eat lots. I have to study every day and it is hard. It is hard to study when I think about other things, but they say I will get a sixth grade certificate if I work hard. They say I do good. I always wanted to do good.

Ma, they ask me about Pa all the time. I cannot figger out why they do that. They ask questions and I say my answers clear and loud and I say the truth every time, but I think maybe someday they will understand.

They say do I know how to make corn likker but I know they do not want to make it. I do not know why they keep asking me. I said to them that I would not be the one to ask on account of I never made none. I keep telling them that.

Ma, I keep thinking is there dead wood that Donald can bust up with the ax? Dead wood will not give heat a long time but I figger it will last thru the winter. And Ma, Uncle Dwight would give you food. Say to him when I get home I can work for him to pay the money it cost. I can rest easier if you would do that. I know he has food to eat and more.

I miss everyone and think about the new baby. I wish Donald had been learned to shoot to get you meat. Ma, I love you and all of them.

~Nathan Junior

The letter from Nate was sent from Benton to Jacksonville and a copy was put on file. A red notation on the copy advised, "Excellent progress and rehabilitation. Tries hard." It was put in an envelope and mailed to the Post Office in River Bend.

It had been days ago that the silent, unsmiling, uniformed officer had taken Nate to Benton. A short train trip, and the rest on horseback. Nate rode in shame with one arm shackled to the saddle horn.

The horse he rode was tethered to the officer's horse. Nate looked at the ground beneath the horse's feet as he rode along. The wind had laid somewhat, and the sun shone warm through his jacket, but there was no chance of removing it due to the shackled hand.

They stopped at a brook for the horses to drink and the officer tipped up his canteen, but Nate was ignored. It did not seem to matter that he was also thirsty. As he rode along, Nate prepared himself for the fact that Abe McCullough had been wrong. If he was not going to be put behind bars, why was he shackled to his saddle horn?

It was late afternoon when they had reached the Benton Correctional Institute. The long driveway was graveled and lined with trees, and the grass had been evenly cut by the sheep currently grazing on the brown remnants.

There were several large, white buildings on the institute grounds, picturesquely set within the groves of tall trees. A group of boys with shovels was digging in a patch of ground. The officer removed the shackle from the saddle horn and attached it to his own arm before marching pompously to the first building.

"I have brought you Nathan Baker, Junior. He's the one that shot the Revenue Officer."

"But he shot my pa," Nate defended.

Both men looked accusingly at Nate and he ducked his head. He was forgetting what Abe had told him about keeping quiet.

The man at the desk told the officer, "Take him on back to the dormitory. And you can take off them shackles. We let 'em walk around free."

The dormitory was full of beds, narrow with solid steel frames. Nate was assigned a bed next to the wall. A locker beside it contained a pillow and some bed linen and towels.

A large man came for him. In a small office nearby, he told Nate to sit.

"Now, son, I got a little advice for you. They ain't no use in you tryin' to get away. They got no bars nor locks here but them as runs away gets hauled back and they got a spend double time at a place where they IS bars and locks. Now, the time you'll be with us, you gonna get clothes you can wear and work you can do and then you gonna study books. Records I got on you say you never got to finish the sixth grade. That'd be the way with most of 'em we get, but you gonna get your chance. You gonna get the schoolin' you never had no chance to get before.

"'Nother thing, you gonna be fed three times every day, all you want to eat of whatever we got. We growed everything right here with you boys tendin' the ground. It's been put up in jars by you boys. Meat's all been butchered by you boys. You bein' here in the winter, you gonna be doin' a lot of manure spreadin' and ground turnin' with a shovel. Come spring, you gonna be helpin' to put in the early crop. That'd be 'bout the most of the rules I got'a pass on to you. You thinkin' on anything you need to ask 'bout?"

Nate had a thought. "Is they paper so as I could write a line to my ma, her bein' worried by now to hear about me?"

The man nodded. "You done got paper and pencil, up top in your locker. Get your letter wrote and hand it to me and it'll get to your ma."

They walked to the locker together.

"Stuff in that locker all mine?"

"Yep, while you live here, that locker'd be yours. You got'a wash them sheets and towels and all your clothes when they's dirty. That's the way we get our washin' done, with everybody doin' his own. The boys take turns helpin' with the cookin'. They'll be a sheet tellin' you when your turn is." The big man looked squarely at Nate and almost smiled. "We ain't gonna give you no trouble less'n you give trouble to us. Then you'd get it back. Double."

It sounded fair enough to Nate. He felt no need of more trouble, either giving or getting.

The man continued, "Next meal gonna be served around supper. You likely hungry now?"

Nate hesitated. He was always hungry, but there had been times when he had been a lot hungrier than he was now, and he certainly didn't want to give this big man any trouble.

The man told him, "Come on, son. I figure you to be hungry. Someone got'a show you where the kitchen is anyway."

Nate followed the man to another building. There were rows and rows of tables with attached benches. The man's booming voice called out, "Give this here young fella somethin' to hold him over till grub time."

A white clad man brought a large biscuit stuffed with sausage and a tall glass of creamy milk. If this was jail, Nate decided, then the guards must be angels.

The next day Nate worked. Hard. He pushed the sharp end of the shovel into the dirt and lifted the resulting clod, turning it bottom up in the hole he had just created, exactly the way he had been shown. A small earthworm wriggled out, then squirmed back into the dirt. Beside Nate, a stocky young man with black hair was doing the same thing.

"Name's Calvin. What's yours?"

"Nate. I mean to say, Nathan Baker."

"What you here for?"

"Shootin'."

"Sure enough? Me, too. Who'd you shoot?"

Nate hesitated and turned another shovel full of dirt. "Lawman," he finally admitted.

"Lawman? No lie?"

Nate shook his head. There was no reason to lie.

"Catch you doin' somethin'?"

Nate nodded.

"What?"

"Me and my pa was makin' moonshine likker."

"No lie! But they caught you? Why'n't your pa shoot 'em?"

"They got 'im first." Nate kept on digging.

"Got 'im? Bad?"

"Dead."

"Oh, man, I wasn't meanin' to say somethin' out'a the way. No offense?"

"No offense."

After a pause, "I shot my pa."

Nate stopped with shovel poised in midair. "Huh?"

"Shot 'em. But I wasn't aimin' to."

Nate waited.

"Iffen I didn't, he was gonna hurt my ma. He was hittin' on her, all boozed up like he was, and I got me the gun. He seen the gun and turned on me."

Calvin dug another shovel full and sniffed loudly. "Never used no gun in all my life. Was thinkin' I could scare Pa into stoppin' what he was doin', but when he turned on me, he was a'gonna get the gun out'a my hand. I hung onto it, thinkin' he'd turn it on Ma, for sure. One of us made it go off 'cause Pa, he fell down dead. Could'a been him, could'a been me. I don't know how to shoot no gun but the law, it said it was me as did the shootin'. Reckon it was, cause I was the only one left alive."

Nate wanted to respond to this painful confession but what could he say?

Calvin continued, "How much time you draw for killin' a lawman?"

"Didn't kill 'im. Bullet just winged 'im. They sayin' I got'a stay till I get to be sixteen. That'd be next May."

"Yeah? But it ain't bad here. Worse thing to me is the dreams. Middle of the night I dream I hear Ma scream 'cause Pa took to hittin' on her agin. I wake up and think 'bout him not gonna do that no more. They keep askin' am I sorry I done it and I say I am, but they's times I ain't. Most times I can rest my mind, knowin' he ain't gonna hit her no more."

Nate nodded. He now thought of something appropriate to say. "We both ain't got no pa."

Calvin sniffed and nodded. "What you gonna do when you go back home?"

"I ain't thought it out."

"You know about makin' moonshine?"

Nate nodded.

"You tell me how?"

"'Tain't somethin' that can be said. Got'a be showed."

"You show me?"

"We got a lot'a time yet to talk 'bout it."

"Where you live at?"

"You know River Bend? You go 'way past there. More'n twenty miles," Nate lied. There'd be time later to change his words. It didn't pay to be too easy with strangers, telling about where your house was. Even strangers as young as Calvin. That's what Pa always said.

Calvin was insistent. "Up a hill?"

"No. Flatland."

"Where at is the still?"

"Hole in the ground." At least that was truthful.

"I got'a come to where you live, sometime. They'd be money to be made at moonshinin', I'd reckon. My pa laid out a lot'a money for a jug. You gonna have a lot'a money, knowin' how to moonshine."

Nate's shovel dug silently.

"Ain't you?" Calvin insisted.

"I ain't thought it out, yet."

"What ya got else to think on?"

Silence hung heavy between them so Calvin changed the subject. "Lucky for you the lawman wasn't killed. You was lucky you missed 'im."

"Aimed to."

"Aimed to miss ' im?'"

Nate nodded. "Didn't aim to hit 'im a'tall. Reckon I was scairt and didn't aim away from 'im, far 'nuff."

"You could'a killed him if you'd'a wanted to?"

"Reckon I could. Be a sight easier'n dropping a squirrel at fifty paces."

Calvin had stopped, leaning on his shovel, and stared at Nate, totally impressed. The supper bell drowned out any need to respond.

The boys took their shovels to the shed and scrubbed their hands and faces in the washroom.

Supper was beans cooked with pork feet, a whole pork hock for each plate. Cabbage simmered tender and potatoes fried with eggs and peppers. And there was pie made from dried apples. There were second helpings for all who could hold them. And milk. There was all the milk that anyone wanted to drink.

Nate ate the food and wondered what was being served at home. If they could just make it until spring, he'd be home and take care of the problems. He wasn't sure just how, but it would happen. It was his duty, wasn't it? He'd get food for them, even if he had to run off a batch or two of moonshine. He really shouldn't have to make very much. Just enough to give him time to make plans. Uncle Dwight never made moonshine and he had food. He'd be the one to ask what to do.

Yep, Uncle Dwight, he'd be the one. He and Donald would just have to work it out. If they could just make the winter....

9

Sunrise saw Floralee and her daughters three miles from town. They ate the cold biscuits as they crunched along the gravel. The mule plodded step after weary step until he reached the brick streets of Jacksonville.

The Jacksonville secondhand clothing store was near to the hitching yard in the court house square, so that was a likely place to start the day. The store was a large warehouse with racks of hanging garments and boxes of tossed and tangled socks, underwear, and flannel shirts with the elbows worn thin.

The girls had to have coats, that was a must. They were growing so fast and the coat Betty Lou wore last year could not be handed down to

Charity. It had fallen apart from exhaustion. The sleeves had pulled loose and there was no fabric to sew them back.

The pleasant, white-haired clerk saw the woman with the fiery red curly hair and the two red-haired girls come into the store and walk toward the winter coats. She saw the swollen stomach of the woman and sighed.

"Can I show you something?" she inquired.

"Reckon we need coats and things, and was lookin' at the prices here."

"What sizes will you be needing?"

"Reckon most all of 'em."

The clerk smiled with understanding. "The girls' coats are here, and the rack beyond has the boys' coats and jackets. Being late in the year as it is, there ain't too much left."

Floralee nodded, and the girls began to look at the coats. "Lookie here, Betty Lou, at this'n. Looks like it'd fit you. Ain't them buttons purty? Here, put it on."

Betty Lou slipped it on. It was somewhat too big which meant it was just right. The scrap of paper pinned to the sleeve said twelve cents. Floralee pressed her lips together and took a deep breath. The coat did look so pretty on Betty Lou, and it was hardly worn at all. The girl was looking at her with eager eyes. She could only answer, "We gonna have to see how things comes out. You find one, Sarah."

Sarah nodded and slipped into the coat made of green and brown plaid wool with brown velvet on the collar and cuffs. It had deep, warm pockets and only one button missing. The price on it was fifteen cents. Coralee turned to the smaller coats. There was a bright red one with a fuzzy black scarf that came with it. She measured the shoulders against her memory of Charity's size and bit her lip. It was also fifteen cents but Charity loved anything red.

"Girls, we gotta go over to the stock barn first and see what comes up in the auction. Then we'll get what we can do after that. Reckon I ought'a be lookin' at the underwear."

Sarah and Betty Lou were accustomed to waiting. They amused themselves by looking at dresses they could never have, and partially worn shoes that really did not fit their feet, but that had pretty bows and buckles.

Floralee began to dig through the bins of tangled underwear. The clerk stood nearby. Floralee lowered her voice. "Ma'am, iffen you had things that nobody wanted to buy after you kept them here a long time, bein' old and all, where would you be throwin' 'em out? I wouldn't be askin' this iffen it wasn't a thing I was forced to do...needin' clothes for them youngens...? Like I do?"

The clerk nodded, sympathetically. "You picked a good day to come in here. The people that own this store said for me to be throwin' out some things that wasn't sellin' too good. You find yourself handy with a needle?"

Floralee nodded eagerly. "My man, he got hisself killed and...."

The clerk touched Floralee's arm. "Oh, honey, I can feel your sorrow."

Floralee nodded without speaking. This was not the time to mourn Nathan. She continued, "And I was gonna say, I was havin' to cut down some clothes of his'n to fit my biggest boy, bein' almost sixteen. Iffen I couldn't use a needle, we'd be in a bad way."

The clerk nodded. "I'll tell you what. You mentioned you had places you had to go, so if you went there and then came back, I could have them 'throw away' things ready for you and you could buy what you wanted after that."

Floralee nodded. "Reckon I'd be wantin' to lay aside them three coats we was lookin' at. Happen we got the money left, I aim to get them for my girls."

There were no other women or girls at the cattle auction barn. Floralee looked and felt out of place, and the girls shrank away against the walls, trying to become invisible. They waited and watched as sheep, goats, cows, and mules were sold. The cows brought a good price, perhaps she should consider selling both of hers, since they required so much feed to get through the winter.

Then came the pigs and sows. Her father had been partial to Hampshires with their black rumps and white shoulders, appearing to be wearing jackets. Since she knew basically nothing about any breed, she hoped to be able to get some Hampshires for a start.

There were brood sows a'plenty, most of them bred, but that was like buying a question mark, and most of them were $4.00, sometimes more. If the sow died from the trip home, there went the $4.00 and she had no more access to pockets containing coins from the selling of moonshine from which she could extract a few pennies here and a few there.

Young pigs came through, but while she was weighing the matter, they were sold and gone. She rashly decided to bid on the next lot coming through the ring if they appeared to be Hampshires. Then came the four young snorting animals with the required white band. She cut off the auctioneer at $1.00 but the price went up to $1.10. She raised it to $1.25, and it went to $1.40. Coralee took a deep breath and raised it to $2.00 and she had four pigs.

Then there was the very skinny sow, trying to feed a litter of six very young pigs. Floralee got the entire lot for $5.50. That was enough to start her hog raising venture. She started to leave, but the next lot was a group of seven, and they were very young. They stumbled weakly into the ring, one of them falling over and refusing to stand. Perhaps it was the maternal instinct that glued her eyes to the tiny animals.

The auctioneer explained, "The sow died a few hours back, and we're runnin' the pigs on through alone. Lookin' for a bid, gimme a bid, gimme a bid, I say...."

The sound of the auctioneer's song echoed out in the huge barn and the fate of the seven tiny animals hung in the balance. "Lookin' for a bid, gimme a bid, gimme a bid. Start somewhere, folks, we ain't got all day. Gimme a bid, gimme a bid...."

Floralee heard her voice as though it belonged to another person. "A dollar and a quarter."

The auctioneer looked in her direction, startled, and other heads turned toward her. Sarah and Betty Lou sank to their knees in embarssment, hunkering down out of the crowd, but Floralee's red hair burned brightly in the sea of cloth caps, hats and greased-down hair.

"Who'll gimme more, gimme more, gimme more? Got a dollar and a quarter, now, who'll gimme more? Anybody? Got me a dollar and a quarter once, got it twice and if you're gonna give me a bid you better do it now. Got me a dollar and a quarter three times and gone, and I sold a litter of pigs with no mama. Take 'em away."

Panic descended upon Floralee. Acting on impulse was a thing she had no experience in doing, and in the heat of the steamy barn, she broke into a sweat and her head began to whirl. The smell and the noise closed in upon her, choking her.

"Ma? You sick, Ma?" Sarah caught her mother's arm and demanded, urgently, "You gonna be sick, Ma?"

Floralee looked at her frightened daughters. "No, I reckon not. We just got'a get out'a here, us havin' all the pigs we gonna need."

Her mind was running on several tracks, simultaneously. How many pigs had she bought, how much money had she spent and how much was left, and was she going to get out of here before she fainted and scared the girls even worse than she already had?

Let's see, four from the first group, six with the mama and seven without a mama made seventeen pigs and the sow. It was clear, she shouldn't have bought the first four. How was the mule ever going to get them home, and she still had to buy some mash to feed them. *Lord a'mercy, I got'a get out'a here.* She paid her $8.50 and promised to be back with the wagon.

The ancient wagon was fairly large, as was required by a large family, but the sow and the pigs completely filled it. She had yet to stop at the feed store and the clothing store.

The one hundred pounds of the wheat bran required to make hog feed for the young pigs was fitted in front of the buckboard seat and they put their feet on it. She bought a pound of turnip seed at the feed store.

"What you want with them seeds, winter comin' on?" commented the clerk, conversationally.

"Reckon they'll keep till spring, don't you speck?"

"Reckon so. Turnip seed'd last a hunnerd years and still sprout, iffen you was to breathe a warm breath on 'em."

At the clothing store, Floralee considered. She now had less than ten dollars, but the coats had to be bought.

The clerk was expecting her. "I got the boxes out back, just bring your wagon around."

"But I need to buy them coats," Floralee reminded her.

"Sorry to tell you, ma'am, but them coats ain't hangin' there no more."

Floralee felt sick again. "Reckon we got'a go look at them that's left over there."

But the sales clerk insisted, "Ma'am, if you was to ask me, I'd be sayin' that next week'd be a better time to be buyin' girl's coats, them over there bein' picked over, you might say. I'd be waiting to get a better bargain, if you was to get the meanin' of my words."

Floralee nodded wearily. Too much had happened today and she had to get home. She directed the mule to the rear of the store and three large boxes were waiting. But where would she put them?

The girls would have to hold them in their laps all the way home, but the clothes, or whatever was in the boxes, were free and she would find a place for them, and she would plan to come back for the coats next week. What was another seven days of cold after a lifetime?

The bone-weary woman turned onto the brick street, but instead of heading east toward River Bend, she urged the mule toward Main Street. There, in front of the ice cream store, she stopped and tied the mule to a lamppost.

The girls exchanged excited glances. Ice cream! Inside, Floralee told the clerk, "Two triple dip cones of chocolate ice cream."

While the clerk was filling the cones, Floralee asked, "How much is a cone with no ice cream?"

"Huh?"

"An empty cone," she repeated. The clerk handed her one, and handed the two full ones to the girls, "Ten cents, please."

Floralee handed him a dime. Then she tipped the top dip of Sarah's cone and then the top dip of Betty Lou's cone into the empty one. They licked the cones slowly as the mule clomp-clomped toward River Bend.

The motherless pigs were shivering in one corner of the wagon and the sow kept trying to stand, causing the wagon to rock precariously. "Good Lord, please make this thing hold together tilst we get it home," Floralee breathed.

"Girls, we got'a put our knee quilt over them pigs. I know we gonna get awful cold, but I reckon we gonna live, and maybe them pigs ain't."

Betty Lou stood up on the buckboard and spread the worn quilt over the tiny pigs and the sow. They quieted down, settling into the bed of the wagon to sleep.

"Ma, reckon they's somethin' in these boxes to put over our knees to keep off the cold?"

Sarah reached deep in the box, feeling for something thick and warm. Her hand touched a woolly garment and she pulled it out. It was the black scarf that went to the red coat Floralee had picked out for Charity.

"Ma, lookie!"

Sarah rammed her arm into the box again and drew out the red coat. The next plunge brought up the blue coat with the pretty buttons. But there was no other coat in the box.

Sarah eagerly searched the next box and brought up a soft brown plaid coat. A woman's coat.

"Ma, lookie, it's the wrong one," she wailed.

"Likely that'n was meant to be for Ma," Betty Lou suggested and Sarah's next reach brought up the green and brown plaid she had liked. The paper price tags were still pinned to the sleeve. Almost fifty cents, total.

"Don't pull no more of that stuff out, Sarah, bein' the chance we'd drop somethin' along the way. I ain't knowin' if what the lady done was right or wrong, but we gonna be thankin' the Good Lord for the gift, and askin' Him to be blessin' the one it come from. I'm bein' sure He'd be the one back of it, somewheres."

It was dusky dark by the time the mule plodded its way to the hill and began the climb. The weary animal leaned into the traces and placed one foot after the other but the wagon scarcely moved.

"We got'a get out and help him, girls. Jump out there, now."

"But, Ma, the clay gonna ruin our shoes, walkin'."

"We ain't gonna be just walking. We gonna push the wagon to help out that old mule 'afore he dies in the harness."

"Push the wagon?"

"Take off your shoes and put 'em on the buckboard." Floralee had already removed hers. "Now jump out and lean on that tailgate. We got us less'n a half a mile to go."

The cold, clammy clay stuck to their feet and squirmed up between their toes, and the sharp rocks ground against their icy feet as they dug in to push, applying their shoulders to the endgate. The cold, wet soil drew the last shred of warmth from their bodies and the splintery bed of the wagon dug into their shoulders. But the new coats were piled safely on the buckboard seat.

Their feet buried to the ankles in the cold mud and their stomachs growled from hunger as they strained against the wagonload of pigs. The timbered woodland was fast darkening around them, the tree trunks turned into pillars of blackness.

Slowly, the wagon full of pigs began to move forward, creeping, inching upward, and its weight cutting into the rutted trail. The sticky clay built up on the wheels in globs and chunks, finally falling off to roll down the hill against bare feet, numbed with the cold.

Sarah clinched her teeth and shoved, her frozen feet sliding in the slick mud, and Betty Lou wiped her ragged sleeve over her face, spreading tears and dirt across her cheek.

The leafless trees were now a bank of blackness against the evening grayness of the woods. Floralee, walking between the girls, straining her weight against the wagon, was no longer conscious of the cold on her feet. Between ragged breaths, she decided, "We got'a do somethin' with this road."

They turned at the curve, midway up the hill, and a light was visible in the cabin window. The thoughts of what could be done to the road absorbed Floralee, pulling her attention away from her icy, bare feet that had no feeling left in them.

"Reckon we could throw limbs and brush on it, keepin' the clay off'a the wagon wheels," she commented to the darkness.

There came a dreaded sound, a vibration in the wagon bed, a sickening crunch, and Floralee's mind refused, at first, to recognize the origin. Then she yelled, "Git back, girls!"

Her warning was seconds too late. Betty Lou's screams startled the mule into a lunge and the sound of it brought Donald running from the cabin. The crunch was followed by the squeaking grind of rusted metal separating from rotted wood, and old planks being torn into splinters.

One corner of the wagon was now dragging in the mud and a wheel rolled drunkenly down the hill.

"Ma, my foot!" wailed Betty Lou.

The sow and pigs had slid toward the sinking corner of the wagon, their weight splintering the rotting sideboard and ripping it away from the wagon bed. Floralee's first thought was of the animals.

"Donald, catch them pigs and don't let 'em run off. Get the big 'ens first."

Betty Lou's foot would just have to wait.

"Sarah, watch out for that sow, she may get mad and turn on you."

Donald couldn't tell big pigs from little ones, as they scattered in the dark woods. He followed sounds that scampered through the dry leaves. The weary, underfed sow presented no problem. She did not try to get up from where she had fallen into a heap of dry leaves.

Floralee saw Charity running toward them. "Charity, darlin', try and catch one of them little pigs. If you can, get it into the shed."

Floralee didn't see Sarah but she knew whatever Sarah was doing, it was something that needed to be done.

"How many pigs did you get, Ma?" Donald asked.

"Seventeen," she shouted back to him. "How many did you catch?"

"Six," came the dispirited reply.

"Come and get this'n. That'll make seven."

Sarah reappeared, "I got them new clothes on inside, Ma, so the pigs wouldn't be tramplin' on 'em. Gonna help catch pigs, now."

Betty Lou sat on the wet, cold ground with her foot pinned under the broken wagon bed. The sow lay beside her, its breath rasping heavily. The girl leaned back and reached behind her toward the side of the road for something to dig with. Her hand located a stiff twig from the oak tree and with it, she began to dig away at the clay from beside her foot.

Using both hands, she slid the injured foot painfully sideways into the hole she had dug. Then, crawling on both hands and the uninjured foot, the girl made her way to the cabin.

Floralee unhitched the mule and led him to the shed. Sheer and total exhaustion had slowed her steps…as steps are slowed in a dream. Maybe this was a dream, or more likely a nightmare. But she must hold on a little longer.

"How many pigs you caught?"

"Eleven."

Floralee went back to the sow. The weary beast did not want to get up. She knew exactly how the unfortunate animal felt, but the nightmare was not over for either of them. She twisted the ragged ears to bring up enough pain to make the animal move. The sow grunted, heaved herself to her feet and stumbled slowly along in the direction she was being pushed. A little farther…and a little farther….

Finally reaching the shed, the sow flopped to the ground again as soon as Floralee stopped pushing.

"How many pigs you find?"

"Sixteen."

"Good job. Just find one more."

The small boy turned and was enveloped into the darkness of the hillside. Floralee went back to the broken wagon. The one hundred pound sack of wheat bran had been thrown clear and was luckily unbroken, but it could not be left outside on the damp ground. She was not sure there was enough combined strength among them to carry the sack, but she had no choice.

"Donald, Sarah, Charity, come help me carry this pig feed. Donald, you get a corner and help Sarah. Charity, you come help me. All together, now." Surprisingly, the heavy bag arose on the eight combined legs and moved along toward the shed.

The sow was still lying where she had flopped. Something had to be done for her. Her life was essential to Floralee's plans for the farm, and whatever sacrifice was needed to be made for her, must now be made.

"Charity, go get me all the milk we got in the house. Bring it in that pail you gathered them chunky pins in."

"All the milk?"

"Yes, darlin'. All of it. And bring a big spoon. The rest of you go look for that other pig."

Charity brought about two quarts of milk. Coralee scooped wheat bran into the milk and stirred it into a smooth paste. The warm, wheat smell of it arose from the bucket. Her own stomach growled in hungry response to the smell. She lifted the spoon to her mouth and tasted it. Its rich, earthy taste was pleasant, so she ate another bite, then another. Then she spooned the mash into the sow's mouth, rubbing the leather ears and throat, encouraging her to swallow. It was most essential to her plan that the mama pig live.

Donald was standing beside her. "Ma, we found that pig."

"Good, son."

"No, Ma. The pig's dead."

"Dead?"

"Yeah, Ma. Wagon hit it when it broke."

"Little'n or big'n?"

"Little'n."

"Take it to the house and find me a sharp knife and have it ready. We gonna have dumplin's tomorrow. You go in and stoke up the fire. It's still gonna take me a little time here, then I'll be in."

Donald left the shed carrying the tiny, limp pig.

The sow grunted contentedly, swallowing the mash Floralee pushed into her mouth. When the mash was gone, the exhausted woman closed the shed and trudged wearily to the cabin.

Donald had a crackling fire going in the cookstove and Sarah was examining Betty Lou's rapidly swelling foot. Charity was carefully removing garments from one of the boxes while wearing the red coat.

Floralee poured water from the teakettle into a pan and stirred in some cornmeal. When the mush had simmered to thickness, she ladled it into bowls.

"Put you a chunk of that butter on your mush, us not havin' any milk. Charity, put them things back in the box till morning, so as we can all look at 'em together, bein' rested."

Finally Floralee was able to stretch out on the feather tick bed and pull the quilt over her. The eternal day was, at last, over. She had the pigs and had gotten them safely home. By some miracle she had yet to consider, the girls had coats, and there were several more usable items and others to be repaired. She could now relax and gain some strength for the demands of tomorrow.

She breathed deeply and closed her eyes. Then in the back of her leg, she felt the familiar pull of a cramp. The pain expanded into a lightning bolt of fire. Easing out of the bed, she extended her foot to the floor. This was going to be a bad one.

Resigned, she put water in the pail to heat. Sometimes a hot foot-bath brought relief. While the water heated, she walked from room to room, attempting to ease the pain.

When the first steam arose from the water, she set the bucket beside the table and lowered her feet into it. Waves of warm relief undulated up her calves and thighs. The grip of the cramp lessened. She leaned her face forward onto her weary forearms and heaved a sigh.

She awakened to the light of dawn filtering through the window. The bucket of water, now icy cold, was still on the floor, so she must have removed her feet from it sometime in the night. Her bare feet, also icy cold, were resting on the drafty cabin floor.

Outside the cabin, she heard horses and the crunch of gravel. What now? She dreaded to look out the window. Surely it was not another dream. She was too weary and drained for the happenings to be other than real.

There came a rapid, light tap at the door.

"Floralee?"

She recognized the voice of Nathan's older brother.

"Come on in, Dwight." Coralee did not care that she was wearing only her nightgown. Weariness had sapped the strength of her reasoning.

The slightly older version of Nathan stepped through the door.

"I see I was a mite too late in comin'. I brung you another wagon, knowin' that one you got wasn't gonna last too long. I see it broke down on you already. Wantin' to give you that mule I got hitched to the wagon, too. That mule'a yours is a bit old for pullin' a loaded wagon up your hill."

Floralee could only stare dumbly at her brother-in-law, unable to comprehend the enormity of the gift.

Dwight continued, "Put you some taters and a sack of beans on that wagon, and a bushel'a pears. Figured you could find a use for 'em."

Floralee still could not answer.

He continued, "Knowd you been needin' things right along, but Nathan'd'a blowed off my head with a shotgun if I'd'a brought 'em to you, him thinkin' I was wantin' to put my hands on his woman."

He paused before making his last offer. "Now, iffen you get down to needin' somethin' you ain't got and can't get, send Donald down to get me and likely I'll be able to figger somethin' out. Now, I got my saddle horse out here so I'll be gettin' back down to work. Mind what I say if you need somethin'." Then he turned to go.

"Dwight?"

"Huh?"

Floralee sighed deeply. "How does a body find words to say thanks for what you just done?"

Dwight grinned, aimably. "You just found 'em.'" And he was gone.

Floralee leaned forward against the solid plank table and began to sob. Tears flowed over her forearms and onto the table. She didn't even go look at the wagon Dwight had left her.

The goats began to bleat for attention and the kitchen stove was stone cold. Floralee squared her shoulders, wiped her eyes and began to build a fire.

"Donald, Sarah, Betty Lou? Get up, now."

Biscuits with apple butter took care of breakfast and now the pork of the small pig was simmering in a large kettle. The delicious smell of it filled the tiny cabin.

The children gathered around the clothing boxes. There were suits of underwear with most of the buttons still on them, and flannel shirts of all sizes. Some of them had no holes at all. There was a large bundle of socks and several of them were mates. There were dresses in the approximate size of Sarah and Betty Lou and a few baby clothes.

There were two pairs of shoes, strangely in almost the right sizes for Betty Lou and Sarah. The prices were still pinned to the garments. *Thank you, Lord, from wherever this gift came from.*

The children prepared to tend the animals.

"Ma, all them little pigs is aimin' to nurse off that sow."

"Allowed that'd happen. That sow got'a be fed extra. She standin' up?"

"No."

"We got'a work on that. Donald, you carry them biggest pigs out to your pen and pick up some acorns for the sow. Betty Lou, let me feel that foot."

The little girl's foot was badly skinned and swollen but she could still hobble along on her heel. Floralee made her soak it in alum water and she wrapped it tightly in a rag, chiding herself that she had not looked at it last night. Her cup of exhaustion had been full to running over, just too weary to think straight.

"Sarah, go out and dip up a kettle of that wheat bran, keepin' it clean, to bring in. Charity, darlin', set that corn grinder up on the table and get them chinky pins you hulled. And take off that red coat, 'afore you mess it up."

The wild chestnuts went into the grinder and came out in a fine, fragrant, slightly oily powder.

"Sarah, you take Henry and Charity and go up the hill and pick up more chinky pins."

"How come?" Sarah could not resist the question.

"Ain't sure, yet. Just go do it."

She wanted them gone from the house. She had explained that the wagon and mule were a present from Uncle Dwight but now she wanted to go examine it by herself.

She wanted to put it away, herself. She wanted to unhitch the young, strong mule with her own hands, and turn him loose in the corral. She wanted to feel the golden smoothness of the pears and the shiny hardness of the dried beans. She wanted to thrust her hand deeply into the beans, cool and brown, and she wanted to be alone with her thankfulness to God and the giver. She set Betty Lou to sewing missing buttons onto underwear, and then she went outside.

First she patted the pale, exploring nose of the mule. For certain, now, the cows would have to go. With another mule to feed, the hay would not last.

At midday, Floralee divided the stewed pork into two quantities, setting half of it aside. She dropped dumplings, light and filling, into half the broth. She measured into the mixing bowl one cup of cornmeal and one cup of chinky pin flour, another of cornmeal and another of the nut flour.

"Ma, what you doin'?"

She did not respond and Betty Lou did not press the question.

The bread rose up in the skillet and Floralee shook the pan to settle the bubbles. When it became solid, she loosened the edges and turned it. It began to rise slowly once more, golden and brown.

Shivers of excitement played on her back and arms. "We shall rise up like a pan of bread, slow, flat and all together," she whispered to herself. "You promised, Lord, and I know You'll be good to Your word." She cut the bread into wedges and put the skillet on the table.

"Ma, this cornbread's different," pronounced Sarah. "Tastes like you put more grease in it."

"Yeah, it don't hardly even need butter."

Betty Lou looked at her mama and grinned. Floralee grinned back. "Reckon we figured out how to make that cornmeal last till growin' season. Donald, you want more of them dumplins? They's lots of 'em?"

Donald extended his plate for a refill.

"Donald, you get through eatin', you got'a go throw some tree limbs on the road. Gather up them you cut off to make the pigpen rails and lay 'em across the muddy places. We gonna take that new wagon and go over to the church in the mornin'. You girls pick out somethin' nice to wear."

"Church?"

Floralee nodded. "We gonna drive that wagon and mule Uncle Dwight give to us. It'll be sure to get us there and back."

She let her eyes move around the table at the six children. The red hair of the Callahan's had left its mark on all of them. Red curls, freckles and sky blue eyes. Six versions of the same coloring. Beautiful, alert and only occasionally disobedient, they were her reason for living.

"Ma?"

"Huh, Donald?"

"Ain't meanin' to make you sad or nothin', but it keeps bein' in my mind to ask. Reckon when Nate gonna be comin' home?"

"Wisht I knowed that myself, Donald. Had it in my mind to check on that but I reckoned it weren't decided. Got'a make a trip into the sheriff, come next week, needin' to find out."

"Ma?"

"Huh, Sarah?"

"You likin' the way Pa's fiddle hangs there on the wall?"

"Hadn't thought on it, Sarah. How come you to ask?"

"Ma, I look at that fiddle and I think Pa gonna maybe come walkin' in and sayin', 'Hey, there, Punkin pie, I'm gonna eat you up, I am', and then I 'member he ain't gonna do that no more." Sarah pressed her knuckles against her eyes and bowed her head.

Charity sniffed, loudly. Betty Lou hobbled hurriedly to the lean-to with Charity close behind. Naomi slid off her bench and hid her face in her mother's lap. Little Henry spooned dumplings into his mouth, bite after bite, chewing with fierce determination.

"Ma," Donald told her, "Reckon I'll be goin' out to pitch limbs on that road." He turned quickly to keep his mother from seeing him rub his eyes.

Floralee called him back. She put her arm around him and pulled him close, "Donald, you been actin' like a big man for five days and you done got behind on bein' a boy what lost a Pa and a brother, and you got tears that ought'a come out."

Donald ducked away from her, refusing to look at her face.

"Donald, you got'a look at me."

He slowly turned toward her, the blue eyes were brimming with unshed tears. She held him with her gaze and the tears flowed down his face. He leaned against her shoulder and put his arms around her neck. She smoothed the tight, red curls as he sobbed.

Henry put down his spoon and came to lean against Donald, whimpering and sniffing. Floralee included him in her embrace until the sobs died away, but her own blue eyes were dry.

She had no tears for Nathan Baker. She missed him, she loved him, and she wished he would come walking through the door, but still she had no tears to shed.

Donald pulled away from her arms and went to the yard with Henry close behind. Floralee put the drowsy Naomi in bed in the lean-to and lifted Nathan's fiddle down from the wall. She smoothed her hand along the worn wood and held it close for a moment. Then she wrapped it in a torn piece of blanket and slipped it under the plank bed.

The children were all out of the room, a rare occurrence. An empty house meant an opportunity to talk privately with God.

"Lord, You was good to give me these youngens, knowin' I'd not be makin' it alone. I was needin' them, and the love I have for them, to keep me pushin' on."

She had sat down for a moment beside the sleeping Naomi when the door darkened. Floralee looked up and saw Nathan's younger brother.

"Hello, Vern."

Vern grinned, "Hello there to you, Floralee, honey."

"What you want, Vern?"

"Tain't what I want. It'd be what I come to give. Somethin' you gonna be needin'."

Floralee watched him and made no comment.

"I just come to say, my brother bein' gone and all, that I know you to be in need of the lovin' you was accustomed to gettin' from him. A good lookin' woman like you, they ain't no need of you doin' without lovin' and me bein' a stone's throw away, you might say. Come time you get them youngens off to school, I can be comin' on over from time to time to help you out, you missin' bein' alone with him."

Floralee moved slowly toward the wall and lifted down the rifle.

"Been thinkin' on doin' a little huntin'," she said quietly. "Beats me how the hair'a your head puts me in mind of a squirrel's tail and me lovin' a mess of squirrel stew. And reckon how it'd look, me and your wife livin' alone up here on this hill with all these youngens, all on account'a you lookin' so much like a squirrel?"

Vern began to retreat backward into the yard, stumbling over a loose stone. His whiny voice chided, "Ain't no call fer you to be so huffy, me makin' you a civil offer like I done. Could be you'll be changin' your mind of a long, cold winter day."

Floralee sighed a long, weary breath. "Don't you be waitin' on it. Right now, I got me a powerful urge for squirrel stew."

By now, Vern was at the edge of the yard and he hurriedly ducked between the trees and was gone. Floralee chuckled to herself as she hung the rifle over the door in its place. On second thought, she might very well go shoot a squirrel. The sound of it was tempting.

She walked out to the shed and noted the old sow was now on her feet, exploring the ground for food. Floralee dropped a handful of the acorns over the fence and the crunch of the nuts in the sow's mouth was like music to her ears. They would rise. They would all rise to the beat of the music of the acorns in the mouth of the mama hog. She and her children, they would all rise just as they had always been meant to do.

However slow it would be, they would rise and it would be on the back of this old mama pig and her noisy brood that they would do it. Just as she had always known it could happen. They had bushels and bushels of acorns and chestnuts and a half a dozen pairs of hands to gather them.

Floralee turned her face upward to the afternoon sun. She felt energy flow into her arms and she raised them over her head. Perhaps, someday she would be like Rev. McCrey had said, and she would run without being weary and walk without feeling faint. But it would be a while, yet.

She went back to the cabin and got the pound of turnip seeds and a rake. She climbed the steep hill behind her cabin and studied the ground beneath her feet. With the rake, she pulled aside the dead leaves, exposing a long strip of earth, zigzagging the furrow through the trees. She scattered the seeds and pulled leaves and raked soil back over them.

Of course, she might get nothing; then, again, she might have very early turnip greens. One must plant if one expects a harvest.

10

It was on a day that Betty Lou did not go to school because of a bad cough, that Donald came into the cabin alone.

"Donald, you come home with Charity?"

"Yeah, Ma."

"Didn't see her. Where at did she go?

"Reckon she snuck up the hill to look at the book."

"What book?"

"The one she brung home."

"School book?"

"Nope. Picture book."

"Where at did she get it?"

"Down at the Mercantile."

"How did she get it? Havin' no money?"

"Took it."

"You mean she just up and took it? 'Thout askin' nor payin' for it?"

"Yep."

"Donald, you lookie here at me. You sayin' Charity picked up a book at the Mercantile and walked off with it? And you let her?"

"Yep."

"Where at she go?"

"Up to the rocks, I reckon."

Floralee sighed and began to climb. She was sure Donald had been right, and that Charity would be in her private place crouched down between two huge rocks. She would be wedged into a crevice not two feet wide. Tidy as a chinky pin inside it's burr. She could hear Charity's voice before she could see her.

"And that one. And that one. And that one. Ma'd get this one. And this one. And this one."

Floralee paused and listened. A page turned. Charity continued, "And them shoes and them shoes and them shoes."

Strange storybook, Floralee thought, but Charity loved all storybooks. But how could she just to go into the store and pick one up? And Charity being her own daughter? The disgrace was unthinkable! Charity's voice went on, "The new baby gonna get this, and this, and this, and…."

Floralee crept around the boulder. Charity was seated in the deep rock crevasse where Floralee knew she would be. She had a very large book in her lap and she turned another page, studying the colorful pictures.

Floralee took another two steps and sighed. At the sound, Charity startled and clutched the book to her chest, staring at her mother over the top of the rock. The name of the book was "Merchandise Brochure for Retail Stores."

"It's mine, Ma. I got it, myself."

"Charity, just 'cause you picked up somethin' don't make it belong to you."

"But old man Jenkins ain't wantin' it."

"He say that to you?"

"No. But he don't."

"We got'a ask 'im does he want it? Folks don't have things in their stores they ain't wantin'."

"He throwed it away!" she insisted, tearfully.

"Now, Charity…honey…."

"But he did, Ma."

"Where at did he throw it?"

"In the burn barrel."

"Are you sure?"

"Sure, Ma."

"Did Donald see you get it out'a the barrel?"

"Yep. He helt me up to let me reach it."

"Let's look at it."

Charity opened the catalog. "It shows pictures of shoes and dresses. I seen baby dresses and dishes and everything. Don't say I got'a take it back!"

Floralee looked at the catalog. It was new but there were black marks of soot from the burn barrel. It must have indeed been thrown away. There were beautiful pictures on its shiny pages. There were shoes and gloves of every color. Everything!

"Ma?"

"What, Charity?"

"Money'd buy them things, huh?"

Floralee nodded.

"I want red shoes. They cost money?"

Floralee nodded again.

"Too much money?"

"Yes, Charity. When we got six people or seven or eight, it'd take too much money to buy red shoes for everyone."

"Ribbons, too?"

"Speck so, Charity. Reckon you got'a just say you got yourself a picture book, just showin' purty things to look at. Put it out'a your mind that them things could be got with money."

"Ma?"

"What, Charity?"

"Come time I get big, I got'a have me red shoes. You want red shoes?"

"Red shoes'd be good, but havin' boys and girls like I got, that'd be even better. Takes money for youngens and money for shoes. Shoes wear out and get throwed away but youngens grow up into people."

"Ma?"

"What, darlin'?"

"Reckon I'd sooner have the shoes, anyway."

"Charity, darlin', you gonna look at them old pictures and feel bad 'cause you ain't got them things? 'Cause if you are, we got'a throw out that old book. There ain't no call for you to be feelin' bad."

Charity pressed the catalog to her chest and her eyes widened. "No, Ma! No! I ain't wantin' to throw out my picture book. I ain't even seen it all, yet. You got'a let this here be my special book!"

Floralee looked from her daughter to the catalog. "Iffen you can think that book is a picture book, then you can keep it. You get to wantin' them things showed in that book, so as it hurts to look on 'em, then we gonna throw it out."

Charity did not take her eyes off her mother. "Mama, you and me, we gonna have us red shoes. I figure to have me lots of money someday, and we gonna have us red shoes. You gonna be glad on account'a me."

"I hope so, darlin'. Now we got'a go down and do our work. Come with me."

Charity carried her picture book under her arm and willingly went down the hill, but later that evening Floralee noticed that Sarah and Betty Lou were turning the pages slowly, discussing the clothes and shoes. The candlelight shone golden through their red curls as they bent to look at the shiny pictures.

It was starting, and it was part of her plan. A year ago it would not have occurred to the older girls to discuss, hopefully, the things they had never enjoyed and saw no hope of ever having. Now, however, some things seemed possible.

Charity stood looking over their shoulders. She spoke softly. "Had me money, I'd be buyin' all them things."

Sarah and Betty Lou didn't seem to hear her. They had ideas and plans of their own to discuss.

11

The days went on, and Floralee was weary all the time, now, totally ungainly and awkward. She was bone-marrow tired from mental and physical exhaustion. The children had worked hard with her and the whole family was meat hungry, though the mountains had small game aplenty.

It occurred to her that there was something terribly wrong about that. Living with a restriction for many years does not make it right, but long time habits seemingly had a mind of their own. They seemed to want to continue long after the cause of them was no longer present. There were certain things in her life that had been lacking, and she was determined to correct the situation. One of those things was the ability to free her thoughts.

Nathan had his own ideas regarding women and guns and didn't believe a girl should be taught to shoot. Her mind was full of the memories of his ways, and his words re-formed themselves inside her head. "Raise yerself a good girl," he had said, "and she gonna get herself a man to do for her, like you got. See, all that fancy shootin' you done when you was growin' up ain't never been needed. Me and Nate on that gun gonna be plenty to take care'a this family till Donald gets some size on 'im."

His words now echoed hollowly through her mind. Through years of experience, her mind had learned not to formulate a response to words her mind told her had no truth.

That day, however, her mind had the courage to retort, "Sure, Nathan, and where be you and Nate on this day? Iffen I only had me strength to be up and down the hill... why, I'd...? Hmmm. Just what WOULD she do?"

Her mind had more to say. "Nathan, why did you say them things to me? Why did I let you? This has got to stop. Them girls of mine, I gotta talk to them. They's things they got'a know that's got'a come from me. I've done 'em wrong. I can't let what happened to me happen to them."

She paused in her thinking as she realized what she would have to do, and how much of the responsibility rested with her. "Soon, I got'a talk to them," she instructed herself. "It'll be hard after all these years and them seein' what they have of the way I was treated... the way I let myself be treated. Them boys, too. They got'a see so's they don't learn from Nathan. That's just not the way'a things. A woman's a person, too."

Then she confronted him squarely but belatedly. "Nathan, it's in my mind you loved me in your way, strange like it was, and you wasn't meanin' to leave me just yet, but....But, Oh! Nathan! I just get so tired... from the memory you left me with. Likely it was how you was taught, but it ain't the way it ought'a be. It's a fact that it was the way I was taught from my ma and pa, too. We growed up thinkin' things was one way, and we were wrong! Girls and boys got equal rights to find their own way, 'thout one bein' the ruler over the other."

Sarah's soft voice broke into her mother's weighty thoughts. "Ma? We mighty nigh got no soap. Speck I ought'a use it on washin' the kettles or save it to wash clothes and baths."

Soap. All it took was ashes and grease, but the supply of grease was low. Grease was needed in the cornbread to cut the dryness, and there needed to be grease for the gravy, it was a necessary thing, needed to keep bodies warm in the winter. It was even possible to do without meat if there was enough grease. She had to have grease.

It was time to put action to her knowledge and cast aside her fatigue and mental exhaustion. There were those depending on her, and their father, weak though he was, had furnished only a small amount of support. But no longer....

"Sarah, wash up the kettles. We gonna make us some soap."

That evening Floralee asked Betty Lou, "You 'memberin' how to make soap?"

Betty Lou nodded, "Sure, but we got'a have grease."

"Sure and we gonna get grease. We gonna have a fat 'possum to render and give us the grease we need to get started. You gonna use half what we got and Charity gonna help you stir up the soap tomorrow. Me and Donald and Sarah, we're goin' huntin'."

"Where at?"

"Wherever they's a 'possum."

Donald had looked from one to the other. "Ma, we need to have us a dog to help hunt. 'Possum'd be easy to find, us havin' a good beagle."

Floralee looked at her son with a mind full of regret. A boy shouldn't have to mourn because he had no dog, but that was for later. Now, he must face the situation that was.

"We got us a dog, Donald?"

"No, Ma."

"Then we got'a do without a dog. Havin' no dog won't keep us from needin' to go find us a 'possum."

Donald sensed an ally and pressed his case. "Uncle Dwight, he's got a good dog. Likely, time he ain't usin' 'im...? Ma, I could...?"

"Donald, Uncle Dwight already done for us and we ain't askin' 'im for the use of his dog."

The boy sighed with resignation. "Sure, Ma."

Sarah had concerns of another sort, and touched her mother's arm. "Ma, you think you ought'a go out there?"

No, Floralee told herself. She knew she shouldn't go "out there," but realities must be faced. Sarah, also, must deal with what was, not what should be.

"Sarah, can you shoot the gun?"

"No, Ma, but...."

"Don't you worry none. Come time we get more shells to stand losin' a few, you gonna learn to shoot. All'a you youngens gonna learn. The exact day your arm is strong enough to yank up the barrel, that'll be the day you learn to shoot. Someone's missin'. Where at's Charity?"

me and Donald went to

Donald pointed up the hill with his elbow. "I seen 'er headin' up the hill. Ain't seen 'er come back down."

"Go up and get her. Ain't no use bein' out there, cold like it is. Go now."

Donald went.

Sarah began again. "Ma, think about if me and Donald went to find the 'possum, doin' all the walkin' it'd take. Then we'd find it and come for you. That'd save you some walkin' and lookin' around."

Betty Lou was nodding as Sarah talked. Sarah's words made sense, and deserved some thoughtful consideration.

Donald burst into the room. "I went like you said and I never saw her tilst I was all the way up the hill. Ma, Charity, she was scrunched down in them big rocks, talkin' things that ain't sense."

"What things?"

"Ma, she thinks Pa to be up there on the hill to talk to." Donald's eyes were wide with concern.

Sarah reached for her coat. "I can bring 'er down, Ma."

"No," her mother told her. "I got'a go. You say she went all the way up, Donald?"

"I can show ya, Ma."

"No. I reckon I best go alone." She put on her coat and buttoned it around her thick middle. "Sarah, you find somethin' warm to wear huntin' tomorrow, so you don't mess up good clothes."

Floralee stepped out into the north wind that came barreling over the top of the mountain. Her coat flapped against her knees and wind tore at the shawl over her head as she lifted one weary foot after the other and climbed the path to the hilltop.

Faintly, the sound came on the wind. Sobs and words torn from the heart of a seven-year-old child were poured forth. "Pa, how come you done things what got you took away? How come, Pa? You said you liked me but you lied, 'cause you ain't here. If you liked me, you would be here." Sobs shook her small body.

Floralee looked at her daughter, crouched on the damp ground and leaning against the cold, gray rock. Only a thin jacket was between her arm and the cold surface of the stone. Words continued to spill forth.

"Pa, you ain't never gonna let Nate come home, are you? I hate you for takin' Nate away from us." She sobbed again. "Pa, you always done what you wanted to, so now you just got'a want to come back. You got'a bring Nate. Nate, he just walked away like he never saw me watchin' 'im.

Nate got'a come back." The little girl leaned back against the rock and looked up toward the sky. She drew her sleeve across her wet eyes. "Pa, you hearin' me?"

Floralee walked softly around the rock toward Charity. She lowered her bulk to the ground beside the little girl.

Charity turned to her mother, "Ma, Pa ain't answerin' me. You speck he ain't listenin' like he weren't always listenin' when he was here? Times he weren't listenin' to me when he was lookin' straight at me. He thought I didn't know, but I knew. Ma, you speck Pa gonna come back, laughin' and singin' like he done, other times?"

Floralee reached her hand out to Charity. The wind blew a tangle of hair into the little girl's face. Her fingers drew back the tangled red curls and her arm pulled her closer.

"Charity, darlin', your pa, he can't come back. He wasn't aimin' to leave you, though. He didn't go away on purpose. He done things that made the bullets come, and the bullets made him go away. When that happens, he don't get to come back."

Charity looked at her mother with an unblinking gaze. "Pa never wanted to go?"

"No, darlin'. He weren't aimin' to go. They's things happen that even a pa got no way'a stoppin'."

"But, Ma...?"

"What, darlin'?"

"Nate did."

"Nate didn't want to go. No, darlin'...."

"He wanted to go. Nate always listened to me and when I looked at him, he always looked back. But he wanted to go with pa, 'stead'a stayin' with me."

"No, darlin'. Nate ain't with Pa."

"But Ma, I looked at him when he left and he never looked at me. He was just like Pa. I looked at him tilst I couldn't see 'im no more. He never looked at me one time."

"Charity, I got'a tell you somethin'. You ever see Nate cry?"

"No, Mama. Nate don't do no cryin'."

"Yes, Charity. Nate does some cryin' sometimes, just like you and me, but he never wanted you to see him do it."

"How come?"

"Nate was ashamed of tears. He wasn't wantin' to go away when he did. He knowd if he looked at you, likely he'd start to cry, wantin' to stay with us. He was thinkin' iffen he let hisself cry, that'd be what you'd always 'member tilst he could come back."

"Ma, he ain't comin' back. He went to Pa. Pa won't let 'im come back."

"No, Charity, darlin'. He thinks about you and all of us. He wasn't wantin' you to see tears in his eyes. Some grownup men are prideful like that and Nate's getting' to be grown up."

"Why?"

Floralee shook her head. "That'd be somethin' that's got no answer. Men have to be like men are, just like you and me, we gotta be like we are."

The cold seeped into Floralee's feet and legs bringing its stiffness, and the short winter evening was becoming night. It was time to get back to the warmth of the cabin.

"Ma?"

"What, darlin'?"

"I was figurin' if I could get Pa to listen, happen he'd send Nate back to us. That ain't gonna happen, now, is it? What we gonna do?"

"Darlin' little girl, Nate gonna be back but it ain't Pa that'll send him. Happen there'll be a day he'll come ridin' in on the dray and we'll go get him with our new wagon."

Charity looked up. "You sayin' that for sure, Ma?"

"For sure. You gonna believe me?"

Charity nodded.

"Now, honey, we gonna freeze iffen we don't go down. They's gonna be two icicles up here and Donald gonna say, 'Charity, I can see right through you, bein' a stick'a ice like you turned into'."

Charity chuckled at the joke, her eyes sparkling. "Aw, Ma!"

"Let's go, now. We got'a walk careful in the dark so's we don't stumble."

Floralee's feet had become numb knobs attached to tingling legs. Shivers of cold trembled from her shoulders to her knees where all feeling stopped. Charity followed behind, holding to her mother's coattail.

They reached the cabin and stepped into the candle-lit warmth. Henry and Naomi stared at them with large, inquiring eyes, but the others looked away in sympathy.

Floralee told them, cheerfully, "I figure this'd be a good night to parch corn on the stove. Donald, put in another stick'a wood. Betty Lou, you get a cup'a corn kernels. No, make it two cups."

The golden kernels of corn were put on the hot stove, a few at a time. With a spoon handle, they were kept moving and when they were smoking brown, they were flipped over. Then when they swelled into a fat, toasted ball, they were raked off the stove onto a platter to cool a little.

The delicious, toasted-corn goodness burst from the crunchy kernels as they were chewed. And parched corn required a lot of chewing.

Charity popped a kernel of toasted corn into her mouth. "Nate, he gonna be comin' home. He ain't gonna stay where he went."

Sarah looked at her and nodded, smiling. "You sayin' right. He's gonna come back."

Betty Lou handed Charity another kernel. "Charity, guess what? You and me, we gonna make soap, tomorrow. 'Thout no help. Just you and me."

Charity looked toward her mother for confirmation. Floralee nodded.

Charity grinned, inserting dimples among her facial freckles. "Really, 'thout no help!" She jumped up and down on her toes and Henry and Naomi jumped up and down with her. A celebration was a celebration, whatever the reason and whomever it was for.

12

Floralee lay awake long after Sarah and Naomi were breathing deeply beside her.

"Lord, you gonna have to show us where that old 'possum is. So, I'm thinkin', iffen you show us right off, 'thout us walkin' all over the county, I'd be thankful. And, Lord, could you make it a good, fat one? You know how it'll be needed for the soap."

After the prayer, Floralee was restless. The cabin was still warm and she eased out of bed and lit the candle, shielding the sleeping girls from the light by setting it behind a crock jar. The water in the stove reservoir was still hot and she took down her special jar of dried raspberry leaves.

She put a small handful of the leaves into a cup and, from the bottom of the jar, she extracted two dried berries. Hot water softened the berries and expanded the leaves and fruit, releasing their flavor together into the water.

Raspberry tea. A small drink of summer. A sip of sunshine and flowers and a memory of the bracing tartness of summer fruit. She sipped slowly, watching the glowing coals in the stove as they blackened around the edges, burning themselves out.

Then the tea was gone and the fire was dying. Her moment of summer had passed on and the wind again whistled around the log ends of the cabin and explored the walls, searching for cracks in the chink. It found them and the room was quickly cooling. She wearily pulled herself to her feet. She blew out the candle and went back to the bed.

Weariness finally pulled her into sleep, and she became a little girl again. Young Florie played with her sisters and learned mountain survival skills.

It was her turn to go with Pa to shoot the gun. Pa was a good shot with a gun, but he was very short on patience. He made a target with a stone on a tree limb and instructed the girl on how to sight the gun.

Young Florie trembled with the anxious effort to please her pa, and her first shots went wild, not even hitting the tree trunk.

"Now, you're not listenin' to what I say. If you did like I told you, you'd hit that rock. Now I'm warnin' you, we don't be needin' to waste more bullets. You lift that gun, you pull that trigger and hit that rock."

With aching arms, she lifted the gun and with trembling fingers she squeezed the trigger. She missed.

"Stupid girl!" he shouted at her. "Just like your mother! You don't listen to nothin' I say till it gets knocked into you. You could save yourself some pain if you'd just listen and do it."

Florie knew what was coming, and stiffened, bunching her shoulder muscles against the blow. The rifle was snatched from her hands and in an instant she was on the ground among the fallen, dead leaves.

"Get up from there, you dummy! Don't just lay there lookin' stupid. Now take this here gun and hit that rock or you'll find yourself getting' more'a what you just got."

Florie pulled herself up from the leaves and took the heavy rifle from her father. Twice more that day she missed, and twice more she was knocked to the ground.

Finally, in disgust, her pa yanked her to her feet and sent her back to her cabin. "Ain't no way to beat sense in a girl-child without knockin' em down."

Before she disappeared among the tree trunks of the hillside, he shouted after her, "You be thinkin' on what happened, and if you want more of the same. Could be a time we'd need you on the end'a the gun, helpin' to protect the family. You just think on it!"

She did. All the way home she thought on it, and knew there was no answer. She did not feel hatred to her pa, who was just trying to teach her what she needed to learn. What she felt was shame that she was not able to please him. He only punished her the same way he punished her mother when he was not happy with her.

Tears of discouragement and frustration were streaming down her face when she reached the cabin. Her mother looked at her, then stepped outside the cabin and studied the surrounding timber. He was nowhere in sight.

She went to Florie and put her arm around her. "Here's what we'll do, Florie, honey. He'll be gone, come time he goes to town or somewhere. That's when you'll take that old gun, and the bullets I got saved up. I'm figurin' you heard all his words about what to do, and how to do it. I was thinkin' this'd happen so I got us prepared."

Her ma stroked her daughter's arms and shoulders. "I know how your arms hurt from liftin' that gun. There ain't no way around that. The only answer for you, and for me, too, is to listen to what he wants and figure a way to get it done." She paused, and then added, "Or get knocked to the ground. Honey, it's just the way of a man to do what your pa done, and it's just the way of a woman to figure how to keep it from happenin' again."

So that was the way that Floralee had learned to shoot. Not from her pa knocking the skill into her, but from her mother's patience and encouragement, and pilfered ammunition.

With fear and determination she had lifted the rifle with her arms stinging with sore muscles. Eyes bore themselves through the gunsight and settled onto the target. Her aim became better and better, and her arm muscles strengthened and refused to tremble.

When her pa once again took her hunting, she brought down the rock on the limb and three squirrels from higher in the tree. He had nodded with satisfaction. "Now, see there? If you'd'a done that from the start, you'd'a saved yourself from the ringin' in your ears."

He wasted no words in telling her she did well… nor did she expect any. He treated her the same as he treated her mother and sisters… with an iron fist.

Maybe it had been a dream, or possibly just deep thought, but Floralee felt the tears flow down the sides of her face and into her hair.

What had made her pa the way he was, and what made Nathan the same way?

What would it be like to live with a loving and kind person? What happened to people to make them the way they were? What could her mother have done about it? And, what could she, Floralee, have done?

She could not answer her old question, but her firm resolve became as hard and cold as the ice on a winter pond. This would not happen to her children! Her beautiful daughters would not be smacked around. Her loving sons would do no smacking. She was not sure how, but she would not let it happen.

They had already seen too much, and she would have to tell them that she, their mother, had been wrong... wrong... wrong...! The words would be bitter in her mouth, but they would be spoken. She would drill them into the children's heads. She sighed deeply and turned on her pillow. She needed to rest.

Tomorrow, God would show her where the 'possum was.

13

Betty Lou carried the ashes to the hopper, actually a decay-hollowed log, standing on its end. The lower part of the log was closed solid and a knothole had opened, extending through to the decayed center of the old log.

"Charity, you got'a stay up wind 'cause ashes burn in your eyes, happen the wind catch 'em and fling 'em there." A cloud of gray dust arose from the log, but most of the ashes had gone inside.

"Now, you pour in the water," Betty Lou instructed Charity, and the little girl dumped the spring water into the log.

"Ain't nothin' comin' out!" Charity complained, watching the knothole.

"It'll come out. You just got'a put in more water, but it'll come out. Then we gonna build a fire under the washpot. Get some sticks like them little 'ens over there. You gonna need to get the coals out'a the kitchen stove, so get 'em now and bring 'em on out here."

Charity brought the coals from the cookstove in the small stove shovel, depositing them carefully on the dry leaves she had put on top of the sticks. The coals caught the dry tender, and soon a blaze licked red and orange flames around the blackened pot.

"Lookie there, Charity! You got lye water comin' out'a them ashes." A small trickle of grayish water oozed through the knothole and dripped into the old bucket.

"We got'a get us a bucket full'a that water to match this here much grease. You gonna need that big stick to stir with."

While Henry and Naomi watched, Charity jumped up and down with the stick, giving vent to her excitement. Betty Lou carefully poured the lye water from the ashes into the melted grease. Charity stirred her stick around and around in the swirling pattern of the grease as it neutralized the lye. The mixture took on the appearance and consistency of gravy.

Betty Lou called to Henry, "Bring over some water. We gonna see if we got soap."

Charity swished her stirring stick in the water Henry had furnished, but there were no soapy bubbles. Betty Lou shook her head, "We ain't got soap. We got'a stir it some more."

Floralee, Sarah and Donald had dressed in their oldest clothes and climbed to the top of the hill. Where would a 'possum be today? Floralee was tired already. Donald had been right. A dog would be a very big help. The boy kept running ahead and reporting that there were still no 'possums.

Exhausted, Floralee sat on a rock to think. If she didn't head back to the cabin right now, tired as she was, she was sure she would never make it.

"Come on back, Donald. We got'a think some more on this."

"But, Ma..." he objected.

"Come," she insisted, and reluctantly he followed her toward home.

When they were in sight of the cabin, they heard Henry squeal, "'Possum! 'Possum!"

Donald called back in disgust, "We never got no 'possum. We come back home instead."

"There," insisted Henry, pointing up into a tree near the goat shed, and there it was in the top of a leafless sweet gum tree, clinging to the topmost limbs. In fact, there were two opossums in the tree, peering curiously down onto the activity below.

Floralee lifted the gun to her shoulder and shot into the tree. Two shots brought down two animals. The globs of yellow fat, stored under their fur had rounded out the sides of the animals, indicating it must have been a good year for them living up among the nut and persimmon trees.

The fat was trimmed away and rendered and added to the soap pot. Charity stirred and the mixture began to thicken more. "Lookie, Ma, we 'bout got soap."

The thick gravy texture was now a creamy white. The contents of the kettle were ladled into the soapbox that had been lined with old cloth. There it would cool and drain away the excess liquid. Within days, it would harden into a firm slab of cleanser, ready to be cut into squares for dishwashing, bathing and clothing.

The opossums, with their yellow fat removed, were nestled in the large roaster pan and put in the oven. Sweet potatoes were tucked around the meat to roast with the same heat.

As Floralee removed the tender, strength-giving meat from the bones and served the children, she apologized silently, *I'm sorry, Lord, for not lookin' up. I asked You for these 'possums, and I ask You to have them be close on account'a my walkin'. Then I went blunderin' up over the mountain like I never even talked to You. I ought'a knowd You'd be bringin' 'em close down to me, bein' the kind of person You are, wantin' to give good gifts.*

At the close of the meal, there was not one morsel of meat left of the animals. Floralee returned the bones to the roaster and covered them with water. The heat still left in the oven would steep the bones and bring out more nourishment. With the addition of a few mountain herbs, the broth from the bones would make a tasty gravy... or a vegetable soup... or, most likely, simmered dumplings, rich and filling.

There were several possibilities to consider when one had the broth from a couple of fat, young 'possums. A delicious dilemma for a growing family.

14

It was during the Christmas holiday from school that the last of the supply of candles were lighted. Floralee was relieved that here, at least, was a necessity not requiring that money be spent and it was a chore the children enjoyed.

"This'n's the last candle we got, Ma," Donald warned as he held a splinter in the stove to catch a flame to light it.

Betty Lou looked up quickly. "You ain't aimin' to make candles 'afore I get home from school to help, are ya?"

"Not likely," Floralee promised. "Bein' that we need all our hands for candle makin'."

"My hands?" questioned Naomi. "I got two, three, five hands."

"Ain't no doubt we gonna find work for your hands, even no bigger than they are," her mother promised.

"Yeah, Ma, and iffen we'd get at makin' them wick cords now, that part'd be over with and done. You figurin' we could be gettin' at it now?"

"No reason not to," Floralee decided.

"I'll be gettin' the fuzzies!" Henry offered. "I can get them fuzzies down out'a the shed beams."

Floralee sized up Henry's height against the height of the rafters of the shed. "Charity, you go with 'im, in case he'd be needin' a boost up."

In a short time, Charity and Henry were back with the burlap bag of thistle down they had gathered from ripe milkweed pods and stored for this occasion.

"Henry didn't need no help," Charity reported. "He shinnied up to get that tow sack off'a the peg and had it down 'afore I got past the shed door."

"Told Ma I could," pouted Henry. "Ain't nobody ever believin' my words, never in my life. I show 'em."

"I believe," Naomi told him. "I believe Henry. I believe Chary. I believe Sary. I believe Betty Lou." As she called their names, Naomi patted her hands against their legs. She continued, "I believe Nate. Mama, I want Nate to be here."

"Naomi, darlin', Nate gonna be here. I promise. He gonna be comin' back."

Naomi ran to the door. "Open it," she demanded. "Nate gonna be here."

"No, Naomi, he ain't comin', yet."

"Mama said!" wailed Naomi. "Nate gonna come. I want Nate."

Floralee reached for Naomi, pulling her into her lap and holding her against her bulging abdomen. "Naomi, darlin', Nate got things he got'a do. He gonna be comin', quick as he can."

"Is Pa through doin' what he has to do?"

"No, darlin'."

Naomi smiled, "Nate gonna help 'im. Nate gonna come. Pa gonna come."

Sarah and Betty Lou went quietly into the unheated lean-to. Donald went outside, slamming the door behind him.

Charity leaned forward to look at her picture book. She poked the index finger of each hand in an ear. Henry opened a sack of thistledown and examined the brown seed pods filled with silky fibers. "Fuzzies," he said softly to the pods. "Fuzzies, fuzzies, fuzzies!"

Naomi repeated her question, "Nate gonna help Pa?"

Floralee rocked back and forth, holding Naomi to sooth her. "No, darlin'. Nate ain't gonna help Papa. Nate gonna come home and help us. He gonna be here soon as he can."

"Papa?"

"Papa ain't comin'."

"Sometime Papa gonna come."

"No, darlin'."

Naomi leaned against Floralee's abdomen and the baby within her squirmed into a better position.

"Mama?"

"What, darlin'?"

"Papa ain't never gonna get through. Nate ain't gonna help Papa 'cause Papa ain't never gonna get through."

"That'd be right, Naomi. Papa ain't never gonna get through but Nate, he gonna be comin'. We gonna go in the wagon to get 'im."

"The new wagon?"

Her mother nodded. "The new wagon. 'Speck we could have us a picnic along the way?"

Why not? The word "picnic" was foreign sounding, but lately, many foreign sounding actions had become possible. Why not a picnic?

"Picnic?"

"Sure, enough!"

"Mama?"

"What, darlin'?"

"Fuzzies. We got'a play fuzzies. 'Enry, I want some'a them fuzzies."

Floralee sighed. Perhaps Naomi's mind was settled for a while. "That'd be right, Naomi. We got'a play fuzzies. Go tell Sarah and Betty Lou to come help play fuzzies."

Naomi slid down from her mother's lap and ran to the door of the lean-to, pounding her small fists against the rough wood of the door. "Fuzzies! Fuzzies! Come play fuzzies! Sary? Betty Lou? Mama said! Fuzzies!"

Sarah and Betty Lou came back to the kitchen. Naomi patted Sarah's arm. "Sary, Nate gonna come home."

"Sure, Naomi, Nate gonna come."

The milkweed floss was carefully removed from the brown pods taking care to keep the floss strands parallel. Three clusters of inch-and-a-half threads were placed in a line, each group overlapping the other in a row on the table.

Hands were greased lightly and the fibers were rolled across the table surface to bond the fibers into a cord. The cords were carefully twisted so the fibers would not separate. The hardening grease helped to hold them in place. The twisting must be hard and firm to make a tight cord which would result in a solid, smooth flame that would not flare up, flicker or drown out in its own wax.

When the cord was about a foot and a half long, it was tied in the middle to another cord of the same length. Now, it looked like a four-legged spider with very long legs.

At this point, the wick makers had to pair up into "holders" and "twist makers." While the holder held the knot, the twist maker molded the cords together, twisting as they were molded. Whirl after whirl was made until a hard, strong wick was formed by the multiple strands. This was repeated until the string was used up and the candlewick was six or eight inches long.

It took a lot of twisting and a lot of care to keep the floss cords from unraveling until they were secure within the knots. A thick, stout cotton cord would work very well for a candlewick, but cords cost money and money could be used for other things that could not be made in the cabin. The milkweed floss wick took a lot of time, but it burned brightly and slowly after being dipped repeatedly into the wax.

As they worked, fine hairs from the milkweed floss began to float round the cabin, tickling noses and causing sneezes. Fuzzies were everywhere. Henry and Naomi blew on them, keeping them floating. They ran around the cabin, laughing and squealing and puffing the floss up in the air.

The flat, brown seeds that had been removed from the flossy threads were saved in a bowl. The more seeds to be returned to the soft earth where the milkweed flowers bloomed, the more floss would be available for harvesting in later years.

The floss of the milkweed was valuable for other purposes. It took a lot of floss to make candles, but it took even more to make the down-filled comforters for the beds. Mountains of fluff were captured between a pieced quilt top and its lining, and "tacked" with stout threads to make a thick warm bed covering. A girl reaching marriageable age would do well to have her comforters made and put away in her marriage chest, along with her embroidered tea towels, pot holders and crocheted lace doilies.

When her married life was begun, and babies began to appear, there would be no time for creating fancy things like embroidery or time-consuming things like making a floss comforter.

Sarah was fourteen and, somehow, there must be a comforter made for her from next summer's harvest. Betty Lou was not far behind. It would be expected for a girl to have a comforter, maybe two, at her wedding day. The thistle down was as warm as goose down in the comforter. It was soft, light and fluffy and it grew in the valley, free for the picking.

Yes, the seeds must be returned to the ground for Sarah's comforter.

Two evenings in the cabin produced thirty-six wicks and their candle maker held twelve wicks at a time. This metal gadget was shaped like an upside down "T" with pegs on the bottom of the crossbar for hanging the wicks. Twelve wicks could be lowered into the wax at one time, building their wax coating, together. Twenty-five to thirty quick and careful dips in the candle wax, created twelve, fat candles that burned slowly and without smoking.

On the following Saturday, Donald and Charity gathered armloads of small, dry sticks to make the hot fire needed for melting wax from the wax myrtle berries.

Sarah and Betty Lou poured the myrtle berries out onto the table, removing stems and twigs before putting them into the steaming water.

The berries shriveled as wax was melted out of their flesh and the empty hulls floated up to the top of the water. The long stick went around and around in the kettle guided by anyone having a free hand. There were two things that absolutely required constant stirring while being cooked. They were applesauce and candleberry wax.

The shriveled skins of the berries collected at the top of the water but were left in the pot until all wax had a chance to ooze out, then they were skimmed off and thrown away and the liquid in the kettle was kept at a full, rolling boil as the steam arose and water evaporated away. As the steam left, the oil became thicker and somewhat gummy, requiring even more careful stirring. Finally, only a thick layer of wax remained in the kettle.

Now came the testing. A stream of wax was dropped into a cup of cold water. If it fell apart in granules, the stirring continued. If it held its shape in long, brittle strings, like toothpicks, the dipping could begin.

A strong, quick arm was needed for the dipping. The T-shaped dipper was loaded with wicks, held firmly by their knots, and was lowered into the wax and quickly drawn out. The wax dip coated the wicks and the cool air hardened them. The colder the day, the better it was for candle dipping.

As each layer was cooled, the dipper was plunged into the wax again. As more wax held to the wick, the candle grew fatter and it took a little longer for the wax to harden.

"I wanna dip," demanded Henry.

"You ain't gonna. You too little," his brother announced.

"I'm big."

"Ain't big enough."

"Mama! I wanna help. Make Donald let me."

Floralee agreed with Donald. "No, Henry. You ain't tall enough."

"Told ya," taunted Donald.

"Donald, you watch that dipper and don't let it stay in that wax too long. No time down in that heat and them candles gonna go back to bein' wax."

"Sure, Ma."

"Ma, I wanna dip."

"Not yet, Henry. When you get nine years old, you can dip. Now, Donald, let Betty Lou have the dipper and you get some sticks for the fire. Charity, you go with Donald."

"Ma, you gonna let Charity dip?"

"No, Henry, Charity ain't big enough, either. Now, you step back out'a the way'a that hot wax. Go find Naomi. Where is Naomi? NAOMI!"

The call echoed in the crisp, winter air but there was no answer.

"Donald, you and Charity find Naomi, first. Charity, you look over the bluff. Donald, look in the hog pen. Henry, look in the shed. Sarah, come out and help find Naomi. Betty Lou, you keep dippin'. I'm goin' up the hill."

By now, Charity shouted back her report. "She ain't over the bluff, Ma."

"Then go look in the cave."

"Cave?"

"Hurry. No tellin' where at she is."

"She ain't in the hog pen, Ma," Donald called.

"Then go down to the cave with Charity. Keep callin' 'er name. NAOMI!"

"NAOMI! NAOMI!"

Donald plunged into the dimness of the cave.

"Naomi? You in here?" The cave held nothing but an echo.

Charity stood on the overhang of the cave and told the sweet gum trees, "Now, Naomi, she don't run off just to be doin', like Henry does, so she got'a be goin' somewhere. Where at would Naomi be wantin' to go?"

Like a flash, the realization came. Charity ran to the road and headed for town.

Donald came out of the cave. "She ain't in there, Charity. Charity? CHARITY? Where at are you?"

"I'm on the road," Charity called back. "I'm a'gettin' 'er."

Donald caught up with Charity at the bend in the road and passed her. Charity called as he ran past, "Reckon she fell off the bridge?"

"Hopin' not. NAOMI! NAOMI!"

Charity echoed, "NAOMI! NAOMI! Where you at? Wait, Donald, I hear somethin'."

Donald stopped.

"Mama?" came a faint, frightened voice from somewhere downhill.

"NAOMI?"

"Chary?"

"Naomi? Donald, I heard her! Naomi, call me agin."

"Chary?"

"There, from over to that rock," called Donald. "Come on, Charity, let's go."

Donald and Charity scrambled under the low limbs to the rock out-cropping. The dead leaves were ruffled and scuffed at the edge and the children leaned over to look down. There, a good ten feet below them, was a small, frightened bundle of red hair and freckles.

"What you doin' down there, Naomi?"

"Fall down!"

"Come on, Charity, we got'a get 'er. No, you stay here and keep talkin'. I'll get 'er." Donald scooted and slid down through the forest of tree trunks to a lower part of the bluff.

Charity stayed on the bluff, looking over. "Where at was you goin'?" she asked Naomi.

"Fall down," Naomi insisted, whimpering.

"You was goin' after Nate, wasn't you?"

Naomi's red hair bobbed. "Uh huh."

"How come was you doin' that?'

"Nate's turn."

"Nate's turn? Turn for what?"

"Dippin'.'

"Dippin'? Like dippin' candles?"

Naomi nodded. "His turn."

"You was a'goin' to get him?"

The red curls bobbed again. "Uh huh."

"You hurt yerself bad?"

"Uh huh."

"The sticker bush done it?"

"Un huh. Bleed all over," Naomi pointed out the red scratches on her arm. "Old sticker bush got my dress."

"Uh huh. Sure did." Charity could see Donald approaching. "Naomi, you hold real still. Donald gonna get you unstuck."

Donald reached Naomi and began to extract her from the clutches of the thorn bush. "Charity, you ought'a run back and tell Ma. She gonna be scairt to death."

"Ouch!" complained Naomi.

"Yeah, I'll be goin'," agreed Charity and she ran up the hill without bothering to go to the road. She shuffled through the deep leaves and tripped over a half buried tree limb. She fell sprawling into the accumulation of leaves, but jumped up, looked at the offending limb, broke off a chuck of it for the candle making fire, and continued running up the hill.

"Ma, we got 'er. Ma!" Charity cupped her hands and yelled upward toward the sky.

"Nate," she announced to her sister.

"You was goin' after Nate?"

"Uh huh."

"You wasn't to do that. When Nate gonna get to come home, we all got'a go get 'im. Ma said that."

"All got'a go?"

"Yep. We got'a go in the wagon and bring 'im back."

"Bring 'im back?" Naomi sought to reassure herself.

"Sure, but now we got'a go back up that hill to Mama. You scairt Mama when you ran away."

When Donald and Naomi climbed up the hill and returned to the candle making operation, the first group of candles were fat and round.

"Sarah," Betty Lou called, "get ready 'cause I'm a'bringin' 'em."

She ran to the cabin with the dipper load of semi-soft rods of wick and wax. She placed them carefully on the table and she and Sarah rolled them gently back and forth, individually, on the flat surface of the table to "round" them and firm up the sides. Charity watched as the finished candles were set aside to harden and the next group of wicks were attached to the dipper.

"Had me some money, I'd be gettin' red candles out'a a book," Charity said in a low voice that no one heard except herself.

"Ma," Donald asked, "can I put in a cedar limb to smell up the wax?"

"Reckon so, Donald."

With a knife, Donald severed a bushy limb from the cedar and shook it to remove dead ends and loose twigs. Holding the stump of the limb, he swished it around in the bubbling wax. The limb turned a brilliant green as its oil was released into the wax, and the rich cedar smell of it permeated the liquid wax and the brilliant green color of the limb became a dull olive. Donald drew the limb from the wax and placed it carefully on a bed of dry leaves.

"You wait, Naomi. When we get that kettle off the fire, I'll be showin' you a purty blaze we can make with that limb. We gonna put that old limb on the fire and that flame gonna shoot all the way up to the sky."

Naomi listened, fascinated. "Up to God?"

"What you say?"

"Fire gonna shoot up to God?" Naomi repeated.

"Ma! You hear that? Naomi said the fire gonna go all the way up to God. You hear that, Ma?"

Naomi looked from Donald to her mother and was rewarded with a smile. "Up to God," she repeated. "Nate go up to God."

Donald sighed, impatiently. "No, Naomi. Nate ain't with God. Nate gonna be with us. I said to you not to be worryin' 'bout it none." Donald shook his head in dismay. Little'ns were so hard headed. Had to be told again and again.

15

It seemed to be a spring day as Floralee stood beside her cabin door. She did not question where the winter had suddenly gone. The new green of the trees was startling after the winter's brown, and the bluejays were squabbling over nesting sites, their fluttering combat causing a sky-blue feather to float down onto her hair. She reached up and plucked it off, moving her fingers over the feather's smooth, cool surface.

She heard the whistling before she saw him through the trees, then he came on toward her with his swinging mountain stride and his special, wide smile. He caught her hand and they climbed to the rocky, mountain peak.

"Lookie out there Florie, baby. They ain't nothin' in that big old world purty as my little strawberry."

His arms tightened around her and she relaxed against him, listening.

"We got us the whole world right here under our feet. You got eyes purtier than that blue jay feather in your hand. Them red curls is lookin' better'n a patch of ripe strawberries. Even purtier'n a October apple."

The sun was warm and the rock was warm. He stretched out full length on the warm rock and drew her down beside him.

"Oh, Florie, baby. They ain't words to say how much I love you."

He drew her closer and she whispered, "Nathan?"

Then hands were on her shoulders, shaking her gently. She forced her eyes open.

"Ma? Wake up, Ma?"

Floralee sat up and the spring green of the woodland disappeared. The cabin was chilled and dark. Tears of disappointment formed in her eyes... tears of disappointment and anger.

"Ma, you was startin' to dream. Did you want me to wake you?"

Floralee reached out in the dark and touched Sarah's face. "You done right, Sarah, darlin'. You should'a woke me like you done. This ain't no time to be dreamin, 'stead'a sleepin'."

"You wantin' me to light up a candle?"

"No, darlin'. We gonna be goin' back to sleep, now."

Sarah was instantly asleep but Floralee stared up into the blackness until dawn was breaking. When would it stop? When would he leave her alone to do the work left for her to do? It was not fair! He was gone, but yet he came! Finally, she was able to drift into a troubled, restless sleep.

It was mid-morning when Donald came running to Floralee.

"Ma, I got me a idea. Iffen I was to take that old busted wagon bed out to the pig pen, reckon I could make a house to keep wind and snow off'a them pigs?"

Donald's tousled red curls were damp from perspiration in spite of the cold weather and his blue eyes were shining with the excitement of his idea.

"Reckon you did get a good idea," his mother complimented him.

His mother's agreement encouraged him to press his case on another matter. "Winter comin' on hard, I'd be needin' to stay home from school to get that pig house done. Yep, reckon I'd be needin' to do that."

Floralee grinned at his conniving seriousness. "Allow we gonna make time to do that little chore after school and on a Saturday. Don't you think?"

"Aw, Ma."

"Be wastin' your breath arguin' with me, don't you reckon?"

Life was getting back to normal, now. The children were beginning to sass and argue in their usual illogical manner. Surely, that was a good thing, wasn't it?

The old sow was looking better, now, and permitting the pigs all to have a turn at her. The nutrition in nuts and acorns seemed to help her to produce at least some milk. The children dug roots from the valley floor to fill out the variety in her diet, and the snorting and squealing of the pigs was a common sound at Floralee's cabin. It strengthened and reassured her. To her, the sound of the animals was better than music and singing.

The children were out of the cabin attending to their duties and she sat wearily at the table, leaning her head forward on her arms in dreamy restfulness. There seemed to be rooting and snorting of wild pigs outside the door.

"Them pigs sure do like rootin' for acorns," she commented to Nathan.

There was no answer.

"I been thinkin' 'n thinkin' on pigs, how fat they get on them chinky pins. It'd seem to me...."

Nathan's voice came loud and angry, "If you're fixin' to be talkin' agin 'bout having pigs on my land, just get your mind off it."

She gathered courage and began again. "But I just know...."

"You ain't 'sposed to know. You 'sposed to do, and I'd be the one 'sposed to know. It's for you to do what I know needs to be done."

The rough, strong hands caught her shoulders and flung her across the room. Her abdomen struck the back of a chair and her body pitched forward. Pain shot like lightning into her hands and feet and then into her entire body.

She screamed, "Nathan, the baby!"

The voice yelled, "Don't talk to me 'bout no baby. Ain't mine, anyways. Wife of mine go messin' around town, likely to have anyone's baby. I didn't tell you to have a baby!"

"It'd be your baby, Nathan. Hear me, Nathan?" She felt the tears start to flow and she squenched her eyes to stop them. Nathan hated tears.

She heard a child cry and startled up from the table, her arms tingling with a cramp. The cabin was empty except for Naomi, who had been awakened from her nap by her mama's loud, frightened voice.

Floralee tried to stand up, but a pain flared across the lower part of her abdomen. She sat down, quickly. "Please, Lord, you 'memberin' I got me three months to go on this baby? Got too many things to get done. You hearin' me, God? I need to be waitin' 'afore I have this baby."

The pain eased a bit. She rose slowly and went to the bed to pat Naomi back to sleep. Outside the window, her pigs snorted and squealed. They were her pigs, and the sound comforted her. Yes, pigs were the answer, but the cows had become a question.

It was becoming clear to her that the cows had to go to the auction. She hated to let them go. They seemed like part of the family, but, like the rest of the family, they ate a lot. And they were worth their weight in pigs and other necessities. It was time to make the decision.

She would tie them behind the wagon and walk slow enough so the cows could make it all the way to Jacksonville. In truth, her land was not suited to cows. Goats were better. The only thing was, the cream didn't come up good on goat's milk, so she couldn't make the best butter. But one could not have everything.

Two more nannies and a really good billy, and she'd have plenty of milk for the children and for giving the pigs a good start. And little goats were not bad to eat, either.

Her thoughts continued. Some of those trees would have to come down so some grass would grow. She'd buy some wheat seeds at the feed store, and she'd get oats and rye, too. That'd make the goats give more milk, eating the green plants.

She walked down to where Donald was busily creating a makeshift pig house out of the rotten pieces of the old wagon. He was not doing a bad job of it.

"Donald, we gonna cut out some of them big trees so as to get grass and brush to grow for them goats."

"But, Ma, Pa always said..." Donald's voice trailed away and he looked down at his feet, apologetically. "I didn't go to say that, Ma."

"I know you didn't. Your pa had his mind on other things, not thinkin' of the good of the goats and how much milk they'd give. But you and me, we have to think on the goats and the pigs. Like the way you had the idea about the pig house."

Donald surveyed his creation with satisfaction. "Yeah, Ma, that's what we gotta do."

Floralee and Donald looked up the hill. "Grass just don't grow good in the shade," she began again.

"Ma, you know how to chop down a tree? I never done it. It was Nate that cut down the wood."

Floralee nodded. "You're right. Likely we gotta wait for him. You bein' only nine, you ain't big enough to swing that axe."

16

The trip to Jacksonville was long and slow, but Donald and Charity enjoyed every minute. The cows kept trying to grab a mouthful of grass only to be yanked back into the road as the wagon moved forward pulled by the young, strong mule.

They followed the trail down the mountain road and crossed the small stream caused by the mineral spring. At Applegate's Mill, the road turned and followed the river all the way to Jacksonville. The children jumped off the wagon and ran to the riverbank, then raced back to catch the wagon and ride a while.

They laughed and squealed in their excitement at having an outing and a day away from the mountain. Away from the rest of the children… feeling special and favored.

At the auction barn, they pushed their way close to the auctioneer. Charity announced to those nearby, "That there's our cow," when their cow was brought in. The men standing nearby chuckled.

The auctioneer's voice sang out, "Gimme a bid, I wanna bid, a bid, a bid, I wanna bid. Let's get started. Five. I got me five, who'll give me more. I wanna more, wanna more, wanna more. Six? Got me six? Who'll go for seven?"

The cow went for $10.50. The other cow went for $13.50 because its calf was near due.

Floralee had $24.00 coming so she waited for the goats to be brought out. She let the first lot go by. They brought a dollar each. The second lot was very young and had a billy and three nannies.

"Who'll gimme a bid, gimme a bid, gimme a bid? Two dollars? Who'll make it three, gimme three, gimme three? I got three, I wanna four, wanna four?" She had to pay $4.75, but they appeared to be well fed and lively. She had to pay twenty cents for a rope long enough to keep them together.

Later, Floralee stopped in front of the stone building where the uniformed lawmen were. Donald and Charity remained in the wagon.

No, young Nate Barker was not there. He had been transferred up state to a school at Benton, but hadn't she got the letter? They had sent it on out to River Bend.

No, she hadn't thought to go to the post office.

It was mid afternoon when they got to the ice cream store. The clerk remembered her and offered an extra cone.

She went down the alley behind the second hand store, just to check. There was, indeed, a large box sitting in the alley. Floralee and Donald lifted the box to the wagon.

"Ma, it ain't got nothin' in it but raggedy things!" Charity complained.

"That's what we reckoned it'd have. Got us a'lot'a need for rags on a farm." They loaded the boxes and were on the way. It was dark when they reached the foot of the hill, but the mule pulled the wagon easily.

"You done a good job on them muddy places, Donald. We ain't even gettin' stuck, like we did last time." It was too dark for Floralee to see Donald's look of pride but she knew it was there.

They unhitched the mule but left the little goats tied to the wagon until the light of morning. Floralee made cornmeal mush with goat's milk and the children went to bed. When the cabin became quiet, she sat down to the table with her list and the candle. She studied the list.

"THINGS I NEED"

Nate was first on the list and she still needed him. Warm clothes? She crossed it off. Firewood? She still needed that. Money? She thought of the almost $30.00 she now had. It was more than she had ever possessed in her lifetime. She crossed money off her list.

That left only two things, and when a woman could write down only two things she really, truly needed, she ought'a be thanking the Good Lord for that.

"THINGS I HAVE"

Thirteen acres. She nodded. *Gonna be some big change on that*, she promised herself. *Cabin needs work. But I got me some ideas*, she told the piece of paper. Five goats. She crossed out the five and wrote "nine." She crossed off the cows.

Mule, old, was next. She added, "Another mule, not so old." Two bushels of sweet potatoes was changed to one and a half bushels and some beans and other things.

Firewood was next. Not enough. No change, there. Eight babies and no more. She nodded her head and smiled. She added more items. Strong wagon. She whispered, "Lord, could You see Your way clear to make it up to Dwight? I know he didn't have nothin' to spare but he brought it on, anyway."

Brood sow and sixteen pigs, all doing good. Nuts. Them hogs sure did like them nuts. Persimmons would be good next fall. All that sugar in them would certainly flavor the hams. Maybe make them sugar cured from the inside!

She turned the paper over to "IDEAS" and wrote. Nut flour is stretching out the cornmeal and that pig food made out of wheat is going to stretch out the flour. Maybe the children don't like it so good at first but they going to eat it and be full. They like being full.

It had been a long day and Floralee closed her eyes wearily. She heard fiddle music and children's voices, singing.

The wind whistled around the cabin corners and shook the windowpanes, but the potbelly stove was crackling and cheerful. Nate, Sarah, Betty Lou and Donald were singing and clapping their hands.

Popcorn and oranges were on the table beside a half eaten cake. She could see everything together and it fair made a picture fit to go on a wall.

"We got a good family," she told Nathan. "Lucky we got two boys and two girls, all of 'em healthy."

"You ain't wantin' no more?"

"We got enough, I been thinkin'."

"What else you been thinkin'? That you could be flouncin' around River Bend, likely Jacksonville, too? Goin' sluttin' around, skinny, with your hair all up? That'd be what you thinkin'? I done told you and told you, ain't no need for you to be thinkin'. You got me t'do that.

"Likely, you been struttin' around front of the preacher, gettin' him to look at you. Ain't no wonder you want to go to that church every week."

Floralee bowed her head in shame, and the children, having no music to sing by, had begun to quietly eat the popcorn, making themselves as small as possible. As they always did when the hateful words began to be said.

It was very soon after that evening that she knew she was carrying Charity, and going to the church every week became more exhausting than she could manage.

Weariness flowed over her body. She felt strange and she sat up in the dark bed. She reached for Nathan and her hand rested on the mass of curls on Sarah's head. Another dream. *Oh, Dear Lord, when would the dreaming stop?*

She lay back on the bed and thought. Nathan had been such a puzzle. He thought she was pretty, but he didn't want anyone to see her.

"Stay up hill away from that 'still'," he had instructed. "Ain't aimin' to ever see you set foot down there. Men come to buy booze and you gonna make 'em think you'd be for sale, along with the booze. Likely, you knowed about that, already."

He had slapped her hard, leaving her ears ringing. "That'd be to help you 'member where a woman ought'a be and ought not to be."

He had said he loved her… but he also loved his fiddle and his gun. He oiled the gun and kept it safely high up over the front door. It was expected to stay there until needed and be instantly ready for use should an unwanted varmit come along.

The same with the fiddle. It was cared for with oil to keep the case from drying and splitting, and the bow was treated, as needed, with rosin. At all other times it was expected to hang quietly on the cabin wall. When he felt the need for it, or had the time to devote to it, the fiddle was expected to be ready to make music. Yes, he truly loved the fiddle… and the gun.

As the years slipped by, Floralee began to realize that the love she had for him was returned to her in the same manner as his love for his fiddle and gun.

The gun never gave him advice on where and when it was to be used, or what kind of ammunition he should provide. It was the duty of the gun to be ready for him to use when he considered it necessary. Always, he was in control.

The same with the fiddle. It had never suggested what kind of music should be played on it, nor had it objected to where it was hung. Neither did it complain when he had no time for it for long periods of time. It waited silently.

Yes, Nathan could love, but only in the manner and at the time of his choosing. It had been a hard and painful lesson for Floralee, and she was doomed to re-learn the lesson, over and over. But he was gone, now, and there was a need for bullets for the gun so she could provide for her family. And the bullets were in the forbidden cave.

Another thought. Even the cave with the mineral water was his, and she was not permitted to enter… just like the fiddle and the gun. But, enough of that thought. She must find the courage to use the cave. Even now, she felt strange when it was necessary for her to go to the valley. She would just have to get over that foolishness.

She was now wide awake. The wind was coming up, howling and moaning as it tore against the ends of the log cabin walls.

There would have to be a new shed very soon. Two cows were gone, but another mule and four goats had been added, and the old shed leaned badly. Goats needed protection more than some other animals. When Nate came home…. The things that needed to be done paraded themselves before her exhausted brain.

She must make her plans and there would be time for everything. If the baby didn't come early…! *Please, Lord, there is so much work to do.*

As soon as she could, she'd cut down trees on the rocky upper part of the mountain and the new little sprouts that grew, come spring time, would be just right for the browsing goats. Nathan never wanted a tree cut. That took away some of the cover and the screening of the still from prying eyes. Didn't need to have folks snooping around unless they were trusted customers.

Floralee didn't even have room among the trees for a kitchen garden. Vegetables wouldn't grow in the shade so she quit trying.

"You find yourself needin' taters and beans, you say so," Nathan always told her, but he brought her such small quantities, she was afraid to cook enough so they could get full. Youngens were always hungry.

Floralee knew she should be sleeping, but her eyes would not close. Too many thoughts. She needed to send word to Martha Maisone about when the baby was due. The luxury of a midwife was one thing that Nathan always permitted. She couldn't spare Sarah or Betty Lou to make the trip to the midwife's house, and Donald was too little. Oh, well, there was time, yet.

She was still busy with her thoughts when the dawn broke over the mountain. Sarah was asleep beside her, her mop of hair a tangle of bright curls on the pillow. Her ivory skin, tinged with pink, and the high cheek bones that were framed with curls.... Floralee shook her head at the wonder of it all. The beauty of her oldest daughter made her weak at the sight!

Reddish gold lashes lay against her cheek. Her pointed chin balanced her up-turned nose. Beautiful Sarah with the strawberry blossom coloring of the Callahans.

When had the freckles disappeared? When had she really looked at her children? They came and they went, they talked and they were quiet, they were good and they misbehaved and she loved them all, but when had she seen them? Really seen them?

This beautiful creature grew out of the knobby kneed, freckle-faced, extremely shy child. Sarah was now fourteen. When did it all happen? But now it was morning... and reality must take the place of puzzled speculation.

While the children were feeding hogs and milking goats, Floralee looked at the wheat bran she had asked Sarah to bring in sometime ago. Today was the day. She squared her shoulders with determination and picked up her batter pan.

She contemplated the wheat bran. It was light brown and almost as smoothly ground as the white flour. It came from wheat and the flour came from wheat. They had been separated, and she'd just put them back together. She measured one cup of flour and one cup of bran, another cup of flour and another of bran, then she stirred in the clabber milk, salt and baking powder, beating with the wooden spoon until it was a fluffy, gummy mass.

With practiced ease, she turned the mass out on the floured board. Without conscious effort, her hands formed biscuits. The two thin, blackened metal pans held twenty biscuits each and there were seldom any leftovers. Certainly, none that lasted from one meal to the next. The way they were growing, she'd need another bread pan very soon.

In the heat of the oven, the bran biscuits began to rise. They were smooth and tan, but not so high and fluffy. She made a skillet of milk gravy and put the bread and gravy on the table as the children came in.

At the table, Donald reached for the three biscuits closest to him and broke them in his plate, ladling gravy over them. He cut a bite with his fork, blew on it to cool it a little, and it was gone.

Betty Lou broke a biscuit and looked at it for a minute before covering it with gravy. Floralee watched them as she fixed food for Henry and Naomi. Charity said, "The biscuits are shorter, Ma." Floralee nodded at Charity, then glanced carefully toward Sarah. Sarah's strawberry pink mouth smiled shyly and the sky blue eye winked at her mother.

Floralee tasted the biscuits. They were different. Not better or worse, just different. And there were leftovers. Everyone got full. Hmmmm. Almost half a pan left over. She had put the two kinds of wheat together and there were biscuits left over… something had happened.

That outcome warranted some thinking. She did a little mental calculation. The wheat bran sack was twice as big as the flour sack and cost half as much. Nathan would not have touched one of these darker, heavier biscuits. "Show me a woman what can't make good biscuits and I can show you a woman goin' back to her mama to learn," he had often said, with a chuckle, though Floralee was sure he meant it. She gave it very little thought, though, as he had been pleased with her biscuits. It was just all of those other things.…

But now was time to stop thinking about what had been and start to concentrate on the future. And that included Nate.

"I got somethin' to say to all of you youngens. I went to see the law over in Jacksonville. Nate ain't there 'cause they moved him upstate to Benton to go to a school."

"School?" sneered the indignant Donald. "Nate bein' almost sixteen, what's he doin' goin' to school?"

Floralee announced calmly, "They told me he was gonna get his sixth grade certificate. They said he maybe wrote us a letter. You, Donald, got'a go over to the Post Office and ask 'em 'afore you start home from school tomorrow."

The necessity of school was still a matter of concern to Donald. "Ma, you thinkin' for sure, I'd be needin' to go to school? Don't need school for pig raisin'."

It was not, however, a matter of concern to his mother. She was firm. "You gonna go to school."

"Aw, Ma!"

Henry was licking the gravy off the ladle. "I'd go. Ma, you could let Donald stay here. I could go to school."

All eyes turned to Henry, grinning and chuckling at the idea.

Floralee didn't laugh. "Iffen it weren't three miles in the freezin' rain, at times, Henry, I'd be thinkin' on sendin' you right off with Donald."

Henry slid off the worn bench and buried his face in Floralee's shoulder and she tousled his tight curls. Shy and embarrassed that so much was made of his offer.

Floralee selected six, huge smooth sweet potatoes and put them next to the firebox in the cast iron stove. Then she took two more potatoes. It was time the children had enough to eat. When the potatoes were gone, she'd think of something else.

"Tain't your worry about fillin' stomachs," Nathan had always told her. "All you got'a do, you be needin' food, is to say it to me."

But it was often days, or weeks, before she got what she needed so she had learned to cook carefully, sparingly. When she mentioned it to him, he dismissed her with, "Ain't we gettin' along? Makes me plum sick to my stomach, hearin' a woman complain when she got no cause to. I done heard all the mouthin' out'a you I aim to put up with."

He reinforced his admonition with a hand against her cheek. His punishment was effective as she quickly learned to anticipate what would set him off. She learned to stay out of his way and keep quiet… just like her mother had.

So Floralee had kept quiet and stretched the food to cover as many meals as possible.

"Eggs'd be nice, Nathan. Youngens need to have eggs to be healthy and the hens'd be no trouble to you, me havin' the time to see after 'em."

He had retorted, "Allow you already got too much time, lettin' you think on things to complain about. Them roosters, bellyachin' of a morning and bone-headed hens, pickin' and pokin' around the mash, droppin' their poop on the leaves? Reckon how many men's be wantin' to buy their likker from me? Just like that fool idea'a yourn to keep goat milk down in the cave, smellin' up the place.

"Cash money from them squeezin's, that's what puts food in the mouths of you and them youngens." He had looked toward the sky as if seeking help from above. "Swear, if I don't think the better lookin' a woman is on the outside, the dumber she gonna be inside her head."

But all of that was in the past.

Floralee determinedly jammed another stick of wood into the stove. The sweet potatoes would be ready just in time for dinner.

"Betty Lou, you be wringin' out a little washin' 'n Charity, you be helpin' with the hangin' up. Donald, you pick up acorns and take Henry with you. Sarah, you come along with me. Get Naomi's hand and bring her along out'a the way."

Floralee, Sarah and Naomi climbed slowly to the top of the hill. The goats paused, stared inquisitively, then resumed their feeding. A mouthful here, a nibble there. A little of this and a bite of that. Some of last year's grass seeds, a dry leaf and a bite of tall moss from under the leaves. Goats had a strange, selective way of eating. Could that be why the cream stayed mixed through the milk and wouldn't hardly rise?

But just wait, with eight goats being milked, there'd be a way to make good butter. She'd keep trying till she got it right. Rich, good butter to spread, dripping, on their biscuits, and she, Floralee, would discover how it was made.

Sarah's voice was soft and friendly as she talked with Naomi, pointing out a tiny fern or a squirrel that was circling the tree to stay out of sight, revealing only a bushy tail.

They climbed over the cabin-sized boulders of white rock, just like goats, until they reached the top-most point of land. The valley was covered with leafless tree trunks, black jack oaks whose dry crackly leaves clung to the tree until spring, and deep, green cedars and pines. They sat down on a sun-warmed rock.

"Sarah, darlin', I got'a tell you some things, you bein' my biggest youngen at home. Reckon it'd be you I talked to, even if Nate was here, now that I think on it." She sighed with the knowledge of what she had just said.

"We got us some money and I got'a say to you what you'd need to be doin', chance somethin' happened to me."

Sarah picked up a twig and examined it carefully.

"We got nigh onto $30.00 and I got it hid."

Sarah looked at her mother, "Hid in that old sock under the bed tick."

Floralee grinned, "Should'a reckoned you'd know that. We gonna likely see Miz Maisone at the church house, to be tellin' her when this baby gonna be due. We gonna pay her $5.00, that bein' the charge. Then we gonna buy us firewood but we still got us money enough to last to spring."

"Ma?"

"Huh?"

"Not meanin' to make you feel bad nor nothin', I got'a say somethin' I been thinkin'. I seen Miz Maisone bring out Naomi and took note of the things she done, Pa not bein' there, 'member? I seen Miz. Massey when she took Henry."

Floralee looked out over the valley to the blue-misted mountains. Her hands massaged her ankles and calves, aching from the climb. "Sarah, darlin'...."

"Ma, it weren't in my mind to make you feel bad. I was sayin' if Miz Maisone weren't here, like if she couldn't come it bein' February and likely stormin', I done seen what happens and could likely do for you, me being the biggest you got. And if you got no one else...." Her words hung pathetically in the air.

Sarah's last words, "no one else," stabbed Floralee's mind. A massive lump formed in her throat. "Sarah, darlin', don't never say to me I got no one, with you settin' right here 'side me. It comin' down to birthin', I done got more help with you than I ever got with your pa. Iffen Martha Maisone ain't able to come, you'd be a comfort to me, knowin' what you do... and all."

Sarah had more to say. "Ma, iffen she don't come, we still got that $5.00 that would'a been paid to her for helpin'."

"That's the truth, Sarah. It'd be somethin' to think on."

They sat in the sun in companionable silence for a few minutes. Naomi had gathered a handful of acorn shells and was placing them in a row. Floralee was looking around at the trees, making a mental note of the ones that should come down to make her garden.

Sarah moistened her lips and looked at her mother, "Ma?"

"Huh?"

"Two more teeth busted out'a the comb, me draggin' out the rat's nests in my hair this mornin'. I was wonderin', not wantin' to put nothin more on you, but iffen there'd be money sometime, could we get another comb? A thick one. And maybe a brush? Havin' hair like we got, Betty Lou and me, comb teeth don't last too long once they start breakin' out. You think we could, Ma?"

Sarah certainly had a valid point and had a right to expect this much from the family economy. "I reckon we could think on that."

Sarah smoothed her hand over her hair, pressing it against her head, but when she removed her hand, the curls sprang out like high-tension coiled wire.

Floralee looked at the ground around her. "Reckon we could take back a lap full of chinky pins, bein' we're up here where they fall. Sarah, you knowd about that wheat bran in the biscuits, didn't you? How come you not to say somethin'?"

"Figured if you wanted somethin' said, you'd'a said it. Betty Lou knowd about it, too, and she didn't say nothin' neither. The taste weren't too bad, come time we get used to it. Don't reckon Donald ever knowd they wasn't the same. If a body had berry jam, they'd hardly notice the difference."

They went slowly down the hill. They reached the cabin to find clothes hanging on the line. Donald and Henry were sitting under a tree.

"Donald, what you boys doin'?"

"We was restin', Ma."

"You done restin', now, so get to pickin' up them nuts."

"All right, Ma."

"Sarah, you and Betty Lou start in on that mendin' and I'll be goin' on down to the cave."

Floralee still felt the uneasiness in the pit of her stomach as she walked toward the valley and its cave with the mineral spring. The trees were dense between the cabin and the valley and, though there was hardly more than 500 feet of distance between them, for Floralee, the cabin and the cave were worlds apart.

Nathan had been firm.

"Don't aim to see a thread of a skirt tail past them trees. The woman's place is in that cabin, not snoopin' in men's business." The words echoed in her head.

"Wasn't snoopin', Nathan. Just wanted the use of the backside of the cave, that you ain't usin', to store goat cheese like my mama makes."

"Floralee, never seen the beat of dumb things that come out'a a head purty as yourn. Men'd say 'Seems like this run'a likker tastes a mite like goat cheese. Reckon we don't need no more.' Now, Floralee, you done been told where to stay and what to do and I ain't aimin' to say no more."

Nathan had again reinforced his words with a hard hand against her face, leaving the red lines of his fingers on her cheek for the rest of the day. Red lines for the children to see… shameful!

A hard, worn path threaded through the trees between the stones of the bluff. The overhang of the cave was covered with grass and shrubs.

The valley in front of the cave which housed the still was about 200 feet by 400 feet and contained several massive oak trees as well as a number of smaller ones, providing a solid canopy of branches overhead. The valley was dark and damp.

She looked up at the trees. Each of the larger ones would provide a winter's worth of wood, she estimated. They'd take out the smaller ones first, she decided, and remove some lower limbs on the bigger ones. What they cut out would make logs for pen building or firewood. Fenced on three sides, with the bluff on the fourth, the valley would serve to pen up a lot of pigs, and it could be done.

Pigs needed cool shade in the summer and plenty of water. Mineral water flowed constantly from the cave. Floralee felt a subconscious twinge of guilt as she thought of pigs invading the sacred domain of the still. But….

The children would have bacon to flavor their gravy, they would have ham with their roasted sweet potatoes, and stewed pork with dumplings. Pigs turned wasted acorns into hams. They turned chestnuts into bacon and sausage.

The oak trees in the valley were so tall she could not see the tops. There were layers of acorns from many years rotting on the ground of the valley floor. Whoever thought they needed the few pennies from the still when they had such wealth as this? *Oh, Nathan, why couldn't you see this?*

Floralee walked slowly toward the cool dimness of the cave. Water trickled from the rock wall, dripping into the spring, then flowing across the valley into the mountain stream. She plunged her hand into the icy crystal water. This water would keep the milk cold and the butter firm. If she ever had a cow again.

She sat down on a bench beside the pipes, tubes and jugs of the still, feeling small against the depth of the cave. Strangely, her mother's voice echoed words from her youth. "Always figure what your man gonna be wantin' and have it waitin'. That'd be the way to make a good marriage. Don't ever go again what he says to do, flat out. Doin' that'll make a man madder than a nest of hornets in the rain."

"But, Mama," the young Floralee had asked, "Happen what he's sayin' ain't right?"

Mama shook her head, slowly. "It don't make no difference. A man gonna smack you 'crost the face quick one way as t'other, be it right or wrong."

So when Nathan had whacked her, just as her mama had prophesied, she knew she had spoken when she should have been quiet.

She thought of her beautiful Sarah… Sarah, with the strawberry blossom skin… and tried to imagine a handprint against her cheek? Nausea spread over her body, gagging her with its bitterness. She stepped out of the cave and was sick at the base of the massive oak. It must not be let to happen.

The winter crows screamed and cawed overhead and Floralee looked up toward the limbs and promised, "No more. This here's where it'll stop and my little girls gonna learn how to fight back."

She walked bravely into the recesses of the cave and found the stash of rifle shells, which meant more meat for the table. The Floralee who could shoot the eyelash off a frog twenty years ago, could certainly hit more than two fat possums in a gum tree.

Donald brought home the letter from Nate.

…The worse thing I got to do is study books. They gonna make me pass the sixth grade before I get out.

Ma, they keep sayin' into me why did I do it and I say he was my pa and I done what I had to do. It don't seem like they got ears because they ask me the same thing over and over.

They going to keep me until I get sixteen and I said to them I needed to get home to plow but they said no. I could maybe help with a garden here, but when I get out in May it'll likely be too late to put out much of anything. I wish I was there to help you but you know what I done was right. I'll write to you again.

Your son, Nathan Junior

Not coming home until May would mean a change of plans, but they would make it.

Sunday morning was cold and sunshiny with sharp, still air. The mule pulled the wagon into the churchyard and Donald tied him to a post.

They entered the church door only a trifle late. Sarah was first. She wore an attractive coat of green and brown plaid. Her hair was pulled back and tied with a green ribbon. A cluster of curls nestled below the ribbon and a fringe of red-gold shorter hairs had snapped back to lie in ringlets against her ivory forehead. The pink lips were firmly set as she searched, with her sky blue eyes, for an empty pew.

Behind Sarah came Betty Lou. The blue coat with the beautiful buttons contrasted the rosy halo of her hair. There was only the faintest tracing of freckles across her turned up nose. Her pointed chin was held high and proud, knowing the blue coat looked stunning on her.

Next came Charity, clinging to Naomi's hand. Long red braids hung over the red coat. Like Sarah, her forehead was fringed with escaped curls, but unlike Sarah, Charity was liberally splotched with freckles that covered her face, neck and ears. Naomi was a smaller version of Charity with shorter braids but just as many freckles.

Henry wore a slightly faded jacket and a warm, flannel shirt. His overalls had no patches. A pile of fiery red curls topped the freckles and his impish grin as he walked down the aisle holding to his mother's hand.

Donald followed behind, a sturdy, swaggering nine-year-old, in denim jacket and overalls.

They filled the bench from one end to the other. The collection plate was passed down the line and each child put in a penny. After church, Floralee chatted briefly with the midwife about helping with the birthing and they rode away.

17

The kitchen chatter in the town of River Bend was delighted with a new topic.

"That Floralee Baker showin' up with her tribe sure was a eye-opener after years of not darkenin' the door."

"Yeah. Likely it was Nathan and not them youngens that was keepin' her out."

Someone else reasoned, "Weren't too surprised, myself, people showin' up at church when they gonna ask for help."

"Didn't see her askin' nobody for nothin'. I seen ever last one of them youngens put into the plate."

There followed a short silence as this information was processed.

"Them girls had 'em good coats. Sure surprised me."

"Yeah. The church was figurin' to have to help 'em, even collected some old clothes to give 'em, but didn't get up there with 'em, yet. Reckon where she got them things at?"

"Ain't it a sight how purty that oldest girl turned out? Spittin' image of Floralee when we was girls, ain't she?"

"It makes a body sit up and take notice how that Callahan hair shows up. Was a solid line of red, sittin' there on that bench."

"Reckon she don't know she gonna starve out up on that mountain? Be no way for her to scratch out a livin' from them rocks. They was dirt poor with Nathan there helpin' and there ain't no tellin' what'll happen, now. Poor things."

"Didn't look too poor to me. Been over a month, now, and they look good. Yeah, mighty good."

"Where you reckon she got them purty clothes. A body'd'a' thought Floralee'd be askin' around did anybody have somethin' their youngens outgrowed."

"But she didn't."

"My Everett said he seen her over in Jacksonville with a couple of youngens and four goats. Likely she sold them goats."

Another woman clicked her tongue sadly, "Bad thing to be doin', sellin' goats when they's growin' youngens to feed. And just to get money for coats. Shame!"

"Reckon what'll happen when they eat up everything on that hill?"

"Likely the town'll have to take 'em in and make sure them little'ns is eatin' right."

"'Speck so."

There was also conversation in the livery stable.

"Nathan Baker's widow found herself in church yesterday."

"Lookin' for a handout?"

"Didn't seem to be."

"She was drivin' a better wagon than the one she brung to the funeral."

"Where'd she get it? Trade it out?" There followed a ripple of chuckles.

"To hear Nathan talk, it'd not be much trouble for her. Kept a close watch on her, he did."

"Allow she's havin' to fend off old Vern, from time to time."

"She acts plum backward. Time or two I tried to say 'howdy' and she just looked down."

"I'd say she done you a favor. Likely if she hadn't looked down, you wouldn't be here right now, jealous like Nathan was over her. And fast with the fire power."

"You'd have to say that was one good lookin' woman. Still is."

"What I wonder is when is that youngen comin' back to run off some likker. Ain't got nothin' left in my jug but the smell."

"Ought not be long, now."

"Wonder if a fellow'd head up the mountain with a little cash, lookin' to buy something and it not be likker, reckon would he get what he went after?"

"Don't reckon it'd be me wantin' to find out. Iffen she didn't take a shine to you, all you'd be was a puff of smoke and a bang. I recollect Floralee bein' a better shot with a rifle than any fellow for five counties away."

"Happen she won't be so uppity come time it gets hungry enough up on that hillside."

18

The younger children had gone to school and Sarah was washing up the dishes, so now was a good time. Floralee picked up the rifle and climbed the hill. She eased quietly around the boulders, straining her keen eyes on the trees. Her bulky body made her slow and breathless but three or four young squirrels would make tasty dumplings for supper.

She moved slowly around a boulder and there, grinning at her surprise, was Vern.

"What you doin' up here, Vern?"

"Waitin' for you, like I promised you. Figured you'd be up here, the sun bein' warm on the rocks."

"Vern, I told you I didn't aim to set eyes on you standin' on my land. Ever again."

"Aw, Florie, honey, I knowd you had'a say them things, grievin' like you was over Nathan. I never helt that agin you."

"Vern, reckon I see a squirrel right back of your head. You want'a get out'a the way 'afore I shoot?'"

"Now, Florie, don't get huffy. Me and Nathan bein' close, he told me things. Ain't no call for a purty woman like you...."

"Get out, Vern."

"Sure, Florie, and you may not feel so uppity, once that youngen gets here. And I ain't one to hold a grudge. You 'member that."

Floralee raised the rifle to her shoulder and aimed at a twig just over Vern's left ear. The bullet whined through the air, clipping several small limbs from the tree.

Vern dropped to his knees and crawled away, reminding Floralee of a snake... a mountain rattlesnake. She put the rifle on a rock and sat down, burying her face on her forearms.

"Oh, Nathan, Nathan. How come you to do this to me? You bein' gone now and me wantin to remember only good about you, and you still come hurtin' me with words from Vern's mouth."

Her dry eyes stung from the pain but there were no tears.

"I loved you, Nathan, all them years, but you done wrung out all my tears with the way you treated me."

She picked up the rifle and looked at the trees. Four shots later she had four squirrels. She removed their furry skins like taking a jacket off a small child. She always hated to skin squirrels for that reason.

She put the squirrels in the pot to simmer and accepted Sarah's praise. "You done good, Ma. Five shots and four squirrels. You done real good."

Floralee smiled at her daughter and then lay across the bed. She was so tired... so very, very tired.

When she woke up, the meaty smell of the stewed squirrels filled the cabin. Sarah had removed the meat from the bones and set the bones to simmer in water that would be added to the broth. There was a lot of flavor in squirrel bones. She could hear the voices of the other children climbing the hill on their way home from school.

A few days before Christmas, Floralee left Sarah with the little ones and went to River Bend in the wagon. She bought flour and bran, a can of cinnamon and two dozen oranges. And raisins. Plump, purple-brown and bursting with flavor.

At the River Bend Mercantile, she looked at a lot of things, finally selecting a blue comb and a hairbrush for Sarah and a yellow one for Betty Lou. She chose a small red purse for Charity and a pearl handled pocket knife for Donald. For Naomi and Henry, she got two boxes of dominoes, perfect for building houses and barns and pigpens on the table during the winter evenings.

The presents came to almost a dollar. Mr. Jenkins told her, "That'll be fifty cents."

"Beggin' your pardon, Mr. Jenkins, but that ain't the price. I got the money right here, same as I added it. Likely, you made a little mistake on the total."

"Well, I...."

"I'd be thankin' you for doin' it, Mr. Jenkins, you bein' a good and thoughtful man, but I hankered to buy these things myself for my children's Christmas."

She couldn't tell him that there had been no presents for years, though she wanted so much for the holiday to be a celebration. How could she buy something, obviously new, without having to explain to Nathan where the money had come from? Stolen penny by penny, so it wouldn't be noticed, during the dark of the night while her husband slept? Presents for the children would betray her secret.

Floralee hid the sack with the presents in it.

"Donald, you and Charity go find me some 'simmins still hangin' on the trees. Get a lot of 'em."

Persimmons still on the trees, had, by now, turned into hard, thin, sugary casings around the seeds. Grainy and sickeningly sweet, they were almost pure sugar. The children brought in about two quarts of the dried up fruit. "Ain't many left, Ma. 'Possums got after 'em."

"This here'll be enough."

Floralee covered the persimmons with water and set them on the stove to simmer and their sharp, winy smell filled the cabin. She stirred and stirred the gummy mass, then lifted out the seeds. She chopped the last two remaining pears into the persimmon pulp, added the raisins and then set it aside to cool.

She combined wheat bran, shortening she had bought in town. Then baking powder and cinnamon. Lots of cinnamon! Eggs would be nice, but there were no eggs. She stirred the mess thoroughly, adding the chestnut flour and chopped hickory nuts. It smelled good already, so she added more cinnamon.

She spread it in the blackened biscuit pans and put it in the oven.

As they ate cornmeal pancakes and baked sweet potatoes, they sniffed appreciatively.

"What is it?"

"Fruit cake," she told them. "It'll be for Christmas."

"I thought we was gonna eat it tonight."

"We got'a wait three days to get to eat it?"

"Ain't it gonna spoil, waitin' that long?"

But Floralee was firm. The cakes were wrapped in a tea towel and set on the high shelf. The thought of the coming Christmas caused her heart to beat a staccato of excitement within her chest. If only Nate were here. But his letter kept saying he was doing fine.

On Christmas morning, she sent everyone, except Naomi, out to do chores. She arranged the gifts around the table at their accustomed places. The cake was cut and put on the table and milk was poured.

Donald came in first and stopped just inside the door to stare at the table. Henry shoved in behind him.

"Ma!"

The girls came next. Naomi tipped her dominos over on the table, squealing with delight. Charity sat down shyly and stroked the shiny red purse with her finger. Red! Smooth! Brand, spanking new, and it never, ever belonged to someone else!

Betty Lou and Sarah looked at each other with shining eyes, their fingers caressing the stiff bristles of the hairbrushs.

Donald looked at the fancy pocketknife in disbelief. He closed his hand over its firm, cold handle and examined the closed blades. Two blades! He'd wait and open it later, to enjoy the suspense.

No, he couldn't wait! One blade was long and wide, the other short and pointed. The blades were sharp and shiny and it was new. It had never belonged to another person! It had only been his!

Henry was building towers with the dominoes. "Lookie, Ma?"

And the cake. Rich, it was, spicy and fragrant, plump with raisins and chewy with nuts. And sweet, sweet!

The gifts were temporarily set aside for the wonder of the fruitcake.

"Ma, this here's the best thing I ever ate."

"Can we have all of it?"

"Let's eat both cakes!"

"Gimme another piece."

"Did it cost a lot to make it?"

But when they were full and could eat no more, there were still several pieces left of the first cake. The rich, chewy cake was very filling.

Thoughts twisted around in Floralee's mind. The children could eat two pans of biscuits unless they had bran in them. The cake and milk were sweet and satisfying and there were LEFTOVERS!

Leftovers were strange things and she had no place in her mind for them. No place in the cabin, either. What did people do with leftovers? And this was only the beginning. The children needed bacon cooked in their beans and meat in their soup. They needed cheese and eggs. Somehow, there would be eggs. Many things were going to be different.

Like the batter in the big skillet. Wet and shiny, moist and flowing. The heat of the oven made it solid and mixed the flavors and it arose. Just like Floralee was going to make her family rise. All together, solid and strong!

Christmas was a day of leisure except for the morning and evening chores. Floralee spent most of the day in the warm kitchen, thinking. She lined up her thoughts and examined them again, for the hundredth time.

She was so very tired, just now, that she could hardly stand. But she would rise. Not on eagles wings, for certain, but slow and steady, she would rise just like that skillet of cornbread. Flat, brown and nourishing, that was how she would be. She would rise.

She thought of the valley below the spring. There was a fence on three sides, but the pigs would root right underneath. If she could cut small limbs and drive them into the ground around the fence line that would stop the pigs. At least, for a little while.

Yes, tomorrow, they would start to do that. All together they would work, and the valley would become hog tight. First they would have their Christmas, and she would get a day of rest.

Henry and Naomi built houses and fences with their dominos and pushed them down, squealing with excited happiness. The plank table had become a world where anything could be imagined and built. Their mother sat beside them, figuring how many stakes would have to be cut to surround the whole valley. One stake driven into the ground every foot, maybe closer, would take a month.

Neither Sarah nor Betty Lou had ever used an ax. It might be time for them to learn.

By mid January, Floralee was tired all the time, and the simple act of leaving the bed in the morning was a major effort.

Sarah made the breakfast and helped make lunches. She washed up the dishes and Floralee struggled down the hill to the valley. Each foot of fence that was fortified by stakes driven deep in the soft, black soil, was one foot less to do later. Donald was eager and begging to stay home and help, and it was very tempting to let him, but she made him go on to school.

False labor plagued her daily. She told Sarah, "Darlin', I been thinkin' on what you told me about watchin' Naomi when she was born. Five dollars is five dollars, like you said, and I speck we could manage. Just you and me."

Sarah looked down, so her eyes would not show fear, "Sure, Ma. I'd be knowin' what to do. And you'd be tellin' me things. Five dollars were, indeed, five dollars."

The first of February brought winds whistling around the mountains and cold driving rains that soaked the hillside and constantly dripped through the trees. Even the girls complained about school and getting wet coming and going, but Floralee made them go.

On the third day of February, the school children left and Floralee told Sarah, "Darlin', this gonna be the day. You still thinkin' we can do this, you not gettin' sick, nor nothin'?"

Sarah nodded. With luck, Henry and Naomi could be occupied with the dominos. She put the toy blocks on a high shelf. "You got'a play with somethin' else now, and later you can play with them again."

They whined and whimpered, but Sarah was firm. Naomi finally curled up beside Floralee and went to sleep. At lunch time, Sarah fed them beans and leftover biscuits, but she, herself, was too nervous to eat.

The vice-like cramps continued, grinding into her lower back. Floralee counted softly to herself between pains. By now, there were few surprises at this stage. "Sarah, darlin', get them flannel squares and have 'em ready. Tie a pullin' rag on the other bed so as we can close the door on the little'ens and leave 'em in the warm room."

The pains were close now, and hard. She wanted to scream and send they away… to fight back… but that would only scare the little ones and terrify Sarah. She breathed deeply, trying to relax. Ragged breath tore at her lungs as she refused to make a sound.

It was clearly time. Taking a deep breath, she pulled herself upright in a vice of agony and walked slowly and carefully into the lean-to as Sarah watched, her ivory skin now a pale, dead white with fear.

The lean-to was cold but perspiration broke out on Sarah's face as she watched her mother's concentration and effort on the pulling rag, which had been knotted to the iron headboard of the bed. Face contorted with the agony of each onslaught of pain. Waiting it out. Forcing breath in and out. Two deep breaths and the pain eased away.

Immediately, it was back. Slashing and tearing her flesh from her bones. Pain… building and building and peaking. Floralee gripped the pulling rag until her arms ached and screams were held in her throat.

As the girl watched her mother, it was like the world and her life had stopped still and her mind was disconnected from her body. Why, oh, why had she said she could do this? She couldn't, of course. She was only a little girl. She would have to tell her mother that she couldn't do this, but when she opened her mouth to speak, nothing came out. Nothing. She opened her mouth wider and wondered why there was no sound.

Floralee felt the building again, and there was no peak. One pain led unceremoniously into the next. It was certainly time. Knives slashed and ripped. Minutes now, and it would be over.

"Sarah?"

"Huh, Ma? What do I do?"

"The baby! Sarah, honey. Get the baby!"

The fourteen-year-old forced movement into her trembling feet and arms. With shaking, fumbling hands, Sarah drew aside the sheet and caught the slippery bundle that was her little sister. Her shaking hands wrapped the baby in a flannel square forcing her memory to produce the instructions for the next action.

She tied her navel and cut the cord, forcing herself to breathe and noting that her hands seemed to belong to another person. The voices of the two children in the kitchen seemed miles away.

Say something, Sarah, she told herself. "Ma, you got a name for a little girl?" she asked her mother in a timid voice, but Floralee was too drained to answer.

Then Sarah saw her hands begin to tremble so badly she was afraid she would drop the baby. She placed the tiny, red creature on her mother's arms and walked out into the drippy February weather. She trembled and quaked and could not stop shaking. The trembling enveloped her from head to foot.

On shaky feet she went over to a backyard tree and circled it with her bare arms, tightening them around the rough trunk of the tree and leaning her body against the strength of it. Holding something strong seemed to steady her weak and shaking body.

"You got'a stop this," she told herself, firmly. "What would Ma think if she saw this, after you sayin' you could do everything?"

She forced her hand to let go of the tree, stomped her tingling feet and took a deep breath. Lifting her chin, she marched bravely back into the cabin. She was relieved to see her mother looking a little better.

"You doin' all right, Ma?"

"Doin' fine."

"What name you gonna give her?" Her voice was getting steadier.

"Maybe Rosie. You like Rosie for a name?"

"That'd be a good name, Ma."

Mother and baby rested until the other children came in from school.

"A girl!" Donald complained. "How come it wasn't a boy? You already had more girls than boys!"

"Wisht I'd'a been here," Betty Lou told them. Sarah said nothing, but there were moments when she, too, had wished for someone else to be there, even an eleven-year-old sister.

Charity poked a finger at the tiny, pink hand and the fist closed around it. "Lookie! She's holdin' onto my finger, already."

Four-year-old Henry had heard enough about the baby. He said, "Come on, Naomi, let's go play blocks."

And five dollars was five dollars. Sarah was absolutely sure she had earned every penny, and then some.

Little Rosie was lovingly dressed in the clothes from the second hand store, saving one nice dress with an embroidered collar for Sunday. She was adoringly passed from Sarah to Betty Lou and the younger children were allowed to hold her tiny hands and feet when she was not asleep. Floralee was encouraged to stay in bed and she gratefully accepted the commands from her older daughters.

"You got'a rest yourself, Ma. You been workin' too hard. We can take care'a things, now."

And Floralee thought, sure enough, she had been working too hard, but why should now be different? She had done too much all her life. But she listened to Sarah and took a couple of weeks off from the pigpen building.

Donald complained, "But Ma, I just made a pigpen. How come we got'a make another'n?"

"That one you made is a good one but it ain't big enough to hold all the pigs we gonna have."

"We gettin' more of 'em?" He was incredulous. There already seemed to be pigs everywhere.

"Lots more," his mother assured him. "We gonna raise up fat, juicy pigs and sell 'em for cash money."

"Back to Jacksonville?"

"Ain't thought that far. Now you get on down to the valley and start workin' your hands, 'stead'a your mouth. Take Henry, he can bring stuff to you."

The four bigger pigs were filled out and growing fast. They "oinked" contentedly in their pen, plowing their snouts through the soft dirt for nuts, greens and roots. Maybe even a few beetles. The twelve remaining little ones had been weaned and were experimenting happily with mash and acorns. The old sow had been moved into a pen by herself to rest and get fat.

Which presented another problem. There was a boar among the biggest pigs and if she kept him, there'd have to be still another pen to put him in before he became mean. So Floralee lay on the bed, resting and thinking.

She could haul the three female hogs back to Jacksonville and take her chances with the auction or she could post a notice in River Bend and wait. Surely there were three families nearby who needed a good butcherin' pig.

Her mouth watered at the thought of the fresh hams and shoulders, but there was no way she could butcher one of them even if she chose to. None of her children had even seen a hog butchered, and among them, there were none who had the size to be of any help. If Nate were only here, perhaps she'd try it, but he was not here.

Anyway, she'd sell the three pigs, trying for $5.00 each. No, make it $5.25. She could wait and see if they would bring that much. The pigs were costing her nothing but time, now that they were off the mash.

Then she'd put a smaller pen beside the one Donald made, getting him started on it as soon as possible. Wouldn't he squeal like a stuck pig, himself, when she told him? The thought brought a small smile. Donald had a lazy streak, but he did a good job when she bullied him into it.

She'd put the boar in the smaller pen and use the other pen for the farrowing sow. The younger pigs would be in the valley and allowed to root it out with the acorns and maybe turnips, if the crop took.

If she got $15.75 for the bigger pigs, she'd go back to the auction and look for another bred sow. Then the boar would be ready by the time the first sow came around again. It all sounded so good, she could feel excitement tingling and strengthening her arms.

19

Nate's letters came regularly, now, and she answered them quickly. They sounded as though he was doing well, and he only complained that he was not there to help her. She told him she was doing all right, and that she had a lot of ideas, but how could she tell him everything she had planned, on just a piece of paper?

He would probably worry, anyway, no matter what she said. When he came home he would understand. Then they would butcher one of the younger pigs, and they would celebrate.

She had allowed herself a long rest, but by the first of March, she was beginning to feel spring in her bones. The urge to be out of doors and the thoughts of planting a garden, obsessed her. There were so many trees that it was difficult to find a garden spot without tree roots criss-crossing it. When the trees were removed, the water would come gushing down the hill and carry away the good dirt. Couldn't let that happen. Some way would have to be found to stop the dirt, and hold it on the hillside.

She spent hours, standing and looking, before the idea came to her. A craggy, dead tree had blown over in a winter storm and was laying crossways of the hill. Leaves and loose dirt had washed in behind it, leveling the ground and a narrow terrace was formed. There was the answer... right before her, but rocks would be better than logs. At the top of the hill were rocks aplenty. They would have to be rolled down, and Donald would be the one to do it.

She sighed. Life was so complicated and she was so tired. Her mind was renewed by the spring but her body was bone weary, completely drained by the winter of work and the pregnancy. Many of the things she wanted to do could not be done this spring, but there would be another year.

She went to the cabin and took a small piece of paper from her hoarded supply and printed on it, "BUTCHERING HOGS FOR SALE. $5.50 see Floralee Baker."

When she read it over, she realized she had put $5.50 instead of $5.25. Oh, well, she would try that first, even though that was top price for a hog.

"Donald, you run by the pharmacy and ask Mr. Markham can you pin this up on his notice board."

The notice having been written, Floralee turned her mind to other things. After all, she was not desperate for cash money at this moment. She was, however, determined to finish the pigpen.

"But, Ma, them baby pigs is gonna run off all their fat off in that big old pen."

"And they can just eat enough acorns and put it back on," was Floralee's answer.

By the last of March, the pen was finished and the twelve babies were let loose in it, disappearing immediately into the brush and piles of leaves.

20

There was talk about Floralee's notice on the board at the pharmacy. That board had more news bearing efficiency than a city newspaper, and gathering groups and individuals came daily and sometimes more often, just to see who had what. And speculate on why?

"See this ad where Floralee Baker got herself a hog to sell? A body'd think she'd be more interested in killin' it to feed that passel of youngens."

"Likely she found herself needin' cash money more'n food, Nathan bein' gone nigh a half a year, now, and her with that new baby."

"Reckon I could use me a little fresh pork right about now, bein' my favorite meat, and bein' of a mind to do her a favor. Would'a helped out 'afore this, iffen she'd'a asked or showed she wanted it. Can't just go forcin' help on folks as don't need it. Figure I may as well go up and get one of 'em hogs off her."

"Where you 'spose she got herself a pig? I know for a fact, old Nathan wouldn't hear to 'em on the place."

"She caught herself a range pig, it'd seem to me. What else could she'a done? Likely, it'll be lean and stringy but them range pigs makes good sausage, and that's always good eatin' of a cold mornin'. Anyway, I've been thinkin' someone needs to help her out."

"That'd be a bit steep of a price for a range hog. But I reckon I feel like you, wantin' to help out Nathan's widow. We could run up there in my wagon and pick up two of 'em and that'd likely keep her goin' till a garden comes on."

It was a Saturday morning and Charity saw the wagon, first. "Ma! Ma! They's a wagon a'comin'. Got two men in it."

Donald picked up the cry. "Yeah, Ma. She's tellin' the truth."

Betty Lou took the baby from her mother so she could go to the door.

"Howdy, there, Floralee," they greeted her.

Floralee recognized the men and knew their names well, but her first instinct was to duck her head and turn away. Instead, she squared her shoulders and lifted her chin, and forced a small smile.

"Howdy, Fred and Josh. What brings you up the mountain?"

"Well, bein' a purty day, we thought we'd get out a bit. Saw your notice about hogs and reckoned we'd take a couple off your hands."

Floralee nodded. "Sure, I got hogs. Got 'em in a pen down in the valley."

The men followed her down the steep path between the rocks and boulders. The pigs had just been tossed a bucket of chinky pins and were rooting noisily into the pile.

"It'd be one of them biggest ones, there. I only got the three ready to butcher."

The men looked at the pigs with wide eyes, then looked at each other. These pigs were clearly not the long-legged range pigs, caught half-wild on the mountain. They were short-legged and wide, with round hams and well fleshed shoulders. Their ears stood up healthy and strong.

In amazement, Fred asked, "Where at did you get these here hogs?"

Floralee hesitated. It was still a man's world, with him demanding answers. "Can't be sure why you'd be needin' to know that, but they's no reason not to tell you. I got 'em over at the auction in Jacksonville when they was little."

"Auction? You?"

She grinned slightly at their surprise. "Reckon I had to. Didn't have me no protectin' angel hankerin' to do it for me. Got 'em last fall and I been feedin' 'em up."

"And it's them pigs you want to be sellin'?"

"Reckon so. Figure 'em to be 'bout as ready as they gonna be."

The men looked at each other. "Gonna be right smart of a tussle, gettin' 'em up the hill and into the wagon."

"Yep. Could be we'd be needin' to make two trips."

Floralee broke into their conversation. It was time to get something out into the open. "Was you fellows thinkin' they was skinny runts, and thinkin' to take 'em both in that little old wagon you brung?"

"Well, we...."

"Is that what you was thinkin', and them costin' $5.50 each? You was thinkin' to give me a handout, wasn't you?"

"But, Floralee...."

"It ain't like that, Floralee."

"Then can you say to me how it was like, comin' up here like this?"

"Honest, Floralee, we wasn't thinkin' nothin'."

"Reckon you wasn't thinkin', t'all. Iffen I was needin' help, which I ain't sayin' I won't sometime, I'd be goin' and sayin' to you, 'I need me a little help right now, till I get back on my feet to pay you back'. But iffen I say I got me a butcherin' hog for sale, at high dollar, then you can believe I got me a hog and not one of them pigs as is all legs and back bone." She smiled to temper the sting of her words.

She continued in a softer voice, "Reckon I ought'a tell you that I 'preciate the thought you had, to help me out. That bein' right neighborly, but I reckon you done forgot the kind of person that was Floralee Callahan. That'd been easy to do, her hidin' inside'a Floralee Baker all these years."

There was a brief pause. One of the men sought to fill it.

"I'll be switched iffen you don't put me in the mind of that girl I used to know by the name of Floralee Callahan," Josh told her, grinning with reminiscence. "Fiery hair and fiery tongue, them is two things I 'member real well."

"Speck you ought to, Josh. Now, iffen you'd take that wagon back down the hill and bring it through the road 'round the brush, you'd be right next to that pen. You'd not be knowin' about that road, not bein' a customer of Nathan's, but I figure to be usin' it right smart now. Figure on havin' a place to make loadin' easier when my Nate gets home to help build it."

A short time later, Floralee watched the wagon pull away, swaying from the load as the two, prime butchering-hogs struggled to keep their footing.

She opened her hand and looked at eleven dollars in cold, hard coins. Her heart pounded and her breath was short. "I knowed it all along, Nathan, but you was too stubborn to listen to your own ears. Iffen you'd listened to what I was sayin', you'd be alive and breathin' right here beside me." She sighed, heavily, and climbed wearily back to the cabin.

Before the day was over, Josh was back with his brother to buy the other hog.

"Good lookin' boar you got there," he commented. "Could be gettin' good money for him, too, if you was a'mind to."

Floralee nodded. "Reckon so, but that'd not be a good idea, me needin' 'im for the brood sow like I got up hill in the other pen, quick as she comes around."

Josh's eyes averted in embarrassment. This was not woman's talk. It was more like what he'd hear over at the livery stable.

"When you thinkin' to let them others go?"

"Don't exactly know, but I allowed they'd hold over till fall."

Josh nodded. "Speck that'd be about right. Thought I'd spread the word, iffen you wanted me to. 'Course, that notice on the board, one that brung me, that'd likely be enough."

Floralee now had $16.50 to spend at the auction if she only had the strength to make the trip. She planned to take the whole family in May when Nate came home, but that was two months away. She needed to make a trip before then.

She could go now, but the weather was too unsettled for little Rosie and she couldn't bear to leave her. Or could she? She had seen nursing bottles for sale at the Mercantile and had smiled at the thought of using one of them when she had much better equipment attached to her own body.

Instantly, her mind was made up. The bottle would help Rosie, and she, herself, would just have to be prepared to bear whatever had to be born.

It was too late to go today, but Monday she would get the nursing bottle and Tuesday she would go to the auction. It would be a long, cold trip and likely amount to a lot of pain, being away from the baby that long. But the pain in her breasts would be offset by the cheaper prices, now, against the warmer days of spring when more people would want pigs to turn out on the grass.

Sarah did not approve. "Ma, you can't be goin' off alone."

"I got'a go alone. You got'a keep Rosie."

"But, Ma...."

Finally, it was decided that Betty Lou would stay home from school and make the trip with her.

"But I'd go, Ma," offered Donald. "That way Betty Lou'd get to go to school. She likes school."

"Reckon you would go, and thanks, but you got'a go to school."

"Aw, Ma...."

They set out before daylight with a ragged quilt for their own knees and another for the pigs they would buy. The $16.50 was in her purse.

Floralee let one good lot of pigs go by, because a brood sow already bred was coming through. The day was wet and dismal and the sun refused to shine. The auction barn was wet, smelly and depressing and not many buyers came.

The auctioneer's voice sang out, "Got us in a pig, here, gonna be a mama. What'll you give, will ya give, will ya give? What'll you give me for the mama pig?" He paused a meaningful length of time, then commented, impatiently.

"Somebody start this thing off! Fifty cents? This ain't no joke, folks."

Floralee bid a dollar.

"Got me a dollar, who'll make it two? Got me a dollar, who'll make it two? Who'll make it two, make it two, make it two? Got me a dollar, who'll make it two?"

"Got me two, I'm'a lookin' for a three. Gimme three, gimme three. Who'll make it three? Two fifty? Got me two fifty, and we're goin', again. Gimme two seventy five."

"Folks, two fifty ain't no price for this mama pig. Ain't gonna be long till there's grass to feed 'er. You aimin' to hurt her feelin's? Who'll gimme more, gimme more, gimme more? Who'll gimme two seventy five?"

Floralee raised the bid. It climbed slowly past three and she bought the sow for $3.10. She was aware that she could have had to pay twice that amount if the attendance at the auction barn had been good. She had been sure she could trade the bad weather and her own discomfort for a good price. And she had.

There were no other pigs small enough or cheap enough to tempt her, but a good looking billy goat came butting and bellowing into the ring. He lowered his head, waving his horns menacingly. She sure would like to have him, but she had no way to get him home.

Or did she? Why not tie him to the back of the wagon? He certainly seemed to have enough energy to make the trip home on his own four feet. It might simmer him down a bit.

Nobody wanted a goat, today. After a few minutes of pleading, the auctioneer got the bidding up to a dollar ten.

"If we can't do better than this, folks, we ought'a go on home. Who'll give me a buck and two bits? Hurry up, folks, it's cold and hungry in here."

His song rang out, "Gimme two, gimme two, gimme two. Who'll gimme two bits?"

Floralee would.

The auctioneer was relieved. "Got me a buck and two bits. Iffen you don't speak up quick, the little lady gonna have herself a handful of billy goat."

The joke brought on a ripple of chuckles. "A buck and a quarter once, a buck and a quarter twice. Gone, to the lady for a buck and a quarter. Gonna charge you men a dime, each, to watch her get this fellow out'a town."

The billy goat lifted his head toward the rafters and emitted a tooth-rattling bellow.

Floralee was forced to buy another length of rope. She tied one end to the billy's neck while he was still held tight in the stanchion. The other end of the rope was tied to his thick, curving horns.

Pulling the ropes high, she tied them together in a large knot directly in front of his eyes. The middle of the rope was attached tightly to the endgate of the wagon.

As the mule pulled forward, the billy was forced to walk with his nose tucked under and his eyes on the ground, unless he walked fast enough to keep up with the mule. There was a murmur of disappointment and admiration among the watching male audience. The billy trotted docilely after the wagon, clip-clopping along the brick street.

"Betty Lou, speck we ought'a have us some hot cocoa to warm us up 'afore we head east." The little sandwich shop was just ahead.

Fragrant steam rose from the rich chocolate as they sipped gratefully. Warmth spread to their feet and hands as they prepared to journey home.

It was while they were in the cafe that the freezing rain started to fall. As soon as the streets, wagon bed and animals were completely

235

soaked, the rain turned to sleet, slashing and biting its way through the mountains.

The angry billy kicked and bucked, losing his footing on the slick streets. He struggled his legs back under him and continued to buck and bleat.

"He'll do better on the gravel," Floralee predicted. "Betty Lou, darlin', you gonna have to ride back there with that sow, keepin' that quilt on her or we gonna lose her in this sleet."

Betty Lou sighed, but was glad she was not wearing the new blue coat. She crouched beside the grunting sow, tucking the sow's quilt around her own legs and over the sow's bulky body.

"Keep back away from her mouth, Betty Lou. Sows been known to snap at people, bein' like her and not knowin' what's happenin' to her. Sure do hope she got herself bred to a Hampshire like herself."

Before they had gone a mile, Betty Lou's feet were asleep and tingling. She stretched out first one leg, then the other, to let the blood flow its stinging needles into her feet. She pulled her scarf over her face and her breath instantly froze it stiff as a board. She could no longer remember the warmth of the hot chocolate as she huddled, miserably, against the hog's back. Between herself and the sow was a small pool of warmth for Betty Lou to insert her frozen fingers.

Floralee was wrapped in the other quilt, but the wind cut through the ragged places and the reins froze in her red hands. She lowered her face into the cutting northeasterly wind that was driving its ice crystals parallel to the ground. The stiffly frozen reins were of no value to direct the mule, but he knew of only one way to go, and he forged ahead.

Finally, Floralee leaned forward and closed her eyes, her head splitting and her breasts aching.

"Ma?" came Betty Lou's faint, concerned voice.

"It's all right, Betty Lou. We gonna make it," was the forced reply. But she chided herself severely for trying to save a little money by making the trip in March, unsettled and unpredictable as March weather always was here in the mountains.

The billy walked a little way, then butted a little way. His angry lunges against the wagon only lightened the load for the mule. Occasionally, he bleated his frustration into the icy blast of air.

Early winter darkness settled in when they were still five miles from home. By now, Floralee's breasts were throbbing and she could no longer feel her feet. She forced herself to stomp until the stinging points of warm blood returned painful feeling into them.

The graveled road gave way to the dirt road past the livery, and then to the narrow two ruts as they disappeared into the tree-covered hill. The red clay road leading to the cabin was frozen tight and hard, and the sure-footed mule slowly picked his way along in the pitch darkness. The angry billy leaned into the rear of the wagon to vent his frustration and pushed all the way up the hill.

The small, eleven-year-old girl huddled against the sow's back, just grateful that she didn't have to get out and push.

The mule headed straight for the shed and the manger of hay and began to mouth the straws before he was unhitched. Donald came running out of the house to help.

"Donald, you unhitch the mule and I got'a have a rope to tie up this billy."

"Billy? A billy goat?"

"Just get me a rope." Floralee had no strength or patience left for explanations.

By now, Sarah had appeared.

Floralee's icy fingers tied the goat to a post before detaching him from the wagon. She could hear Rosie's angry wails coming from the cabin. *Just a minute longer, Rosie,* her mind promised, but Rosie screamed on.

"Donald, tuck that other quilt around the sow and leave her there in the wagon till mornin'." Floralee's feet, with a mind of their own, began to carry her to the cabin.

Sarah had cooked fresh young turnip greens and cornbread. The brown beans were thick and rich in their broth and there was milk. But first, the screaming Rosie was put to her breast, where she smacked and gurgled, eagerly.

When everyone had eaten, there were leftovers of everything. Floralee was too exhausted to wonder about it. She huddled against the warmth of the fire, cuddling Rosie to her aching breast. The food and warmth revived Floralee, and the full stomach made Rosie drowse and yawn.

In time, she surveyed the table where her children had eaten. Leftovers! Again it struck her on how strange it seemed! She looked from the contented children to the food left on the table. It was truly a miracle! One handed down to her by the Good Lord, and certainly He should be properly thanked. And she would do that just as soon as she got warm enough to thaw out her mind. Properly.

She let the school children stay home the next day but she made Donald go up the hill and pitch rocks in a row to terrace the dirt. The wind, the rain and the feet of animals would loosen the disturbed soil and it would be caught behind the row of rocks. Next spring, or at least soon, there would be a kitchen garden for greens and fresh vegetables. The effort helped Donald work off some of his energy.

Then came Saturday and the sun broke free of the cloudbank, spreading living gold over the mountains. The coating of crystal ice that encased every twig and pebble reflected the sunbeams into rainbow colors, casting them about into the clear mountain air, but by noon, the trees were dripping with melted water. By mid afternoon, the sparkle had gone and the gray twigs and rocks were beginning to dry out.

Sunday morning at breakfast, Floralee told them. "Tomorrow we gonna butcher us a goat."

"Us, butcher?"

"A goat?"

"That big billy?"

"No," she told them. "The little billy."

"How we gonna do it?"

"Ma, did you ever butcher anything?"

"No, Charity, but we gonna."

"I could stay home and help," Donald suggested, hopefully.

"Yes, Donald, you can stay home one day. We gonna need all hands to help."

Floralee spent Sunday in the bed, resting. "Lord, I sure wisht I could go over to Your house, but this here little Rosie, bein' so young and all… reckon I'll have to invite You to come to my house, today."

On Monday morning, she bravely took up the rifle and made the children stay inside.

"Aw, Ma!"

"Mind me, now, Donald."

One shot brought down the little billy. The back legs were tied together and the rope thrown over a tree limb dragging the carcass up the trunk. With sharp knives, she and Donald began to remove the white, wooly skin.

The corn grinder was attached to the table and the meat-grinding blade was inserted. Grinding was usually considered the best use for goat meat.

Sarah and Betty Lou took turns on the handle, grinding the meat. They formed patties and fried it brown in the skillet, carefully saving all the grease.

Donald stood by the hanging animal, cutting away slabs of meat. Charity edged close to catch the carvings and carry them, running, into the house.

When there was a mountain of fried patties and pans of grease, Floralee began to pack the patties into the deep crock, the way she had seen her mother preserve them. She packed several layers, then poured rendered grease over them to cover them, pressing down to remove all the air bubbles. With all air removed, the patties would keep fresh for weeks.

Most of the meat was packed into the crock. The bones were cracked and put to simmer in the largest kettle. By late noon, the steam from the simmering broth blended with the aroma of the fried meat, tempting hungry mouths to an unbearable degree.

The wealth of rich broth was so great that she was forced to seal up several of her canning jars full. The sight of the gray-brown liquid in the jars sent a comforting sense of wealth through her body. Broth… for gravy, or soup, or dumplings, or …? Totally without forethought or planning, she could pick up a jar of the broth, open it, and use it for the next meal. *Oh, Nathan, why would you not listen to me one time? Or maybe several times?*

Floralee made biscuits and brown gravy.

"How many meat patties do you want me to put on for dinner?" Betty Lou wondered.

"All of them," came the startling reply.

They ate the meat, sucking the juice from the fragrant patties and making sandwiches with a split biscuit. They chopped them up in their plates, smothering them with the brown gravy.

Floralee watched them eat and whispered, "Lord, I ain't sure how this happened, but I figure You to be in the back of it somewheres, knowin' my youngens needed meat. Now, Lord, iffen You got any ideas on how I could get us some chickens…?"

There were meat patties leftover and she broke them up in gravy to put over sweet potatoes for supper. The thick, rich broth from the bones would make dumplings for two days. And the several jars of the broth, now under her plank bed, were a source of hidden wealth. Something she could open and use to make a meal without even thinking of the next day… and the next.

On Friday of the same week, a fat young buck leaped the fence and was browsing on the dry grass with the goats. One shot brought it down. All day Saturday was spent butchering him.

Large slabs of meat were hung over the potbelly stove to make jerky ("Ma, ain't this here the stuff that Pa didn't like?") and the rest of it was ground into patties and fried down. It totally filled another crock.

Floralee was too excited to sleep. She spent most of the night keeping a steady fire under the jerky. Removing as much moisture from the meat as fast as possible would improve the flavor of the cured product. It seemed that the Lord not only giveth, but kept on giving until the little cabin on the hillside was overflowing.

The next Sunday dawned warm and bright as it often did in the mountains. The Bakers filled their accustomed bench and contributed to the collection plate. Tiny Rosie fussed only a little.

21

By Wednesday, the new sow was carrying sticks in her teeth, obviously about to farrow. Floralee made Donald bring baskets of fresh, dry, dead leaves to toss into her pen.

All day Thursday, the sow circled in the leaves, tromping them into powder, and by Friday morning, she had nine squealing pink babies, though she was equipped to feed only eight.

The squirming pink runt was brought into the house. He was happy enough to get a chance at the nursing bottle that Rosie had rejected.

If all nine pigs lived, she would have 21 pigs, two sows and a well-patterned Hampshire boar. Twenty-one times $5.50 was over a hundred dollars. Floralee refused to allow herself to think in amounts of that magnitude.

Late into the night she sat before the plank table with the candle burning before her. The cabin was alive with the sound of breathing, sleeping children. She held the scrap of paper on which she had made her lists six months ago, smiling as she read the entries under each column.

She held the list close to the flame of the candle and watched as the fire caught the corner. It spread evenly, turning her words into whispery black cinders, crumbling and falling on the table. When the paper was completely burned, she swept the ashes up in her hand and tossed them into the ashbin.

Rev. McCrey had suggested that she would mount up with wings like an eagle and it had seemed preposterous. She thought she would be content to be as the cornbread, warm and substantial, rising fragrantly in her skillet, but she had done better than that.

Certainly she was not an eagle, but perhaps a winter crow? Noisy and healthy, the ebony-colored birds fluttered about in the freedom of the treetops, existing on whatever nature put before them. Yes, she was a winter crow. Thank You, Lord.

22

At the Tuesday Sewing Circle in the church in town, someone reported, "Good to see Floralee Baker out with her new baby last Sunday."

"Likely she was gettin' cabin fever, not bein' able to get out on account'a the weather. Never liked winter babies, myself."

"Happen Floralee never got the chance to pick when that baby come. Or whether it come."

"She put a purty name on her, 'Rosie'."

"Baby got red hair?"

"Does a rooster crow?"

"Strange thing, them youngens puttin' money into the plate every Sunday, sure as shootin'."

"Reckon where she had somethin' to put in?"

"Hard to say. She ordered ten ricks of wood from my boy and he's gettin' a dollar a rick, delivered. He's been crossin' fingers that she's got the money when he's got the wood."

"We got us a butcherin' hog and paid her for it. Reckon she's got that money."

"What'd you do with the hog? Make sausage?"

"Strange about that. Figured we better grind it up, likely bein' tough, but it turned out fat and tender. Best money we ever paid out for pork. Hams that'd cut with a fork and the fat back two inches thick. Two strips'a lean through them jowls."

"Hmmmm."

"Reckon she'd'a liked that new youngen to be a boy, her bein' short on male help up on that hillside."

"Speck her brother-in-law does for her from time to time?"

"Does what?"

"Yeah. Likely, he gives her a bit'a trouble in some ways."

"How's that wife of his'n? Always been a queer sort."

"Who wouldn't be? Married to Vern."

"I heard she was strange 'afore he married her."

"Must'a been, or she'd'a turned 'im down. Would'a thought that havin' youngens'd be a help to her, and then she never had none, did she?"

"Speck Floralee'd glad of any company, even a little queer, stuck up on that mountain the way she finds herself."

"Ham's purty good and juicy, huh?"

"Likely the best I ever ate."

"Sure could use me some good pork, 'tween now and when my fryers come on."

"She ain't gonna have no more butcherin' hogs till fall, my Josh told me. Said he told her to hold one for us."

"Too bad. I'd'a liked to get one. We'd could'a paid her cash money."

"Well, that's what it'd'a took to get 'em. They weren't cheap."

"She was lucky, that baby comin' while the storms was here. Likely she got plenty to be doin', once it fairs up."

"Yeah, I reckon. You folks got your garden plowed up, yet?"

23

The weather indeed had become fair and the sun finally spread its golden warmth over the mountainsides. The black jack oaks had finally dropped their leaves, being pushed off by the new, swelling buds. That was a sure sign of spring. The pussy willows and redbuds, the dogwoods and the violets gave color to the brown of the dead leaves.

Four more days and Nate would be released.

Floralee walked down to the valley and sat on the overhang of the cave. She caught an occasional glimpse of a pig, snorting and rooting, crunching tubers, grubs and tender twigs. Twelve growing, fattening pigs were just about lost in the big pen.

Through the leafless trees, she could see the cabin where Vern and Elaine lived. Strange person, her sister-in-law.

At first, Floralee had tried to be friendly, but was never able to communicate. Elaine would answer Floralee's attempts with a "yes" or "no" or a puzzled look. Finally, Floralee gave up trying to be friendly.

To make matters worse, Elaine remained childless as well as withdrawn, while Floralee produced children biannually. Elaine never came out of the cabin, sitting, instead, at the window just staring toward the valley.

Floralee seldom thought of her anymore, and was not thinking of her now. She watched tiny rabbits skipping and hopping on new spring legs. Suddenly, she was hungry for fried rabbit, young and tender, fried crisp and tasty. One of the best and tastiest treats of a mountain springtime, for a fact.

Strange, really, to feel hungry for rabbit when she had goat meat and deer meat at the cabin. But there had been occasional rabbits nibbling at her tender, young turnip greens and there were likely some there right now. She sat a moment longer but restlessness forced her to her feet.

Climbing the hill back to the cabin, she picked up the rifle and several shells, then headed farther up toward the top. There were no rabbits at the turnip greens, so she climbed still farther. The goats were looking fat and healthy, the white of their hairy hides standing out against the gray and brown of the rocks. She stood watching their delicate noses sniff at twigs and newly unfurled fiddle ferns, selecting this bite and rejecting that one. Their long lashed eyes rested on her as they chewed contentedly.

A voice from around the rock startled her.

"Glad you came up here, Florie, honey. Been watchin' for you, thinkin' it was comin' time." The ingratiating voice of Vern broke raspingly into her meditation.

"What you doin' here, Vern, after me sayin' to keep away?"

"Now, Florie, honey, I don't hold them words agin you, knowin' a woman makes herself feel better to say 'em. I knowed soon this purty weather'd make your blood rise, and you'd be comin' up here to me."

"Get out," she said calmly.

"Aw, now, Florie. You been alone too long. Let me kiss them purty, pink lips."

"Get out."

"Don't be skeerd. Can't nobody see us in these big rocks. Just lay down that gun and come on over here. Let me hold you."

"You get away from me, Vern Baker, 'afore I blow off your head."

"Florie, you look so purty standin' there in the sun, that purty red hair so shiny."

"Vern, I said to you what I'd be sayin' to Elaine, you comin' over here botherin' me."

"Aw, you wouldn't be doin' that. I knowd you was just talkin'. Elaine, she ain't purty like you and they ain't nothin' can make her mad, like you get."

Floralee began to tremble with anger. "Turn yourself around and start walkin' 'cause I'm a'fixin' to shoot, right there where you stand."

Floralee lifted the rifle and leveled it at Vern's head. She lined up the sight with his grinning face.

"Aw, Florie, now you don't...."

The whine of the bullet had an unreal sound and, in exaggerated slow motion, she saw the grin disappear from Vern's face and his knees buckle under him. He crumbled to the ground at the base of a large rock, blood running down his face.

Floralee slid her hand over the barrel of the rifle. What had happened? She only meant to scare him off. Why, the gun was not even loaded. He was joking, of course, and he would get up laughing... tormenting her!

No, this was a dream. Of course, it was. Over and over she had lived through a frightening scene, only to wake up safe in her bed. She sat down on a rock, waiting to wake up. She waited a long time and finally she began to sing, to maybe help her to wake up faster. Any minute now, Sarah would shake her awake.

But it was Betty Lou who came to her in her dream.

"Ma? What you shootin', Ma?"

She saw her mother sitting on the rock and came over to her. She saw the crumpled body of Vern and her eyes flew open and she pointed.

"Ma!"

Don't be scairt, Betty Lou, darlin'. I just been havin' a bad dream and you got yourself into it. We both gonna wake up any minute now."

"No, Ma, it ain't no dream."

"Sure it is. This here gun didn't have no shells."

"We heard the gun, Ma."

"No. It weren't no shot. You just got yourself caught up in my dream."

Pale and terrified, Betty Lou slipped away and ran, breathless, down the hill. "Sarah! Sarah! Ma's done shot Uncle Vern. Killed 'im."

Floralee heard Betty Lou'a frightened cry and smiled. Dreams could seem so real! So very, very real, and so scary if you didn't know it was a dream. But this time, she knew.

Within minutes, Betty Lou was back with Sarah. They came and sat on either side of her, acting very strangely.

"We got'a go, Ma." They took her arms and walked beside her to the house.

Sarah told Betty Lou, "We got'a get somebody. You stay and I'll go."

Floralee told Sarah, "No, darlin', don't be goin' nowhere. There's no need."

Floralee went into the cabin and picked up the crying Rosie. She saw Sarah hitch the mule to the wagon and drive away but that was all right. It was just part of her dream... her very, long dream.

Betty Lou went about the cabin, doing this and that, so Floralee lay down on the bed with Rosie. Naomi curled up beside her and she smoothed the little girl's red curls. Slowly she relaxed. Maybe if she went to sleep in her dream, she would wake up again and the dream would be gone. Finally, she dozed with Naomi and Rosie on either side of her.

Sarah didn't know where to go. All the way into town, she thought about it. She could knock on someone's door. She could go to the cafe or the Mercantile.

Or she could go to the livery stable. That would be it! There were always men around the livery and someone would know what to do. That would be best.

She reined the mule in toward the livery and stopped at the door. She went up to a group of men and they stopped talking to look at her.

"Please, I got'a get help."

"Someone get hurt? Ain't you Floralee Baker's girl?"

Sarah nodded. "My Ma shot someone."

"Floralee...?"

"Shot someone?"

"What you sayin', girl?"

"Who got shot?"

Sarah found her voice. "Uncle Vern. Please hurry!"

"He hurt, bad? Is he bleedin'?"

"Dead?"

"Dear Merciful Lord!"

"Speck we better hurry on up there."

One of the men drove Sarah's wagon and others came in another one. Sarah sat trembling on the bench. She couldn't stop shaking. Maybe it was a dream, like Ma said. She heard a noise and knew it was her own teeth chattering.

The mule was impossibly slow. She felt she should say something to the man sitting beside her, but she had no more voice, so that probably meant it was a dream. She hoped it was a dream. Lots of times, voices didn't work in dreams.

Finally, the wagon reached the top of the hill. Betty Lou was standing in the doorway and she ran out to the wagon.

"Ma's asleep," she told Sarah.

Sarah looked helplessly at the man beside her. The other wagons stopped and the men got out.

"Young ladies, my name's Josh. Where at is... the... where at is Vern?"

"Up there," the girls pointed toward the mountaintop.

"Reckon we better have a look." They walked up the rocky hillside, with Sarah and Betty Lou following, not knowing what else to do.

"Likely his wife knows by now," Josh said, but the girls shook their heads, wide-eyed.

"Reckon I ought'a tell her then."

They walked to her cabin.

Elaine opened the door. "He be dead, now," she told them in a dead-pan voice.

Josh nodded. "Ought we...? You want the body here?"

"Might's well," was Elaine's unemotional reply.

The body of Vern Baker was carried to his cabin and placed on the bed.

Elaine stood looking at Vern. "Now I reckon you gonna stay put," she told him, sternly.

"Yes, ma'am, he gonna stay put tilst we get up here with the casket. Be bringin' help up to you, right away."

"Don't need no help. Don't bring no casket."

"Huh?"

"Reckon he gonna stay put, keepin' to his own cabin."

"What you mean?"

Elaine firmed her lips and stared at the men. "I had me a thought to get that red headed woman at the same time. It'd only take me another bullet."

"Red headed...?"

"Yep, should'a got 'em both."

"Both?"

Elaine continued, "But then, I seed her try to run 'im off. Picked up her gun to 'im. That was when she done wrong. It weren't her place to shoot 'im dead. Vern be my husband. Up to me to keep 'im home. Up to me to shoot 'im, that bein' the only way to do it and make sure he stays. He gonna stay put, now."

The men looked at each other and then at Elaine.

"You sayin' you ain't wantin' 'im buried?"

"Ain't no need."

"But...."

"Go," Elaine pointed to the door.

"But...."

Elaine reached above the door and took down her rifle.

"We'll be runnin' along, now, Miz Baker." The two men scurried through the door, running toward Floralee's cabin. They knew too well what happened when Elaine pointed her gun.

Floralee woke up from the nap and was staring at the wagons in the yard. This was the longest, strangest dream she had ever remembered. She saw Josh and the other man running toward her.

"Floralee, you didn't do it!"

"Do what?"

"You didn't shoot Vern."

"Knowd I didn't. The gun weren't even loaded. 'Sides, how come you to know that? It was my dream."

"Dream?"

"Josh, what you men doin' comin' up the hill to my house?"

"Floralee, we got'a sit down 'cause I got'a say somethin'. Vern Baker was shot and he's dead."

"No, Josh, that was the dream." How many times would she have to tell them?

"No, Floralee. He's been shot and Elaine done it. She done went out'a her mind and she didn't even let us take the body away."

"She's apt to be comin' over here totin' a gun after you. We got'a go get the law at Jacksonville. Ain't wantin' you left alone up here, 'side'a her."

Floralee objected. "I got youngens to get fed. Reckon we gonna be safe."

"Floralee, I ain't likin' to say this, but I ain't lettin' you stay. Reckon you could go over to Dwight's?"

Floralee sighed, "Sure thought I was havin' a dream, but I ain't leavin' the hill. I got a supper to cook." She looked at Sarah, standing by the door, watching her. It was then that the scene became clear.

"Sarah, you went down town and it weren't a dream. Oh, Sarah, darlin'. You thought... and Betty Lou? You... oh, dear gracious Lord! My little girls!" Floralee shook her head, sadly.

"Josh, you go do whatever it is you got'a do. Ain't nothin' gonna happen up here that I can't manage."

Josh was inclined to agree and finally left, though reluctantly. Floralee watched Elaine's cabin through the trees as darkness fell. No light showed through the window and no one stepped outside.

In the early light of dawn, the four uniformed lawmen surrounded the cabin and closed in. In a little while, they brought out Elaine, one on each side, urging her along, then they brought out a pine box and put it on the wagon. Floralee watched as the wagon disappeared into the trees.

She sighed a long sigh. Now, she was really alone on this side of the mountain. Alone with seven children, and it wasn't a dream.

Poor Elaine. Poor Vern and poor Nathan. And now another funeral would be held.

It was a warm, sunshiny day at the cemetery. Floralee and her children stood near the grave, dug so close to that of Nathan's, and listened to Rev. McCrey's words. "Friends and neighbors, we have gathered here to pay our last...."

The grass had not yet grown on Nathan's grave because there had been no summer, and Floralee stared at the red dirt of the grave, so like a bleeding gash that had wounded the mountainside. Rivulets of blood-red soil had drained away from the mound by the washing of the winter rains. New grass was coming up under foot and in a few weeks, the vulgar red mound of dirt would be green. Beside it, Vern's would also become green.

Oh, Nathan! Why... why...?

Dwight's family and hers were the only kinfolks present. It was clear now that Elaine would never be able to function in the outside world. There was a home upstate, where she could be taken, and if she had family to care about her, Floralee did not know of them, nor would she try to visit her.

"....and so we commend this body to the ground and this soul to its maker."

The minister stepped back and paused, respectfully. Floralee looked at Dwight, and he looked back to her. He motioned for her to come with him and together they stepped forward and each took a handful of clay. Each dropped their clay into the gaping hole and stepped back. They were then free to turn away from the awful scene and the shovels began to scoop the dirt onto the lid of the pine box.

Floralee's children were in the wagon, ready to roll away. The mule was chomping a mouthful of the new grass, dripping green juice from his lips.

Dwight came to her and spoke, softly. "Floralee, there's the matter of Vern's place up there. Elaine ain't gonna have need of it, seems like, and it'll be a matter of time tilst it'll be in your hands and mine. I'd be wantin' you to think on it, but it'd be my feeling that you ought'a make use'a the place where Vern's cabin was. That other'n, the one I left to come to town, I figure you'll think'a something to do there. It ain't no use to me, and no one'd buy a place shaped the way Pa cut that'n up.

"I don't see me nor my youngens ever havin' a need for it, so I'd consider it a favor if you was to see after it, maybe run goats over there, so as it don't go back to brush.

"Wouldn't'a stopped you to listen to this on the funeral day, but it was in my mind that Vern's passin' couldn't be too much of a pain to you, bein' nothin' 'tween you two over the years. Had nothin' much 'tween him and me, neither."

Floralee bowed her head, respectfully. It was hard to look at the bare soul of a man, and Dwight was speaking with painful openness.

He continued. "Had me two brothers and buried 'em hardly more'n six months apart, lovin' 'em both but not understandin' neither one of 'em. Life plays painful pranks, throwin' folks together that hadn't ought'a ever met.

"Well, I got'a be runnin' on, but you go ahead and feel like that place is yourn to use. Spring comin' on, they'll be good browse for the goats."

Floralee had no words to respond and the conversation seemed complete. She extended her hand and he shook it, then she turned and went to her wagon.

Donald was holding the reins and Betty Lou was patting tiny Rosie against her shoulder. Henry and Naomi were leaning over the endgate, trying to see how far they could lean without falling off. Charity scolded them like a chattering squirrel. But Sarah was not in the wagon.

Floralee looked around at the milling groups of people, standing in twos and threes, renewing acquaintances and recounting the bizarre incident causing this funeral.

Ah, there was Sarah. Floralee opened her mouth to call her, then closed it again.

Sarah stood, looking at her hands and fiddling with her handkerchief, listening to something a young man was saying. Floralee couldn't hear the words but she saw Sarah's smile. And she saw the young man. He was a little taller than Sarah, but very thick in the shoulders, and his overalls and new shirt were clean and not faded much.

His hair was bleached to the color of straw from being in the sun, and he smiled a broad, relaxed smile. He said something else and Sarah looked up at him, then glanced toward the wagon. She made a move to come to the wagon, but the young man caught her hand and she did not pull away.

"What're we waitin' on, Ma?"

"Just wait, Donald. We got lots of time and your sister's talkin'."

"Shore, but she was talkin' all the time you was talkin' to Uncle Dwight, and I figure she could'a got it all said by now."

Floralee glanced at Betty Lou, whose blue eyes twinkled. "Boys couldn't be expected to understand, could they, Ma?" her eyes seemed to be saying.

Now Sarah pulled her hand away and turned to the wagon and the young man came with her, smiling at Floralee.

Sarah asked, "Ma, Freddie, here, asked, could he come up to see me of an evenin' sometimes, and I said I'd like it but I'd need to be askin' you. Reckon he could?"

Floralee smiled at Sarah, "See no reason why he couldn't." Her words made two people happy. Freddie waved to her and walked away, glancing back several times.

"Now can we go?" asked the impatient Donald.

"Reckon it'd be you we was waitin' on, now," his mother told him, tousling his hair.

"Ma, we gonna go 'afore daylight, goin' into get Nate in the morning?"

"Seems to be a good idea."

"You gonna let me drive all the way?"

"Donald, I reckon you to be the only one wantin' to."

"Me," called out little Henry. "I'd drive that mule. I could make him run."

Henry ducked his head at the chuckles of his sisters. "Well, I would," he insisted.

A small spring rabbit jumped from the grass and hippity-hopped down the road in front of the wagon. Floralee thought again of the crisp, succulent fried rabbit she had been hungry for. Donald broke into her thoughts.

"Ma, one of them boys at school goes huntin' with his pa. Says I could come along if I was a'mind to. I told 'im I'd ask."

"Ask what? Iffen you had a mind to?"

"Aw, Ma."

"Reckon you'd be big enough to go, you goin' on ten, now."

Donald braced himself for the next request. "Said I'd need me a good huntin' dog."

"But you ain't got no dog."

"I could get me one."

"Where you thinkin' to get a dog?"

"Same fella. They got a beagle, had herself a litter. One of 'em could be for me."

"Reckon it could."

"Likely they'd be scraps and things it could eat."

"Likely. And the hillside is full'a rabbits if he got hungry enough."

"Ma, you sayin' I can get me a dog?"

"Was you askin'?"

"Oh, Ma! I got'a 'member to tell Nate I got me a dog!"

"Reckon he'll see it when he gets home, don't you think?"

"Reckon so. And Ma?"

"Huh?"

"That same beagle had herself a big litter. They'd be enough so as Nate could have one of 'em, too."

"Now, Donald, happen they wouldn't be wantin' to let two of them pups go."

"Yes, they would, Ma. I done asked if they'd be two we could get, makin' one for me and one for Nate. 'Course, I'd be gettin' first pick'a the two."

"'Course."

Floralee thought, again, of Nathan. Very often now, her thoughts drifted to him, mostly in regard to something he did not like or permit that had no reasoning behind it. Nate and Donald had always wanted dogs, and mountain hound dogs usually supported themselves, often becoming providers, but Nathan did not like dogs. Too noisy. But things had changed.

Donald was so certain, now, that the rules had changed that he had taken the liberty of asking for not only one, but two, of the pups. *Oh, Nathan, Nathan, why...?*

The mule turned to go up the hill. Steady and sure-footed, he climbed through the newly green trees. Past the valley pigpen, they came. Floralee studied the tree where she planned to construct the loading chute. It would be wide as a grown hog, and have short sidewalls. The floor would have saplings laid crossways so the pig feet could get traction as they climbed into the wagons of customers. Nate would help her build it.

The mule walked into the shed out of habit, though he was no longer fed hay. Clumps of green grass dotted the hill, and the turnip patch, grazed down continuously, was still trying to grow. Floralee would have to get someone to pull the turnips and pitch them to the hogs. It was time to plant more.

She would not let her eyes stray over the fence to Vern's land. Later, when she could deal with it, she would decide what to do. Tomorrow they would go to Jacksonville to get Nate.

24

The early May dawn was bright with sunshine, noisy with birdcalls and the excited chatter of children. In the gray of the dawn, they had come through the edge of River Bend and turned west. Along the river road, they plodded, pulled by the mule.

Little Henry was permitted to hold the reins for a while, but he was soon bored. The excited children could not sit still in the wagon and kept jumping down to walk a while, then to run to catch up. Donald sat, sturdy and tall, holding the reins and calling encouragement to the mule.

At the roadside spring, they stopped to eat their breakfast of cold biscuits with deer meat patties. The children climbed rocks and jumped off, then ran to the river to watch the swift current carry away leaves and twigs. They were going after Nate!

Floralee had rested on the buckboard seat, then on a flat rock beside the spring, with Rosie nestled in her lap, cooing at the movement in the trees. It was a holiday filled with shouts and laughter. Free of nagging worries. Her mind was as light as the butterflies and busy as the squirrels. So many possibilities to think on.

Beside her, in the lunch basket, there was a mountain of biscuit sandwiches, their meaty fragrance beginning to attract ants. Leftovers were still strange things, but not so much as before. It happened so often, now. The biscuits just lay there in the basket, ignored. Perhaps the children would snack on them on the way home.

The girls were looking forward to a stop at the clothing store. Everyone was looking forward to the stop at the ice cream store. Floralee longed to go to the auction, but how would she have room to bring anything home? Besides, she hadn't decided what she needed next.

They re-boarded the wagon and the mule plodded on. Floralee and Rosie sat beside the serious Donald as the others decided to ride or walk. With Donald at the reins, she was free to think and plan.

Twenty-one growing pigs and two brood sows were a good start, but space had become a pressing problem. With growing children, it was necessary that the supply meet the demand. She would likely get to buy Dwight's place and that would mean three fenced homesteads for her three sons when the time came. In the meantime, she could use it for free.

The girls? Well, there would be special things for them when they found husbands and left her. Freddie was coming to court Sarah and other young fellows would follow. Then there was dainty little Betty Lou. After that, the prim and fussy Charity would go. But first, she had to have the talk with them. She sighed at the thought. And Naomi and Rosie, too, when the time came, but now she must think of tomorrow and the next day.

She needed to make a list of expenditures for the year, all the things they would need, for certain. Then she could determine how many pigs would be required to supply the money. Also, how many would be needed for their own food and how could she possibly get some chickens so they could have eggs? Somehow, they had to have eggs. It was hard to keep chickens away from the varmints, up on the wild mountain the way she was.

There was the valley part of Vern's land, now to be hers to use. It would make a good pigpen, since the same tall oaks grew there as grew on hers. How many pigs would that support?

Naomi got tired of walking and Sarah lifted her into the wagon. Henry and Charity were far up ahead, planning to be in Jacksonville first. Betty Lou and Sarah were talking about dresses and the wonderful things they would find at the secondhand store.

Like mist rising off the river, allowing the sun to shine through, the idea settled upon Floralee, fully formed and clear. The cabin! Vern's cabin! It was small and two roomed and it had a tight-fenced yard. It would be the perfect chicken house!

Her arms tingled at the thought and became bumpy with ripples of excitement. Chickens and eggs! It was too bad about Vern and Elaine, but leaving the cabin empty out of pity would not help them.

Baby chickens were small and wouldn't take up room in the wagon. She'd get them, today. Now she, Floralee Baker, was so excited she almost got out and walked! But she didn't. She had to decide how many to get. Having cash money in one's purse made so many important options possible.

Just ahead they could see Jacksonville. The bus that was to bring Nate was expected at noon, leaving over two hours to wait, so there was the clothing store, then the hatchery. Plenty of time for everything.

The white-haired lady was in the clothing store. Floralee watched the girls hurry excitedly to the racks of dresses. Even Donald became mildly interested. Floralee, herself, needed a dress for church. Maybe two dresses.

The price tags were five and ten cents and several nice dresses were twelve and fifteen cents. Four good dresses were as much as a young pig, but they needed clothes. One could not wear a pig!

Sarah and Betty Lou tried on dresses, squealing with uncontrollable excitement over a perfect fit or a becoming color. Shapely Sarah blushed before the tall mirror as she turned this way and that and saw that all views proved that her shape was becoming more than adequate.

Betty Lou found dresses with fitted bodices and full, flouncy skirts which reduced her tiny waist to a mere nothingness. She held her hands high and whirled around from the sheer excitement of it all. The full skirts fanned out like the petals of an exquisite flower, opening among the dry leaves of a tree-shaded woodland. Naomi jumped up and down and clapped her hands, begging Betty Lou to whirl again.

Charity went, alone, down the racks, refusing this one and that one, looking for special colors and rich, silky fabrics. She held them against her body, smoothing them with her small hands. Her mother watched and puzzled it all in her mind. What would Charity choose? And why?

Then on the heels of this puzzlement, came the startling remembrance. Six short months ago, she had been desperate for assurance that Charity and the others would be reasonably warm and not overly hungry and now she was concerned that an acceptable dress be found. Oh, Nathan! The answer had been there all along. Why wouldn't he listen… ? Why! Why!

There were always concerns that every mother had for her children. It was only the priority of concern that shifted.

Charity found a dress of ivory velvet trimmed with lace and black ribbon. She found a dress of 'water-mark' taffeta which glistened and changed shades as she moved, its raised grain whispering softly. She found a dress of delicate, whispery dimity in baby pink with blue and yellow rosebuds embroidered on the collar. It was marked twenty-two cents, as much as three of the plain cotton dresses.

Finally, Floralee selected several practical dresses for Charity's school clothes and let her have the three she wanted.

Naomi was happy with anything and Rosie didn't care what she wore. The boys had overalls and shirts, underwear and jackets.

Shoes and shirts were placed in piles and overalls were put beside them. Floralee waited, nervously, while the prices were totaled. Four dollars and twenty cents, almost as much as a fed-out butchering hog, but she counted out the coins and gave them to the clerk. Sarah and Betty Lou eagerly helped fold them into the brown boxes.

They went to the hatchery where Floralee agonized over her decision. One hundred chicks would be right for a start, but what kind?

The tall, dark red Shanghai roosters were a beautiful sight with their shiny blue and green tail feathers, glistening in the sun, but her chickens were not for looking at. They were for eggs and for eating, and for that, there were none better than the Domineckers. Their fat bodies made juicy eating and their eggs were large and brown, even their black and white feathers were perfect for pillow stuffing.

She paid for the one hundred chicks. That was another dollar spent, and a bag of chick starter mash was seventy-five cents, but now she had her chickens.

It was still too early to pick up Nate, so they went back to the courthouse square to wait.

Naomi walked back and forth on the low brick wall by Floralee's bench. "Lookie, Ma. I ain't fallin' off!"

Donald and Henry were at the water fountain, squirting water on each other.

Charity sat on the wall surrounding the goldfish pond, watching the sparkling creatures swim among the water lilies.

Sarah and Betty Lou sat on a bench some distance away, talking in low tones.

A young man stood leaning against a tree, watching her girls. Sarah was wearing a blue dress with white dots and she had a white ribbon tied around her curls. Her hair sparkled and glistened in the May sunshine, and her lips and cheeks were the warm pink of ripening strawberries.

The young man licked his lips nervously, and took his hands from his pockets. He took two steps toward the girls. Suddenly, Betty Lou jumped up and went to the gold fishpond. She sat down by Charity to watch the fish.

The young man went toward Sarah and stood behind the bench. She turned slightly toward him. Floralee couldn't hear their words, as she was busy with her own thoughts.

She was going to have to talk to those girls, soon. It was going to be very hard to do, but she would do it.

She would tell them that when they were tiny, she spanked them so they would learn what they should and shouldn't do. But now that they were bigger, she didn't spank them anymore.

She would explain that grown up girls should not be hit by anyone and that she, Floralee, their mother, should not have permitted anyone to hit her. That would be the hard part. They would remember the many times when Nathan had.... But she would tell them. It was her duty.

And when a young man came to court them, they should be careful to make him listen as well as look, because girls had good ideas, too. She'd have to tell the girls, hard though it would be, that they must never, never allow anyone to hit them or yell at them to shut up.

No one must ever tell them that their ideas were worth nothing. If the young man did not listen to them, the way they listened to him, then that was not the young man for them. Generally speaking, things did not get better as time went on, and courting time was decision time. They must think clearly and not be dazzled by flattering words.

The young man talking with Sarah had to leave, and it was now time for them to go to the bus station.

A pillar-shaped cloud of road-dust followed the bus into the station yard and Nate stepped from the vehicle. He was taller and broader, and his hair was cut neatly and combed. He was wearing a new shirt and waist pants with a shiny belt. All in all, he was strikingly beautiful.

Immediately, he was hidden within many pairs of loving arms.

"Ma! The baby!" He looked at them all with moist, tender eyes. Everyone had to touch him.

Then they went to the ice cream store.

"Chocolate triple dips for everyone."

The clerk looked at tiny Naomi, "Even that one?"

Floralee nodded, "Iffen she'd need help, chances are somebody'd be there to help her."

Charity tugged at her mother's sleeve. "Ma, if I could have pink ice cream...?"

"Make one of them cones pink."

Eight cones came to forty cents, almost enough to buy a pig. They went back to the courthouse benches to better enjoy the treat

Nate stared at his mother. "Ma, I plum forgot how purty you was! I was so lonesome that all I could think of was comin' home. And you know what, Ma? They'd'a let me come home sooner, but they kept talking about something they called environment, and whether I was gonna shoot someone else, even when I told 'em I only done what I had to do.

"They said I had to get my sixth grade certificate and I had to study a lot but I got it. They kept askin' if I knowed how to make moonshine and I told 'em I never done it in my life, but they kept on askin'." Nate sighed with relief to be away from the questions.

They picked up the baby chickens at the hatchery, all counted out and boxed.

"You got chickens, Ma? You always wanted them! Didn't speck there'd be money. And all them good clothes! I was worryin' if you and the little 'ens had somethin' to eat."

Floralee smiled, "We got lots to say to you, Nate, and they ain't time to say it on the way home, 'cept that we gonna put a lean-to on the other side of the cabin. You boys is gettin' too big to sleep in the loft."

Back at the spring, they stopped to water the mule. Floralee set out the basket of sandwiches. The leftovers!

Nate was impressed. "They got meat in 'em, Ma!"

Floralee nodded, "They's a time to say everything, Nate. Don't worry yourself, none. I kept sayin' to you that we was doin' good."

"Yeah, Ma, but I figured you was sayin' that so as I'd not feel so bad, leavin' you."

As they came through River Bend, a young man called out, "Miz Baker, I got them ten ricks'a wood ready to start bringin' 'em on up."

"Bring 'em on," she told him.

"Firewood, Ma? How come you to order wood, and me comin' home? It ain't even winter. Summer's comin' on. You hadn't ought'a done that, Ma. I could'a took care of it 'afore winter." Nate's scolding tone grated on her nerves. His voice was becoming so like…. Floralee shook her head to drive away the disturbing thought.

"Nate, darlin', don't ever be tellin' your ma what she ought'a done, no matter if it be out'a love for her. We got money to pay for that wood and they's things you need to be doin' that'll be worth a sight more to our family than choppin' wood."

Nate stared at his mother, his sky-blue eyes wide with amazement. She continued.

"Fact is, you ain't gonna have time this summer to be layin' ax to wood. You got bigger things t'do."

Nate continued to stare at his mother, sitting straight and slim on the buckboard beside Donald. The setting sun shone through her hair like a rosy halo and her eyes were clear and as deep blue as the evening sky. She smiled at him.

"Yep, Nate, darlin'! You come home just in time 'cause we got a summer full'a important things we gonna do."

In her purse, Floralee had just over $17.00 left, almost exactly what she had last fall, but now the family had clothes and they ate meat and spring was coming on. It had been a lot of hard work for everyone, but was it not expected that they would work?

They would have goat meat, chicken and pork and more money when the pigs were sold. *Oh, Nathan, why...? So many years lost!*

The setting sun dipped below the mountain just as the mule turned off the main road. Outlined against the sky was an old storm-broken craig of a tree with a wide nest in its upper limbs. Over the nest stood a tall bird, hovering and poised, offering food to the fledglings in the nest.

The bird lifted its head and spread its powerful wings. Thrusting up into the wind, the feathered body began to soar in wide spirals, riding a warm air thermal into the dusky sky. With a scream of triumph, it disappeared into the depth of the heavens.

Floralee looked behind her at the healthy faces and ahead of her at the leaf-canopied trail leading up to her cabin and she thought her precious thought. It had happened! Truly happened!

"I will mount up with wings as the eagle. I will walk and not be weary, I shall run and not faint. But, Lord, that ain't no surprise to You, is it? You knowd it all along!"

The young mule placed one foot after the other, steadily climbing the mountain, bringing the family home.

1

Taming the Wilderness Historical Fiction Series

Night Flight

Caravan

JOANN KLUSMEYER

NIGHT FLIGHT

Roberta stood in the garden, covering her eyes to shield them from the last rays of the bright, late-February sunshine.

She and the soon-to-be-five-year-old, Alecia, had been harvesting some of the last of the winter turnips to store in the root cellar and perhaps make into pickles to vary the late-winter diet. It would soon be time to break ground for the new planting.

Blinking against the sun, she felt her lungs tighten and her muscles cringe at the sight of two wagons heading up the hill toward the mountain farmhouse. Taking the little girl by the hand, she led her toward the house and toward the trouble, whatever it was. Two unexpected wagons in the mid-afternoon could be only one thing... trouble.

Apprehension mounted as she recognized her brother's horse, Dancer, being led, riderless, beside the first wagon. She felt the tingle of her scalp tightening with fear.

With a mountain woman's continuous attention toward preparedness, acquired during her twenty-two years of life, she dusted the loose dirt from her apron and held it ready. At a raised palm from the driver of the first wagon, she wrapped her apron before the face of the child, turning her and hurrying her away from the dreaded scene.

"Papa," she called to the man working in the barn. "Would you go see to the wagons out front? We're takin' a little stroll."

The older man walked as rapidly as his years permitted toward the approaching vehicles, and the little girl looked up at Roberta with questions in her eyes.

"It's all right, honey. We'll go see if we can find where old Cockle Bonnet hid her nest. She's likely gonna be bringin' in a new family any day now."

Reluctantly, the little girl allowed herself to be drawn into the search for the hen's nest. It was necessary for Roberta to occupy the child until the first of the preparations were made at the house. Ten or fifteen minutes should be enough. Meanwhile, her mind raced in many directions. How bad was it... what to do about it... and what to do with the child? These were decisions more immediate than the location of the nest of the brooding hen.

"Honey," she addressed the girl, "let's go see Grandpa Ned."

The child's small hand tightened in hers as she instinctively hesitated. The wide, blue eyes looked up into Roberta's.

"Just for a little while, darling. I'll be comin' back to get you 'afore suppertime. Can you do that?"

"Why?"

"Big Papa and I have some things to do."

"I'll help…."

"No, darling, not this time. But I promise I'll come to get you. Now, don't be cryin'. Grandpa Ned won't like to see tears in your eyes. Make a big smile. That's my girl!" Roberta encouraged with a forced smile of her own.

They walked down the steep hill and picked their way over the brook, stepping then on a path of flat stones. The trail rose immediately up a steep hill to the mountain cabin. On the porch of the cabin sat an old man, his eternal jug beside him, but he seemed in possession of his wits.

"Brought the girl, eh?"

"For a while. I think she'd like to see the new puppies. I'll be back to get her before supper. Bye, now."

Roberta loosed her hand from the girl's reluctant one and stepped away. After a pause, Alecia walked on toward the porch where the old man sat.

Roberta's heart pounded as she turned and retraced her steps down to the brook and up again. What would she find waiting for her? Not good, that was certain. Her father was standing at the crest of the hill, watching for her.

"Bertie, I waited too long. I know'd it was time to be leavin', and I didn't go. Rob paid the price."

"Really bad?" A cave-in at the coal mine could mean death or dismemberment, or it could be only a cloud of black smoke to add to the rest of the blackness of the coalmine. For the one escaping loss of life or limb, the inevitable result was a layer of coal dust in the lungs and a cough that followed the miner to his grave.

The old man walked along in silence. His daughter insisted on an answer.

"Papa… was it bad?"

The question was too much. Like a mighty cedar tree that crumbles to the earth when a forest fire has burned away its roots, the old man sunk to his knees on the ground and bowed his face into the dirt, sobs tearing themselves from the bony frame. His daughter fell to the rocky path beside him and wrapped him in her arms.

"No, Papa! No! It can't be!" But she knew it was and pulled herself to her feet, drawing the old man after her. She squared her shoulders, resolutely marching toward the mountain cabin… toward the men who stood waiting with heads bowed and hats in hand.

Dreams must play themselves out, and even nightmares continue to force themselves into the thoughts of a night. So must the actions of the day continue, but there is a difference. A new life appears each morning as the nightmare fades, but the ravages of an actual day can leave torn lives to be dealt with forever.

Some years ago, her strong, beautiful brother, the laughing Eldon, three years older than Roberta, had been brought home in the wagon, barely alive, and a week later he was buried. He was stolen from her by the coal seam that ran through the mountain and beneath her own cabin.

Now her twin brother, Robert….

Both her brothers… gone… and only she was left with her papa. It was indecent, somehow, for the child to die before the parent. Especially the beautiful Eldon, and now the quiet, sensitive Robert, her childhood playmate and the sharer of confidences over her whole life. Gone.

It was truly startling, the speed with which thoughts can race through the head. Between the sight of the flock of chickens, scratching in the backyard, and the shape under the sheet spread over the bed, a million thoughts had whirled… and uppermost among was the hope (prayer?) that Papa had been wrong, and Robert had only been severely hurt. Hurts can be healed.

But that was not to be. The white sheet covered her brother from his feet to the top of his head, extending up and over the unruly mop of red-gold wiry curls.

The dreadful weight that had been whirling in her head now suddenly dropped with terrible finality into the pit of her stomach. Gone… first Eldon, whose death had also taken her frail mother from the grief of it all… now Robert, her soul mate. And one other thing. Her mind thumbed its way through the pages of her thoughts, searching for another date. Two years ago it was, counting from last December, that the only man she had ever loved had walked away from the mountains and from her.

But, like nightmares that cannot be stopped, this day must be lived through, and she lifted the corner of the sheet to look at the mangled body of her twin brother. There was no time for tears, as there was Alecia, Robert's daughter, to be thought of.

From the barn, she could hear the hammering of nails into the wood, and it drummed into her mind the necessity to make plans for Alecia. She had promised to go get her, but that would mean the child would be brought into the house. She would see a sight that would bring nightmares into her dreams as long as she lived. For the child, losing her mother at three was something that could be dealt with, because she still had her father. Now he was gone, but she must eventually be permitted to see him, or she would think he had gone away and left her because he did not love her. What to do…?

A discrete tap at the door told her they had arrived, the women folk of other miners, and they had come to help her through the next days. Just as she and her mother had gone to others in the time of their loss. Just as they had come when Eldon….

She opened the door and wordlessly permitted the silent forms, clad in work dresses, aprons, shawls and bonnets, to enter. Words were unnecessary, and there was nothing to be said that had not been already said over and over and over.

Large, comfortable Annie McDougal, who had buried a husband and son, placed a leather-skinned, calloused hand on Roberta's arm as she looked into her eyes. No words were necessary.

"Annie…?" Roberta pled, uselessly.

"What, sweetheart…?" The arms spread wide, and Roberta was pulled toward the pillowy bosom. The tears she had pushed aside now found their outlet, drenching the fabric of Annie McDougal's wool shawl.

When the sobs died away and she was able to speak, Roberta whispered. "Annie, his little girl, she's got'a see her pa. You know? To give her a picture in her mind to look back on? Can you…?"

"Yes, honey, I can. Now you go tend to your papa. He's not got youth like you got, and it'll hit 'im hard this day and likely harder tomorrow."

Roberta slipped away and joined her father in the kitchen.

"Papa? Papa? I wouldn't be botherin' you, but I got'a go get Alecia. I promised."

Wiping his eyes, the old man nodded. "Yes. You go on."

Two

So soon the eternity had passed, and they were in the cemetery.

Roberta stood with her father as the last prayer was spoken by the preacher and those in attendance had gathered around the three of them. The little girl hid her face in the front of her aunt's dress. Words of intended comfort were said as the trio climbed into the buggy. The horse moved out onto the road, leaving others to the filling and leveling of the grave.

"We're leaving." The old man made the announcement as though discussing the weather.

"What, Papa?"

"It's time and past time. We're leaving."

"Papa…" Roberta glanced knowingly toward the attentive ears of the little girl, and her father nodded his understanding.

"Yessirree, we're leavin' that cemetery, 'afore the road gets dusty from all them other buggies."

The little girl looked at the ground and grinned at the joke. "Aw, Big Papa, there ain't no dust. This here ain't summertime!"

"This ain't summertime?" He pretended surprise.

The small fist pounded on her grandfather's sleeve. "No, Big Papa! It's wintertime."

"Oh," he exclaimed. "That must be why I'm wearin' a coat!"

"Big Papa! You're so silly!"

Leaving, huh? The word had stuck in Roberta's ears. Old Eben Carlile had often spoke of leaving; in fact, he had brought it up just about once a month since his wife had passed on. Virginia Carlile, never strong physically, had been the force that had held Eben together for the greater part of his 56 years of age. She had been his link to the rugged mountains around the cabin, but his tie to the rocks and trees had been severed when she was put in the ground.

Roberta knew about links. She'd had some of her own. One link had been severely weakened when the man she loved had walked away, promising he would come back for her. It had not happened.

When the little girl was tucked away in bed, Roberta joined her father around the miniature parlor stove. The weather was unseasonably mild, but a small fire had been laid to take the chill off the room. Fresh coffee filled the parlor with a fragrant, roasted-nut smell. The coffee was made from the package of coffee beans brought by neighbors, along with the other food, to the laying-out. A friendly mountain custom.

There was talking to be done.

Roberta sat on her mother's small sewing chair and looked at the flames in the miniature stove. Her father spoke.

"South. That'd be the place. Around water and boatin', like there's plenty of, over to the river. An old man could find jobs a'plenty."

"Jobs, Papa?" Did she have to remind him of his 56 years? Remind him that he was not strong and young anymore? Did she have to mention his accelerated decline since her mother's death?

"Little girl, your old pa, he ain't done in yet. They's fishin' net mendin' to be done and cleanin' and calkin' the leaks in the boats. Old man like me, he'd find job's a'plenty. Us three that's left, it wouldn't take too much to take care'a us."

"You thought this through, Papa? Like what to do with the place here? You think there's some kind of a rush to get on the road?"

"Bertie, child, think on it. For you and me, likely there'd be no rush. For that youngen in the next room, we're down to days, the way I figure it."

"Days?"

"Days," he uttered with finality. "The Doughertys, they might not be no swifter in the head than the average box-turtle, but it ain't gonna take them more'n a week or so, and they'll see that with her pa gone, we ain't got no more legal hold on that little girl than they got. That happens and they'll be here to get 'er."

The horror of the thought silenced his words, and Roberta felt her stomach muscles clench like the steel claws of a wolf trap. A panorama of scenes flashed through her mind of robberies and other unsolved crimes that seemed to point toward the Doughertys, of the frequent jailing of their male members and the shy little Letha who often slipped away and climbed the mountain to play with her when they were children. Also among the vivid pictures were those of the grownup Letha, pregnant with Robert's second child, staring into Roberta's blue eyes with her own gray ones, sharp as steel knives.

"Somethin' happens to me, don't you let 'em take my little girl!"

"Hush, up, Lee! You're gonna be fine. It ain't like this here was your first baby!"

But Letha had been insistent. "Don't you be tryin' to jolly me out'a what I got'a say. YOU KEEP MY LITTLE GIRL! I got'a hear you promise me."

Roberta did, and she remembered those words again as she had stood beside Robert at the grave of lovely Letha and the baby that she had not been strong enough to bear.

She glanced at the old man as he stared into the fire, its orange and red flames reflecting against the tears on his face and in the moisture pooled in his swimming eyes. "I ain't lifted a gun agin no livin' human, and I ain't aimin' to start now, so what's left for us is to get out. Don't say nothin' in front'a the girl, but you get together in your mind what you got'a take, as much as'll go in a wagon, and you leave the rest to me."

"But, Papa...."

"Hush, child. The less you know of it'll be the less you'll say. Likely there'll be times you'll be sayin' to folks what you and me'll do, but this here's a time that I say what's to be done. Sometime this week, you take 'er across the valley one more time, to see the youngens over there, but don't be leavin' 'er alone."

"Sure, Papa...."

There'd be no sleep for her tonight. With a pencil and paper, she walked around the room, checking what could be removed without an explanation to the girl. It wouldn't be easy.

"Bertie, child...."

"Yeah, Papa...?"

"Likely be easier to do your plannin' if you was to know we'll be leavin' in the night."

"Night?"

"For a fact. The through-train to the south goes past here at one fifty, barrelin' on down the valley less'n it's been flagged. Station don't open at night. A body wantin' on that train got'a do the flaggin' hisself."

Well, yes, that would make the planning easier. Alecia could be put to bed, and there would be time to load up if she had her list made up already.

"Papa, how're we gonna get all our plunder on that train, this bein' only a flag stop?"

"Bertie, child, that ain't your worry. You figure out what'll go on that wagon and I'll tend to gettin' it off."

Put like that, it would be simple. So she started the list. Boxes. Trunks. Her mother's sewing rocker. Alecia's stuffed bear that had been made by her grandmother, and the rag doll she herself had made for her last Christmas. Their clothes, the dishes, the....

"Papa, the parlor stove?" Likely not, but she was hopeful.

"Put it in. It hardly ain't much bigger'n a stewpot."

She paused in her list-making as a memory stabbed her. The jar! She couldn't leave without the jar. A glance at the window reminded her of the full moon, furnishing plenty of light, but still, Papa would want her to light a lantern. Then he would want to know what she was doing.

He still stared into the flames, so Roberta went to the lean-to kitchen and moved a few pots, making a fair amount of noise. What man noted any sound that came from the kitchen?

Easing silently through the door, she hurried across the yard and down the path toward the outhouse. Stopping halfway, she walked toward the large oak. Clearing away the leaves with her hands (Papa wouldn't like that! Snakes can hide under leaves), she felt the reassuring hardness of the glass jar with the tight-fitting zinc lid. The coins inside whispered, clicking metallically against each other.

Cradling it carefully in her apron, she took the jar into the kitchen and set it inside her soup kettle. That took care of that.

"More coffee, Papa?"

"Might as well. Still got a lot'a thinkin' to get done."

Three

Early in the morning, Eben Carlile paid a visit to his neighbor on the next farm.

"Eli, you always had a hanker to add my farm to yourn; what'll you give me if I was to sell?"

"What'll you take?"

"A two hunnerd dollar bill. But if'n you'll do me a favor, I'll split that two hunnerd half in two."

"What'd the favor be?"

"It'd be that you don't say nothin' about this for a week, givin' me time to get away."

"Why'd it need to be kept a secret?"

"The Doughertys. I find myself needin' to get away, maybe earn a little hard money, and I had me the idea the river'd be a place to do it."

"The river?"

"Yeah, down to the south where the fishin' is. Figured they'd be needin' a old codger like me to kick around and do the dirty work. Need a way to take care'a my girl till she gets herself a man, and there's the least'n to be thought on."

"Not gonna leave the little girl here?"

"Think on it, man! Bertie bein' the only ma she's knowed, and now her pa's gone? It'd be shameful to leave her, though likely she'll be a peck'a trouble. Maybe later…."

Elias Weatherby nodded his head knowingly. Good of Eben to take on the responsibility of a youngen—and her hardly out of diapers.

"Tell you what. I'll take you up on that if you can make a trip into Hilltop first thing in the mornin' to sign the papers. You'll be gone in a week? Well, this place'll miss you."

"Aw, not much, 'n there'll be the comin' and goin' for visits, the youngen still havin' kinfolks here."

Elias nodded again. "What about your farm plunder? What'll you do with it?"

Eben chewed on a straw and spat the broken end onto the ground. "This and that. Got a place to get rid of some of it on west'a my place. Got'a deliver it today. Gonna be some of it left around up there. Anything still there when we leave, that'll be yours."

Elias nodded. This was turning out to be a good day.

Eben returned to his cabin and inspected the practically new wagon stored under a shed out of the weather. Good paint job. Color of a grasshopper, and they'd teased Robert when he brought it home.

He inspected the undercarriage. Wheels been kept greased. His son had bought himself a good wagon, Eben had to admit, and the span of bays he bought at the same time drew a second look most anywhere they went. Likely he'd paid too much for the wagon and horses and for the new clothes he'd got for the little one out of the money from selling his place. Leastwise, he didn't seem to have any left.

Eben rubbed the hay dust off the shiny paint and sighed. When Robert's wife died, that should have been the time to leave the mountain, but change is hard, especially when a man is past 50 years old and he's bone-tired of life. Then, too, there was Roberta, still thinking that young man would be back. Everyone else had thought so, too, but things happen. Young men get themselves killed, or there could have been a dozen other things to keep him away.

Anyway, two years was long enough to wait, and Eben didn't have to be hit over the head to know it was now time to go. Time and past time. Elias was getting a bargain, but Eben did not have the luxury of months to shop for a buyer, and now he needed to load the wagon.

A few plow points and a strong shaft, buckets, a roll of lightweight rope, axel grease, part of a roll of wire. On and on, picking up this and that, Eben was occupied until noon.

Over dinner he told his daughter, "Gonna be headin' west with stuff I thinned out. Could be late getting' back."

At her raised eyebrows, he added, "Takin' the grasshopper."

So Robert's wagon was to be sold. She nodded. "You have to, Papa? Sure, and it's best, I reckon."

Alecia forked green beans into her mouth. "Big Papa, grasshoppers make wings out'a their legs and that's how they can hop or fly."

"Who told you that?"

"Grandpa Ned."

Eben buttered a biscuit and wondered why people lie to a child when the truth would be easier told. Well, that would stop in five days.

He left the yard with the bays pulling the green wagon, and the saddle horse was tethered behind. Roberta glanced at it with a bit of regret, but Papa had decided, and she hoped he was doing the right thing.

Eben watched the gait of the horses ahead of him. Good, even gait. Not excitable. Robert was a good judge of horseflesh. You could tell by watching them that they had set Robert back a pretty penny. Still, there should have been a little something left from the sale of his place.

At the edge of Pinetop, Tennessee, the old man stopped in front of a hardware store, buying two full sets of side clamps for holding cleats to a wagon. At the lumberyard, he selected ten tough, springy strips of wood, two very large canvas tarpaulins and two buckets of heavy oil, which he stowed in the wagon beside the tar.

On to the livery stable he went to conduct his final business.

It was dark when he left Pinetop and near midnight when his tired saddle horse climbed the hill to her warm stable and hay. The two hounds, Pete and Pokey, were left behind him at the livery stable.

"Papa! I was about to get worried. I been loadin' into the wagon, figurin' if we was needin somethin' to ride, we could use the buggy. I was thinkin' what I'd use to cover the stuff, Alecia askin' questions like she does."

"You done good. Don't be concernin' yourself. I took care'a it. It's covered with a canvas I picked up."

"Our buggy, Papa? What about…?"

"Don't you be worryin'. I got stuff disposed of the best I know'd how."

Four

Then it was the last day.

The roosters had hardly finished crowing when a light tap sounded at the door. Roberta left her biscuit dough to answer it. There stood old Annie McDougal.

"Come in. You alright, Annie?'

"Right as rain. All exceptin' my old ramblin' brain. Could'a give you this at church next Sunday, but like as not, I'd'a forgot it agin. Then, too, the sight'a it could'a plowed up grief best left to deal with in private."

"What is it?" Certainly it must be important, as it brought Annie up the hill almost before daylight.

"It's this, honey." She drew a handkerchief from her apron pocket. "It was at the layin'-out that I looked at that young man, whilst I was a'combin' that curly hair, and I said to myself, 'Annie, they's a little girl in there that lost her papa, and what'll she think later when she tries to remember what he looked like?' So I got me the scissors and clipped some of them curls. Then, when I got'a 'em home, I tied 'em in little bunches, so's they'd not muss up when they was put away."

The gnarled old hands tugged apart the knot in the cloth square and spread it on the table. There, laying on the cloth, was a pile of red-gold curls, likely enough to fill a teacup. How had she been able to cut so much hair and have it not show? And what a loving and thoughtful thing to do… to think of the future that way. And of Robert's little girl.

"Annie, I got no words to thank you."

"Sure you have. You just said 'em. Now I got'a be getting' on."

"Wait. I got a present for you. You bein' such a friend to my mama, I want to give you something that was a thing she liked."

Roberta reached up to the wall and took down a picture. It was a scene painted on glass, its vivid colors depicting a bird nest and a pair of bluebirds hovered around a trio of open mouths. She was surprised to note the square of unfaded wallpaper behind the picture. The bright square blazed out from the faded roses of the paper. Annie noticed it, too.

"But you'd not want...."

"I want you to take it. That's what I really want, and when you look at it, think of my mother." She would have liked to have said 'think of us,' but Papa had said to TELL NO ONE.

"Well, honey, if you're sure... and thanks."

And Annie was gone. Roberta tied the rosy caramel-colored curls, the exact shade of her own, into the cloth and tucked it into the jar, then hesitated. No, the curls might get squashed... yes, it was the place for them. Right there in that jar with the coins left over from the sale of Robert's farm. He'd told her, "Bert, you take this and hide it. In the mine like I am, there'd be a chance some day I won't come out. The money's to take care of my little girl."

The glass jar was wrapped in a cloth and buried in the trunk full of clothing.

After breakfast, Roberta suggested, "Let's go see Grandpa Ned and the cousins."

At Alecia's hesitation, she added, "Then we'll look for that nest old Cockle Bonnet hid out."

As the girl played with the other children, her cousins, Roberta fought for words to say to be polite to the old man. Words that would not involve the future of Alecia, but it was not to be.

"Losin' 'er pa'd put the lassie in a new light, us bein' kin the same as you. She could just as well's to be here with other youngens to play with."

Roberta forced herself into calmness. "That's the truth. 'Course, that'd be a thing for you and Pa to be settlin'. I ain't got no say in the matter." Tension made her breath thin and thready.

The man picked up his jug, took a gulp, and set it down again. "Speck the thing to do'd be to leave 'er here tilst the talkin' got done."

Think, Roberta, THINK! "You know, that' be a good idea, too, 'cept for one thing."

"What'd that be?"

"That girl, she's got so spoiled to her stuffed bear to sleep with, likely no one'd get a wink'a sleep for her caterwalin'. We shouldn't'a let a kid get that'a'way."

That wasn't a lie, was it? A whole lie? Sure, she slept with the bear, but certainly she wouldn't cry for more than a minute or two if she didn't have it for a night. However, she might find other reasons to cry.

The old man was considering his options… getting his way or losing sleep from the crying child. Sleep won.

"Wal, I don't tucker to spoilin' a kid, but that can be took care of. Bring the blasted thang on over when you bring her."

Roberta sighed and nodded. "Sure thing."

"And don't you be thinkin' to forget about it, neither. You and your pa'll both know I got ways'a makin' somethin' happen."

Roberta nodded again. "Like I said, don't you worry none. Pa'll make sure nothin' happens. He ain't wantin' no trouble." She wasn't certain she convinced the old man.

In the late afternoon, Roberta poured warm water in the washtub by the stove and set Alecia to taking a tub bath. Who knew when her next one would be? As the little girl splashed, soaped, and poured water from one cup to another, her aunt and grandfather stood in the kitchen and talked.

"You 'bout ready?" he asked.

She nodded. "Poor little thing's tired. She'll be asleep by seven. Give me four hours after that and I'll be ready to pull out." She fingered her list, twisting it apprehensively.

"Good. You tell me when she's asleep, and I'll move her to the buggy."

"Buggy? But I thought…?"

"Don't think. Pack. All I got'a do is wait for the fire to die down and take the stove. You're fixin' food right now?"

"Don't I always? Fixin' to make more biscuits right this minute. Don't reckon they serve food on the train."

"I reckon not."

Then they were ready, and the lanterns were lighted and hung on the buggy and also on the side of the wagon. The horses knew the trail, and the wavering light from the kerosene lanterns was enough. Roberta sat in the buggy beside the sleeping girl, waiting while the fancy parlor stove was cleaned of ashes and wrapped with canvas to be stowed in the buggy.

- END OF EXCERPT -

ADDITIONAL BOOK SERIES BY JOANN KLUSMEYER

The Great I Am Bible Story Series for Kids
6 books

The Young Pioneers Adventure Series for Kids
5 books

The Wentworth Triplets Mystery Series for Young Teens
3 books

Footsteps in the Canyon Adventure Series for Young Teens
4 books

Burnt Tree Junction Historical Fiction Series for Adults
6 books

Ozark Mountains Historical Fiction Series for Adults
7 books

Taming the Wilderness Historical Fiction Series for Adults
4 books

The Sheltering Stones Historical Fiction Series for Adults
5 books

The Trilogy of Wishbone Hollow Historicial Fiction Series for Adults
3 books